drive

drive

Raymond Ahrens

Tasora

TASORA BOOKS
5120 Cedar Lake Road
Minneapolis, MN 55416
952. 345.4488
Distributed by Itasca Books
Printed in the U.S.A.

Drive

Publisher's note: This is a work of fiction; and while all fiction is culled from the writer's experience, and as such resonates of real-life characters, conversations, and causality, any resemblance in this novel to actual people is purely chimerical.

Author's note: Any comparison between *Drive's* governor and former Governor Jim McGreevy of New Jersey, is coincidental. Any comparison between *Drive's* governor and politics as we know it, is completely by design.

The author's effort to present a factual account of Mount Freedom's Jewish resort history was thwarted by the scant narrative that remains, relegating history more to fiction than fact.

ISBN 978-1-934690-64-2

Book design by Patti Capaldi.

A special thanks to my wife, Sara, for allowing me to sneak into my den to write all these years, without suspecting perverse or deviate behavior; Don Gervich, my writing coach, who rescued Willie by helping me cure, or at least mitigate, my writing inhibitions; and to Lucretus, who two thousand years ago deduced that the Earth traveled around the sun and that the universe is infinite and glorious. (Or something like that.)

Playlist

MUSIC PLAYS A principal chord in this novel. Long before the storytellers told their tales, the drummers kept the beat. Words separate us from nature, while music makes princes of us all. Many of the chapters are titled after songs. Some songs create a comic note, some set the mood, while others add melody, message, and meaning to the chapter. Yet some songs worm their way deeper—finding their way into our inner self. "Fall on Your Knees" is meant to play as you read the chapter, while an acoustical version of "Like a Rolling Stone" plays as a portent for Willie's escape. "Whaling Stories" adds tenor to the section "Revive," drifting in and out of Willie's epiphany. Jim Steinman's "Heaven Can Wait" is woven into the fabric of the story—possibly becoming the story. If you hear a word or phrase that rings of song, it might have been placed there by nuance or happenstance. Either way, as Beethoven was purported to say on his deathbed, "Play on."

The songs are attributed to the artists who recorded them, not the songwriter.

It's My Party	Lesley Gore
American Pie	Don McLean
White Rabbit	Jefferson Airplane
Cat's in the Cradle	Harry Chaplin
Voodoo Child	Jimmy Hendrix
This Kiss	Faith Hill
New York, New York	Frank Sinatra
Sweet Dreams (Are Made of This)	Eurythmics
Chimes of Freedom	Bob Dylan
You Can't Always Get What You Want	The Rolling Stones
Chase Scene	Keystone Cops
The Road to Nowhere	Talking Heads
Like a Rolling Stone	Bob Dylan
It All Makes Perfect Sense	Pink Floyd
Crosstown Traffic	Jimmy Hendrix
Golden Slumbers	The Beatles
Sunday Will Never be the Same	Spanky and Our Gang
Everybody Knows	Leonard Cohen
For Whom the Bell Tolls	Metallica
Road to Hell	Chris Rea
The End (Petition the Lord with Prayer)	The Doors
Under the Broadway	The Drifters
I Am Pegasus	Ross Ryan
My Heart Will Go On	Celine Dion
Our House	Crosby, Stills, Nash & Young
Christmas	The Who
Amazing Journey	The Who
In the Arms of an Angel	Sarah McLachian
Unchained Melody	The Righteous Brothers
Eleanor Rigby	The Beatles
Forever Young	Bob Dylan
O Holy Night (Fall on Your Knees)	All Choral Versions
We Will Rock You	Queen
What a Wonderful World	Louie Armstrong
I Shall be Released	Bob Dylan
Whaling Stories	Prochol Harem
Somewhere Over the Rainbow	Judy Garland
Heaven Can Wait	Meatloaf (Jim Steinman)

See the U.S.A. in your Chevrolet
America is asking you to call.
Drive your Chevrolet through the U.S.A.
America's the greatest land of all.

The Dinah Shore Show

If the American Dream is truly a dream
Then someone put me to sleep.

Anonymous

Drive

I'll Cry If I Want To

IT'S AN ORDEAL listening to a grown man cry—a cry the Haitian aides working at the Morningside Nursing Home compare to the sound of screeching tires in the instant before a deadly crash. So as they led a wailing Willie Easelman through the hallways of Morningside, shadowed by his remorseful daughter, Anna, one of the Haitians rushed ahead, closing doors and warning residents loitering in the corridors to cover their ears. Fatigue usually overcomes these remonstrative newcomers as their screams dissolve into sobs and finally into private silences. But at eighty-six years old Willie still possessed remarkable lungs, and for the following month the hallways at the Morningside reverberated with Willie's tormented screams. Cries of "Where's my God-damn car?" or "Anna's stealing my fucking Impala," echoed day and night, bringing indignation to some residents and childish giggles to others.

But it was Willie's pauses, pauses that hung in the air before worming their way under one's skin, that most unsettled the residents and staff of the Morningside. Willie stopped crying and the ensuing silence spread through the passageways of the Morningside with flu-like alacrity. Often these silences were interrupted with Willie's child-like queries: "Why am I here?" or "Where am I going?" Willie's voice resounded with such innocence that even as far away as the kitchen the cooks hesitated in preparing casseroles and tilted their heads with warm-hearted woe. If a sympathetic aide rushed to Willie's side, trying to explain to the confused old man that the Morningside was his home, Willie would shake his head vigorously and plead, "So this is it?"

Willie also created a buzz among the Haitian aides by the devilish way he snuck up on them. Willie, being slight of build and a yarmulke shy of five feet tall, blended into the contours of the velvet curtains or the fake foliage of the dusty plants that crowded the lobby. When an unsuspecting aide passed by, a raspy voice hissed, "Gotcha!" To the Haitian aides, Willie's disembodied voice carried the ring of voodoo, and Willie became known to them as the "invisible one." Many were convinced Willie's body was inhabited by a mischievous but good-natured demon. But when Willie began calling the female aides "Anna," his daughter's name, and damming their wickedness with outbursts of "slut" or "whore," the female Haitians began to gossip that Willie's body had undoubtedly been taken over by a more sinister, possibly even evil, spirit.

Willie taunted the young aides, many of whom had been orphaned by the earthquake that plundered their island. With eyes flaring, Willie pounded his thin chest and threatened, "I'm going to change my will, Anna!" or "I'll leave you and your brothers zip!" One afternoon he leaped from behind the piano in the lobby, startling a young aide with, "I'll haul your skinny ass into court, Anna." The startled girl, whose ass was anything but skinny, was so traumatized that blood gushed from her nose.

Eventually Willie worked himself up enough rage to swing at one of the Haitian aides. Thankfully the good-natured woman, who was more than twice Willie's size, grabbed his wrists and held them apart—a mother restraining her child. But as she walked away, Willie sent shivers through the huge woman, shouting, "I'll see you drown in Hell!" When Willie saw the woman hesitate he added, "Drown in your own blood." The aide fled, but later, at the dilapidated house the Haitians rented in Newark, she terrified her co-workers when she revealed that Willie's eyes had turned "red as a rooster's comb."

As complaints from Morningside residents mounted over Willie's incessant crying, not to mention the growing anguish of the Haitian staff, the administrators decided to take action. They summoned Willie's daughter, Anna, threatening to expel her father from their "well-mannered" facility, as if Willie was a truant schoolboy.

"Your father must learn to behave if he is to become part of the Morningside community," one of the administrators scolded Anna.

"He's quite the spoiled brat, you know," piped in another.

Anna, who knew her father could be difficult, nodded as if she were on trial.

"Maybe your father would be happier in a different nursing home?"

"The kind that isn't as kindly as the Morningside?"

Anna was near tears.

Solutions, however, are often acts of desperation, not to mention the impressive pension and stock portfolio Willie brought to the table from thirty-five years of selling life insurance to the businessmen of Manhattan.

"Maybe we should try giving him back his car?" Anna sheepishly suggested.

"His car?" the administrators bellowed in unison. "Why, that would be criminal!"

"His car, but not his keys," Anna continued, noting that his car, or lack of car, prompted much of her father's grief.

"Interesting," one of the administrators mused.

"Kind of a token of our trust," another offered, as the three retreated in private to discuss Anna's proposal.

Anna looked around at the Morningside residents slouched in the worn armchairs that lined the perimeter of the lobby. She had visited her father infrequently since he was admitted, and during those rare visits she scurried through the lobby, avoiding eye contact with residents. But now their pale faces overwhelmed her. One lady, sitting alone, gazed longingly out a bay window, as if awaiting a special visitor. A man dressed in a suit and sporting a spiffy bow tie, seemed to be ogling her breasts. And someone was playing snippets of Broadway musicals on a piano tucked in the corner, her face eclipsed in shadows. Anna sensed the residents were eavesdropping;

these old folks were cunning enough not to stare. But something in the manner in which they extended their necks towards her made her suspicious.

After a short discussion, the three administrators returned. With one eye on a solution and the other on the bottom line, the tallest administrator extended his hand to Anna and announced, "We have a deal."

Later that day the administrators sent a Haitian to pick up Willie's car from Anna's yard. The administrators then took Willie's 1986 white Impala for a short spin around the town center of Mount Freedom, New Jersey, before parking it beneath his window. The three leaned against a maple tree and waited, lurking like kids scheming to snare a bird beneath a cardboard box.

From his room high on the third floor, Willie watched. As he blinked wide-eyed at his cherished Impala below, a whisker of a smile broke across his parched lips. He pressed his forehead against the window to better observe the three youngsters conspiring under the tree. He might be old but he could still smell the stink of a trap. The men were gabbing on their cell phones as if their empire would collapse without their continuous attention. He knew the type well, or at least their Manhattan counterparts who made these aspiring sharks appear like guppies.

"Term insurance, always term insurance," Willie whispered, as if recalling the mantra from some past life. He remembered flogging term insurance by the bucketful to suckers like these. Or rather to their wives, whose eyes bulged when he mentioned the "million dollar" pay out. That number was magical. Oh how the word "millionaire" slid off their lipstick-caked lips with the promise of possibility. "A millionaire." It ignited daydreams of Florida resorts and nights of jitterbugging with Latin entertainers. Willie caught his reflection in the window. He chuckled as he remembered dickering with the husbands who squawked at those hefty insurance payments. How he phoned their wives in the evenings and found a check waiting on his desk the next morning.

But fate was fickle for those wives. Cigarettes, martinis, and steaks heaped thick with butter can't get you a free pass to paradise if your husband is alive and kickin'—after all, term insurance does have limits. Unknown to those women, the game was rigged. For it didn't matter what toxins their husbands crammed down their gullets; a century that began with a life expectancy of fifty and ended with eighty meant his company could lob darts blindfolded and still make a killing. Capitalism, it is said, operates in the margins. But with the war over, prosperity booming, and a wonder drug called penicillin, life insurance was second only to plastics as the next sure thing.

Willie found it ironic that in the end he was left with nothing more than a 1986 Impala he was forbidden to drive and a yellowing stack of stocks he couldn't cash. Yet if one of his boyhood Brooklyn buddies had prophesied on the grungy streets of Flatbush Avenue how one day he would achieve so much, Willie would have called him crazy. For Willie had exceeded the expectations of a skinny Jewish boy whose father barely spoke English. Once again Willie found his reflection in the window and grinned, amused that the endgame only becomes obvious at the end of the game.

Willie waited till he felt the gaze of all three administrators upon him. Leaning against the window he flashed them the OK sign. The administrators put down their cell phones and gawked, yet suspected the old man might still be hiding a few cards up his sleeve. When Willie shot them the OK signal again the administrators remained cautious. After struggling to open the window, Willie leaned out. The administrators, fearing their clever plan would turn catastrophic if Willie fell, held their breath. Willie teetered. Savoring the drama he contorted his arthritic body to lean out further. He reveled in their groans, concealing his snickering in the pit of his arm as he stretched even further.

But Willie had no intention of jumping, even though the specter of him spread-eagled on the hood of his precious Impala did cause him to compose a line or two of his obituary. And so he threw two thumbs to the sky and slipped back into his room, but not before one final slip, which left the administrators gasping. Then, to the delight of the staff at the Morningside Nursing Home, the residents, and the three administrators trying to catch their breath, Willie winked at his reflection in the window and never cried again.

American Pie

WILLIE EASELMAN DIDN'T end up at the Morningside Nursing Home overnight. His decline, as with most people his age, was gradual, beset with the usual bumps and potholes in the road. First came the simple absentmindedness, which everyone thought was cute, followed by frustrating senior moments searching for his car in parking lots, convinced someone had stolen it, until finally the dreaded word "Alzheimer's" began to slither its way into Anna's conversations with her oldest brother, Andy.

Willie, the tough World War II veteran, lived alone in the garden apartment in Mount Freedom, New Jersey he had moved to after his beloved wife died. When his "better half," as he always referred to Jeanie, passed away after more than fifty years together, he sold his house in Jersey and never looked back. Anna lived in the adjacent town and swung by a couple of times a week to check up on him, even after he started calling her "Anna the Horrible," while she referred to him as "bonkers" to anyone willing to open a sympathetic ear to her sad story. He still drove his trusty '86 Impala, although he pledged to Anna to drive the car only to the supermarket or on

Sundays to the Mount Freedom Diner, where he and the "breakfast boys" teased the young waitresses with veiled sexual asides.

Willie's freedom ride, however, was about to come to a screeching stop. One Sunday morning, after a breakfast of Belgium waffles and pork sausages, Willie took a wrong turn down the only one-way street in town. The policeman who stopped him, the grandson of one of Willie's breakfast buddies, was on the verge of letting Willie go with a warning until Willie boggled the registration exchange, handing the officer a crumpled restaurant receipt by mistake. When the officer once again asked Willie for his registration, Willie rambled about "taxes without representation" and "crooked politicians who line their pockets with pig grease." Yet it wasn't Willie's ranting that convinced the young policeman to reach over and remove the keys from the ignition; it was Willie's grin, for it was a smile wide with exaggeration but thin on cognition, similar to that of a toddler whose hand is caught in the cookie jar.

His buddies at the diner were convinced that Willie's world collapsed that day as he sat on the curb waiting for his daughter to drive him home. Later, Anna returned with her husband to drive the Impala back to their house, where it ended up parked in the back yard next to the rusting swing set. That night the couple's conversation centered on her father's deterioration.

Anna's husband asked, "How can he stay in his apartment without a car?"

Anna scoffed, "He can if I babysit him every day."

"Maybe he'll agree to Meals on Wheels."

"He'll starve before he'll eat that stuff."

"We could stock his cabinets with cereal," her husband proposed, trying to calm down his wife. "He loves cereal and it stays fresh for months."

"And I'm supposed to be his milkmaid?"

Exasperated, Anna closed the door on their discussion with, "How can anyone in America live without a car?"

The harder Anna tried to find a solution, the more unsolvable the situation seemed. It began to consume her and soon even her simplest task felt impossible.

Anna didn't want her father to move in with them. No, her house was small and, although her first child was away at college, she still had two teenagers at home. Furthermore, her dad had never been much of a grandfather; his crisp dollar bill on birthdays was about the only thing he ever gave her kids. Willie never attended a soccer match or a little league game, even when her oldest was the starting pitcher in the all-star game and Willie drove by in his Impala. It was no wonder that her boys and her father weren't close, and Anna no longer corrected her boys when they giggled about how "Grandpa smelled funny." More significantly, her husband was a private man and she knew that her dad's presence would wedge them more apart than they already were.

Anna's brother, Andy, who had always been her father's favorite, owned a huge house on the Maine coast and his children were grown and gone. But Andy repeatedly dodged Anna's hints that Dad should move in with him. Anna knew that her brother's wife wanted no part of the old man. Her sister-in-law believed that Willie was certifiable—continuously citing a visit a few years back when Dad became belligerent, convinced that Andy was plotting to steal his car.

"Over my dead body," Dad growled, taunting Andy by dangling his car keys in his face. "Shoot me now and take me out of my misery."

As for Anna's other brother, well, he was as good as useless.

In the weeks following the officer taking his keys, Willie began to suspect his daughter had joined the conspiracy, suspicions that Anna believed were morphing into paranoia. Willie barred Anna from his apartment, jeering at her behind locked doors with cries of "Lizzie Borden." When Anna countered that it was the police who took his keys, Willie just sneered, "You've been fucking that cop since high school."

Anna was on the verge of calling health authorities when Willie relented and opened the door. Inside, Anna found unopened bags of Meals on Wheels scattered throughout his apartment and letters strewn across the kitchen table addressed to his congressman. The barely legible letters were incoherent, rambling about his "unalienable rights" that were being stolen from him or how driving a car was a Second Amendment right.

Anna tried to reason. "But you're going to starve if you don't eat!"

Pounding his chest, her father shot back, "My only regret is that I only have one life to give for my country."

"And what good is that if you're dead?"

He shook his fist in his daughter's face. "What good is any man who can't drive?"

"But the officer did it for your safety."

"That kid's nothing but a God-damn messenger boy. It was YOU. You always wanted my car."

Willie started to cry and, consumed with grief, reached for Anna's arm. The touch of his hand flooded Anna with memories of her father's gentleness while growing up. Her father always took her side when she fought with her mother; took her side even when he knew his wife's anger would later turn on him. A slight tear now settled in Anna's eye as she heard her father's tirade begin to fragment, like the letters on the table, into incoherence, and a sadness overwhelmed her as she watched her father stagger to his worn armchair and collapse, too weak, too exhausted, too old to go on.

Anna called Willie's doctor, who responded to each incident she detailed with a weary but detached, "Oh my!" Later that day a social worker met Anna at Willie's front door with a nurse, two policemen, and the chain-smoking superintendent, who brandished a ring of keys, bragging about the apartments, as if he was the owner. The group barged into Willie's apartment after the briefest knock, and while the social worker pulled a bewildered Willie aside and talked to him in a soft, patronizing tone, the two policemen shoved their way into Willie's bedroom and stuffed two suitcases with his belongings. As Willie was being led off, he turned to Anna standing by the doorway.

"Rot in hell, you harlot," he spat.

Anna averted her eyes. But when her father stumbled, kept from falling by the two policemen, Anna grabbed the railing with both hands and wept.

Seeing this, her father sneered, "Your mother always said you'd never amount to much."

With a policeman on each arm, they lifted a muttering Willie Easelman into the cruiser and strapped him to the back seat. Yet, as they started for the Morningside, Willie squirmed his way to the window. "You'll get yours," he threatened. When that failed to get a reaction from Anna, Willie pounded on the window. "You'll get yours," he fired, "like when that Meyer kid stuck it up your dress on prom night."

Hide-and-Seek Sneak a Peek

IT WAS TAMMY Adler, the Morningside social director, who discovered the secret of Willie's fixation with hiding. Even after Willie stopped crying, he continued his annoying habit of leaping out and tagging the female Haitian aides. But over time Willie developed a variant of that game. For hours on end, sometimes as long as an entire day, he would hide, concealed behind a vacuum cleaner in the janitor's room or inside piles of laundry, which now had to be inspected before being placed in the large commercial washing machines. Willie's hiding heightened the Haitians' stress, which worsened the longer Willie remained hidden. Sometimes, when Willie stayed hidden all day, the tension would reach the point that the aides refused to go into closets, a choice hiding spot for Willie. The Morningside staff reprimanded Willie, especially when he violated a resident's bedroom with his hiding stunts. An appalled Doris Manheim fretted about finding Willie under her bed and demanded that a female aide check it before she would fall asleep each night. Since Willie rarely chatted with other residents he became easy prey to rumors and suspicions spread by those who alleged that Willie's hiding wasn't all so innocent.

Willie's favorite hiding place was the kitchen, where he spent hours in the cabinets. To the good-natured Haitian cooks, all of them men, Willie became a mascot, and while they went about the drudgery of preparing meals, they would joke "Where's Willie?" or "Willie's got us fooled this time." Although these comments brought muffled giggles from deep inside the cabinets, Willie never popped out until the cooks cried, "We give up!" and Willie emerged victorious.

It was a cold December day when Tammy Adler went to the kitchen to make herself a cup of hot chocolate. She heard rustling. Thinking it was Wilma Fogerty's cat, who routinely escaped from Wilma's room, Tammy flung open the cabinet door, surprised to find a wide-eyed Willie staring back at her. Although Tammy knew Willie, the Morningside being a small, intimate facility, the fact that Willie rarely spoke to anyone other than the Haitians meant they had never talked.

"Good afternoon, Willie."

Willie blinked. Peering around to find the cooks gone, he made a bee-line for the swinging door. But Tammy, knowing Willie's zeal for playing tag, tapped him on his shoulder, shouting "Gotcha!"

Willie turned and tagged Tammy on her arm. "Gotcha back," he hollered with delight.

"Gotcha back a triple-time, no nickel-and-dime," Tammy shot back, and Willie's body went limp with defeat.

After gulping down two cups of hot chocolate, smothered with whipped cream and stirred with a candy cane, Willie looked up at Tammy. "You know this place really hasn't changed one iota."

Tammy gave Willie her patient, understanding smile. "What are you saying, Willie?"

Willie looked around, a dab of whipped cream stuck to his nose. "Uncle Al found it: a place where you could get a warm kosher meal, a clean room, and a bellyful of laughs for less than a buck. My uncle was a shyster. Bragged up and down Flatbush Avenue how he stole the place for fifty cents a night."

"Fifty cents would be quite a bargain," interjected Tammy, going along with Willie's fantasy.

"My uncle was a fast talker. The only thing he paid top dollar for was Kansas City steaks. My mother called him a shnorrer, a one-arm Jew who can't find his wallet."

"But fifty cents, Willie?"

"Uncle Al watched peep shows for a nickel. Knew uptown girls who charged half what the floozy bowery babes charged."

Tammy's face blushed to a mid-western shade of red. "So Uncle Al found the room?"

"Here."

"The Morningside?"

"Not this shit hole, the other Morningside."

Tammy, thrilled with her sudden breakthrough with Willie, ignored his crass comment. "And so Uncle Al found the Morningside?"

"We piled in the Desoto—me, my dad, and Uncle Al. We took the ferry to Hoboken and topped off the tank. Handed the man a crisp five-dollar bill."

"Your Uncle Al has a Desoto?"

"A Desoto Six. Swindled it from a widow after the crash."

"A wrecked Desoto?"

"No, stupid, after the stock market crash. Her husband had ordered the car from Detroit before the crash."

"So your uncle bought the car from a widow?"

"Her husband flew tweet-tweet out a Wall Street window. Uncle Al got the car for a song—and a bonus back-room romp with the shiksa."

"And the three of you found the Morningside in his Desoto?"

"Me, my dad, and Uncle Al. The roads were rutted back then. We drove all day. My uncle said the Grand View was a rip-off and Mrs. Levine a baleboosteh. But the Morningside was cheap. He haggled Mrs. Lieberman down to fifty cents a night."

Suddenly it made sense to Tammy. Willie had been here as a boy. The Morningside Nursing Home had once been the Morningside Hotel. It started as a Victorian farmhouse that rented rooms, but became a full-fledged hotel in the 1920s, when the Lieberman family bought it. They expanded the hotel in the '30s, adding a two-story wing in the rear. They ran ads in the Brooklyn newspapers, enticing city dwellers to the countryside with catchwords like bathing, fishing, dancing, and, of course, kosher food. The Liebermans retained the original character of the house, converting the parlor into a lobby with velvet sofas and armchairs, while carving out an arched alcove for Pauline Lieberman's office where she greeted guests and tallied bills.

Tammy Alder also knew a bit about Mount Freedom's history, about how in the '30s the rural town became a favorite for city residents trying to escape summer's heat. Being close to Brooklyn, the region became known as the "Borsht Belt," as Mount Freedom and a string of other towns in northwest Jersey began catering to Eastern European Jews, recent immigrants who found the countryside here nostalgic. For kids like Willie, who lived in crowded tenement houses, these two-week stays were escapades into a world of forests and streams, frogs and turtles, a magical place where they could play games past bedtime while their parents jitterbugged to the swing bands. Every hotel, regardless of size, provided entertainment, and many a band, crooner, or comedian got their start by booking one-night stands at these welcoming venues. These first "hotels" were little more than rooms to rent in a house, but as roadways improved and the automobile became dependable, some grew into fashionable destinations like the Sains and the Sunrise, which at their peak in the '50s commanded more than 100 rooms.

"Uncle Al loved his Desoto Six," Willie went on. "Four doors, 55 horsepower, and a spare tire to boot. Mom said he worked twelve-hour shifts at the bakery, six days a week, so he could parade his car down Flatbush Avenue on Saturday nights. I got a nickel to wash it and a penny when I scrubbed the whitewalls with Ajax. Uncle Al let me switch on the electric wipers and beep the trumpet horn at pretty women. On holidays we took the Desoto uptown to visit the girls. They gave me candy when Uncle Al went upstairs; then he gave me a dime to tell my mother we were fishing off the piers."

"Fibbing to your mother is naughty, Willie," Tammy intervened, a bit taken aback by Willie's story.

Disturbed from his daydream by her outburst, Willie replied. "My mother's dead!" which left an uneasy silence between them.

Deciding this was enough of a breakthrough for one day, Tammy returned to her task of hiring the Frank Sinatra impersonator, a favorite with the Morningside's residents, most of whom believed he was the original. In her haste, Tammy left her red scarf dangling on the stool. Willie snuck back inside the dented stainless-steel cabinet. But he didn't close the doors all the way. Peeking through the crack, Willie continues to journey back, back to his days at the Morningside Hotel.

It's the year of Willie's Bar Mitzvah. Saturday night and the Big Bands are going to light up the Sains. Most of the parents are going there, or if drinking is their pleasure, to Little Broadway, where liquor is available. Both are a short walk from the Morningside, along a torch-lit path. As parents dress for a night on the town, the kids gather, knowing the hotel will be theirs for the evening or until their parents return from the Sains singing "The Dipsy Doodle," or from Little Broadway, just plain tipsy.

It is the custom at the Morningside that on the Saturday night before Labor Day the kids play one final game of hide-and-seek. This ultimate game begins in the lobby with the ceremonial drawing of the "Schmuck Card." Willie knows all of Morningside's best hiding places. Last year he won the contest by contorting his slender body into the concealed compartment of the piano bench. It was a daring strategy, since the piano nearly touched the antique oak tea table designated as home base. But the plan worked, and Willie became the first kid in the history of the Morningside Hotel not to be found.

Tonight his idea is equally novel. The kitchen, with its kosher recipes and exotic smells, has always been off limits, not because of any rule but because it's just plain creepy. As the door swings shut behind Willie, the lingering odor of stale bread causes his stomach to sour. Pushing aside pots and pans, Willie slips into the stainless-steel cabinet, leaving the doors slightly ajar so as not to be taken by surprise. He's been hiding there for a while when he hears the kitchen door creak. It's dark, but he sees shadows moving towards him.

Peering through the slit in the cabinet, Willie sees Suzie Isenberg with a boy. She's older, sixteen, and no longer plays games with the kids. Willie is nervous. Years ago Suzie cornered him on Albany Avenue and pulled down his pants to amuse her friends. It's one of Willie's earliest memories. He remembers running home and telling his mother, who was playing mahjong with his aunt. They burst out laughing and called him a putz. "Every boy wants his pants pulled down by a girl," his aunt cackled. Uncertain why he became so upset, Willie refused to eat dinner that night, even though his mother was frying chicken livers. Since then Willie kept his distance from Suzie, even after stories circulated that she lets you peek under her blouse for a dime.

Suzie and the boy unroll a beach towel and in the midst of a jingle of giggles lay down on the kitchen floor. Willie knows a bit about kissing, even though he's never observed his parents doing it. Willie is surprised by the way they kiss, how they greedily search out each other with their mouths open. They also roll around, both struggling to end up on top. When Suzie's there she strokes the boy on his cheek and floods his face with kisses, but when he's on top he slides his hands under Suzie's blouse, something that puts a halt to the kissing.

"But I won't see you till next year," the boy begs. Willie recognizes the voice, a lifeguard at the Sains Hotel.

"You can wait forever, for all I care," Suzie balks, as she tucks her blouse back in.

"Give me a little something to remember you by. Something to last the year."

"I'm tired," Suzie whines.

"I'll do the work."

"All the boys say that," Suzie snickers, then takes the lifeguard's hand and places it on her breasts. His eyes come alive. "Remember these when you're bored at school," she teases, then bites him on the neck. "Ouch!" he cries. Suzie kisses the red spot on his neck, then parts her legs slightly so he slips between them.

Although technically considered a grown man, by virtue of his recent Bar Mitzvah, Willie doesn't have the whole shtup thing down. He knows men and women do things when they're alone, things which are strange and forbidden. The rabbi had hinted about them during his Bar Mitzvah studies, but Willie hadn't understood when the rabbi winked at him and spoke about the "temptation of the apple" and "the evils of Eve." Last year, behind PS 109 Willie paid a nickel to an eighth grader to gawk at a magazine showing naked women. He knows women are different. They have tits, something that Uncle Al was fond of playing with. "Tits nourish you as a baby, but nurture you as a man," Uncle Al told him. But beyond that, this man and woman thing is a real mystery to Willie.

When Suzie pulls the lifeguard's hands off her breasts, he chides "You're a tease."

"So I'll do the teasing," Suzie answers, as she runs her hand up the boy's leg. She sits up and under the dim light of the clock starts undoing the buttons of her blouse. One by one she unbuttons them, while watching the boy's face go numb. She's wearing nothing underneath and Willie sees her tits. They're not as big as the women's in the magazine, but Willie is overcome with the urge to touch them. The lifeguard's mouth devours them and as Suzie leans back and draws him on top of her, Willie reaches down and undoes his zipper.

The lifeguard tires of her breasts and tries sneaking his hand up her skirt. "No!" she says, so emphatically that Willie stops what he's doing.

"Just a touch?" the lifeguard pleads.

"When it's time."

"It's time for me."

"Well it's time-out for me."

Suzie goes back to kissing and the lifeguard to touching her tits.

"Have you done it before?" Suzie innocently asks.

"Have you?"

A grin rises across Suzie's face. "That's for me to know and you to find out."

Willie's eyes remain glued on Suzie's face as she lets the lifeguard stay on top. From inside the cabinet he watches their bodies fuse together. They find a tempo, their hips grinding back and forth in rhythm. Suzie's eyes close, as the lifeguard thrusts harder into her thighs. The window is ajar and Willie hears the swing of the distant saxophones. Suzie's mouth is inches from Willie; he sees her teeth biting hard on the boy's shoulder, though he appears not to feel it. The sax blends with her groans, shrieking madly as the boy's hands roam freely beneath her skirt. With the jitterbug whirling in the background, Willie grips his shvantz, pulls down his pants, his hand beating to the rhythm of Suzie's sighs.

When the boy pulls down her underwear, Suzie hesitates. Willie stops, though his body aches to continue. Suzie reaches down and takes the boy's hand, positioning it deep between her legs. She utters a moan deeper than the saxophones, as she begins to move the boy's hand back and forth. Willie feels his own body swell beneath the spell of her body. He clenches himself harder as Suzie gasps for breath. Her skirt is above her waist and the darkness between her legs draws him in. The lifeguard tugs to remove his jeans but they become tangled in his shoes. The harder he struggles the tighter they wrap his legs. Willie can see the lifeguard's shvantz rising. Suzie reaches over and grips it with both hands, teases him with her teeth. He tries to roll back on top but she turns him aside with a yank. His body quakes as she shakes his shvantz harder and then mounts him. She hovers above him. His body arches towards her but she pushes him to the floor with the palm of her hand. Willie grows woozy with her groaning, as she guides the boy's shvantz between her legs, and then slowly descends on him.

Willie trembles. The urge is overwhelming. He shuts his eyes and penetrates her. The saxes are screeching, as he freefalls into the mysteries of her darkness. He pushes deeper, experiencing a world never entered, never experienced, as the music screams to a crescendo. Suzie gasps, her fingernails dig into his chest. Willie mutters "fuck" into the chaos of his erupting body.

Curled within the cabinet, Willie watches Suzie withdraw herself from the lifeguard. The lifeguard starts to speak but she silences him, pushing him aside with a simple shove. Rising to her knees, she turns, peering into the slit in the cabinet. She runs her hand through her tasseled hair. Sweat rolls down her naked body. She kneels in front of the cabinet, her breasts choking Willie with desire. She places a finger to her lips, licks it with her tongue, then reaches over and shuts the doors, sending Willie into the shadows of his imagination.

Willie lays there spent, his body curled in the cabinet. The Big Band has grown silent; the screech of the saxophones resound in some unknown part of his brain. He opens the doors. A red scarf that wasn't there before, drapes the stool. Suzie is gone, although her fragrance lingers.

"Gotcha," a voice whispers in his ear.

Willie freezes, wondering if he has won.

White Rabbit

FOR MONTHS AFTER her father was confined to the Morning-side, Anna would awake from a dreadful nightmare, believing her father was being tortured. Her father's torturers were always different: a doctor, a boss, even her mother. Her dreams were so real that she would lie in bed, trying to piece reality back together, as if her mind was a puzzle. These nightmares were particularly vivid on the nights preceding her visits to her father, which Anna detested. Her father might see her as an uncaring bitch of a daughter, but from the start of his decline Anna was there for him—whether he knew it or not.

For years Anna had accompanied her father on his medical visits, trying to impress on his doctor her father's declining condition. From time to time she even got his doctor to run a few cognitive tests, ones her father thought were childish.

"How can they ask me how many fingers Jack is holding up, when I don't know who Jack is?"

Shocking to Anna, these tests always ended up inconclusive.

"Your father's brain still functions," the kindly physician would tell her. "But he's no spring chicken."

"But something's wrong," Anna cried, wringing her hands.

"The brain is still a mystery," the doctor sadly noted, as they watched Willie motoring around the waiting room driving a Big Wheel.

Anna concluded that her father's deteriorating mental state was beyond the scope of his small-town doctor, so she persuaded the general practitioner to refer her father to a specialist.

After a two-month wait for an appointment, Anna arrived at the specialist's office with her father, where she was presented with a fifteen-page questionnaire, asking everything from the age her father reached puberty to if he had been bullied as a child. While Willie sat amused by Oprah's show featuring run-away teenage girls who fall prey to prostitution, Anna fell prey to questions which highlighted the fact that Anna knew little about her father's life. She scarcely knew his mother's maiden name, and for her grandmother's birthplace she simply wrote "Russia." History, it occurred to her as she struggled with the questions, is erased as fast as it appears—disappearing ink that leaves us strangers to ourselves. "A nation of gypsies," she muttered, as she made a mental note to write down what she could recall about her parents' lineage.

By the time the receptionist informed Anna that the doctor would see her, she was exhausted. The specialist was younger than she expected and yawned continually through his fifty-minute evaluation. Although he scoured the questionnaire methodically with the tip of his pencil, and had Willie's medical history from his primary physician, the specialist never spoke directly to her father before declaring he had stage-three dementia. Annoyingly referring to Willie as "Dad," the specialist droned about the slippery slope Dad was skidding down. In the specialist's opinion, nothing could be done but pick a nursing home or, "if his finances were sound," assisted living. If, on the offhand chance she was a "guiding angel," who wanted Dad in her home, something he strongly recommended against, then she should start making arrangements now.

"Leave Dad to the professionals," he said, closing the book on her father. "Dad's a drowning man. He'll take you down with him and you won't get as much as a thank you."

Anna wanted to argue, wanted to tell the specialist how much her dad meant to her. But with a glance at his watch, the specialist anticipated her hurt.

"As the offspring of the unfortunate, we yearn to give them the care they once gave us. When a baby cries, our instincts tell us to rush to their crib. But with the elderly it's different; their cries wake us to our own mortality. It's a cry few can listen to." And with that wisp of wisdom, the specialist scribbled his name on a scrap of paper, handed it to Anna, and scurried from the room, apparently late for his next appointment.

On her way out of the office, Anna was stopped by a sympathetic receptionist, who offered her condolences, along with a handful of tissues, and a $650 bill, which Anna was expected to pay before leaving.

To Anna, who had endured the symptoms, diagnosis, and eventual cure of a host of childhood illnesses contracted by her three children, this "nothing more to be done" prognosis was unacceptable.

"Give him something!" she pleaded to his doctor, who stood fidgeting with his stethoscope, before writing a scrip for a popular antidepressant.

During the months that followed, she pestered his doctor with names of drugs she read about in magazines or over the Internet, some of which he begrudgingly prescribed. She left messages with his receptionist about miracle cures that the FDA had yet to approve and herbs from the rainforests of the Amazon, all guaranteed to improve memory. She started sprinkling ginkgo leaves on his Cheerios and became friendly with the salespeople at the nutrition store, who never ran out of helpful suggestions. When each promising drug turned to disappointment, despite the impressive list of physicians who indorsed them, and nothing slowed the "slippery slope," Anna became convinced that her father needed a psychiatrist, preferably a renowned one. After months of unreturned phone calls and warnings about "Medicare's paltry reimbursement policy," Willie's overworked primary doctor finally provided a referral.

The six-month wait for an appointment with the psychiatrist was excruciating. Her father's condition worsened by the day and Anna began swallowing her father's pills, which he adamantly refused to take, to alleviate her growing anxiety. No one understood her situation, how her father's mindless giggling at an afternoon prize show caused her to snap at her children watching a reality show. She worried herself into more pills with fears about her father burning down his apartment house or plowing his Impala into a busload of school kids. Yet she survived the six-month ordeal, at the expense of her relationship with her husband, although as she applied make-up in her hallway mirror the morning of her appointment, mounting doubts of ever finding a cure caused her to down a pink pill she recently purchased over the Internet.

Anna found the renowned psychiatrist, Dr. Weimer, on the twelfth floor of an Upper Eastside Manhattan medical building, whose lobby was a replica of a Renaissance Italian villa, complete with a four-tiered marble fountain that apparently served as a wishing well. The psychiatrist's waiting room was adorned with soft leather chairs and mirrored the Italianate theme of the lobby, an expansive set of Palladium windows providing an unobstructed view of the East River. Anna observed the meticulous detail that extended to the human anatomical Da Vinci prints that lined the faux stone walls, although the eerie sense of being watched caused her to study the pale-blue reproduction of "David" for a hidden camera.

The receptionist offered Anna and her father coffee and a tray of pastries. Willie gobbled down the strawberry croissants with both hands, leaving a spot of jam on his shirt, which Anna tried to remove by licking her handkerchief and dabbing at the stain, something her mother used to torture her with. The questionnaire came bound in burgundy leather and was more comprehensive than the one Anna completed for the specialist. It took Anna two hours, during which time her father stood fascinated by a colorful display of salt-water fish swimming around a ceramic pirate ship.

"Row, row, row your boat, gently down the stream," her father annoyingly sang to the fish over and over, forgetting the second line of the song that every schoolboy knows.

Anna didn't know if she should laugh or cry as she watched her father's face, distorted by the water of the fish tank, waving at the fish with the wonder of a four-year old. What if he regresses any further? But Anna got hold of herself before her fears started to freefall any further by taking deep breaths, although when she was unable to answer the first question, a spiraling sense of dread made her surreptitiously slip her hand into her purse and swallow another pink pill.

When she finally completed the questionnaire, an assistant with an Ivy-League style of dress, entered and led them into a private room where he went over with Anna the minutia of her father's life, while leaving Willie free to fidget with the strawberry jam stain on his shirt. It was clear from his synopsis of her father's condition that the psychiatrist's office had received accounts from both her father's primary doctor and the specialist. When this ordeal was completed, the assistant took Willie by the hand, leaving Anna alone with a stack of magazines highlighting everything from Florida fly fishing to Milan's spring fashions.

Sitting alone in the windowless room, Anna began losing track of time. The fashion magazines soon bored her as she struggled to keep her eyes open. Adrift in thought she began to believe that her father could be cured with one visit, one magical pill that only Dr. Weimer possessed. She saw her father emerging from his session as a young man, strong and protective. Anna's dreams were so life-like that she didn't hear the assistant enter, he awakened her with a gentle shake of her shoulder, led her down a twisting hallway and through a series of arched mahogany doorways with oversized brass doorknobs on the open doors. Anna was ushered into an expansive room where her father sat in an armchair alongside an impeccably dressed man that Anna took to be the famous psychiatrist, Dr. Weimer. A massive, hand-carved desk, with a glistening marble top, took up a good portion of the room, although, with the exception of the burgundy folder she had filled out, the desk was empty. The assistant remained, standing in a corner taking notes.

The middle-age psychiatrist lifted himself with difficulty out of his leather armchair and strolled over to Anna. Extending his hand with a weak but welcoming shake he introduced himself, without so much as a nod in the direction of his assistant, who seemed to disappear into the Italianate wallpaper.

"Your father and I have had a most productive chat," the psychiatrist began in a crisp Eastern European accent Anna found difficult to understand. "He's had a rather remarkable life, something I trust you, as his daughter, are well aware of." Turning back to Willie, Dr. Weimer flashed him the OK signal, as if in their short time together they had developed a private bond. Willie returned the signal, peering foolishly through the circle his finger and thumb made.

"Your father's condition is extraordinary," Dr. Weimer began to Anna. "As Dr. Adams previously diagnosed, your father has stage-three dementia, although I suspect that in the months since that diagnosis your father's condition has noticeably slipped. I see your father's physician prescribed a scattering of pharmaceuticals and homeopathic remedies, none of which apparently has worked."

In the ensuing silence Anna nodded.

"Yes, the world never tires of miracle cures," the doctor spoke in the direction of his assistant. "Apparently it's part of the human condition."

The psychiatrist glanced over at Willie, who had scampered over to the bank of windows which filled an entire wall of the office. There he looked through an antique brass telescope aimed at the river below. Amused, Willie swung the telescope around and looked through the other end.

"Yes," the doctor replied. "One end of the telescope makes you larger, and one end makes you small." Satisfied that Willie was entertaining himself, Dr. Weimer turned back to Anna.

"But let's back up, shall we? You were recommended by your father's physician, who observed deterioration in your father's psyche."

"It's pretty hard not to notice," Anna shot back, nodding towards her father who was waving to people twelve stories below.

Smiling admiringly at Willie, the doctor continued. "We here at the Memory Institute owe our origins to Dr. Fredrick Drinkinheimer, a turn-of-the-century German psychiatrist who was a contemporary of Dr. Alzheimer, and I might dare say, a man of infinite compassion. While Dr. Alzheimer waltzed into medical fame on the strength of a single patient's diagnosis, Dr. Drinkinheimer was exiled to obscurity, usurped by the pharmaceutical companies whose profits came to dominate our field. Dr. Drinkinheimer's approach to dementia was both novel and simple. He believed that human consciousness was essentially a story we have told ourselves about ourselves and that memory disorders could be cured, or at least modified, by retelling the story the patient has regrettably forgotten. He was a pioneer in reconstructive memory, a giant of a man who unfortunately died before many of his theories could be substantiated."

Anna wrung her hands in her lap. "But certainly there's a medical component to my father's condition."

"Undoubtedly," Dr. Weimer replied. "But Dr. D, as we at the institute fondly refer to him, wasn't concerned with the physical side. He believed that although the patient's story, his consciousness, had been ravaged by illness or by age, substituting a new story could create a new self every bit as real as the forgotten one."

Anna rubbed her forehead. "A fictional self?"

The psychiatrist hesitated, having caught his reflection in the huge mirror propped against the wall. "If one can make that distinction, yes, fictional."

"But why not recreate a patient's real but forgotten past?" Anna asked.

Fidgeting with his tie, the psychiatrist chuckled. "Excellent question, my dear. Dr. D wasted an exorbitant part of his career attempting just that. His office was cluttered with photo albums and memoranda of his patients, but unfortunately this path always led to dead ends. Apparently humans are hard-wired to take a road but once."

"Hence, the road not taken," his assistant dryly interjected from his corner.

"But would my father be the same person? I mean if my father was to be given a new ... story, wouldn't it be like creating a new person?"

The psychiatrist laughed to himself "Who am I? Ah, that's the great enigma—a riddle that even the great Odysseus couldn't answer."

"Well, I know who I am," Anna replied defiantly.

Still struggling to get his tie perfect, the psychiatrist glanced at Anna, with a patronizing smile. "You must understand, Ms. Tanner, that we're dealing with a most difficult situation. We are not creating a new story, so much as altering a forgotten one. But if it becomes a choice between a buccaneer," and here Dr. Weimer nodded at Willie who was waving a plastic pirate's sword, "and someone spouting Shakespeare, which character would you prefer to call 'Dad'? What might be fiction to you becomes fact to your father."

"You can do this?" Anna hesitantly asked.

Apparently pleased with the knot of his tie, the psychiatrist turned from the mirror. "We've had our successes."

"So you can do this with my father?"

Anna's question seemed to trouble Dr. Weimer. He shuffled over and pointed out something to Willie on the river below, who after a crisp, "Aye, aye, Captain," rotated the telescope in that direction.

"What makes your father's case so unique is that he appears to lack any notion of time. His memory, on the other hand, is spectacularly intact, with one caveat: he has no idea when that memory occurred. Thus a trip to the grocery store that he took as a young boy becomes confused with a trip he took to the supermarket yesterday."

"But on his good days my father's aware of his surroundings. In fact, he is often quite normal."

"That's because on your father's good days he is experiencing the present and not the past. Thus he is often capable of conversing with his buddies or driving a car, although I would emphatically discourage driving. Your father's problem, if we define it as a problem, arises when he is experiencing the past. We so-called normal people utilize the past, make projections base on it, but we keep it phenomenologically isolated from the present. But your father, having lost that separation, apparently can process the past in a unique way."

"But don't dementia patients do that—live in the past?" asked Anna.

The psychiatrist turned back to the mirror, as if searching for an answer in the depth of the looking glass.

"Yes, dementia patients do remember the past, often with remarkable detail. But their past is frozen; it's a world that's accessible, but unalterable. Mother is always mother; the family dog always ends up getting hit by a car. Childhood memories, either horrors or harmonies, remain locked in a state of perpetual stasis."

"And my father?"

"Your father apparently has the ability to alter his past by reliving it in the present."

"Possibly creating a new story in the process, ergo a new self," butted in the assistant.

The psychiatrist's gaze remained fixed on the mirror. "To be perfectly honest, Ms. Tanner, we're not completely certain what your father's psyche is capable of creating."

Anna rubbed her temples, while trying to present the impression that she understood.

"Maybe my assistant can clarify."

"We all see the outside world from within," the assistant began after the briefest of coughs. "What you call the 'I,' or what we at the institute refer to as the 'I Am,' is, in fact, nothing more than the story you tell yourself about yourself."

"I am therefore I am," Dr. Weimer chanted into the mirror with a snide snicker.

The assistant continued, "It's this story which makes us human. And, like a story, it is imperative for one's narrative to have a timeline. One doesn't go from diapers to college and then back to grammar school. Time, in the usual sense, is an arrow moving in one direction, which gives effect to cause. Without time, events would appear to be random, much like how demons and gods spontaneously materialized in the cortex of pre-consciousness man."

"Are you talking hallucinations? My father doesn't hallucinate."

"Not yet," cautioned the psychiatrist, "but in time, or rather without time, I suspect he will."

Anna collapsed into her chair, tugging at a loose stitch in her blouse. "You mean my father doesn't know the difference between a memory and something happening now?"

"Precisely. You sitting here in your chair and a childhood memory of you in a high-chair blend and blur to him."

Anna slumped deeper into her chair.

"What's more, my examination reveals that your father can't determine his own age. That is, when your father awakes in the morning he could see himself as an eighty-six-year-old man in the mirror, but then again he might be looking at a six-year-old boy. On the bright side, your father probably will remember you, unlike those unfortunate souls afflicted with Alzheimer's."

Struggling to see any bright side, Anna said, "But you can fix him, right? Give him a new story?"

Lost in the mirror, Dr. Weimer flicked a spec of dust off his shoulder. "You must understand, Ms. Tanner, that even our most promising patients have a low cure rate. Our modus operandi is in its infancy."

"But my father?"

The doctor glanced at his assistant, a look that Anna took as not too promising.

"As my assistant explained, time is essential to our story, to consciousness. Dr. D believed that the processing of time was the evolutionary leap that gave rise to modern consciousness."

"But if my father is not processing time?" Anna asked, afraid of the answer.

Dr. Weimer turned from the mirror and answered Anna firmly. "Then from our perspective we would be just wasting our time. Pardon the pun."

In the silence that swallowed up the room, Willie pointed to a ship moving up the East River. "Are we going to take that ship to America?" he asked.

The doctor smiled. "We are, but first you need to take your daughter to school."

Willie turned to Anna. "Did you do your homework, Anna?"

The doctor coaxed Anna into replying.

"I've done my homework, Daddy."

Willie nodded. "Then you can eat your cake."

"When will we arrive in America?" Willie went on.

"When we see the large woman raising her arm," answered the psychiatrist.

"Is there anything we can do for him?" asked Anna, the magnitude of her father's condition crashing down on her.

"The brain is a marvelous enigma, Ms. Tanner. In fact, we know more about the workings of the first second of the universe, thirteen billion years ago, than we know about the human brain. It's a galaxy unto itself, and infinitely more complicated. We can poke it, knock it, shake it about, but it remains elusive, an elegant black box, as Dr. D liked to call it. Like gravity, we can measure it to the nth degree, but, as with gravity, we haven't the slightest notion how it actually works."

"And his ... prognosis?" Anna asked, pleased that she sounded slightly more professional.

The doctor walked over to Willie who had locked his telescope on a photograph of the Statue of Liberty hanging on the wall.

"Medically, we can expect a continual decline, although your father's condition is rare, which makes any prognosis rash."

"And psychologically?" Anna asked, the tenor of hope drained from her voice.

"That is pure speculation. Throughout his career, Dr. Drinkinheimer operated on the fringe of traditional psychiatry. But during his last years he became distant and aloof. 'Mad Fred,' colleagues began calling him. It was during this period that he advanced his more curious theories on time."

Dr. Weimer looked through the telescope at the photograph. "Yes, that's our lady, the one with the torch."

Willie mumbled something.

"It says, 'Bring me your tired, your poor, your huddled masses yearning to breathe free.'"

"Is she wearing underwear under the robe?" Willie snickered.

"You'll have to ask the French. They dressed her."

"I'd like to undress her," Willie went on. "Are they real?"

Dr. Weimer shook with laughter. "As real as real can be."

"According to his unpublished journals," the assistant interrupted, "Dr. Drinkinheimer believed that if time collapses in the mind, so that the past and present become actively fused, it would bring about a condition he called 'singularity.'"

"Is that good?" Anna asked.

"Dr. D hypothesized that singularity would mirror many of the chimerical time riddles revealed by relativity. His unfortunate quote, 'The future is the grandfather of the past,' was ridiculed shamelessly at the time."

"It sounds ... "

"Absurd?" interjected Dr. Weimer, his eye still locked on the telescope's eyepiece. "But let's not forget that the good doctor also held a doctorate in particle physics and no one can deny his contributions to the emerging field of quantum physics. He practically wrote the book on virtual particles."

"Something that is now common knowledge," interjected the assistant.

Ignoring his assistant's interruption, the psychiatrist continued. "It was Dr. D's belief that without time, the event horizon of the brain would collapse, creating 'vistas' into the future. We're all a bit sketchy as to the specifics, but Dr. D insisted that there was conservation of time and space, much like how energy and mass are conserved."

Anna looked at her father, who had taken back the telescope.

"These vistas into the future?" Anna murmured.

Dr. Weiner once again left it to his assistant.

"According to Dr. D, singularity was the operating principle in prophets; Nostradamus was his favorite example."

"You believe my father's a prophet?"

"Maybe not so much of a prophet, but a ..."

Willie interrupted the talk with his tenor tone, breaking into song:

> *My lass has the tits of a mermaid*
> *And the legs of a Parisian whore*
> *But I'd sail the seven seas in a teacup*
> *To plug her right there on the floor.*

The rest of the session was a blur to Anna, much like how a deep afternoon nap can bring on the strangest of dreams. While the doctor's assistant enthusiastically elaborated on the theories of Dr. D to a perplexed Anna, Willie and Dr. Weimer swapped sailor songs and jabbered like pirates.

"One curious note from our examination is that your father apparently remembers every song he's ever heard."

Anna forced a smile. "When we were kids Dad played Sinatra until he drove us crazy."

"But he retains them all, and his pitch is remarkable. I'm not sure if it's a consequence of his condition or a caprice of memory."

"Nostradamus was reported to know more than 2000 folk songs," the assistant added.

"Something undoubtedly ripe for publication in one of those pseudo-scientific journals you and your cohorts subscribe to," the psychiatrist blurted. "One more thing, Ms. Tanner. Dr. Drinkinheimer's followers tend to be mostly atheists, like my assistant James here, or agnostics in the more complicated use of the word. Their personal perspectives undoubtedly influence their interpretation of Dr. D's more esoteric works. But a smattering of, let's call them transcendentalists, view these vistas into the future, these singularities, as glimpses into an afterlife. Twisting Dr. D's words, they postulate that a person's final second would appear as an eternity to them.

"An eternity?" repeated Anna, bringing her hand to her forehead as if to arrest the spinning in her head.

The psychiatrist broke into a coy grin. "Did you know, Ms. Tanner, that a computer can exceed a thousand trillion calculations a second?"

"But…"

"And if each calculation represents one second of our time, then one computer-second worth of calculations would represent a span of time that exceeds the age of the universe. Time, Ms. Tanner, doesn't always behave as it ought to."

Anna's head was now whirling out of control and from the vortex of her chaos emerged her mother's nighttime reading voice:

Why it's simply impassible
Why don't you mean impossible?
No, I mean impassible. Nothing's impossible.

With his grin still plastered on his face, Dr Weimer turned to Anna and added, "What all this means I haven't the foggiest idea, but I thought you ought to be aware of it."

Anna's mind, riddled with perplexity, was too scattered to reply, and what thoughts she could muster up were drowned out by a voice in her head shouting, "Why sometimes I've believed as many as six impossible things before breakfast." Dr. Weimer's grin transformed into a wide simper of a smile as he shook hands with Anna. Then, rotating on his heels, he gave Willie a crisp military salute, before exclaiming to him. "The sea is a sea we are all able to see."

"We see sea shells down by the sea shore," Willie answered.

"Say that six times fast and see where it gets you."

"Aye-aye, Admiral," Willie bellowed back, clicking his heels.

The assistant shut his notebook and led Anna and Willie back through the maze of arched doors, somehow ending up back at the lobby. The assistant wished them luck and told them to keep in touch. Anna, who had concluded that the psychiatrist and his assistant were as bonkers as her father, nodded politely as she helped her father on with his coat.

The receptionist appeared out of nowhere and handed Anna an embossed envelope with Anna's name scrolled with calligraphy, containing a bill for $1,600, and a friendly reminder that they take both MasterCard and Visa. Handing the receptionist a credit card, Anna felt surprisingly relieved knowing with surety that her father wasn't going to get better and that her adventure into the world of cures had come to an end. But as Anna rummaged in her purse for her pillbox, her thoughts drifted to a peculiar question: what story would she wish for her father, if she could wish her father a new story?

Overcome and slightly dizzy, Anna stepped into the elevator. Her father pushed the "L" button and then peered at Anna for approval. As the elevator descended her father hummed, "Row, row, row your boat gently down the stream."

Looking like a kid awaiting his prize for good behavior, Willie grinned. Anna, her head swirling with contradictions, couldn't resist the urge to hug him. The elevator chimed with each passing floor, creating a melody, and causing them to break out in a duet.

Merrily, merrily, merrily, merrily, life is but a dream.

Cat's in the Cradle

THE MORNINGSIDE NURSING Home was "a nice place to
live out your golden years," according to the hand-carved sign in
the lobby that the administrators had paid fifty bucks to the high
school shop class to make. Located in Mount Freedom in pastoral
northwestern New Jersey, a town where legend is that George
Washington named it as he waited to cross the Delaware, although
legend also has it that many of the smaller hotels in town got their
start during prohibition when liquor "bubbled up from the countryside," giving a different slant to the origin of the town's name.
The town had once been a popular resort spot and the old-timers
still talk about the days when a skinny Frank Sinatra crooned or
Henny Youngman brought the house down with his quirky jokes.
With the advent of highways after the war, however, people could
drive further and the Catskills became the "in" place. Sadly the hotels of Mount Freedom were shuttered, as these once lively estab-
lishments became irrelevant; yet the Morningside Hotel was saved
from the wrecking ball by a group of small-town investors whose
accountants convinced them that nursing homes were the next
sure thing.

The Morningside was a nice facility, as nursing homes go, with the bulk of the work done by Haitians who commuted thirty miles from Newark each day in a couple of unsafe vans with rusted-out floorboards. Morningside was divided into two wings—one for those who could partially take care of themselves and one that was always kept locked. The locked wing was filled with Alzheimer's and dementia patients, with a few folks bedridden from falls. Since only one registered nurse was on duty at any one time, and never at night, Morningside had no chronically ill residents. When a resident dropped to that level of care they were unceremoniously transferred to a sister facility in Trenton, where they more or less disappeared.

Residents of the Morningside often gathered to gossip about the horrible goings on behind those locked doors.

"They force feed you in there like babies," remarked one woman.

"And no one ever visits."

But the real terror of the gossip was reserved for the residents living there.

"They've forgotten how to talk."

"They grunt like pigs."

"They don't remember their own children."

Sometimes in closed circles their gossip gravitated to sex and their suspicions of what went on behind those locked doors.

"It's done quite regularly," a silver-haired woman whispered.

"And they don't remember a thing in the morning," snorted another.

"Might have saved my marriage," a third woman added, to the snickering of all three.

While most residents at Morningside believed their lives were empty and their friends and relatives had abandoned them, when they saw those locked doors they knew things could be worse. But when those doors swung open, the residents in Wing #1 would stop what they were doing and gawk, fearing that one day those doors would open for them.

When a screaming Willie Easelman checked into the Morningside, he was temporally placed in Wing #1, although the odds were immediately put at 2 to 1 by the Haitians that he would end up behind door # 2, or the "wacky ward," as they fondly referred to it. When Willie was still screaming after five days, the odds went to 4 to 1, as Morningside's irritated residents eagerly joined the betting. Even Doris Manheim, the resident "goody two-shoes" who preached gambling was a road leading straight to Hell, placed a five-dollar wager on Wing #2, confident that Willie's destiny had been ordained by a higher power. Willie's crying added volatility to the bottom line and in the Haitian's van the odds changed regularly. When Anna's unorthodox suggestion to give her father back his Impala actually worked and his crying stopped, the money in the Haitian coffee tin was divvied up and Willie was permanently assigned a room in Wing # 1. Willie's placement in that wing probably had little to do with the Morningside's doctor who concluded that Willie's "fragmented frontal-lobe dementia" did not pose a risk of flight, but was likely due to the fact that Wing #2 was over capacity, a fact only one shrewd Haitian took note of.

Henri Pascal, the Haitian aide who won big betting on Willie, took a special liking to the old man and rearranged his small room so Willie could keep an eye on his Impala from the comfort of his armchair, the only piece of furniture that survived the move from his apartment. For weeks Willie sat in his armchair and gazed at his car. He rarely conversed with any of the residents at the Morningside, apparently content to slip into his private silence. Since he never bothered the staff or attempted to escape, his name was never brought up in the monthly staff meetings when heart-wrenching decisions over which patients would be taking the one-way journey to Wing # 2 were made, a journey into a different kind of silence.

While Willie kept mostly to himself at Morningside, he did form a friendship with Henri. On Saturdays, when Henri's short work day meant waiting four hours for his return ride to Newark, Henri often relaxed in Willie's room, listening to him reminisce. Willie, despite his silences, was also a great raconteur whose stories could mesmerize. Henri listened as Willie spoke about his old days in Brooklyn, lacing his boyhood adventures with Yiddish phrases that Henri found captivating. As a kid Willie had been a devoted Brooklyn Dodger fan, but his real zeal was for hating the Yankees. "Hate," he told Henri, "is stronger than love. It's the spice that flavors the stew, the bouquet that makes the wine." Willie once confided to Henri that he hated the Yankees more than he hated the Nazis.

"The Nazis might shoot you, might even rape your sister," he told a spellbound Henri. "But the Yankees, they rip out your heart."

Yet sometimes his stories seemed contrived, like the one about sneaking into the Polo Grounds during the 1936 World Series. It was the Giants against the Yankees and Willie's voice was thick with suspense when he detailed how he evaded the attendants at the turnstiles by carrying a stack of newspapers and posing as a newsboy.

"Planted my rear-end right down in the first row with all the big wigs. Game two of the Series. The Giants had won the first game. Win today and they'd have the Yankees on the ropes. Of course, the Giants end up losing the damn game by about a zillion runs. I loathe the Yankees, but you knew there was no way they were going to be outscored by those losers. Hell could freeze over, but those damn Yankees would just put on ice skates and glide to victory."

The staff at Morningside believed these conversations to be therapeutic, for the stories kept the pathways to Willie's past open. The staff even secretly recorded some of Willie's sessions with Henri in the unlikely event that state health officials—or worse, their lawyers—challenged Morningside's decision to keep Willie in Wing #1. On slow days the aides sometimes pulled out these tapes and played them, knowing that even though Willie's stories were probably imaginary, they were at least quite entertaining.

Henri didn't care if these stories were true or not. He loved how Willie brought his adventures to life, as if he was actually living them. Willie combined the timing of a stand-up comedian with the tenderness of a father reading a bedtime story, something Henri had never experienced. Henri fell spellbound to Willie's cadence, rhythms, even the smacking sound he made with his lips as he told tales of people like Mrs. Goldstein, "a woman wider than she was tall," whose celebrated pastries enticed the entire neighborhood to her stoop. Or his stories about kids like Pee Wee Gurstle, who having peed in his pants to avoid taking a math test, got suspended from school and a life-long nickname, "all on the same day." Most of Willie's accounts were events seventy years old, about people who, if they ever did exist, were probably dead now. But he spoke with the reverence and wonder of a child whose memories hadn't dimmed with age. Time, it seemed, had no place in Willie's universe. Time was a stranger to the cobblestone streets and gas streetlights of Brooklyn and to the kooks and crazies who still inhabit those streets in Willie's mind.

Sometimes when Willie told his tales, time collapsed and his memories began to slip into the present. Pee Wee Gurstle was no longer the skinny kid from Brooklyn, but lived down the corridor in the Morningside. Suzie Isenberg was a waitress at the Mount Freedom Diner, spellbinding Willie and his buddies with her accounts of playing strip poker under the bleachers. "Win or loose," she'd say with a shrug, "you end up a winner."

"Let her have her fun," Willie confided to Henri. "She'll be married with four kids in no time, and the shtupping won't be so good."

To Henri, whose uncle was a practicing voodoo houngan, Willie's time jumping was nothing new. Ancestors were always playing tricks on you. You could be on the deck of the Santa Maria sailing with Columbus one moment and then back to geography class the next, the earth changing from flat to round with the whim of the spirits.

"Elvis isn't dead," his uncle was fond of saying. "He's drinking Piña Coladas with the Pope and singing ballads with the troubadours."

Often on lazy afternoons Henri closed his eyes and, with Willie's stories as a musical background, drifted back to when he ran with his brothers barefoot through the narrow streets of Port-au-Prince. Here were the brightly painted shacks that lined the streets, which Henri's memory transformed into majestic mansions. And as the warmth of Willie's voice carried Henri further back into the mysteries of childhood, Henri heard the squawking of chickens, fishermen's wives singing the catch of the day, and the sirens of tides calling him to play. In moments like these Henri became immersed with the joy of music, as Willie's voice smelted past, present, and future, as the ancient storytellers once did when they wove yarns without the bondage of time.

Willie sometimes cut his stories short when he detected a certain smell originating from the kitchen. "I've been here before with my father," he'd tell Henri, as he sniffed out the odor like a bloodhound. Henri, who didn't know Willie's history of vacationing at the Morningside as a boy, believed this was probably a quirk of Willie's mental state. But if Willie persisted, Henri would tell him what his uncle once told him. That "smells sail you to places, your mind has long forgotten."

"Tell me about your father," Willie prodded Henri one day, as he sat in his favorite armchair.

"My father?"

Accustomed to the lure of Willie's sing-song voice, Henri found Willie's direct question unsettling.

"Your father!" Willie repeated. "Everyone has a father."

"My father, he was a simple man," Henri began. "He never read a book. He fished off the pier, which was always crowded at dusk. He taught me how to put a worm on the hook, told me a real fisherman catches a fish even when the man standing next to him catches only a cold. He was always around the house when I was small. My mother used to complain he was there more than our rooster. But there was little work in our village and as our family grew bigger my father had to travel to find work. Suddenly he was never home."

"He went to the States?" Willie asked.

"He went to the far side of the island. My father built stone walls. But many people built stone walls in Haiti, so he went to where they were cutting down the forests for firewood."

"Firewood? I thought Haiti was warm."

"At night the ocean carries a chill."

"My grandfather made charcoal in the Ural Mountains of Russia," Willie added. "Do you know how they make charcoal?"

"No, Mr. Willie."

The old man shifted in his armchair to explain. "They cut down whole forests and burn them and when the trees are smoldering they smother them in sand."

"Charcoal pays well?"

"Better than firewood," Willie replied with a caustic laugh.

"My father made little money cutting trees. Sometimes they paid him with rum."

"Rum?"

"A bottle a day, my mother said. She said the rum demons got into his brain. They're worse than voodoo spirits, you know. My parents began arguing and one day my father was gone."

"She booted the old man out?" Willie asked.

"Yes ... booted him out," Henri sadly repeated.

"Did you ever see him again?"

Henri went over to the table and straightened the papers that were strewn about, letters to Willie's daughter, started but never finished. "Once on Easter he brought me a chocolate bunny taller than me."

"You shared it with your sisters?"

"I shared it with my stomach and the Easter spirits punished me with a tummy ache. But my mother was with a new man, a man with a good-paying job in Port-au-Prince. Things were better. We moved into a real house."

"And your father?"

"My mother said he moved to America. New York City. Told me he owned a taxi cab, but I knew she was making that up. I saw him begging in the streets, saw him stumbling around talking to himself. The rum demons had messed with his mind."

With difficulty, Willie pushed himself out of his armchair and ambled to the window. He stared at the bright afternoon sky hovering over the distant meadow before dropping his eyes to his Impala. Henri watched a tear form in the old man's eye and in a hopeful burst said, "I have two children back home. Someday my family will join me. America is a great place. We will be a family again. There are cheap houses in Newark where my wife and I will raise our family."

"How old are your children?" Willie asked, still staring out the window.

"Jamie is six and Tina two."

"A boy and a girl. Nice."

"The Lord has blessed us."

"The Lord giveth and the Lord taketh away."

"The Lord has given me much," Henri replied.

"The Lord is my shepherd."

"He is everyone's shepherd."

"I shall not want."

"In America no one wants who wants to work."

"The Lord is a tall tale," Willie spat with disgust. "He's nothing but a crappy bedtime story."

"The Lord is my father."

Willie's eyes were glazed as he turned from the window. "Fathers are frauds!"

"Fathers do their best."

"The hell they do!" Willie pounded the table so hard his tea cup tipped over.

Henri wiped up the spill with his sleeve.

Willie staggered to his armchair and collapsed, on the verge of crying. Henri felt uncertain how to calm his friend.

"Fathers are human," Henri added.

Willie sat there, his breathing abrupt and irregular, as he scoured the room looking lost and confused.

"My father came from Russia. He came to America after the great forests were cut down. In Russia there was a revolution, which meant the poor got poorer. Little food and with the forests gone there was no more charcoal to make, no more work for my father. What could he do? So he left my mother and traveled to America. He found a job in Brooklyn where he shared an apartment with ten Russians; his only possession was a lumpy mattress. When he saved up enough money he returned to Russia. He braved the cold, traveling from St. Petersburg to his old village on horseback. He bribed the corrupt officials and got his wife and her sister out of Russia. My father was less than five-feet tall, but everyone at the synagogue called him The Bear."

A pause infused the room. Henri moved to the door, uncertain if the old man finished his story. Willie's lips moved, but Henri no longer could hear what he was saying. Believing the old man would soon be asleep, Henri opened the door. But as he stepped into the hallway Willie shouted after him, "That son of a bitch could have given me a hug!"

Voodoo Child

TO THE STAFF at Morningside Willie was a model resident except for his only fault—the annoying game of hide-and-seek he continuously sprung on the Haitians. To the Haitian men, who didn't find the game threatening, Willie's behavior was just the eccentricity of an old man. Everyone fortunate enough to reach Willie's age has quirks and if you accepted that then everything went smoother. If a resident insisted on taking a bath fully clothed, then it was easier to change his clothes than to argue. The female aides, however, kept a wary eye on Willie, holding suspicions that became fertile grounds for rumors.

Convinced that an evil spirit had taken up residence inside Willie's frail frame, the Haitian woman began to conspire. The aides were unsure what the evil spirits meant. Though raised Catholic, they were fascinated with voodoo's web of spells, even though their priests condemned it as witchcraft. Since most of the Haitian women had come to America at a young age, they had only an elementary understanding of voodoo. But Willie's bloody threats for revenge on Anna awoke deep rooted fears in these women; and as they stirred the pot of hearsay and legend, they convinced themselves that Willie was someone to be feared. Phone calls were made to relatives in Haiti and eventually a consensus was reached that it was the devilish spirit Kalfu who had taken over Willie's body.

To protect themselves from the powerful Kalfu, the women gathered monthly to perform voodoo rituals they concocted but took seriously. They danced late into the night, often waking in each other's arms come morning. Having been told by mothers and grandmothers that Kalfu was notorious for mounting the bodies of women and making them perform unnatural acts, they weren't going to take chances with the crazy old man in Room 27. Some remembered how the priests in Haiti always warned of Kalfu's power to seduce, scaring them with stories about how the slippery scoundrel slips into the beds of girls at night to share in the sexual fantasies of their dreams. In the belief that blood quells the urges of the Dark One, the women took to sacrificing roosters and kept vials of rooster blood pressed against their breasts as they slept. They also added chants to their nightly prayers, ones they remembered hearing as children, meant to pacify their own desires and to placate Kalfu.

And so voodoo became both the problem and the solution. Everyone became a master of the ancient rites. Voodoo, which most of the female aides learned about in the same fashion children in America learn about trolls, goblins, and witches, no longer carried the wink of a bedtime story. With each telephone call home, the specter of Kalfu, and the fear of Willie, grew more real.

As their apprehensions grew, the acts attributed to Willie multiplied. At first these doings were harmless: the burning of a Sunday roast, a power outage, the stubbing of a toe when passing Willie's room. One night, however, an aide returned in tears to the house the Haitians rented in Newark. Her name was Simone and she had come to America after her entire family perished in the island's earthquake. She was sixteen, but her fair complexion and delicate features made her appear younger. Simone revealed that while she had been cleaning Willie's room she felt a strange presence. Turning, she saw a man staring out the window.

"I thought he might be Mr. Willie's son. I asked if I could help him but he just chuckled. Then he turned towards me. He looked powerful and his skin was the color of a man badly sunburned."

"What did he say?" one of the older Haitians asked.

"He asked me my name."

"That's all?"

"He said I was as beautiful as a freshly plucked rose."

The girls giggled.

"He came over to me and took my hand. His breath smelled like the sea."

"Was he good looking?" the older Haitian asked.

"Yes," Simone said beginning to cry again. "But when I started to leave the room he grabbed me. His hands were strong and he reached under my blouse. He touched me all over."

Knowing that Simone was a virgin, the women sighed a collective hush.

"I tried to push his hands away. It was the touch of fire," Simone continued. "He untied the string on my pants. I was nearly naked."

"Why didn't you run?"

"I couldn't move. Some power gripped me."

"Kalfu," Simone's friend Jacqueline gasped.

Now the women's faces turned serious as they closed around Simone.

"He was so strong. He lifted me up like I was a feather and carried me to the old man's bed."

"You let him take you to the bed?" asked one of the Haitians.

"I was his prisoner," she pleaded. "Helpless, I closed my eyes."

"Where was Willie?" Jacqueline asked.

Jacqueline had come to America with her mother and had remained in Newark after her mother returned to Haiti. She had taken on the role of big sister with Simone, partially due to Simone's sad story but mostly because they shared a fun-filled approach to life. Their giggles filled the Haitian's van during the early-morning commutes to Morningside, waking up the men quicker than strong coffee. Simone had a spark in her eye, a twinkle that never let her personal tragedy get in the way of a good belly laugh. Jacqueline always told Simone, beautiful and thin, like a younger sister should be, that one day she would be a famous dancer.

"Mr. Willie was sleeping in his armchair," Simone replied, looking straight into Jacqueline's eyes.

"Did he do it? Did Kalfu do it to you?"

"I crossed myself. I ..."

"Did he do it?"

"You should have called for Jesus," a chubby aide said.

"I did. I shouted 'Jesus,' as loud as I could. The man was furious, swearing in Creole. I covered my ears."

"He stopped?"

"He got so mad I thought he was going to hit me. But I kept shouting, 'Jesus, Jesus, Jesus!' That's when he bit me."

Simone opened her blouse, showing the teeth marks on her tiny breasts. The women closed in to comfort the terrified girl.

"And you were naked?" Jacqueline asked, putting her hand on her terrified friend's shoulder.

"I still had my underpants on."

The woman laughed, releasing some of the tension.

"Was Kalfu naked?"

Simone looked away from her friend. "His pants were down and his thing was out when the old man came into the room."

"Mr. Willie?" Jacqueline asked.

Simone didn't meet her friend's stare. "No, not Mr. Willie. He was older than Mr. Willie. He had a dog with him and walked with a cane. He threatened the man in a tongue I couldn't understand. The man spat at him, but when the old man raised his cane, the man ran from the room."

"Without his pants?" the chubby aide mocked.

"Legba," Jacqueline whispered.

"And your screams didn't wake up Mr. Willie?" the chubby aide continued.

"He ... he slept through it," Simone answered. "Although I thought his eyes were open ... maybe a tiny bit."

"So his powers are growing," Jacqueline pronounced.

"Who?" the women asked, their eyes large as their curiosity.

"Mr. Willie has been taken over by Legba, not Kalfu."

"Legba?"

"He's the gatekeeper who rules between the spirit world and our world," Jacqueline explained.

The ring of women tightened, their foreheads nearly touching.

"Legba is old. Some believe he's older than the earth. He's fond of young girls, virgins like Simone, because they make him feel young." Jacqueline touched Simone's hair with the tenderness of a mother. "He's more powerful than he looks and often fights with Kalfu, especially over a pretty girl."

"But he handed me my clothes. He didn't want the sex."

"Legba is clever. He wants the sex, but he wants you to crave it. He wants his virgin to take off her own clothes."

"I never want that!" Simone said, so emphatically that the circle of women giggled.

"Some say Legba is no threat, that he's a kindly old man who obeys his wife. If you're good to him he'll let you talk to your ancestors."

Simone wiped away her tears. "My parents? My brothers?"

"But be careful. Legba can seduce girls with his sweet talk, telling them what they want to hear."

"About my family?"

"Maybe he shooed away Kalfu so he can enjoy you himself."

"I'll never do that," Simone balked.

"Oh, you'll do it," the chubby aide scoffed. "Just not with an old man like Legba."

But Simone was adamant. She grabbed the Bible off the coffee table and swore on it that she'd never do such a nasty thing.

"Swear on as many Bibles as you like," one of the older aides mocked. "The woman within writes the chapters."

"And we all know how that chapter ends," laughed another.

"But I don't want the sex," Simone stammered, on the verge of tears. "Never!"

Jacqueline put her arm around her young friend and led the trembling girl to her bedroom. "Don't tell the boys about this," she whispered, as she folded the quilt back to let Simone slid between the sheets. "They'll tease you."

"Do you really believe in the voodoo?" Simone asked.

"When I was young I didn't believe in voodoo. My father told me tales about the spirits, but I thought they were just ghost stories. But voodoo's real; I feel it in my blood. You must be careful, Simone. You're young and sweet, the kind Legba wants to bed. He'll promise you treasures. He'll make you laugh, make you feel special. He'll even let you talk to your dead family. But he wants just one thing. Never go into Mr. Willie's room alone."

"I won't. But I don't believe in voodoo. I believe in the Jesus."

"Maybe it was Jesus who saved you today?"

Jacqueline lit a candle and after chanting something in Creole she placed it on the window sill. "This will scare away the spirits."

Simone sank deeper into the sheets. "Jacqueline," she whispered, hesitantly. "When I was trapped beneath my house after the earthquake I prayed to Jesus."

"And Jesus answered your prayers, yes? Everyone said it was a miracle that you survived."

"But ... but I only prayed for myself. I didn't pray for my brothers. Maybe if I ..."

Jacqueline placed a finger on Simone's lips to silence her. Immersed in the glow of the candle she was a child yearning to be hugged. Did voodoo or Jesus really matter, compared to the pain this child had lived through? Jacqueline's imagination curdled to the terrors that Simone must have experienced during those long nights beneath her collapsed house.

"Tonight Simone, think of your family watching over you. Hear the strumming of your father's guitar playing for you. Let his songs stir the joys of your youth, the memories of yesterdays, which, once upon a time, were filled with laughter."

Jacqueline sat on the edge of the bed, watching Simone. With a mother's dread, Jacqueline felt the quivers rocking Simone's body as she slipped into slumber. She was beautiful, a natural born dancer. With her hands folded under her head she was the picture of innocence. Jacqueline leaned over and whispered, "Sleep tight, my child, everything will be all right," tucking the covers around her shoulders. Simone nodded drowsily, comprehending the tone, but not the meaning of her friend's words, before wandering off to the torments of her dreams.

This Kiss

ONE SPRING SATURDAY, as the temperature pushed unseasonably over 70', Henri and Willie were sitting in their usual chairs overlooking the parking lot when Henri asked Willie if he wanted to visit his Impala. Henri knew the car keys were stashed in the desk drawer of the reception office and that after a long winter the car needed a good work-out. The two were soon tip-toeing down the back stairs, but when they reached the Impala Henri grew tense. Branches from the budding lilac trees and a coat of winter grime covered the car, making it appear discarded and forlorn. Willie approached the car tentatively. He stroked the fender, tracing the curves of the car like a young man exploring the mysteries of a woman for the first time. And then he smiled.

Henri, seeing Willie's joy reflected in the tinted glass of the windshield, offered Willie the keys. Willie hesitated, as if they were foreign, possibly dangerous. But he came around, giving Henri a conspirator's wink as he took the keys and unlocked the door. Sliding into the front seat, he centered himself behind the steering wheel, all with the grace of someone who had performed this ritual countless times before.

Henri watched through the open window as the old man, face rapt with wonder, glided his hand over the upholstery. Back and forth Willie's age-spotted hand rubbed, the simple act of touching seemingly restoring his spirit. His hand lingered on the chrome latch of the glove compartment, before coming to rest on the steering wheel.

The rev of the engine heightened the music swirling through Willie's brain. At first Willie's humming barely rose above the threshold of silence. But as his humming grew bolder, Willie's lips began to mouth a song. Lost in the fog of a world inaccessible to everyone he had ever known, Willie was trying to sing.

Henri stood by the open window. The song sounded familiar, maybe some childhood lullaby his mother once sang. Dazed and distant, Willie chanted the verse, rocking back and forth in the front seat of his Impala, like a cantor chanting on holy days. Spellbound, Willie stared straight ahead, the windshield transformed into a silver screen of yesterdays. Henri leaned closer, trying to recognize the song, the catchy little jingle snaking its way through Willie's age-ravaged brain.

Smiling, adrift in a world of altered remembrances, Willie kisses the hub of the steering wheel. She is his again—all his. The thrill of his first car, the promises that lay ahead on the open road, the dream that in America everything is possible—all converge with this kiss. Everything that has transpired, conspired, inspired, or acquired to make this slumped-over man Willie, is transformed in this instant. "Term insurance," he whispers, from deep within the cobwebs of his mind, a final curtain call heard by no one. Then, lifting his voice with the music worming through his brain, Willie bursts forth with song:

See the U.S.A., in your Chevrolet!
America's the greatest land of all.

New York, New York

THE MORNINGSIDE HOSTED two celebratory dinners where, if you could "walk, crawl, or roll out of bed," you were expected to attend. Christmas and Thanksgiving dinners were always held on an off-day, so they did not conflict with those residents whose families brought them home for a holiday meal, something that gave these residents status at Morningside. But there was one event everyone was expected to attend, everyone with the exception of those poor souls in Wing #2. The Morningside Variety Show was held once a year in mid-June. Why the tradition started had long gone the way of many of Morningside residents' memories, yet it remained the quintessential activity in Morningside's rather gloomy social calendar.

The theme for this year was Broadway and sequined Rockettes were stretched like paper dolls along the hallways, giving a refreshing sparkle to the otherwise pale green institutional walls of the Morningside. Although any resident could participate, regardless of talent, the musical numbers and theatrical skits were exclusively performed by the women. The heavily outnumbered men at Morningside, however, did their part by dressing in their finest, though outdated, suits, even though their preference would have been to be asleep. And so as June 20th rolled around and summer passions began to dance in the fantasies of the Haitian workers, the Morningside Nursing Home held its annual variety show.

With dining room tables stacked away, a small stage was rolled out and the upright piano brought in from the lobby. The residents sat on folding chairs while the staff stood at the perimeter, leaning against the cinder-block wall. The Haitians, who looked forward to the show, hooted and encouraged the shaky participants, clapping wildly after each skit no matter how botched, bungled, or blown the performance was.

Lisa "Legs" Linksy, who actually possessed musical talent and was rumored to have can-canned her butt onto Broadway at the scandalous age of sixteen, started the night off on a high note with a piano piece she had memorized. Although she played the song from "Westside Story" flawlessly, she couldn't recall the title, referring to it as "A little something by a little someone." Lisa then invited Betty Towers on stage to accompany her with a medley of Broadway hits. Squeezed together on the piano bench, the same bench that seventy-five years ago a youthful Willie Easelman had won hide-and-seek by hiding in, Betty played the bass notes of the piano with her left hand while Lisa played the treble with her right. They did struggle with page turning, though, often playing tug-of-war over a page, which brought a chorus of he-haws from the Haitians. Their last number, "Wash That Man Right Out of My Hair," from "South Pacific" was a smash and their theatrical washing of each other's hair with their free hands even brought a spattering of laughs from the local staff.

Yet after that promising start, the variety show began to collapse in predictable ways. Mrs. Heimlick recited an original poem, a cliché-riddled story about her childhood, full of green pastures and Jersey cows that talked, even though everyone knew she had grown up in Queens. Worse, she read the poem in a child's voice and spoke hunched over, mumbling into her crumpled piece of paper. She recovered at the end of the poem, however, finishing with a flourish.

When you're young and fancy-free
The treasures of the world are guaranteed

Old age is as distant as the Emerald City
Adrift in fantasy it shimmers so pretty.

Mrs. Kline then marched on stage to deliver a melodramatic reading of the "Pledge of Allegiance," which after a heart-felt opening line deteriorated into an exercise in absentmindedness, ending with "one nation under dog, with barks and growls for all." Not to be patriotically upstaged, Mrs. Oppenheimer sang "America the Beautiful" in her alto-tenor voice bronzed by more than seventy years of chain-smoking non-filtered Camels. Her performance was surprisingly first-rate and would have been the highlight of the night if she had not gotten carried away by the applause and made a bumbling attempt at the second verse. Jannie Hightower who, at seventy-two, was the youngest resident of Morningside and, in her mind, the most attractive, then struggled through a painful, single-fingered rendition of "Chop-sticks," all the while fluttering her eyelashes at the men napping in the back row.

After that, anything went, culminating with Doris Manheim's "Morality Play in One Act." In her play Doris brushed the hair of three naked Barbie dolls, while making catty comments about many of the female residents of Morningside she was convinced were on "a one-way street to hell." Generously applying lipstick to her dolls, who Doris referred to as the "Three Harlots of Hookerville," Doris pulled out a Ken doll, who engaged the three dolls in a tasteless Donkey Show. But when Doris called Lisa Linsky "a Jersey whore, who shows more tit than Zsa Zsa Gabor," she was politely led offstage, leaving behind her naked dolls in a ménage a trois of arms and legs. Having snored continuously throughout the show, Walter Wilder suddenly woke up and shouted, "I'd rodeo those three cowgirls bareback into hell." Doris rushed back on stage and pointed a crooked finger at Lisa, stammering, "Girls like you get what they deserve!"

Lisa responded by playing the opening chords of a Vaudeville melodrama, before calmly asking Doris, "And what do girls like me deserve?"

"You deserve IT!" Doris spat, as she was once again escorted offstage.

After the dolls were cleared away and, to the relief of the yawning locals, no one moved to grab the stage, Tammy Adler, the poorly paid but enthusiastic, overweight social director at Morningside, thanked everyone who performed. The social director cooed when she confessed how something stirred inside of her when she heard Mrs. Oppenheimer sing "above the fruited plain." Tammy was planning her own exit as she concluded with a mushy, "And don't we all have so much to be thankful about in America—this fruited plain we call Morningside where we live out our golden years," when Willie Easelman stood up and started walking straight towards her. The Haitians afterwards claimed that Willie actually leapt on stage, although most believed this was an exaggeration since Willie had enough trouble just standing with his arthritic knees. But in the aftermath of the night's strange events, the Haitians stuck to their story, embellishing it with whispers of voodoo and heated speculation over which demon had taken over Willie's body.

When Willie Easelman leaped, hobbled, or as some Haitians swore, flew onto the stage, Tammy Adler didn't know how to react. Willie certainly wasn't the type to be driven on stage by vanity. Tammy pondered if something she said had set Willie off, common enough with her slightly confused friends. She also wondered by the possessed look in Willie's eyes if he might hit her. But Tammy thought of herself as a courageous social director, one who was more concerned about her elderly friends' welfare rather than her own. So she stood reconciled to take the hit for team Morningside when Willie halted, his chest nudging hers, and Tammy asked in her sugar-coated voice, "Is there something you want to add, Willie?"

Willie ignored Tammy and snatched the microphone from her. Some of the Haitians swore afterwards that the two struggled, with Willie ripping the microphone away with a mighty tug. But everyone at Morningside clearly remembered Willie turning to Tammy and in an unruffled tone say, "I'll take it from here, sweetie."

Disturbed, but relieved that Willie hadn't struck her, Tammy drifted to the wings, leaving Willie alone on stage. As the audience settled down, Willie loosened his tie but remained stiff, and those in the front row later remarked seeing him perspiring profusely as he mouthed words which refused to come out. One of the Haitians shouted, "Give 'em heck, Willie," and Willie acknowledged the remark with a shaky thumbs-up. As the hush thickened and started creeping uncomfortably through the audience, Tammy decided to rescue "her poor little Willie," even at the cost of a slap to the face. And so she marched back on stage, her institutional shoes clomping through the awkward silence. But as she neared, Willie raised his hand, stopping her in her tracks with, "It's all part of the act, sweetie, all part of the act."

Turning from Tammy, he pivoted back to the audience and, with the nonchalance of the great entertainers of the '40s, began.

"I married my wife out of revenge," his voice now crusty with a Yiddish accent. "Maybe all men marry for revenge. All I can say is that the sex was good and since revenge never grows old, neither did the sex."

"My Jeanie was from England," Willie continued. "It was wartime; that's WW2 for those of you too young to remember," as he tossed a still-fuming Doris Manheim a twinkle.

"She had a thing against Jews, my Jeanie did. Said the Jewish butcher in her village always left his finger on the scale when no one was looking. I told her: so what, it probably tastes like baloney. She laughed, and since I didn't have a big Jewish schnozzle, she confided with me. 'All Jews are thieves.' So I decided right then and there to get even—and so I married her. I took her back to Brooklyn. Talk about Jews. There were a million of us in Brooklyn and now we had one proper English woman to gawk at. Well, maybe she wasn't totally proper. But she was properly good in the things that mattered, if you know what I mean, Doris." Willie gave a suggestive wink to Doris, who blushed at the innuendo.

"But this was wartime and if you're going to die tomorrow in some trench, then you might as well touch a little bit of skin today."

"Touchy feely!" one of the Haitian shouted.

"Oh I touched my share of skin over there and I can report back that it felt pretty good. Strange how sex and war go together like a horse and carriage. How's that for a Broadway song, Lisa?"

Lisa flashed Willie some leg and Doris whispered, "Broadway call girl," loud enough for all to hear.

"Besides, who's watching during those blackouts?" Willie went on, "Oh, those timely little blackouts. They say the night is the way into a young girl's heart … but I say it's the way to a few more prized parts of a woman's body."

Willie gave the audience a big grin. "Now all parts of a woman are precious, although some are more precious than others. Some parts even glow in the dark."

One of the Haitian men let out a thunderous belly-laugh. Swinging his arm around the buxom woman standing next to him, so that his hand came to rest on her breast, he joked, "I can read in the dark with these."

The woman turned and scoffed, "Well you'll need to learn your ABCs if you're going to read with these."

The chorus of hoots nearly jolted Willie out of his rhythm. But as the laughter piped down, Willie regrouped and extended the joke, saying, "And that's an alphabet they don't teach you in kindergarten."

"But talk about revenge," Willie continued. "They say Jews never forget. But they say that about elephants, too, so go figure."

"Elephants have big noses," one of the Haitians good-naturedly shouted out.

Willie struck back, a masterful comedian being heckled. "What, you call this a nose? I'll tell you about noses. My Uncle Al had a schnoz, a real downspout of a snout. Now some said it gave him character, but we knew better—it was just a place to stash his shekels. Talk about cheap. He used to bum cigarettes from the nafkehs up on 42nd. Told them the cigarettes were for his ailing mother. Uncle Al always said that hookers have a soft spot for their mothers—and Uncle Al liked to amuse himself with those soft spots."

"Is that true?" Doris hollered at Lisa, who ignored the comment.

Willie pulled out a handkerchief and patted his forehead. "Yes, my Jeanie was quite the shiksa. Never complained—not even in the back seat of my Chevy when we ended up in positions that might have gotten us jail time. Gave new meaning to 'four on the floor.' But I always suspected my Jeanie was more comfortable with the buzz of German bombers than with the buzz of Brooklyn Jews. So we Jews complain a lot, is that a crime? Annoying, yes, but a crime—I don't think so."

"But a million Brooklyn Jews weren't as imposing as one Rabbi Chankier, not to be confused with Ravi Shankar. No, Ravi played the sitar, Rabbi Chankier played your soul … and believe me when I tell you he was terribly off-key. If the man ever cracked a smile, it must have been when he was sitting in the bathroom. Scary? We kids called him Rabbi Canker ... and that was being kind. I mean a canker is only skin deep—Rabbi Chankier got under your skin. When he met my wife for the first time he looked her straight in the eye and said, 'So you're the goy who's killing Willie's mother.' Rabbi Chankier didn't mince words. Talk about old school, the man made the sphinx look like a kid."

Singling out the Haitian who had heckled him, Willie said. "I'd take voodoo over Rabbi Chankier any day. I mean, what're a few pins in your chest compared to a knife in your back?"

The Morningside residents were laughing it up and Willie felt their gaiety in his bones. His pauses lengthened and his punch lines became crisper. But he wasn't through—no, Willie wasn't through by a long shot.

"Ah, the war. It got me out of Brooklyn. Saw the world too, compliments of Uncle Sammy, although a one-way ticket to that hell hole doesn't sound like a tag line for a travel agency. But don't confuse me with those hero types. No, the real heroes came from Queens, not Brooklyn. We weren't the kind to jump on a grenade to save our buddies. Hell, I was just a wide-eyed boy from Brooklyn who shined shoes on the street corner and was jealous of the boy hawking news- papers because I thought that's where the real money was."

"Well I brought my Jeanie home—my bissel of a bride. My mother thought she was too thin and my father, let's just say after three weeks he was still muttering, 'Why me, Lord, vhy me?' But things change, beliefs weaken, and though he always called her 'my little goy,' he came to love her—or at least he loved to peek at her tuchas...and you know how that peek goes, Doris?"

Doris, brimming at the attention, blushed. Feigning overheat- ing, she undid the top button of her blouse.

"No, I wasn't much of a hero ... although I saw what was left of them when they were mailed home in a bag. War is hell, but luckily the army didn't trust me with even a bit part in that theater. My job was the laundry. You laugh? What, you don't think the army stinks? Well, it does and my Jeanie worked at the only laundry in town. The army bean-counters decided it was more cost effective to use English labor, rather than have a skinny boy from Brooklyn botch the bleach. Of course we always suspected the English of putting a finger on the scale. But it was war time and we were allies—and, as my father used to say, 'If you can't shmendrick a friend, who can you shmendrik?' "

One of the Haitians yelled, "We're all being shemendriked."

Willie quipped him back, "You got that one right, brother." Willie then changed keys, the comic's smile that had accompanied his shtick turning serious as he repeated, "You got that one right, brother," a couple of times. But Willie had the pulse of the audience and wasn't about to let go.

"How many of you kids grew up in the Big Apple? Come on now, Mrs. Hemlick, we all know your first step was on asphalt and not cow dung. Quite the place, New York. The city that never sleeps. Well, let me tell you, Brooklyn in 1945 was no New York. It not only slept ... it snored."

Willie made his way to the piano as he talked. He began pecking at the piano with one finger, searching for a melody.

"This is a tune I first heard in Hoboken or Hackensack or who knows, maybe Atlantic City. But it's a catchy number, so don't blame me if you find yourself humming it in your sleep tonight, Doris."

Doris stood up and blew Willie a kiss, which he caught in his hand and slid into his pocket adding, "Later, baby, later," to the knee-slapping hysterics of the Haitians.

Turning back to the piano, Willie struck a couple of keys with his fingers and then with his thumb. His eyes closed as he played these five notes over and over, building to a melody.

"As the ol' sage Satchmo used to say, 'The melody's gonna make me fly.' So let's soar, to a place where music rules the joint and the gods break out in song."

As Willie talked he continued to up tempo the same five notes, which were forming a familiarity with the audience.

"Some say this song is magic. Critics call it trite. Me, I think it's the national anthem ... the greatest, craziest, zaniest song ever sung."

In that breath of an instant, it dawned on the audience what song Willie was playing, and the maestro, tuned to his audience, knew that they knew. He smiled, gave the crowd an acknowledging nod, and then brought both hands to the keyboard and sang:

Start spreading the news.
I'm leaving today.
I want to be a part of you,
New York, New York

"Yes, that's the ticket. But I need a little help. I can't play the piano and sing at the same time. Maybe our Lisa can lend a hand? So let's put one hand together with the other for Lightning Fingers Linsky."

Lisa stood up and bowed, strolling to the piano where she raced through a ten-finger prelude to "New York, New York" that surprised even her.

"That's one scorching intro, Lisa," Willie added, touching the piano with his finger and then shaking it as if burned. But when he cooled his finger on Lisa's naked shoulder, Doris Manheim strutted to the rear of the room, where she folded her arms over her flat chest and fumed.

"Now let's do it Satchmo's way, with a li'l bit of soul and a ton full of boogie."

Lisa followed suit, her fingers flying so fast that Willie stepped out of her way.

"Yes, that's the way they do it down in N' Orleans," Willie shouted, giving Lisa a double thumbs-up. "The Big Easy got nothing on you, babe."

"Yes, 'Pops' Armstrong, the grandson of slaves and the only black man in America to want to change places with a Jew—regrets to Sammy Davis, Jr. Did you know that Satchmo spoke Yiddish with a southern drawl? Not bad for a schvartze."

Willie brought the microphone to his lips and imitated the deep, gruff voice of Armstrong, while skipping through a soft-shoe step that drew cat-calls from the Haitian women:

These vagabond shoes
They're longing to stray
Right through the heart of it
New York, New York.

Willie changed keys again, leading Lisa to the sound of Big Band conductor, Cab Calloway:

These little town blues
They've all melted away.
I'm about to make a brand new start of it
Right here in old New York.

Willie leaped fearlessly into the audience and grabbed the sulk-
ing Doris, and to the envy of every woman in the room, he swirled
Doris around Gene Kelly-like. Doris melted into his embrace, although Willie wasn't prepared for the provocative way she wrapped
her leg around his and drew him into the folds of her dress. Willie
squirmed away, passing Doris off to a leering Mr. Holden. Turning
matchmaker, Willie began pairing the men and women. Since there
weren't nearly enough men, the women paired off or sought out
a Haitian, who was only too eager to oblige. When Mrs. Oppenheimer and her partner Sally Simpson kicked it up a notch, Willie
shouted "Jitterbug," and Lisa buried them both with a jazzy adapta-
tion of "New York, New York" that left everyone wheezing for air.

The Haitians, not to be out-partied by a group of past-their-
bedtime octogenarians, retreated to the kitchen, emerging with an
assortment of pots and pans that they banged as they wove their
way through the crowd, Mardi-Gras style. Tammy Alder broke into
the dance line, and with flaying arms and pulsating thighs, took the
dance to what some said was a sexy and others said lewd level. Impulsively Tammy turned and gave Willie a kiss, leaving a smudge of
lipstick on his forehead that he wore like a war medal. And through
it all Willie kept singing, calling out the names of Big Band leaders
like Benny Goodman, Count Basie, and Duke Ellington as if they
were life-long buddies. Even Ginny Blanchard got into the act, spinning her wheelchair around and around on two wheels. Sadly she
had to be restrained after shouting, "I can dance! I can dance," as she
leapt from her wheelchair, but ended up groveling on the floor.

The Haitian drummers picked up the slack as Lisa abandoned
the piano to showcase some of her patented can-can moves. Amazingly she didn't fall as she let loose and kicked for the stars. Lisa's still
shapely legs proved too much for Walter Wilder, who slinked out of
the wings and started to grope them. Walter, who had made and lost
a fortune in the stock market, but who now gave everyone the same

advice, "Buy Xerox," had to be subdued by the Haitians, a task made harder by Lisa coaxing him on with more leg.

Stuck like a broken LP, Willie kept repeating, "I'm king of the hill, top of the heap," over and over in delirium. He pushed on, dazed, like a boxer who refuses to go down. Tight-roping on the edge of the stage, Willie swayed back and forth, the beat of the drums keeping him upright. "King of the hill," he kept singing, until Lisa's ruby shoe flew across the stage and smacked him on the side of his head. He saw a swirling flash and the drums went distant. Suddenly Willie was alone, and when he opened his eyes—Brooklyn.

Back on Flatbush Avenue, back as a boy. The street is alive with the calls of pushcart venders hawking their wares. Ira Goldman walks with his mother to violin lessons, lessons that Willie knows will end with Ira cramming his violin down a sewer and crying to his mother that the Negroes stole it. There's Suzie Isenberg, the soon-to-be class nafkeh, who, after developing breasts at an early age, dazzles the boys of Miss Gunner's seventh grade with a private session of "show and tell," a show that still gets a rise out of those boys as they traverse old age. Over there, buried in a pile of potatoes, the "half-idiots" Isaac and Norman sit, apparently placed on this earth to husk corn at their grandfather's vegetable stand and shoo away the street urchins trying to snitch fruit. Willie can feel his feet moving as his buddies race to catch a trolley to hitch a free ride to Jones Beach. "You'll break your leg," a mother scolds from a third-floor window.

Willie hangs on to this rollercoaster ride of remembrances, where past and present play as one. He does not straddle these two worlds; he inhabits them equally. Breathing in the smells of the streets of Brooklyn, Willie is not reminiscing—he's there.

Overwhelmed, Lisa raised her arms and let out a boisterous cry. Walter broke free from the Haitians just in time to catch her as she fell backwards into his arms. Her skirt lifted, Walter drooling over lurid possibilities hidden beneath her ruby-red underwear. "Get us a room, Wally," Lisa nibbled in his ear; and Walter felt a slight surge swell within him.

And through it all Willie kept dancing, shuffling his feet as he remained stuck on the line "King of the hill, top of the heap." Willie might have questioned why his daughter Anna was belly dancing at the center of a circle of the breakfast boys or wondered why Ira Goldman was accompanying him on the fiddle. He might even have found it odd that Suzie Isenberg was on stage petting heavily with the lifeguard, while clad in a red scarf that barely covered her breasts. But when Willie opened his eyes Ira was still playing the violin, Suzie was still necking, and Lisa was sneaking offstage with Walter. It didn't matter if nothing made sense or that Willie's grandmother was dancing the polka, shouting "Der mensch trakht un Gott lahkht."

Willie lifted his arms to his adoring crowd. "Willie's the man," the Haitians chanted. Willie smiled benevolently before signaling Louie Armstrong, whose trumpet poked out of the curtain folds, to take the song to its crescendo, and in a voice so rousing that even Suzie Isenberg withdrew her hand from deep within the lifeguard's pants, Willie sang:

If I can make it there
You know I can make it anywhere
Come on, come through
New York, New York, New York!

Sweet Dreams
(are made of this)

DORIS MANHEIM LEANED against the dining room wall, tapping her foot as the Morningside Variety Show dwindled to a close. Alone, Doris was stewing over Lisa Linsky's seamless seduction of Walter Wilder. Doris shook her head, a vile taste in her mouth as Lisa went through her routine, revealing enough leg to reel in that despicable man. "A marriage made in hell," Doris jeered, "Lucifer and his tag-along whore of a wife." The show was breaking up as Lisa's hand gripped Walter's belt and led him out of the room, presumably to hers.

Doris never had a man in her room in her five years at Morningside. She never had a man in her room in her thirty years at her Hoboken apartment, either. In fact, she never had a man in any bedroom, either his or hers. The closest she ever came was on a church hayride in her early teens. It was a cold night and in a crowded mix a boy's head found its way onto her breast. She tried to squirm away but the tangled bodies made it impossible to move without a fuss. When she felt his hand slip under her dress, she wanted to scream but the coziness of the night made it feel acceptable. As the group sang Christmas carols, Doris mouthed the lyrics, closing her eyes to the thrill of the boy's touch. She never looked at him, believing her pretend indifference preserved her innocence. She didn't resist as the boy tugged on her underwear and when their cramped positioning thwarted his advances, she moved her legs slightly apart to accept his greedy hands, biting her lip to keep from gasping.

Days later, riddled with guilt, Doris confessed to her mother. "Shame on you … you trollop," her mother spat. Her father was horrified and stopped talking to her for months, never again calling her "my littlest angel." Sobbing with shame, Doris pledged to her parents and to the Lord never to let another man touch her, a pledge she dutifully kept for more than seventy years. But now as she watched Lisa's cheeks go red with desire, she had her doubts.

Recently she had been visited in her dreams by a man who sneaks in through her open bedroom window. In her dream she is seventeen and her parents are sleeping in the next room. She wants to shout for her father but the man puts his finger to her lips and whispers, "Hush."

When the man slides his hand beneath her nightgown, it makes her giggle. "You're a naughty little lass," the man says, as he warms his hands on her breasts. "The kind me mother warned me about." Her bed is narrow and when he struggles with her nightgown she shifts her body so he could pull it off, believing that a proper girl always removes her own clothes with a man. She closes her eyes to the pleasures of his explorations, believing she is safe in the realm of dreams. She grabs his shoulders and pulls him towards him. "Not so fast," he teases. "A man like me doesn't do it with just any tart." She grips him by his hips, tries to press him to her but he resists. She pleads with him to enter, exhales with pleasure when he finally does. The next night he forces Doris to beg harder, brings her to tears before ripping off her panties. One night he makes her pray on her knees like a schoolgirl. "Our Father who art in heaven," she chimes, as he lifts her nightgown from behind. Three times he makes her repeat, "Deliver us from evil," before she feels the thrill of him slipping into her. Once he tells her to call her father, and hiding beneath her sheets, the man fondles her roughly and whispers dirty things into her ear, as her father tucks her in.

Doris's mother always told her, "Dreams are the brush strokes of Satan." Maybe the devil was tempting her, like he had Eve? She turned towards the stage, towards Willie. She noticed similarities between Willie and the man in her dreams. "Everything happens for a reason," her mother also said.

But how could she interest Willie? Lisa made seduction seem easy, effortless. She lifted her skirt and Walter was putty. But Willie? What would it take to get a real man like him? She closed her eyes. Would he be as crude as the man in her dreams? Would he make her beg? Would he want her to dress like a school girl or do those nasty things she wished the boy in the hayride had done to her?

Chimes of Freedom

WILLIE LAID BENEATH his sheets still wearing the clothes he wore to the variety show. He had never thought about escaping. His word was his bond; anyone who knew him from his insurance days would vouch for that. He had accepted the administrator's contract: they returned his car, he stopped crying, and implicit in the contract was that he wouldn't escape. He had no intention of reneging—until tonight. What brought this on he couldn't say. But the game had changed and so must the rules.

Willie knew from his contract days that the devil lurked in the details, yet in this busy multi-tasking world nobody bothered with the small print. He chuckled at the loophole spinning around his head, that being given a car implied driving the car. "Can I borrow your car?" meant that the borrower was asking to DRIVE the car, not let it rust in a parking lot. Yes, this was his way out, the backdoor breakout that led out of here.

The lawyers in the firm would be pleased; they'd say old Willie still had it. How many times had he dug those company lawyers out of their muck holes? He was a master at finding arcane clauses buried deep in the insurance contracts, or turning an obscure phrase into an excuse to deny a claim. Boilerplate, oh how he loved the enigmatic language of the boilerplate. Text obscured by double negatives, time twisted by a string of heretofore, aforementioned, and hereinbefore, not to mention the assault on clarity by a jumbled matrix of "whether to for," or "have before or in so future of a time be," so in the end even the lawyers were baffled. The actuaries, who kept to themselves playing cards in the lunch room, were impressed with his skills, especially for someone who never attended college. Oh, the scotch will flow again, like that day his boss broke open his private vault to celebrate his ten-million-dollar year. All the single malt a man could drink. Yes, they'd be slapping him on the back, saying old Willie's back.

Willie knew that the solitary aide on duty after 2:00 AM would be in the laundry room sleeping on a pile of towels. Willie tied his sneakers in the dark, curling his shoelaces around his thumb as he muttered the verse his mother had taught him ages ago. He thought about a farewell note, but after contemplating one, decided he had nothing important to say. He retrieved the bag hanging in his closet, snacks stolen from the cafeteria for no particular reason other than stealing was fun. He reached into his drawer for the special pair of socks stashed there. He slipped his hand into the folded socks, removing the keys. He brought the keys to his ear and jingled them.

The rattle of the Impala's engine jolted him. Everyone, even a sleeping aide in the laundry room, would hear that. He held his breath and counted to ten, but thankfully the night held onto its silence. He rubbed his military blanket that protected the front seat of every car he ever owned. He shifted the Impala into reverse and backed up.

Willie hadn't the slightest idea where he was going. No, that part of his plan was sadly absent. But now that his escape was on the threshold of succeeding he found himself asking, "What's next?" And yet he knew from thirty years of feasting at the banquets of the insurance gods that the future was a smorgasbord stuffed with surprises and anyone foolish enough to believe he knew the next course was asking for indigestion.

Willie crept towards the slanted streetlight that cast more shadow than light on the narrow exit. There he hesitated and rolled down his window. Looking back on the edifice that over a half-century ago had initiated him to the mysteries and magic of sex, but which had become his prison, Willie flipped his middle finger, then put the pedal to the metal and peeled out, the screech of his tires punctuating the night with the cry of freedom.

You Can't Always Get What You Want

DORIS KEPT HERSELF awake by reciting nursery rhymes. She lay in her twin bed waiting for the corridor to settle down. "Not a creature was stirring, not even a mouse," morphed into "Three blind mice," until "She cut off their tails with a carving knife," spun wildly in her brain. Eventually all was still and she snuck out, looking the part of Christmas Past as she drifted down the corridor, her white nightgown floating above her knees, her pallid face, white as new-fallen snow.

But what to say to him? Men were so different. She had always felt insignificant in their presence. Even at work, when she knew her calculations were correct, she always deferred to men. Men were the bosses—she was the bookkeeper. She could add columns like a machine, but when they asked her opinion, her voice would go mute.

She turned the doorknob and slid her slender body inside his room. The room was dark as she tugged nervously on the pink bow of her nightgown. Doris was thinner now than when her mother bought her the "honeymoon gown," and with barely a shake she heard the gown rustle to the floor. Trembling, she glanced at the clock, trying to silence her mother's voice scolding "nothing good happens after midnight." She walked towards the bed like a sleep-walker.

Reaching through her insecurities, she lifted the blanket and slid in. The coolness of his sheets reassured her as she murmured "My soul to keep." She closed her eyes, awaiting the thrill of his touch, the joy she had only experienced in the realm of dreams.

The sound of the motor startled her. Rushing from the bed, she threw open the sash. Gripping the curtain, she started to sob. "Willie," she whimpered, her voice barely powerful enough to pass from her lips. Wrapped in his blanket, she thought he waved, then watched the rear lights of his car rise into the hills. She yearned to say goodbye, remaining at the window long after his lights had vanished. Framed in the open window Doris stood like a child, praying for miracles, but receiving only silence.

Chase Music from the Keystone Cops

LATER THAT MORNING no one was able to explain how Willie Easelman successfully navigated the thirty miles over back roads in the dark to end up on the Garden State Parkway, not Trooper Scott, who was called in to investigate Willie's unsanctioned leave, not the administrators, who were worried how this episode would tarnish Morningside's safety record, and not the Haitians, who the administrators were convinced were complicit in Willie's escape.

Trooper Scott showed up early Sunday morning at the Morningside Nursing Home carrying a grainy black-and-white photo of a confused, old man chucking a fistful of change at a toll booth on the Garden State Parkway. Trooper Scott put the cocky administrators on the defensive by noting that Mr. Easelman's driver's license had been revoked well over a year ago for "age-related reasons," before he pounced on the fact that Mr. Easelman was driving a car that was uninsured, uninspected, and with Maine plates registered at his son's residence. When the administrators tried to shift the conversation to Morningside's exemplary safety record, Trooper Scott raised his huge hand and asked, "And knowing all of this, you still let Mr. Easelman drive?"

Stumbling over the details of the deal they struck with Mr. Easelman's daughter, details that now sounded quite foolish, the administrators tried to worm out some wiggle room, but Trooper Scott stopped them.

"So you gave Mr. Easelman back his car so that he would stop crying?"

"At his daughter's suggestion."

"A car he was forbidden to drive?"

The administrators continued to nod, like a trio of bobble heads stuck to a dashboard.

"A car more for show than to drive?"

"Exactly," one of the administrators piped in.

"And yet somehow Mr. Easelman, whom I'm told suffers from dementia, was clever enough to get hold of his keys," Trooper Scott concluded, as he slapped the incriminating photo of a wily-looking Willie down like a trump card.

Trooper Scott took pleasure in watching the stunned administrators pass the photo between themselves. It was the joy of a prosecutor tripping up a star witness, and as the administrators squirmed, Scott wondered if he was still young enough to go to law school, even though he was only a few years shy of retirement. But Scott wasn't the only one enjoying the show. The residents of Morningside, who had been startled by the trooper's bullish entrance, were regrouping. And as the administrators huddled over the photo, a sprinkling of giggles leaked from the far side of the room.

Trying to regain their composure, the tallest administrator reached into his pocket and slid a set of keys to the officer. "But you see, officer," the administrator challenged with a smirk, "we still have *our* set of Mr. Easelman's keys."

The onlookers gasped, while someone on the piano threw in a suspenseful Vaudevillian lick.

Trooper Scott took the keys and held them up to the light before depositing them into an oversize envelope marked "evidence."

The tall administrator went on. "Mr. Easelman's daughter might have something to add to this conversation. It's only conjecture, but his daughter could have slipped him the keys. She was distraught over institutionalizing her father, and Mr. Easelman rarely had anything good to say about her. Embezzling was mentioned, rumor, mind you, but talk nevertheless. You'd be surprised the guilt that riddles these daughters of the afflicted, these poor souls forced to do the dirty work. She probably thought she was doing the right thing by giving him the keys."

"Really?" asked Trooper Scott.

"These old folks wear you down. They beg for something every time their kids come for a visit—candy, popcorn, some old photo that's been lost for decades. They're more persistent than kids," the administrator went on, sadness cracking in his voice.

The irony of the administrator's words was not lost on Trooper Scott as he pressed on. "But giving him keys?"

"I'm certain the poor woman never thought her father would actually use them."

As the administrator sensed a softening in the trooper, he once again boasted of Morningside's safety record.

"Safety records, my ass," a voice resonated from the shadows. "How hard can it be keeping a bunch of cripples locked in the slammer?"

Ignoring the comment, the administrator went on to emphasize that Mr. Easelman did not have their permission to drive the car.

"Permission?" Scott scoffed. "You give a grown man a car and then you forbid him to drive?"

"You tell them, copper," the voice in the corner rang out.

Back on the offense, Scott played to his audience. "And how can you be sure that Mr. Easelman didn't make a habit of these forays, especially since your facility is staffed by just one poorly paid aide at night?"

"We pay a fair wage here," the tall administrator shot back.

"The hell they do," the unseen man interjected among a chorus of giggles. "Illegals, all of them. Might as well be living in Mexico."

When the administrators faltered, Scott pounced on what he saw were three twerps in designer suits. "Maybe Mr. Easelman learned to navigate the back roads during these midnight rides?"

"The British are coming, you stupid bobby," the voice rang out; then in the ensuing silence he chimed, "One down my leg, two in my shoe."

Although the administrators wanted to disclose their suspicions that the Haitians were involved with Willie's escape, they were hesitant to go that route since the Haitians were illegal immigrants and knowingly hiring illegal immigrants was a criminal offense in New Jersey, the word "knowingly" no longer sounding as smug as when their Manhattan lawyers used the word. Besides, the administrators were concerned that the police might take a dim view if it became known that they were paying the Haitians below minimum wage, something that undoubtedly would be exploited by the news-starved local rag.

As Scott jotted down the administrator's comments, he began to feel edgy. He heard the squeaking of walkers closing in on him and felt the hairs on his neck tingle. He glanced over his shoulder at faces that averted his gaze, ghostly faces void of expression. Scott was reminded of a low-budget zombie movie he had recently rented where the creatures feasted on unsuspecting pizza delivery boys who were lured to their grotesque deaths by the zombie's use of computers, since apparently zombies mumbled on their cell phones.

When it was the Haitians' turn to be questioned, they confided in Trooper Scott their belief that voodoo was to blame for Willie's escape.

"If you want to catch the culprit," Willie's friend Henri explained, "find the person who holds a grudge."

When the police officer asked, "Who at the nursing home holds a grudge?" Henri bluntly answered, "Frank Sinatra."

Scott stiffened but held his composure. "But isn't Sinatra dead?"

"So is Jesus," the man in the shadows chuckled, "and he's still preaching."

"That's just the point, officer," Henri calmly replied.

"You hear the one about Easter, copper? If the Easter Bunny sees his shadow it's six more weeks of winter. Or maybe it's eight. Rabbits don't have fingers to count on."

Both Henri and the trooper ignored the outbursts and Henri continued. "It's always the dead who are behind these kinds of things. Mr. Frank Sinatra's spirit was awoken last night. And you know how nasty spirits get when they're disturbed."

Playing along, Scott asked, "And why was Mr. Sinatra's spirit awoken?"

Henri hesitated, trying to find the right words in English, a language unsuited to describe supernatural occurrences. He then answered, "Because last night Mr. Easelman sang "New York, New York" better than Mr. Frank Sinatra ever did. Spirits are jealous. They're worse than wives, you know."

"You got that one straight, wetback," came the voice in the corner. "My wife was so jealous she had to take off her clothes—with strangers."

"Are you saying voodoo made Mr. Easelman do it?"

"Probably Papa Ghede. He's a bit of a clown. But you never know. Maybe it was a more devilish spirit?"

"The devil made him do it, flatfoot," the voice rang out.

"But how could Mr. Easelman become this ... this Papa fellow?" asked the officer, aggravated that he was prolonging this nonsense.

"Papa Ghede entered Mr. Willie's body."

"Take, eat, this is my body broken for you," the voice scoffed.

"Papa Ghede likes to entertain."

"This is my blood. Christ, are we talking vampires or voodoo?" the voice rambled.

"And last night Mr. Willie was on stage."

The voice intervened. "This great stage of fools and tools. Did you hear the one about the female screwdriver? She had two nice gadgets that drove you nuts when you screwed her."

Trooper Scott tried to sum it up. "So this Papa fellow enters Mr. Easelman's body?"

"Yes. Mounts him."

Trooper Scott had heard enough voodoo, but resisted the urge to demand to see Henri's Green Card. "Better keep things simple," he told himself. Bring Homeland into this and we'll still be here when it snows. He made a mental note to avoid mentioning voodoo in his report; the boys at the barracks would burst an artery.

While he was finishing up his notes, two Haitian girls approached him.

"Excuse me, sir policeman. About, Mr. Willie?" the older of the two girls asked.

Trooper Scott looked up and nodded.

"My friend, Simone, wants to talk with you."

Trooper Scott's gaze summed up the girl. She was noticeably nervous as the older girl nudged her.

"I think my friend wants to talk in private." Peering around at the residents who had crept closer, she whispered, "These old people gossip like magpies."

Trooper Scott led the two girls to a corner.

"I know Mr. Willie would never hurt anyone," the older girl, Jacqueline, began. "He is a kind man. But tell the officer, Simone. Tell him what you told me."

The trooper looked at Simone with a father's eye. Her face reminded him of his own daughter at that age. She seemed so innocent that he smiled, hoping to put her at ease.

"Last week I worked late," Simone painfully began. "I saw Mr. Willie's door open. He was crying. It hurts me to see the old people cry."

"And what happened?" the trooper asked, trying to speed things up.

"He was in his favorite chair. His head was in his hands. I asked what the matter was. He said, 'They have all forgotten me.'"

"All the old folks say that," Jacqueline interjected. "They tell you family secrets. Squeal on their kids."

Simone continued in a monotone. "Mr. Willie says his daughter steals from him."

Seeing the story wasn't going anywhere, Trooper Scott interjected, "Anything else?" in a tone meant to wrap things up.

"Tell him, Simone. Tell the policeman."

"So I go over to Mr. Willie and tell him that his daughter loves him. I tell him we all love him. But still he cries. I put my arm around him, but he just shakes his head and pats the cushion for me to sit down."

"You should never have sat down," scolded Jacqueline.

"But I feel sorry for Mr. Willie."

"Mr. Willie is no longer Mr. Willie."

Now Scott was curious. "Then who is he?"

"He's either Kalfu or Legba," answered Jacqueline.

"No, he's not!" protested Simone. "The Jesus came and now there's no more voodoo."

"Tell the officer what happened."

Simone, fidgeting with a button on her blouse, looked away. "So I sit down and Mr. Willie kisses me."

Trooper Scott stiffened. "How did he kiss you?"

"First like a father. Then harder."

"Kalfu!" shouted the older girl.

"No, he's not Kalfu," stomped Simone.

"Is that all he did?" asked Trooper Scott.

"I felt his tongue go down my throat. It was sharp."

"Did you struggle?"

"I couldn't move."

"See!" said the other girl. "The spirits invaded Mr. Willie's body."

"Is that all?" repeated Trooper Scott, fearing to hear more.

"He lifted my blouse off. Undid my bra."

"Did he fondle you?" asked the trooper.

"His hands were everywhere. He untied my pants." Simone looked frightened. "I tried to call out for Jesus, but I had no voice."

"Did Mr. Easelman pull down your pants?"

"It wasn't Mr. Willie; it was Kalfu," Jacqueline stammered.

"Did he pull down your pants?" Trooper Scott insisted.

Simone looked away. "I closed my eyes. I felt his thing." She started to weep.

"Did you try to stop him?" asked the trooper.

"Tell the truth," said the older girl.

"I ..."

"Did you tell him 'no'?"

"Tell the policeman the truth."

"I tried to stop him the first time."

"The first time?" a shocked trooper asked.

"We ... we did it twice."

Trooper Scott's mind burst. By regulation he was required to put her statement in his report. Hopefully she was of age.

"How old are you, Simone?"

Jacqueline took the younger girl's arm. "Tell the man the truth."

"Sixteen."

Trooper Scott muttered a swear. By rule he was now required to write up the girl's statement. It was rape, either statutory or second

degree by an old man in a nursing home. The papers would spin this
into a sideshow. Christ, on a slow Sunday it might make the lead on
the 6:00 news. The boys at the barracks will choke. Voodoo, illegal
immigrants, child labor, and now rape. Christ, the list was growing
faster than Scott could scribble. This was a full-blown circus.

"It's not her fault," the older girl blurted. "She was under the
spell of Legba. He tricked her."

Having heard enough voodoo for a lifetime, Trooper Scoot
hissed, "Twice?"

"Legba's crafty—a leech. He preys on sweet girls like Simone.
Takes over their dreams."

Seeing a possible way out, Scott looked intently at Jacqueline. "Do
you think your friend dreamed this up? Could she have imagined it?"

In unison Scott and Jacqueline turned towards Simone, who
bowed her head. Simone's face was wet with tears. She felt abandoned, naked, and wanted to go home.

Twenty-five years on the force and Scott's career now depended on how he handled this … this side show. Was this the last tango
of an old man gorging himself on Viagra or the sexual fantasies of
adolescence? Either way he was trapped. Report the incident and
he'd be the joke of the barracks and play the part of a clown when
the media turned this into a circus or bury her statement and, if this
thing broke, he could kiss his pension good-bye.

Scott shut his notebook, concluding that only Willie Easelman
knew the whys and wherefores, and Willie was missing. He thanked
the two girls and told them to keep the story to themselves. "Once
we locate Mr. Easelman, we'll get to the bottom of this."

Simone asked in her squeaky voice. "Will Mr. Willie get in
trouble?"

Scott was too riled to answer. As for Easelman's escape, Scott
had already spent too much time on a dead-end case going nowhere.
Undoubtedly the administrators bore blame, but who would lodge a
complaint? His daughter, who probably was glad to be rid of her father? Hopefully they'd find the poor guy before he did any damage.
As for these Haitians, screw them and their stupid voodoo.

Trooper Scott felt his neck tighten and he loosened his tie. This
old folk's home was giving him a big-time case of the creeps and the

sooner he got out of here the better he'd breathe. The residents were watching his every move and their milky complexions gave them all a ghostly hue. The wise-ass in the corner snuck up and whispered, "Buy Xerox," into his ear. When Scott whirled around, the old man, dressed in pajamas, flashed him a toothless grin.

"That's enough, Walter," one of the Haitian aides said to the man in the pajamas.

"Three times I nailed her," the man bragged.

The hairs on Trooper Scott's neck were electric as he stuffed the grainy black-and-white photo of Mr. Easelman back in its folder. In his haste to leave, the trooper's knee bumped a wheelchair, nearly flipping it over. The woman gripped the chair as it spun across the lobby, pointing a finger at the trooper and hissing, "Arrest that man for hit and run!"

"Stick 'em up, copper," Walter smirked. "You're under arrest for the disappearance of Jimmy Hoffa."

Scott turned to apologize to the woman in the wheelchair, but slammed into Doris Manheim, who had leaped out from behind the curtains to confront the trooper.

"You'll never take him alive," Doris spat, before collapsing.

The piano player shifted into a riff from the "Keystone Cops."

"Take who alive?" Trooper Scott asked, spooked by the unnatural angle of the woman's dangling arm.

Trooper Scott extended his hand to Doris, but she latched onto Trooper Scott's pants with cat-like strength. Looking up at the towering trooper, Doris cried, "You won't take my Willie alive." Before adding, "He's a nursing home freedom fighter."

"Ma'am, I'm just trying to investigate a disappearance."

Doris's one good eye swelled like an enraged rooster's as she clung to the trooper's leg. "He's our Paul Revere."

Walter groaned. "The British are coming and so am I"

"I'm sure he is, ma'am," Scott said, patting the tiny woman on her head.

"You know these nursing homes aren't the hoity-toity place they're made out to be," Doris said, swinging from the trooper's leg. "The devil in sheep's clothes is what they are."

Trooper Scott didn't know how to extricate himself from the

frail woman without hurting her, something sure to raise a ruckus at headquarters.

Doris's finger swung like the needle of a compass towards the administrators. "You should lock these scallywags up," she urged, which brought a burst of laughter from the residents and an "off with their heads," from Walter.

"Please, ma'am," Trooper Scott begged in an official voice.

But a feisty Doris held her grip, and the piano player broke into the "Keystone Cops" chase scene. Doris, whose pulsating eye had a creep factor all its own, spat, "You mess with my Willie, mister, and you mess with me. Understand?"

"Comprende, padre?" Walter giggled.

Scott nodded and Doris let go of the trooper's leg, falling backwards onto the crushed velvet sofa. Scott raised his hand, but Alice Keegan stood and pointed at the officer's pants, gasping, "It's escaping!"

Scott followed Alice's finger to his open zipper. Walter saluted the trooper. "So you Polly-wagged the old sow, too!" Walter chirped, to the suspense of the "Keystone Cops" music.

With one hand covering his zipper, Scott opened the door. Doris called after him, "And my Willie won't be taken by a tenderfoot like you."

Alice, whose wagging finger was following Scott's hasty retreat, exclaimed. "Stop that THING before it escapes!"

Doris, having scaled the pillows scattered on the worn couch, stood. "If I know my Willie, he's halfway to Florida by now." But fearing she might have said too much, added, "Unless he's planning to come back here, in which case he's nuttier than a fruitcake."

Trooper Scott shook in the doorway, his 6'3" frame eclipsing the morning light. His neck was pulsating and his heart thumping, as he made one last effort to take control. But he could only manage a high-pitched, "Yes, ma'am," words accompanied by a military retreat played on the piano.

On the sofa Doris raised a fist to the departing trooper. "If you find my Willie, tell him I'll wait till the end of time," as she free fell into a cloud of dust.

Grinning, Walter stuck a finger up his nose and sneered. "Your Willie-boy went bye-bye, church-lady. He flew the coop."

Doris shot back, "You should be locked in a chicken coop, you filthy old man!"

"Filthy enough to know what a slut like you wants," Walter slung back.

Doris lifted herself to her knees. "Sticks and stones will break my bones, but names will never hurt me," she taunted, hurling a pillow at Walter, striking him square in the face.

"Sticks and stones may break my bones, but your tits are too tiny to hurt me."

Doris fumed and whipped a second pillow at the fleeing Walter. "And there's more where that one came from," she cackled.

Trooper Scott was gasping for breath as he raced down the cement walkway, his head grazing the forest-green awning that gave the Morningside a funeral-home appearance. His hands were trembling as he flopped into the front seat of his cruiser, accidentally flipping on the siren. The siren seared the Sunday silence and brought a chorus of cheers from the residents inside. Scott shot up the narrow turnaround, slamming on his brakes when the old man in pajamas leaped in front of his cruiser.

"Come again, copper" the man called, as two Haitian aides grabbed hold of him. "We'll tag-team that harlot into submission."

The black-and-white photo of Willie Easelman, grinning like a kid at an amusement park, slid off the front seat. Trooper Scott gunned his cruiser, his tires shrieking in retreat. The two aides lifted a kicking Walter up by his elbows and gently carried him up the stairs.

"So you had quite the ride last night, Mr. Wilder?" one of the Haitians good-naturedly laughed.

Walter proudly replied, "Rode that bucking bronco till she squealed."

"You're a legend, Mr. Wilder," the second Haitian chuckled, patting Walter on his back.

"They'll be singing your song for a hundred years," added the other.

As the three men returned to the lobby, Walter, breathless with excitement, blurted out, "And tell the other wetbacks I did it without Viagra" in a voice loud enough for everyone to hear.

Survive

Like a Rolling Stone via The Road to Nowhere

THRILLED WITH HIS escape, Willie flipped on the car radio, hoping it would keep him awake. The variety show had been a jolt of adrenalin, but it was wearing thin. The country roads were dark and the curves were leaping out at him without warning. He turned the dial. How about some comfort music? Sinatra. A perfect ending to a perfect day, he thought, humming "New York, New York," as if to recapture some of the stage magic of his performance.

Not bad, he mused, escaping that hellhole of nitwits. No way could those rookies hold Willie Easelman down. And those three greenhorns. Love to see the look on those stooges' faces come morning. Try messing with me. He reached over and patted the glove compartment. "Try messing with us." Those guppies should try flogging life insurance.

But late-night radio wasn't dishing out any Sinatra. DJs, more impressed by their own voice than by any music, filled the airwaves with chit-chat. He found a country station, but country music always sounded like a bunch of losers who can't get their shit together. "Buck up!" Willie screamed at a singer who whined about losing his woman to an overweight banker from St. Louis. "You think you're the only person who lost their lover?" Willie hit the dial when the wimpy cowboy moaned, "I would have given you the world, but you settled for crumpled sawbucks and a curd custard pie."

The dial landed on a young preacher. "This is the Reverend Tell-it-like-it-is T. T. Teller, telling you that Jesus saves."

Willie, who found religion even more despicable than country music, perked up. "Tell it like it is, Rev! Give the audience a taste of what they're dying to hear."

"Yes, this is T.T. the Teller, telling you that all you need for free admission into the Kingdom of God is to say that Jesus died for your sins."

"Jesus died for my sins," Willie answered.

"Why, it's as easy as driving a brand-spanking new Cadillac down a highway."

Willie jeered at the radio. "How about a not-so-new Impala?"

"As easy as opening a flip-top can of Coke."

Willie slapped the dashboard and laughed. "I remember when you had to use a church key."

"Everyone thinks it's hard as chores, but it's so simple a child can do it. Just believe that Jesus died for your sins."

"I believe," murmured Willie.

"Believe that Jesus is the son of God."

"Oh, I believe."

"Believe that in the Kingdom of God, everyone drives a Cadillac. A cherry-red Coupe Deville."

"I'm riding shotgun with you on that one, Rev."

"And that all the women you loved—ever wanted to love—will ever love, will be waiting for you on the beaches of paradise."

Willie reached to change the station.

"Even the one that still haunts you in your dreams. The one who got away."

Willie's hand hovered above the dial.

"But do you really believe? Believe in the face of fear? Like when you were a kid and fear was hiding under your bed at night. That, my friend, was fear, the kind that sends you scampering into your mommy's bed. So how do we defeat this bogeyman?"

"By giving?" Willie scoffed.

"That's right, by giving—so you know the Big Fella upstairs will be there when you find yourself alone in that desert, dying of thirst."

"Amen."

"So let it shine."

"Shine on."

"Let the altar shine."

"Shine on, Brother."

"Show the Lord that although we're all sinners, we still know how to give."

"Drive it home, Rev."

"Send as much as you can. No, send more than you can. Give it up for the Lord, so the Big Guy can give it up for you."

"Amen."

"Yes, Amen, brothers."

A chorus broke in. "Give it up, give it up, give it up for the Lord."

As the chorus chanted in the background, the Reverend spoke in his rich, baritone voice.

"So send a check, send a money order, send cash, send food stamps. Send it C.O.D. to G.O.D. No return address necessary cause the Lord knows where to find you. Let the altar shine—it shines for you. And as you're writing that check, let's check in with our own Mr. Johnson, who'll lead us in..." and the station dissolved into static.

Not bad for an amateur, Willie chuckled, but he'd starve in the insurance business. Selling redemption is child's play compared to selling life insurance. The Rev has God on his side. "Got God"—now that's a T-shirt that would sell a million.

Willie laughed so hard he had to slow down. Religion might offer eternity, but insurance offers legacy. Sell a man into believing his estate will last forever and you'll have a customer for life—or at least until he can't afford the premium.

Turning the dial, the radio skipped to another station. The opening piano chords ... Sinatra? He turned an eager ear to the music. Not the Chairman, but it wasn't that country crap, either. He thought he knew the song but static devoured it after the opening line.

Heaven can wait
Got a band of angels wrapped up in my heart.

Struggling to keep the melody alive, the riff was interrupted by the Reverend's parting words, "Let the altar shine."

Where had he heard those words before? The Bible? God had a thing for altars and all that burning bush crap. And He was quick with the advice, always calling from the mountaintop choice sound bites like "Don't screw your neighbor's wife" or "Honor your God-damn father." Honor your father, maybe kids were different back then. He should try raising kids these days. You give them everything and then they take away your keys.

God loves altars—God loves Praise

But kids love indulging in the American way

"Crap. All crap," he cried, striking the steering wheel and nearly driving off the road. "Uncle Al was right. 'Rather shit on a stick than the shit carved in a stone.' Go fuck your commandments, Moses."

The night turned darker with his growing fatigue, and Willie's forehead bumped the windshield as he struggled to see. Huge trees with centuries of girth crowded the side of the road, their bark gouged by cars, each gash a tragic story. He hoped he was heading east, but he wouldn't be surprised if a compass pointed west. A roulette wheel would be better. Where was he and where was he going? Shadows teased and taunted him. The road split and he went left, the road split again and he went right. The radio cleared. Not the music of the Big Bands, but he knew the song from being stuck inside the car with his kids. He rolled down his window and sang along each time the singer called out, "With no direction home." The song cut out, but Willie continued:

> *How does it feel?*
> *How does it feel?*

Keeping the beat with the beep of his horn, Willie livened up the night with a rousing crescendo:

> *To be on your own*
> *With no direction home*
> *Like a complete unknown*
> *Like a rolling stone?*

A breeze flowed through the open window, chilling him with doubt. He looked at his hands, the hands of an old man. He gripped the steering wheel harder. Was this a stupid blunder?

He took a deep breath. But no, he was Willie Easelman. THE Willie Easelman. The kid who went off to war at seventeen, did ten million in '55, sent Andy to Harvard. He grabbed hold of a Sinatra drift and sang:

I've lived a life that's full
I traveled each and every highway

"Try taking that from me!" he shouted, at the imaginary inquisitor riding shotgun. Patting the glove compartment door, he scoffed, "I'll do it my way."

Willie stumbled upon the Garden State Parkway by accident. The huge sign shined above him—a beacon lighting up the sky. He headed north for no particular reason other than New York sounded better than Delaware. It had been years since Willie had driven on a highway and a decade since he had driven on one at night. Clinging to the slow lane, he struggled to keep up his speed, knowing that the troopers would be on the lookout for dawdling drunks at this hour. Speed kills, but dillydallying gets your ass hauled into jail. He knew the highways around Newark would be frightful, but smiled at the idea of dropping in on Henri and the other Haitians. What a hoot. Swing by for breakfast. What do Haitians eat for breakfast?

The highway was empty and he sank deeper into his seat. Out in the distance flashes of lightning erupted in volleys, followed by an eerie darkness. Sometimes the whole panorama lit up and what was nothing, suddenly was. The summer solstice? The Haitians had used those words all day. It was the end of the road for the sun ... and yet oddly summer had just arrived.

"Let there be light," Willie called out. And when a bolt answered him, Willie chuckled, "And there was light."

Under the glow of mercury-vapor, the toll booth stood as a cement monolith. Willie lifted his arm to shield his eyes, weaving wildly. Confused by lanes marked in different colors, he ended up in an exact-change lane where he scoured his coffee-cup holder for coins. He threw a handful of quarters into the basket and thankfully the light turned green.

Newark was impossible, with tentacles for roads and bypasses built for cruelty. When Willie slowed, horns blasted him from behind, while oncoming cars blinded him from the front. The road was a maze of entrances and exits, a highway to hell lined with fortify barriers that were closing in on him. No longer driving, now he was surviving. The glare was impossible, as he peeked through parted fingers. Dust swirled. Awash with anxiety he gripped the wheel with both hands and braced for a crash.

Yet in the height of this pandemonium Willie suddenly found himself calm, a captain amongst chaos. Traffic slowed, curves straightened, and tranquility settled in his body. He closed his eyes, floating above the traffic, as he drifted into his past.

Willie waits for the old man to leave. The man locks the register, even though Isaac and Norm had been told a thousand times not to sell fruit in his absence. They can put the fruit in bags, but a sale has to wait until Zayde returns from the bank.

Entering, Willie picks up an apple.

"Got to vait, got to vait for Zayde," Isaac and Norman chant like twins joined at the hip.

Willie puts the apple back with a shrug.

Four eyes follow Willie as he moves through the cramped fruit stand. He knows that Isaac and Norman will never tire of watching him, since he's the kind of kid their Zayde continuously warns them about. The twins stop husking corn and follow Willie. They march in single file weaving their way through a labyrinth of torn cardboard boxes and wooden display crates.

"Do you know why God picked the Jews as the chosen people?" Willie asks, casually pinching a pear to test for ripeness.

The twins haven't a clue how to dress themselves, don't know how to navigate the six-block route from their home to the store by themselves, but fifteen years of studying the Torah has made them surprisingly knowledgeable on the subject. They peer at Willie, then at each other. Their hand motions are synchronized, reminiscent of a Vaudevillian stage show Willie's uncle took him to, and Willie struggles to suppress a laugh. The twins suspect a trick but the question intrigues them, and their suspicions gradually yield to their curiosity.

"Why us?" Willie repeats, the seeds of his ruse now sowed.

It's the WHY of the question that confuses them. They know their facts. The twins can recite Abraham's linage down to the New Testament; they know the good and the bad of every ancient nation that has ever helped or fought Israel. But WHY God chose the Jews baffles them. While the twins blink blankly at each other, Timmy and Jacob slip in the front door. The cat-and-mouse game begins.

"Because we believe in Him?" Isaac tentatively asks.

"No."

"Because we worship Him?" Norm replies..

"No."

"Because the Jews celebrate the coming Messiah?" they ring in unison.

"No, no, no."

Willie draws them closer with a theatrical curl of his finger, glances over at the pyramid of apples disappearing into Timmy and Jacob's pockets. He waits until his buddies exit and they're safely out. He cups his hand, as if guarding this great secret. The twins hold their breath.

"Because."

"Because?" the twins echo.

"That's it ... because. God did it because He can."

The twins stare at each other, the color in their faces drained by bewilderment. "God did it because He can?" they repeat, chewing on the uncertainty of what this great truth means.

Willie lifts a finger to his lips, drawing them deeper into his drama. A séance of silence surrounds them. "That, and because Mary was a whore."

The twins giggle mercilessly at the word "whore," and in the swirl of their giddiness, Willie snitches the pear and heads out the front door.

Later, as Timmy, Jacob and Willie devour the apples, their feet dangling over the muddy waters of Wallabout Bay; they all agree that the apples taste special. "The best I've ever had," Jacob mumbles, as he bites into his third.

Willie sits by the river after his buddies have gone. He hears the distant screams of the twins being thrashed by their Zayde over the stolen apples. "They must learn to protect the fruit!" Willie's stomach aches. He asks himself, if we really are the chosen ones, why did God create Isaac and Norm? Maybe he should ask the rabbi, but he'd just give him some abracadabra about Abraham.

The first hints of night conspire in the east. The twins have stopped squealing, sent to bed without their dinner. Willie wishes he could return the apples. He hears his mother calling. Drowning in thoughts too complicated for his young mind, Willie throws his last two apples into the river, then heads for home.

Willie opened his eyes. Newark was in his rearview mirror. He breathed in the intimacy of the Impala's smell that age had woven into the fabric of the upholstery. Rubbing the dashboard, Willie smiled.

Sleep was at his doorstep, as Willie coasted into the Montvale rest area, parking in a deserted area far from the service center. His tongue glided over his parched lips as he pulled the coarse green blanket over his chest. Somewhere a piano played. Accompanied by remembrances both imaginary and real, Willie shut his eyes to the backbeat of his heart, which was pounding with an unfamiliar rhythm. Struggling for breath he loosened his collar, gently wiping away the sweat that gathered there. No longer a hostage of time, Willie slipped into a deep sleep, free to explore the mysteries of the cosmos, one universe at a time.

It All Makes Perfect Sense

TROOPER SCOTT WAS halfway back to the barracks before he noticed his right hand was trembling. He slammed the steering wheel, hoping the shock would stop it. Damn, how close he came to hurting that old lady at the nursing home! A public panel would probably call it an assault. This was madness. He was a decorated senior state trooper whose career might be derailed because a frail, old lady leaped in front of him. Christ, she could have cracked a hip.

As Trooper Scott fought to control his worries, he wondered why he had been called in to investigate in the first place. Why send a state trooper thirty miles off the highway to investigate a nursing home escapee? This Easelman fellow wasn't a prisoner or a ward of the state. With the exception of driving without a license, hardly a capital offense in Jersey, the man hadn't broken any laws. This was a case for social services, not police. Even if this was a case for the police, the locals should investigate it; this was a small-town situation for small-town police. Yet his lieutenant had summoned him and not his sergeant; that was odd. And his lieutenant called from his cell phone and not over the radio. Something didn't add up. But what? Maybe this Willie Easelman fellow was more important than he appeared?

The spot on his thigh where the old woman had grabbed him began to throb. What did she shout? That Willie Easelman was a "freedom fighter?" No, A NURSING HOME freedom fighter, whatever that was. Was the state of New Jersey worried about an eighty-six year old starting an uprising? Trooper Scott chuckled at the notion of those ghoulish characters at the Morningside being freed by this Willie Easelman. What a sequel to "The Night of the Living Dead." Well, whatever was up, one thing was for sure: this Morningside Nursing Home was one creepy place.

Scott looked at his note pad. "Christ," he muttered, as he glanced at his notes on the Haitian girl, the word RAPE prominently underlined. He should report her to the lieutenant. But was voodoo sex the same as real sex? It was probably just a figment of an adolescent girl's imagination—a confused mix of craving and curtailing. And could an eighty-six year old man with dementia be charged with rape? Christ, they're all loons back there.

As Trooper Scott drove, the question continued to nag: why him? Possibly it had something to do with him serving on the governor's security team. But if this Easelman fellow was of interest, why not send a detective?

His cell phone beeped. He didn't recognize the number.

"Ed Davis here," the voice said. "Hook onto anything?"

Trooper Scott was stunned: Colonel Davis was the head of the State Police. He had only talked with the colonel a few times. A few years ago, when Davis was a captain, he debriefed Scott concerning the sex scandal that threatened the governor. Davis was an old college buddy of the governor and wanted to know if Scott had observed any foul play. Damn. This investigation of Mr. Easelman was moving up the ladder faster than a Corvette up the Garden State.

"Sir?" Scott replied.

"Any laws broken?" the colonel shot back.

Trooper Scott hesitated, wondering if he should bring up the Haitians. "We might have a case against the nursing home. Illegal immigrants."

"Tell me something I don't know, Scott. Can you name me one nursing home in Jersey that operates without them?"

"No, sir."

"They're as indispensable as diapers."

"Yes, I mean, no, sir, I ..."

"Jamaicans?"

"No, sir, they're Haitians."

"Good. You can't trust the Jamaicans. They'll steal you blind and then give you that smiley face. And they smoke dope till it's coming out their ears. Something to do with their religion. High holidays, no doubt. But the Morningside. Anything fishy there?"

"Seems like a well-run place. The residents are a bit odd, but ..."

"Scott, it's a nursing home, not a book club. Hell, you'd be odd too if you ate canned peaches and strained to crap all day."

"I'm not certain I know what I'm looking for, Colonel."

"Something we can pin on the nursing home. And don't give me that illegal immigrant crap. My Aunt Amy has her house cleaned by illegals and we're sure as hell not gonna haul her ass off to jail."

"I'm not sure ..."

"Try finding an American who cleans windows, let alone cleans shit."

"But ..."

"How about the car? How did this Eastman fellow get hold of it?"

"It was his car, sir. Apparently it was parked on premises. Something about the car made him stop crying."

"Christ, I'll be crying too when they come for my keys. Tell you a story, Scott. We stopped a guy in Trenton last week. Ninety-three years old. The guy hadn't renewed his license in twelve years and had the eyesight of a mole. Turns out his wife was sitting in the passenger seat directing him when to turn. Apparently she said "right" for something and he thought she meant take a right. Ran three stop signs and a red light before plowing into a check-cashing storefront, but when we went for his keys the old fart went nuts. Nearly bit the trooper's finger off. I'm telling you, Scott, these old people fight dirty. It's life and death when it comes to their car. But the keys? Did the nursing home actually give Easelman the keys?"

"They denied it. Tried to pin it on his daughter."

"Daughter? Now that's the crap we're looking for. So the old man has a daughter who slipped him the keys?"

"I can't … say."

"So the daughter slips her old man the keys. Gives them to him, but knows his license has been revoked. I'm not a lawyer, Scott, but it smells like a felony to me."

"Sir, I didn't interrogate her."

"Maybe you should. It's at least a misdemeanor."

"Sir, this is all conjecture."

"Good work, Scott. Anything else?"

Without thinking Trooper Scott blurted out "voodoo."

"What did you say?"

"The Haitians thought voodoo might be in play," Trooper Scott already regretting his candor.

"Voodoo? You're not smoking that Jamaican weed are you?"

"No, sir, I just wanted to …"

"Voodoo. Good one. You got me on that one, Scott."

"Sir?" Trooper Scott started, hesitant to bring up the Haitian girl.

"I'll take it from this side. Voodoo! That's rich, Scott. Maybe we'll find this Easelman fellow pinned to his car." The colonel laughed and the line went dead.

Trooper Scott cradled his cell phone. He was now more confused. Why did the brass choose him? And the colonel? This was no ordinary escape. Must be connected with the governor. The scandal? Scott had been a witness, sworn under oath that he had seen nothing—no foul play in the Atlantic City hotel where the governor stayed with taxpayer's money. The Democrats had dug up some skanky call girl who testified that the governor had cornered her in his room. "Snookered her," was how she put it. The headlines in *The Daily News* that day read: "Jersey Gov Snookered Her in the Shower." But Scott had seen nothing and nothing came out of the investigation other than a waste of taxpayer's money. The lieutenant, the colonel, would the governor be calling him next?

What about this "nursing home freedom fighter?" Should he have mentioned that to the colonel? No, the woman was a loon, and so too was that Haitian girl. The colonel had mocked him when he mentioned voodoo. What would he say to an eighty-six year old "snookering" a sixteen-year-old aide at a nursing home? That was the stuff of comedians, not crime blotters. He tore out the two pages of the girl's statement and crumpled them in his massive fist before chucking them out the window. So much for her.

Near the entrance to the Garden State, Scott glanced at his watch. Four hours remained in his shift, plenty of time to go home and drop Elaine off for three o'clock mass. Father Kelly, who was approaching ninety, would probably conduct it. He was infamous for skipping the liturgy and mangling the scriptures, while his sermons were little more than childhood recollections. Maybe he could drop Elaine off and squeeze in nine holes before the cookout.

But storm clouds were gathering in the west, the kind that might put a damper on golf. He didn't mind if the cookout was rained out. His daughter was pregnant with her third and with her husband out of town she would probably bow out. That left Elaine and his dad. Three people sitting around a picnic table hardly warranted being called a cookout. His dad would have forgotten about the cookout and, with the Mets playing a doubleheader, will want to watch the game on his lucky TV, even though the Mets were a hopeless twelve games out of first and playing their worst ball of the year. If he called to remind him, Dad would insist on driving. That would bring Elaine into the fray, who was convinced that Dad behind the wheel of a car was a suicide bomber with a license to kill. All this for burned burgers and the season's first tasteless corn on the cob from Georgia?

Scott picked up his cell phone, but before calling his wife he deleted the colonel's incoming phone number. Elaine had a suspicious streak and nothing got her going more than an unrecognized number on his cell phone. It wouldn't be beyond her to dial the number.

Someday he'd have to tell Elaine. Would she forgive him? He doubted it. But what confused him the most was how one stumble fifteen years ago could destroy a marriage of thirty-eight years? Was marriage so fragile? Were the laws of God so intransient? Thou shall not!!! Could all those cherished memories—the births, the illnesses, the Pop Warner football games—be reduced to ashes by a single slip? "To death do us part?" Yet even if the marriage limped on, she would never really forget. It would gnaw at her, fester, a cancer in remission. A sin was a sin and this sin was beyond forgiveness

He turned onto the on-ramp of the parkway, but as he slowed to call Elaine he noticed the blinking sign towering above him. How could he be so dense? Suddenly it all made sense. The colonel, the investigation, even the governor, the whole absurdity of this Willie Easelman guy. Scott pulled into the breakdown lane started to laugh at the farce of it all. Yes, it all made perfect sense.

Crosstown Traffic

THE HAITIANS' RIDE back from Morningside was bumpy and long, but filled with the energy they savor on Sunday. Yet this wasn't any ordinary Sunday. It was the summer solstice, and the promise of lazy beach days lay ahead. Outside the day was burning as sunshine reigned. The Haitians were anxious to get home, and with windows open and wind in their faces, laughter escaped the van as they sped through the dingy streets of Newark. The men up front sat four abreast, relieved they had survived the cross-examining of Trooper Scott and dodged a one-way ticket back to the Hades that Haiti had become after the earthquake. Jacqueline and Simone lay together in the spacious back floor. Three of the men were mocking the trooper.

"That trooper really ate up that voodoo stuff you were feeding him," one of the Haitians said to Henri.

Another laughed. "You mean that Frank Sinatra bullshit?"

"Strangers in the night, exchanging glances. What were the chances, we'd be dodging fuzz before the night was through?'"

"Stop it!" scolded Henri. "Mr. Willie is in trouble and voodoo can help."

The first Haitian snickered. "By sticking pins in the trooper's tire?"

"By summoning Mr. Willie's ancestors."

"Not Frank Sinatra?" a second Haitian added to a chorus of giggles.

"They'll lead him home," Henri said seriously, "to the Morningside where he belongs."

"Maybe Mr. Willie doesn't want to be at the Morningside," Jacqueline said from the back. "Maybe he wants to be home with his daughter."

Henri sighed. "They all want to be with their children."

"Maybe Mr. Willie wants to be with Simone," teased the first Haitian. "I think the old man has a little surprise up his pants for her."

Simone ignored the dig, but Jacqueline stood up for her friend. "It wasn't Mr. Willie; it was the voodoo."

"Right. The devil made him do it?"

"That and a fistful of those blue pills."

Jacqueline punched the front seat. "He didn't do anything."

"Is that true, Simone?" the second Haitian mocked.

"The voodoo has taken over Mr. Willie's body," Jacqueline continued.

"This is my body, which is given for you," ribbed the first Haitian, making the sign of the cross.

"Stop it!" warned Jacqueline.

"Oh, the good Catholic girl doesn't want to be mounted."

"Take this in remembrance of me," snorted the first Haitian.

Jacqueline swung wildly at the boys. "Shut up!"

"You know how the old men get when they corner a sweet one like Simone."

"They're all hands."

"They still enjoy a treat from the cookie jar."

"Isn't that true, Simone?"

Curled in the back seat, Simone didn't answer.

"Shut your filthy mouths," shot her friend.

"But the priests say the voodoo can't touch good Catholic girls. They say Jesus protects them."

"Maybe it was the devil?"

"Or maybe our sweet Simone isn't as innocent as she pretends?

Maybe she craves a late-night visit from Kalfu?"

"Maybe you'd like a foot up your ass," Jacqueline hissed, kicking the back of the seat violently.

"Maybe our little Simone is becoming a woman," the second Haitian added, reaching back and caressing Simone's leg.

"Keep your dirty mitts off her."

"It's Mr. Willie's hands you have to worry about."

"Or Kalfu's. I hear he's quite the beast."

"Jesus saves," cried Simone.

"Or maybe it's Alberto who saves."

With the mention of Alberto the van went silent. Realizing they had gone too far, the men returned to making fun of Trooper Scott, while Simone spent the rest of the ride in silence.

It was a dilapidated Victorian in a poor section of Newark that the Haitians pulled into. It was on a street once referred to as "Banker's Way," a long, winding road that curled up a hill overlooking Newark. The houses on the street were massive, too large for one family to maintain, so over the years many of the rooms had been rented to boarders. The houses began to run down during the '30s and '40s following the stock market crash, but it was the exodus to the suburbs in the '50s that delivered the knockout punch. As the doctors and bankers were lured elsewhere by the promise of fenced-in back yards and colonial reproductions with towering columns, the houses they left behind deteriorated faster. As the decay spread through Newark, immigrants like the Haitians took up residence in these once majestic but now aged elephants, as they searched for their own version of the American dream.

The stillness of the house greeted them as the Haitians entered through the back door. In a house where fifteen people lived, silence was the last thing one expected to hear. A note on the refrigerator read, "Summer's here. Beer and soccer on the beach." The men rushed to their rooms, changed into their swimsuits, and were back teasing Jacqueline, who enjoyed their attention. Everyone's mood was sky-high—everyone except Simone, who to a chorus of nays said she was too tired to go.

Jacqueline hugged Simone. "See what those nasty boys did."

One by one the boys apologized and Simone mustered a faint smile.

Simone strolled to the living room, watching the van bounce down the road with Jacqueline's bare feet dangling out the rear window. Simone couldn't remember the last time she had the entire house to herself. The silence was refreshing, the house suddenly intimate. And after the two weeks that she had gone through, being alone felt therapeutic.

Simone remained at the oversized window long after the van disappeared. She often wondered about the first owners of the house. She knew Newark had long ago been prosperous and the original owners must have been rich to build this place. Once upon a time these rooms were filled with the laughter of children, children of privilege and promise. Simone imagined the girls growing up and marrying here, descending the central staircase in white gowns. But the rich people had moved out, although Simone believed their ghosts still haunted the house. Lately she had heard children's voices at night. But it wasn't the voodoo, wasn't the stupid Kalfu the girls were always clamoring about. The Bible talks about voices. In Revelations the dead speak to the prophets. Simone heard spirits in her dreams, the cries of her mother trapped beneath the rubble of their house.

Simone moved from the window and peered into what was once the dining room, but was now a make-shift bedroom. Blankets nailed to the walls covered the windows. The smell of men permeated the dark room. She had never entered this room. Stepping over the threshold, she sighed. Five single beds crisscrossed the room, clothes scattered everywhere. Alberto's unmade bed was at the center. She leaned over and smelled his presence.

She had not meant to lie to the trooper. She had not wanted to talk bad about Mr. Willie. It was Jacqueline who made her speak, made her retell her fib. She hoped this wouldn't cause trouble for Mr. Willie. She liked the old man, especially his stories about when he was a boy. His eyes weren't dead like so many at Morningside. She didn't even mind when Mr. Willie leaped out from behind the plastic plants and shouted "Gotcha!" or when he pinched her ass.

Hearing a noise, she scampered out of the room. She stopped at the base of the winding stairs and called, "Anyone there?"

She placed her hand on the newel post and caressed the petals of the carved sunflowers. The post had never been painted and its rich wood reminded her of the old-world hotels back home where mahogany beams crisscrossed the ceilings. She heard a second sound, yet convinced herself it was only the creaking of an old house.

Starting up the stairs, she felt the railing swell in her hand. She lingered at the landing. Often when she awoke at night, she took these stairs, rather than the shorter way down the backstairs to the kitchen. Dressed in her robe and blanketed by the night, she would imagine her wedding here. Jacqueline was her maid-of-honor and Alberto was waiting at the bottom of the stairs, his eyes greeting hers with tenderness. She stepped slowly, the train of her gown filling the stairwell as a piano played. Candles lit the way while her childhood priest stood ready to join them. Her parents and her brothers couldn't be there, but as a tear formed she wiped it away knowing they would be watching.

But the thought of those men in black robes jarred her as she hugged the newel post with both hands. The hate in their voices staggered her. She covered her ears, but lost her balance, saving herself by clutching the handrail. Why did they despise her?

Simone staggered to her bedroom and collapsed. The room was swirling with voices. She sank her face in a pillow and started to cry. She hadn't meant to lie to the trooper. It was Jacqueline's fault. But Jesus would forgive. Jesus knows she didn't believe the girls and their stupid voodoo. Jesus will forgive.

Simone reached under her bed for the wooden box her grandfather carved for her when she was born. Her treasure chest, it held the trove of precious things she had brought to America. She carried the chest into the bathroom and shut the door. In the congested house the bathroom was her sanctuary, the one place she could be alone. Her hands were trembling as she lifted the cover.

She removed the vial of sand. She scooped a handful of sea shells and made a cross on the pedestal sink. She took out the only photo that survived the earthquake. Her older brother was grinning, a crab hanging from his nose by its claw. Her brother always made her laugh. He could say the stupidest thing and they'd laugh hysterically. Even when her father went missing at sea for three days, he made her laugh.

Simone gazed into the mirror, searching for vestiges of the "little princess," her father always called her. She saw her cheekbones were rising, her lips thickening. The beautiful woman in the mirror surprised her. Alberto called her "pretty face" when they were alone. Did he still see her that way?

But those nasty men hated her. She can see them vividly in her mind. They called her horrible names. One shoved a cross in her face. Alberto slapped it away. She could still hear the cross shattering on the pavement. A man swung a shard of the broken crucifix at Alberto. Simone shuttered as she watched the blood drip from Alberto's arm.

Simone took the rosary beads from the chest and kissed them. She loved the taste of the beads, their coolness, and how whispers of her reflection shimmered in them. She rubbed a scrap of fabric between her fingers, what remained from her baby blanket. Covering her nose with the cloth she inhaled deeply, the aroma enveloped and comforted her.

The sound of a door closing alarmed her. Simone held her breath. She heard feet on the stairs. She contemplated rushing over and locking the door but was too frightened. The footsteps continued. They were searching, looking for someone. Thoughts of ghosts and men in robes gushed through her as she brought her hand to her mouth. The doorknob turned.

"Pretty face?"

The door opened.

"Alberto," she cried, sliding the rosary beads back into her treasure chest.

"Tanned and back from the beach."

He was wearing his swimsuit with a towel wrapped around his head in a turban; she laughed. He strolled up to her and lifted her onto the sink.

"You belong on a pedestal."

"Please."

He reached beneath her blouse and caressed her waist. When she tried to protest he kissed her lips. "It's been too long, pretty face," he said, unclipping her bra.

His smell was intoxicating and she felt herself go weak. She placed her arms on his shoulders and he removed her blouse.

"It's been too long," he repeated, as his mouth engulfed her breasts, pleased that her nipples had stiffened.

"Alberto. It hasn't been long enough," she pleaded. But when he continued, she felt her body ache for his. "Do you still love me?" she gasped.

"Nothing has changed, pretty face."

"But those men. I hear their voices at night! They visit me in my dreams," she pleaded, covering her breasts with her blouse. "They're real."

"They're nothing but bad dreams."

"I see them ..."

"They're nightmares."

"But they know."

"What do old men know about the joys of a man and woman?"

"They know what we did."

"God created pleasures for us to enjoy."

"And the baby? I lost my baby!"

"We will have many babies once we're married."

Simone searched Alberto's face for the truth in his words. He loved her; she knew it from his smile.

He tenderly took the blouse from her and cast it aside. She watched it float through the air, landing on the rim of the bathtub, its empty sleeve swinging. He untied the string of her pants. She loved the feel of his hands, remembered the first time he undressed her, piece by piece. She felt her underwear slip away. She wanted to say more, wanted to beg his forgiveness for their unborn child. Engulfed in his arms she leaned back and felt the coolness of the mirror on her back. She reached for his shoulders and drew him in. Their bodies begin to move as one; her breath flew away. She gazed skyward. The stained glass window above her was crisscrossed with cracks. Her father's little princess. Her father's little princess had found love and it came with all the joys and complications of being a woman.

Golden Slumbers

WILLIE SITS IN his Impala at the Montvale rest area, engine idling, eyes shut to the assault of passing trucks, a blind man lost at sea. Music swirls in his head, persistent piano playing that isn't Sinatra. He doesn't have the drive to wake up, to stir consciousness from its slumber. The smell of the streets is intoxicating, flooding him with memories. He cocks his head. He hears voices. Shouts coalesce. Brooklyn.

Willie was a junior in high school and it was the first Saturday of the month, "money day," when he collected for the magazines he delivered. *Life* magazine, the ultimate circuit, was his. Luck had played her hand in him getting the route, but Willie had made the most of his best friend's accident. His friend had slipped off the trolley and ended up in traction. Willie never fully accepted the role luck played in his life. "Luck might open a door," he was fond of saying, "but crossing through that threshold is the stuff of the American Dream, something you do with your own drive."

Willie made more money in one week delivering *Life* than he did in a whole month of shining shoes. He loved the jingle of change in his pocket as he strolled through the tenement houses, convinced

he could distinguish the sound of quarters from dimes. The music of
money struck a chord deep within him. He was no longer just a shoe-
shine boy kneeling for loose change. He was a young man of means
and it amazed him what money could buy. He could cheer up his
mother by buying her a bouquet of carnations from Ginsberg's Flo-
rist, or enliven his little sister by buying her a second-hand bicycle. Yes,
money bought things, but it also bought respect. He felt the weight
of his quarters in his sock every night before he fell asleep. As the
sock grew heavier, it spurred fantasies of promenading down Flatbush
Avenue driving his own car. Lately he had begun saving dollar bills
under his mattress, "silver certificates" he called them, as he coveted
the growing pile of bills he would one day exchange for a car.

Life magazine in 1940 was special. The pages were large and
glossy and colorized the lives of people whose world was drab and
profitless. The women in the neighborhood couldn't get enough.
They cherished each page as if the articles were about them. They
were awed by the storybook tales of the rich and glamorous, dazzled
by the girl who happenstance had placed at the corner soda shop at
just the right moment to be discovered. Success, to these housewives,
was luck not merit and for a couple of hours each Saturday they sat
on their front stoop and fell into the Wonderland of possibilities. And
though by suppertime they were back washing dishes or scrubbing
floors, as night fell they would close their eyes and return to that
world where everything was possible.

On the first Saturday of the month Willie went door to door,
collecting the forty cents; one dime was his. The work was too easy
and he routinely whistled as he walked the walk. Later, when coun-
seling rookie salesmen about success in the insurance business, he
stated that his success was a consequence of his days delivering magazines. "Business is business," he chanted. "Whether it's Wall Street or
Main Street, money has no address but long hours and hard work."

Willie kept customers' accounts on paper slats that hung from a
ring attached to the belt loop of his jeans. He would initial the date
of each payment in pen, not pencil, so there was never a question
about payment. When a customer fell a month behind, which was
often the case in those days, he personally delivered the bad news.
Yet he often cushioned the blow by giving the cancelled customer

free samples. Because of this, Willie was known around the neighborhood as a genuine guy, someone who could be counted on—at least for a month or two.

One housewife was always being terminated, Elizabeth Hirschhorn, whose husband ran a smelly butcher shop specializing in cheap chicken parts. Yet somehow she always scraped up the money to reinstate her subscription, probably raiding her husband's blood-stained smock for loose change. Elizabeth was younger than most of his clients and Willie knew her slightly since she had been in the same grade as his older sister. Her story was similar to many girls. In her haste to escape an overcrowded home life, she latched onto the first man who showed attention. She married within weeks of graduating from high school and now, scarcely a year out of school, she had to care for a baby.

Willie felt sorry for Elizabeth. Often when he made his rounds he found the blinds to her cramped one-bedroom apartment tightly drawn. Her sadness seemed out of place for a young mother. How they started flipping through *Life* magazine together he no longer remembered, but he made her laugh and her laughter made him feel special. Saturday was a busy day for Elizabeth's husband, so the butcher never disturbed them as they sat together on her hand-me-down sofa, awed by the photos of enchanting places.

Life magazine often featured an actor or a famous person on its front cover. Willie felt Liz's passion when she declared that one day she would design wardrobes for the stars. Liz owned a foot-powered sewing machine that her grandmother had given her and made all of her son's clothes. Although not yet walking, her son had an endless array of outfits. Willie's favorite, a blue and white sailor's suit, was topped with a seaman's cap that Liz knitted. Once, when a summer issue highlighted swimsuits, Liz turned to Willie and asked "How do you think I'd look in this?" She pressed the full-length picture of a skimpy bathing suit against her body and sauntered around the room. "You'll be the belle of the beach," Willie roared. Liz, who was thrilled that her breasts were still large from breastfeeding, thought so too. If she ever got the opportunity to wear such an outfit, she would strut down the boardwalks of Atlantic City, with the grace and style of those Hollywood actresses.

When they sat together on the couch, Willie hid his fear of her husband barging in. Willie watched the front door of the cold-water flat wondering "Does the butcher bring home his meat cleaver?" Some nights Willie had nightmares where the butcher chopped him up and sold his parts at discount. Willie concocted a plan where if the door burst open, he would grab his pen and say in a goofy voice, "And I hope you enjoy your free subscription, Mrs. Hirschhorn," knowing the chicken butcher would be delighted by anything free.

The man in the Impala grips the handle of the door with both hands. It is uncertain if he is trying to escape or simply confused. But on further inspection an outside observer would notice that the old man is fast asleep. He twitches and turns, acting out his dreams, like an actor playing his part. He is unaware of the storm gathering in the west, its distant rumbling approaching fast.

Willie looked forward to their Saturdays together, especially when Liz put the baby down for his nap. Conversation was easy when it was woven with the pictures of far-away places they both fantasized of someday visiting.

"You'll never find me in that snake-infested river," Liz said as she squirmed at photos of the Amazon jungle.

"Anacondas grow to thirty feet," Willie whispered menacingly.

"Why they'd swallow a girl like me whole," Liz gasped, gripping Willie's arm as if the snake was ready to strike.

"How about climbing that?" Willie said of a wispy black and white photo of Mount Everest.

"Too cold."

"Maybe I'll be the first to conquer her," bragged Willie.

"Second wouldn't be too shabby," chimed Liz.

First on Liz's list of places to visit was Paris and she worshipped the special edition of *Life* that chronicled the city.

"Isn't Paris beautiful at night?" she said with a French accent. "The city of lights."

"I'd climb that giant Erector Set," Willie bragged, pointing to a picture of the Eiffel Tower.

Liz chuckled. "Why climb it, silly, when you could ride the elevator to the top?"

"You'll never get me in that claustrophobic box."

"They say it's a ride you'll never forget."

Even though a subway outing beyond Brooklyn had been adventure enough for both of them, as they sat on Liz's thread-bare couch, everywhere seemed possible. The world was enormous, but inside the pages of *Life* magazine even the most exotic places seemed possible; after all, Paris and London were now just a plane ride away.

Automobile ads were particularly exciting to Liz and Willie, full-page advertisements where dignified men and stunning women highlighted success. Liz found it hilarious that in the automobile ads the women always rode in the passenger seat, while the man drove.

"Women can't drive," Willie teased Liz, who snatched the magazine and hit him on the head.

"A woman can do whatever a man can do," shot back Liz.

Willie smiled at Liz's sudden boldness. "Try changing a tire."

"Try having a baby."

"Try making a baby," Willie snapped back without thinking, shocked with his words.

Liz ignored his outburst and continued. "And I suppose women can't smoke either."

"A particular kind can," Willie coyly replied.

"And who might that particular kind be?"

Willie cupped his hand over Liz's ear and drew her near. "A nafkeh." Whispering that forbidden word created a secret conspiracy between them, although Liz tickled Willie until he took the naughty word back. And though Willie shivered with the thrill of her touch, his eyes remained locked on the front door, consumed by the fear that the doorknob would turn and in would rush the chicken butcher, meat cleaver and all.

Willie always boasted how one day he would own a car and was adamant that the only car for him was a Chevrolet, although he wouldn't say no to a Cadillac. Willie traced the curves of the cars in the magazine with his finger, coveting the chrome-fin fenders that highlighted the luxury sedans or the sleek freedom of the open road invoked by the convertibles. Willie knew the make and year of every car that drove past Liz's window, and he never tired of impressing her by calling them out.

Asleep in the driver's seat the old man watches her move around the apartment in her polka-dot dress. He hums the tune that refuses to leave his head. Reaching out for her, he grabs the mother-of-pearl button that conceals her breasts. She feigns escaping, then leans towards him and giggles in his ear. Her laughter excites him, as his agile fingers slip the button through the buttonhole that leads to paradise.

One Saturday afternoon, after Liz fed the baby and put him down for his nap, she returned from the bedroom with the top portion of her polka-dot dress open. She picked up the magazine on the sofa and started leafing through it, her foot tapping to a lively beat. Willie peered at the curvature of her breast nestled in the white cloth of her bra. Liz was more animated than usual as she shared with him an article about an Africa tribe. The natives in this remote village dance for days during their fertility rite, and the near-naked women wore jewelry crafted by the warriors seeking their affection.

But Willie heard nothing. Watching Liz's undulating breasts, Willie was growing dizzy. Liz leaned forward, her breasts begging to be touched. She grabbed hold of Willie's thigh to point out a nighttime photo of the tribe dancing around a bonfire. The men looked to be in a trance, their eyes locked in darkness. "I wonder what makes them look so crazed," Liz asked, her lips puckered with innocence. Willie was too breathless to speak, yet he focused on the image of the dancing tribesmen, their bodies ecstatic with flames.

His arthritic hand strokes the Impala's dashboard. He opens his mouth to draw her in, to once again feast on her tenderness. His fingers trace the mysteries of her waist, the slight rise of her belly where enigma and magic converge. His hands drop to her hips and he draws her near, the blood rushing through him carries the vigor of youth. Outside the storm ignites the sky with flashes of fire. The piano plays on.

Liz changed the record and cast aside the magazine; the African rites no longer interested her. Her polka-dot dress flowed with music; her breasts swelled as the ceiling faded away. The fragrance of her skin was intoxicating. She whispered something, her voice drowned out by the beating of Willie's heart.

He reached out for her; the touch of her body sent him swirling into the unknown. She smiled and slowly undid the buttons of her dress. Taking his hand, she led him to her breasts. Her softness enveloped him, a softness so delicate his soul quaked. She said something, but everything was spinning too fast for words. His mouth found her nipples, his body trembled to the resonance of her gasps. He closed his eyes—the softness of her body enveloped him.

Keys rattled and they froze. He saw the terror in her eyes as she covered up. They heard the sound of a door opening. Rising from the couch, he shielded her with his body. But it was the neighbors' door. She giggled with relief, laughing as she buttoned her dress. She picked the magazine off the floor and kissed him on the forehead. He opened his mouth, hoping to draw her in like Suzie Isenberg had with the lifeguard. She broke away and whispered, "Later."

The man in the Impala arches towards her. The piano is reaching a crescendo; the dashboard light illuminates his hopes. Her softness that has remained fallow in the garden of remembrances for all these years overcomes him. He calls her name, begs for her to stay. She smiles with the mystery of the moon, fastening the buttons of her polka-dot dress she begins to fade. He aches to touch her again, to dance with her around the bonfire of his imagination. But she's gone. The storm rages, rocking the Impala. Flashes of light tear open the night. Thunder drowns the music. He struggles for breath but finds none. He draws his knees to his chest and covers himself with his blanket, hoping for one last touch to sooth his body.

Sundays Will Never
Be the Same

SUNDAY LUNCH AT the Morningside Nursing Home was always well attended, always held at 11:00 AM sharp. The smell of baking chicken permeated the hallways as residents, drawn by its aroma, began gathering outside the double doors to the dining room. The administrators sat huddled in the corner of the lobby crafting responses to Trooper Scott's charges and hatching strategies to minimize the damage caused by Willie's escape. The three agreed their best defense was a strong offense, as they jotted notes to submit to the Bureau of Elderly Affairs come Monday morning.

Blame, the administrators agreed, should rest squarely on Willie's daughter, Anna. They knew the Bureau was inherently suspicious of family members, since family members regularly steal from their helpless relatives. More importantly, it was the daughter's idea to give Willie back his car. The administrators marveled at their ingenuity as they conspired to back-date a letter of protest to Anna's plan and plant it in Willie's file.

The administrators snickered when they discovered that Willie's daughter had committed her father without properly procuring guardianship. Although a mere technicality with dementia patients like Willie, legally it was kidnapping since it was done without her father's permission. They could also leak to the newspaper that Anna had been remiss about visiting her father. The administrators could hardly contain their giddiness when the logs revealed Anna hadn't visited her father in six weeks. Six weeks would undoubtedly be viewed as unconscionable in the scrupulous eyes of their small-town readers, the majority of whom read the police blotter more religiously than the Bible.

"How about the headline 'Daughter Questioned in Father's Disappearance'?" scoffed one of the administrators.

"Or 'Daughter Key Suspect in Father's Escape,'" said another.

The tall administrator then summed it up with, "Daughter Key to Missing Father's Whereabouts."

As the administrators schemed, the residents of Morningside grumbled. Sunday was the meal of the week, and if one thing rankled them, it was Sunday dinner being served late. Now they might gripe about the food, grumbling how it was unfit for dogs, but "Be late and be hate," was how the good-natured Haitian cooks put it, knowing that complaining was the only thing left for most of the residents. So when the combination of the late-night variety show, Willie's thrilling escape, and Trooper Scott's brunt interrogation of the administrators put the kitchen staff an hour behind schedule, it wasn't surprising that the Morningside residents were raising canes well before the first piece of undercooked chicken hit their plates.

Walter Wilder led the protest, riling up his group of buddies. "A man needs cake, if he's going to fornicate," he bellowed, pounding his chest like an alpha ape. When his followers started chanting "fornicate," Walter pulled out a bottle of blue pills and shook along, cabasa style. Julia Banner threatened to call her private number for social services and protest dinner being late and Mary Maysinger began demanding seconds, even though she rarely did more than sniff her food. The Haitian cooks laughed at the escalating complaints, but turned the oven up full blast, hoping for the best, while knowing if the chicken burned there'd be hell to pay.

Ignoring the growing chaos, Doris Manheim sat on the settee fretting over Willie. She wanted her Willie back, but she also feared what would happen if that trooper got his hands on him. These conflicting wants baffled Doris. She clasped her hands in prayer; but after a shaky "Dear Lord," her mind remained blank. She gave a spiteful glare at the crowd outside the dinning room and thanked God she wasn't like them. She heard Walter Wilder's boasts and begged God to please send that horrible creature straight to hell. Doris gripped her hands harder but she couldn't squeeze out a prayer. She gazed at the stained-glass window, a trick that often helped, but still nothing came.

What came, however, was admiration for Willie, her newly crowned prince. She pictured in her mind how he leaped on stage and snatched the microphone away from that detestable monster of a woman. He sang and told jokes with the good manners of the legendary entertainers she adored. But most of all Willie had become her champion because he had chosen *her*. He had singled *her* out, and not Lisa Linsky, that showboat tramp who flaunted her tits as if they were public property. No, Willie held *her* in his arms, had danced with *her*, and had twirled *her* around to the envy of all the girls.

As the crowd outside the dinning room boomed louder, Walter Wilder became more belligerent. He yakked at the Haitians through the closed doors. "If you don't open up we'll ship you wetbacks back to Cuba." When that insult was met with silence, he pounded on the doors, chanting, "U.S.A., U.S.A.," a cheer that everyone eagerly joined. The chant gathered steam and soon even Mary Maysinger was pumping her pencil-thin arm into the air and squealing, "U.S.A., U.S.A."

But be careful of the line separating grip from chaos, and when Walter Wilder wrestled a walker from one of the residents and rammed the doors, the administrators acted. They rushed over and admonished the crowd with an old-fashion scolding. But as the administrators returned to their corner, Mary Maysinger taunted, "You're nothing but a bunch of party-poopers," and the grumbling started anew.

Doris's hands were white with worry as she continued to press for a prayer. She knew she had to be careful. She couldn't just ask the Lord outright to send Willie back to her. God doesn't listen to those who plead for themselves. Doris knew this because all the relatives she had prayed for were long dead. Prayers worked but they had to be correctly addressed. Suddenly the sun sliced through an opening

in the clouds, flooding the lobby with amber light, and in that instant
Doris was reminded of the Easter Miracle.

She was just a little girl on that day before Easter when the pet
mouse she shared with her sister lay motionless in its cage. She and
her sister poked the mouse, thrilled with even the slightest shiver
of its legs. But as the day wore on, and the shaking dwindled, their
father took them aside and warned them what to expect. The girls
spent the rest of the day crying. Late that night, as her sister slept,
Doris went to her open window and prayed. But she didn't pray
for herself; she prayed for her sister's half of the mouse to recover.
And in the morning it did. There among the hidden jelly beans and
chocolate rabbits, their mouse raced around its cage like it had been
reborn. The girls were overwhelmed. Their mouse had grown spots,
a sign from God their mother solemnly told them. The Easter Miracle, her sister called it and all agreed this was the best holiday ever.

No, she couldn't plain out ask God to help her. She had to pray
for someone else and then maybe, just maybe, she would get her
Willie back. But as Doris clasped her hands so tight her knuckles
went white, the double doors opened and a man with a Haitian
accent announced, "Dinner!"

Whoever said the elderly hold the keys to etiquette never
watched the Morningside residents seat themselves for Sunday dinner. For no sooner had the word "dinner" left the server's mouth
than the stampede began, if people advancing in walkers and canes
could be classified a stampede. The first person into the dinning
room was Ginny Blanchard, who had strategically positioned her
wheelchair near the door, her wheels in gear and ready to roll. However, as Ginny shifted her weight to rotate her wheelchair in the
direction of her favorite seat, thereby denying it to her archrival
Renee O'Shay, her rear tires snagged the door. If the residents simply
waited for the Haitians to free Ginny, then much would have been
avoided. But they didn't. In the rush Ginny was shoved from her
wheelchair and trampled by the various devices invented to help the
elderly walk.

As Ginny groaned on the floor, the residents began pounding
on their tables. Someone flung a dinner roll at one of the aides who
was wiping blood from Ginny's forehead. Though the roll missed,

the thud of it striking the cinderblock, followed by a chicken wing flying across the room, signaled the food fight was on.

"Stop it!" the administrators barked as the three streamed in to quell the commotion.

The room fell silent, as the residents hung their heads in shame. The taller administrator reprimanded them on their bad behavior, a speech surprisingly similar to the lectures the residents once delivered to their own children. Even Walter Wilder was regretful, as he covered his face which was smeared with mashed potatoes. Some residents wept openly. And not a giggle leaked out as the Haitians pushed poor Ginny out the door, the bent wheel of her wheelchair squeaking in counterpoint with her moans.

This roomful of remorse greeted Doris Manheim as she strolled into the dining room. She walked to the exact spot where Willie delivered last night's monologue, although the stage was removed. The room was thick with repentance as Doris waited for the pots in the kitchen to stop clanging. As the hush drifted towards self-reflection, appropriate for naughty ones on Sundays, Doris turned to her audience and in a tone so heartfelt that even the three administrators bowed their heads, began: "Let us pray."

Everybody Knows

TROOPER SCOTT SAT in his cruiser on the entrance ramp of the Garden State Parkway, staring up at the signboard blinking "SILVER ALERT WILLIE EASELMAN 1986 WHITE IMPALA 413-782." He laughed—today was the start of the governor's much-heralded Silver Alert campaign. So this is why the state police were called in—Willie Easelman was the guinea pig. Scott picked up the black-and-white photograph and looked into Willie's eyes. It was the expression he frequently saw in his father. The "gone-fishing look," as Elaine referred to it. With luck Mr. Easelman had made it to a neighboring state and was now their problem. But if he's still in Jersey, Doris's "freedom fighter" was not only a menace to the highway but to the governor himself.

The Silver Alert campaign was hatched six months ago after a horrific accident on the Garden State. The crash was the fault of Bill Cassidy who, at ninety-two, should have been confined to a wheelchair rather than propped on a pillow in his car. But here was "Wild Bill," as the media came to call him, careening down the turnpike doing 85 m.p.h., until his joy ride was cut short when he rear-ended a vacationing family of six from Rhode Island. In the aftermath of the accident that killed everyone, the media pounced on the fact that despite being legally blind, diagnosed with stage-three Alzheimer's, and swallowing a daily assortment of thirty questionable pills, Mr. Cassidy still possessed a valid New Jersey driver's license. The outrage was immediate. Soon the newspapers were competing to outdo each other by printing photos of the most heinous crashes caused by seniors. The Wreck of the Week, as it was known, became a staple in the local news-starved papers. Sensing controversy, the networks jumped in, often prefacing their graphic videos of cataclysmic wrecks with a blinking "inappropriate for small children" warning. Editorials turned bolder, some proposing an outright ban for all drivers over eighty.

The governor was squeezed. The media howled to halt the carnage; meanwhile seniors were the most dependable voters. No governor had been elected since 1918 without carrying the demographic. They voted in vast numbers and were chauffeured to the polls in specially equipped buses. Election day at the nursing homes had become pageants, with politicians waltzing the walk down dingy corridors like dignitaries, hailing everyone as the country's "greatest generation."

A referendum to revoke the licenses of the elderly would be suicide for the governor, especially when his private polling group showed that ninety-five percent of the elderly opposed even minor restrictions on their right to drive. Seniors organized and protests escalated. Elderly marches became a staple of the six o'clock news, since no one tired of those folksy sound bits.

"If I can get my ass into the driver's seat, then no governor is going to kick my butt out," became a popular slogan. And no protest was complete without a circle of seniors singing, "My car, my car, my car. Never apart, never afar," as they burned their driver licenses.

The tug-of-war in the media reached a tipping point when a disoriented senior drove the wrong way on the Jersey Turnpike, somehow surviving six miles, as oncoming cars, scrambled down embankments and into ravines. The incident went viral when "Toad's Wild Ride," as YouTube called it, was captured on a teenager's cell phone. "ENOUGH!" the newspapers balked and even the usually passive legislature demanded that the governor act.

It was Christmas Eve and news was being handled by third-rate amateurs when the governor made his speech. The state would place thirty Silver Alert signs on the highways to inform citizens when an elderly driver was at risk to himself or to the community.

"Our intent is to reach out to those seniors in need," the governor intoned, as he sat in a rocking chair with his beloved yellow lab sleeping at his feet. "No responsible senior needs to fear their right to drive. The right to drive is a family matter and not something the state needs to pry into. Government is never the solution—it is the problem."

The "Christmas Eve snow job," as the governor's speech was referred to in political circles, was a success and the Silver Alert sign blinking on the entrance ramp was a brilliant example of how a governor tackles a highly sensitive issue.

But this mess was falling smack into Trooper Scott's lap. He had to find Easelman before the old man hurt someone. Now it was clear why the colonel wanted dirt on the Morningside. It was a back-up plan to blame someone, anyone, other than the governor. Scott thought those cocky administrators at the Morningside would make good fall guys and the media would delight in wiping those despicable smirks off their well-shaved faces.

The thought of a crazed Easelman plowing into a troop of Girl Scouts flashed across Trooper Scott's mind, an image superimposed with his own father driving. How bad would it look at headquarters if it was his father doing the plowing? His dad, who had battled dementia for years, was on the verge of losing the war, the repercussions of which made Scott cringe. He needed to talk with his father, needed to take his keys. But before he could lament further, his cell phone beeped.

"Davis here," the phone barked. "New York doesn't show shit on Easelman entering the state. No surprise there since their stuff is as high-tech as a telegraph. You remember the Connelly case? The serial killer was commuting over the Tappan Zee like a Wall Street broker for three months without them knowing it. CSI NY, you know what it stands for, Scott? 'Can't Solve Shit In NY.' But if New York's got it right, we've got a problem. We're short-staffed today so I need you to take the Garden State to the border. Understand?"

"Sure, sir."

"Check the rest areas. God knows how these old people like to snooze. Head straight to Monmouth, then work your way north to Montvale. Maybe we'll get lucky and someone will call in on the Silver Alert." A pause, then a scorning laugh. "Who knows, maybe the taxpayers will get their ten-million worth."

"Yes, sir."

"Remember, Scott, the governor's head is in the vise on this one. The first day of the program—friggin' amazing. Couldn't have planned it better if it was a Hollywood movie."

"I'm on it, sir."

"Politics. Christ, I didn't know how good I had it when I was just Joe Trooper riding the wheel. Up here everyone has an agenda. If this Silver Alert crap goes south, they'll be swarming over the governor like drunks at a football game. The back stabbings are more routine than in the back alleys of Newark."

"Sounds like fun," Scott replied, without a hint of sarcasm.

"It'd be funny if my job wasn't on the line. But you got to chuckle knowing the governor's balls are in the hands of an eighty-six year old lunatic joy-riding through the countryside like a reborn Paul Revere. Only in America, Scott, only in America."

"You can count on me," Scott added, his words sounding hollow.

"I know that, Scott, but we need a plan B."

"What?"

"If we don't locate Easelman before he makes hamburger out of the luncheon crowd at McDonald's."

"Not sure I follow, sir?"

"Leave the thinking to me. But you're on to something with this daughter thing. I've talked with a few boys in legal."

"What do we have on her?"

"Contributing to the delinquency of an elder."

"What?"

"If she gave her father the car keys, knowing he was incompetent, then she's guilty of something. The legal boys are working out a strategy as we speak."

"What about the nursing home?"

"A dead end. Christ, every nursing home is guilty of something.

Goes with the territory. The whole bunch of them are lawsuits waiting to explode ... except for one thing."

"Sir?"

"Where do we put them? Christ, these old folks live forever these days. My Aunt Amy is doing Tai Chi at ninety. Says she wants to see the Great Wall before she gets too old. But the daughter. Now that's sweet poetry."

"I'm not sure I follow."

"No need to, Scott. All we need is a ten-second clip of the daughter being hauled off in handcuffs and the governor's off the hook. I mean the average American's attention span is down to a few nanoseconds. Besides everybody knows it's always a family member that did it; check out CSI. By the time the courts say the daughter's clear, the public will be watching 'Dancing with the Stars.' It's beautiful, Scott, beautiful."

"I guess."

"Politics. Don't try to figure it out; better to just air it out."

"Yes, sir."

"But let's not lose sight of the prize. Find this Willie pinhead and our asses are aces."

"I'm on it."

"And call the daughter. Snoop around; squeeze her a bit. See if she'll admit to giving the old man the keys. Remember admission trumps confession."

"Yes, sir."

"And dig deeper into this Easelman fella. These nursing homes have turned into sugar shacks with those little blue pills. Last month we had to pry a bottle out of an old codger's hand. The guy was eighty-nine and had more sister-wives than a Utah Mormon. Find out if this Easelman fella has a something on the side."

"Not sure how that figures in."

"TV. If this thing ends poorly, and trust me I'd bet a month's wages that it will, the media will turn Easelman into a villain and by association the gov. But gramps with a mistress draped on his arm has the look of a champion. Christ, I can see his picture plastered on a box of Wheaties. It's all one big reality show."

"I guess."

"Heroes might be tragic, but everyone loves them. Ask Shakespeare."

"He did have one admirer, a Doris Manheim. Told me Willie was her nursing home freedom fighter."

"That's the ticket. I bet he's tapping her."

"She doesn't look like the ... the tapping type."

"A nursing home freedom fighter. It's got a certain flare to it. Could see Stallone playing the part. Mowing them down with an assault rifle as he sits in his wheelchair."

"I'll check it out, sir."

"Five mistresses. I tell you, Scott, those pills can raise the dead." And the phone clicked off.

Scott opened his notebook and dialed Easelman's daughter's number.

"Ms. Tanner? Ms. Anna Tanner?"

"Yes."

"This is Trooper Scott from the New Jersey State Police. I'm investigating your father's disappearance. I wonder if you might have any idea where your father might go. Perhaps some favorite spot?"

"My father has dementia, Officer Scott. I doubt even he knows where he is."

"Yes, we're aware of your father's condition. But sometimes people like your father want to return to a favorite place. Maybe a choice fishing spot. Often their recall of such places is quite extraordinary."

"No, my father wasn't much into hobbies."

"A special house?"

"No, everything was work with my father." There was a pause before Anna continued. "He speaks a lot about Brooklyn."

"Reminisces about the old days, does he? The Brooklyn Dodgers?"

"I ... don't know how to say this, but it's more than memories. It's as if he's actually back in Brooklyn. His eyes dart about when he talks about those days. I'd swear he's actually reliving it, actually ... being there."

Scott weighed the heaviness of her pauses. "One other thing, Ms. Tanner. We're trying to piece together a timeline of your father's ... disappearance ... his escape. How he got hold of his keys. The

Morningside still has theirs. Any idea?"

"No. I gave them my only set. It's possible that my father stashed a second set. He's sneaky like that."

"Maybe you gave him the second set and forgot?"

"Perhaps, but I don't think so. Those were troubling times, as you might expect. My father never got over them taking away his car."

"Then you didn't take away his car?"

"Thankfully the police did. It might have killed him if I had."

"Understandable."

"I wasn't exactly on my father's favorites list. But I'm sure there was only one set of keys."

"I understand, Ms. Tanner."

"Until you do it yourself, Officer Scott, you'll never understand. It's a crime against nature, committing your father."

"But the Morningside seems like a pleasant place."

"Let's leave it like that, Officer."

Trooper Scott squeezed his phone. "One last thing, Ms. Tanner."

"Yes?"

"Your father's car has out-of-state plates. Maine plates registered to your brother's address."

"Yes."

"Apparently he's registered his cars in Maine for over twenty years."

"Is that a crime?"

Scott heard the defensiveness in her voice. "Technically it's just a fine. But ..."

"But?"

"But if your brother knew about it and if, let's say, there was an accident, it might end up in court."

"In court?"

"Everybody sues these days. More lawyers advertise on TV than used-car dealers. Sign of the times, Ms. Tanner."

Scott welcomed the pause on the other end.

"What does it all mean?" Anna struggled to ask.

"It means your brother could be held liable for aiding and abetting. The penalties could be quite severe."

"Such as?"

"Your brother could lose his house."

As Anna's thoughts raced through the sixteen rooms of her brother's seaside estate, Trooper Scott glanced at his reflection in his rearview mirror, satisfied the seeds of worry had just been planted. If Easelman's daughter knew anything, these seeds would quickly sprout.

"Well I'm sure this will all turn out fine, Ms. Tanner," Scott said, sympathetically.

"Officer Scott, when you find my father, promise me you'll be understanding. He might try something foolish ... to protect his car."

"I understand," Scott answered in a fatherly tone.

"In a way, it's all he has left."

"I have a father of my own."

"Officer."

"Yes?"

Silence, the kind Scott knew often precedes a confession.

"My father ... my father might have ... a gun. When we cleaned out his apartment we couldn't find it."

"Do you think your father is armed, Ms. Tanner?"

"My father's not a violent man. He may have some strong political views but I'm certain they'd never reach the point of violence."

"But he has a gun?"

"I don't know. Maybe he misplaced it. He bought it years ago during the riots. To protect his family. But if he thinks someone is taking away his car..."

Scott could hear her holding back tears. "We'll be careful, Ms. Tanner."

"Thank you."

"Trust me, Ms. Tanner, this will all turn out OK."

Trooper Scott flipped on his flashers, ignoring the need for his siren. He had four rest areas to check before Montvale. Hopefully, Easelman was off the highway. Brooklyn would be fine—NYPD's problem. Either way he was bound to show up soon. How many '86 Impalas are still on the road?

Trooper Scott rubbed the spot on his thigh where the old woman had clung. He tried to block out her crazed look as she squawked, "He's our nursing home freedom fighter!" What were these the strong political views his daughter mentioned? He had to disclose the gun to the colonel. The Haitian girl, he was having doubts about deep-sixing her story. And now the governor. This case was widening, not narrowing—moving fast. Trouble was brewing; he could feel it burning in his gut along with the four cups of coffee.

Trooper Scott rang his wife. He told Elaine things were tight for 3:00 Mass, although the cookout still looked good.

"Jim, Dad is insisting on driving himself to the cookout. I told him I'd pick him up, but he says he's not a child. When I asked again he shouted, "You're not the boss of me!" He got so riled up. You've got to do something."

"Later, honey."

"He's a menace. Susan saw him run a red light on Washington Street."

"Honey."

"Sailed right through it without slowing down. There're kids around, Jim. What if he hits one? Maybe we should call the police?"

"Right now I need both hands on the wheel."

"OK. Be safe; we'll talk later."

Talk later? For fifteen years Scott wanted to have that talk. The toll was growing. Someday he would tell her—needed to tell her—even if it ended their marriage. He pondered the events of fifteen years ago. He loved his wife, loved her more than she knew. He was a cop, with a cop's tough skin. But inside his silence was gnawing at his gut.

As for Dad? Soon he'd be in a home like Morningside. Soon he'd have that same ghoulish expression, the same loathing for him that Easelman feels for his daughter. But he has to take his keys, has to take the keys now. Scott shuddered at the thought of the struggle, a frail wisp of a man standing his ground against his son, gripping his keys like his life depended on them. But try buying a loaf of bread in America without them.

For Whom the Bell Tolls

REBORN FROM HIS nap, Willie whipped his '86 Impala back onto the parkway. The road was ghostly quiet and Willie kept his speed dead on 65. What day was it? He glanced at the broken clock on the dashboard, whose miniature arms were frozen at 4:13. Age had caused havoc with his internal clock, dividing time into just two parts—day and night. The Morningside staff was always trying to recalibrate his clock into unnecessary segments, telling him it was dinner time or bed time or pill-taking time. But Willie wasn't having any of it. Time seemed rather stupid. If time stopped he'd still be the same person.

Signs appeared and disappeared into the night. Fog hovered in the fields, creating a mood that reinforced a sense of familiarity. He had been here before. He studied the terrain with the guile of a guide trying to remember his way. As Willie straddled the break-down lane, something stirred as he murmured "Upper Saddle River," the cadence of the words resounding with significance.

He pulled his Impala over and got out, staggering over to the exit sign that towered above him—"Upper Saddle River." Crows squawked in the distance, disturbed from their sleep by the sound of a car door slamming. One flew out of the fog and circled him. Eyeballing the intruder with its yellow eyes, the crow swooped low and scrutinized the tottering old man before returning to the mist amidst a punctuating series of cackles.

"Home," he whispered, like a child tasting a new flavor. The word felt good on his lips. He recognized the sound, knew how to shape the single syllable word with his mouth. "Home," he repeated. The word began to crystallize with meaning, his tongue quivering with implication.

Jeanie and he called it "The Big House," bought when his income reached six figures. It sat on a hill with gigantic columns, which everyone said were grander than those at the White House. They had been out for a ride and had seen a sign. Jeanie was ecstatic, said the house "completed her." She never initiated lovemaking, but later that day she did.

The urge to see that house again gathered in his chest. He took the exit, his headlights slicing through the dark curves. It was all coming back as he weaved through the maze of turns. Lefts followed rights through a progression of quiet lanes until he rolled to a stop in front of a colonial. The hill wasn't as high as he remembered it, the yard not so grand, but as he got out of the Impala the word "home" hung on his lips.

He knew Andy would be impressed by the house. It was Christmas vacation when Andy brought that girl home from college. They stayed in his room, coming down only for meals. They giggled and talked in secretive tones. Andy announced he was going to become an architect. Suddenly everything in the house was "provincial." Yes, that was the word they used when he caught them chuckling about Jeanie's Hummel collection.

Christmas Eve. Jeanie was so proud, telling the kids over and over that their new living room was larger than their entire apartment on Flatbush Avenue. We were on our second bottle of wine when Andy, standing by the fireplace, said, "You know, this house is like a split-level on vitamins. It's big, but it really doesn't have any soul." The girl struggled to contain herself, but as she brought her slender hand to her mouth a few drops of red wine fell on the new white sofa. Andy and his girlfriend stood watching as Jeanie sprinkled salt on the cushions. Jeanie said it was nothing, but a week later a new sofa arrived.

Willie tottered up the slight incline to the house, his arms flopping for balance. The columns were thin, barely the thickness of a couple of two-by-fours, and the house was in need of paint. Under cover of night, he snuck to the rear entrance and lifted the mat. No key. He tried the door. Locked.

The scent of freshly cut grass drew Willie away. How many times had he cut this grass, sweated under July's sun? Suddenly it dawned on him this wasn't the big house; it was his first house after leaving Brooklyn. The swing set was still there. Home plate was the oak tree.

"Look, Dad," Anna exclaims, "Pokey's a pup again."

Pokey, free from the leash of the city, bounds tirelessly after each ball the kids throw.

His boys, shirtless with enthusiasm, edge each other to chuck the ball into the neighbor's yard. Standing to the side, Willie marvels at his boys' maturing chests, but is aggravated over their pathetic throwing arms.

"You two throw like girls."

Andy takes offense and tosses the ball as far as he can.

"Pathetic. You'll never pitch for the Dodgers throwing like that."

Andy whips a second ball, which rolls short of the first. Pokey stands by, his ear cocked to the laughter.

"Like a girl," Anna snickers.

Dropping their baseball gloves, the three kids circle Pokey, waving wands of dandelions. The seeds drift with the summer breeze, messengers of mirth of this new land. The kids make up a song.

> *Float high*
> *In the sky*
> *And be my eyes*
> *As you fly—away.*

It's Sunday. Jeanie is in the house cleaning. The sun is shimmering; the fragrance of freshly cut grass permeates the air with well-being. Laughter is general throughout the yard. A squirrel scampers across the lawn perfecting the moment. Pokey, slowed by a life of leases and cement sidewalks, gives chase.

The first car grazes Pokey. The second car swerves, its horn slicing Sunday's silence with alarm. Pokey stands shaking in the middle of the road, his loyal brown eyes staring questioningly at the kids. When the third car strikes Pokey head on, time stands still.

Willie stood in the dark watching the squirrel scamper away, its tail fluttering with meaningless indifference. The moon peered out from the clouds, illuminating the yard with a touch of iridescence. Willie spotted the clumps of crabgrass sprouting through the patches of neglected grass. Angry, he turned and stumbled back to the door and pounded. The kitchen light flashed on. A man's face appeared at the door, his wife glaring out from behind the man's shoulder.

"What do you want?" the man asked, rubbing his eyes.

The question confused Willie.

"What are you doing here?"

"Doing here?" Willie repeated.

Seeing it was just an old man, the woman pushed her husband aside and shouted. "Get off my property!"

"He looks harmless," her husband remarked.

"I don't care if he's a God-damn saint; we have kids sleeping upstairs."

The man opened the door, keeping the screen door locked between them.

"You've got to go, mister. We've got kids."

Willie blinked at the shimmering figures watching him from behind the screen. "I lived here," he murmured, his words as confusing to him as disturbing to the two.

"I'm calling the cops!" the wife barked, disappearing from the doorway.

The two men remained staring at each other.

Willie noticed the slit in the screen sealed with scotch tape. "Jeanie told me if I don't fix the screen the mosquitoes will bite the children."

"You've got to go, mister. My wife's calling the cops."

"When the mosquitoes bite the kids they get sick."

The man stood in his pajamas peering at the old man framed in the doorway. He felt the urge to invite him in, share a cup of coffee at the kitchen table. The old guy said he lived here. He must have stories to tell, adventures of raising his own kids. But their kids were upstairs sleeping and his wife was calling the cops. He slammed the door shut.

Willie remained in the doorway blinking, as the kitchen light turned off. Willie turned to the night that enveloped him. Pokey was buried here, somewhere in the backyard. He heard a distant siren and headed for his car. Opening the door he hesitated and turned back. The house was grinning at him. He picked up a rock. Winding up, as if he was pitching game seven of the World Series, he chucked it, chuckling at the thud the rock made when it struck the house. "You can have your stupid shit box!" he shouted. Slamming the Impala in gear he raced into the night, retracing his tracks back to the highway.

Willie entered New York and the highway forked. In the instant of indecision Willie weaved right. Any hint of familiarity vanished and he traveled on in a haze of uncertainty. He scoured the horizon for a landmark, a gas station or restaurant, but saw nothing. Thankfully the roadway was deserted. As Willie drove among the shadows of looming hills he spied the tinge of dawn and smiled.

The sun was nudging the horizon as he approached the Tappan Zee Bridge, its steel legs knee-deep in the mist that swirled over the river. How many times had he crossed this bridge? How many trips had begun here? He felt the spark of memory surge with the changing pitch his tires made as he started across the bridge. He remembered waking the kids to witness the spectacle of the mighty Hudson. A quarter was the going rate for anyone who could hold their breath across the bridge's majestic span. Andy tried the hardest. That's why he succeeded. He saw a seven-year old Andy in his rear-view mirror, his face red with determination. Willie cracked the window and inhaled the river's scent. "Why is the mighty Hudson salty, Dad?" Andy asked.

To his left, the Palisades were coming alive with oranges and red. The five hills overlooking the Hudson were a perfect fit for the painting his mother took him to see. "A very famous painting," his mother confided. Yet the painting was just a bunch of trees with a path disappearing into them. He studied the painting, trying to unearth something "famous" in it, but it remained just trees. He asked his mother where the path led, but she pinched his earlobe and told him to hush.

To his right, the city was waking. Vaporous buildings shadowed in the smog, stood like a dream on the threshold of becoming real. His fingers tapped the steering wheel, a beat he carried to the dashboard. Da, da, da, da dum—"Start spreading the news." Lisa's piano remained in his mind's ear. He watched her hands gliding effortlessly across the keyboard. "I'm leaving today."

Willie places his three kids into the backseat of his Chevy. "We're going to our new home, going to own a piece of the rock"

"In New Jersey," Anna states, matter-of-factly.

"What's wrong with Brooklyn?" Andy asks.

A three-year old Anna turns to Andy. "It's dirty and yucky, and they steal your hubcaps. We're going to own a piece of the rock, right Daddy?"

The kids stop arguing as they drive over the George Washington Bridge. "They're called sky hooks," Andy tells Anna. "Those wires hang from the sky and hold up the bridge."

"Really, Daddy?"

"All bridges have them."

"Is our rock made of rock candy, Daddy?" Anna giggles, as the three kids wave good-bye to Brooklyn.

"Sweeter than candy."

Somewhere out there was Brooklyn. Undoubtedly Isaac and Norman were still guarding the family fruit stand, husking corn and shooing away street urchins. Ira Goldman was now a master violinist, his mother having pawned her wedding ring to replace his "stolen" violin. Suzy Isenberg would be telling Yiddish folk stories to her twelve grandchildren, her wanton escapades of show-and-tell to the seventh-grade boys, just a memory. The squealing of streetcars filled the air as they circled back over the Manhattan Bridge. A woman shouted not to ride the rear of the trolleys. "You'll break your leg." The stoops swarmed with old men playing checkers and kids flipping baseball cards in the alleys. Willie stood on the sidelines inhaling the gaiety, glad he wouldn't be sent off to the Morningside.

Fear riveted Willie as the toll booth popped up before him. He jammed on the brakes, the screech of his tires stripping away his daydream. He swerved into the adjoining lane and continued skidding, stopping at the last instant. Had the toll keeper noticed? But the keeper, his face hidden in a cloud of cigarette smoke, didn't look up, even as Willie struggled to pull out his wallet.

"Five dollars," the toll keeper said in a gruff voice, his outstretched arm limp with indifference.

"Five dollars?" Willie stammered, still tugging for his wallet. "I remember the time when a man could feed his whole family steak with five bucks."

The toll keeper ignored him. His hand was almost resting on Willie's shoulder as Willie dug through the folds of his wallet. He found a ten-dollar bill buried among the yellowed business cards. He handed it to him. The toll keeper snatched it, slipping five bills back into Willie's hand with the stealth of a magician.

The keeper's head bobbed to the music oozing out from beneath his black earphones. Willie felt the music's scorn stab him in his chest, but fought the urge to say something about "real music," about Sinatra and the Big Bands. The light turned green, but Willie sat, watching the thick lips of the keeper mouthing a string of vulgarities.

A horn blasted from behind, aggravating Willie. He shot his middle finger through his open window. More horns joined in, creating a cacophony of chaos. Willie stuck his head out the window and shouted something incoherent. Willie could smell the toll keeper's foul breath. Willie tried making eye contact, but the keeper avoided him, his opaque sunglasses a divide between them.

"You know that's not real music," Willie stuttered.

The dissonance of horns swelled. Someone yelled, "Asshole!" Gasping, Willie hissed, "You hear me, stupid, it's not real music."

The keeper stood like a manikin, nodding to his music. The car behind Willie swung into the adjoining lane, almost slicing off Willie's bumper. "Get a horse, you fucking old man," the red-faced driver stammered.

"It's nothing but crap!" Willie clamored, slapping the dashboard hard. The glove compartment door dropped open.

Willie reached inside, feeling the trigger slide comfortably around his finger. The crescendo of horns was disorientating. He wanted to silence them. Show those derelicts what an old man was capable of doing. When the keeper mumbled more lyrics, Willie fired back, "It's nothing but shit!" while squeezing the trigger with anger.

The keeper looked straight ahead. The horns were going ballistic, as the keeper chanted his rhyme with indifference:

"Whole families slaughtered for five presidents in coin
Red, white, and blue babies destined for porn.
Christened with greed,
They cry for their Moms
Whose tits tattooed green—drip with disease.
Abductees
Absentees
Adoptees of hate.
They'll left at the gate
Of a twenty room estate."

Willie heard a crash.

"That's not music," Willie spat, as he drew the gun out of the glove compartment and jammed it at toll keeper.

The keeper glanced indifferently at the gun.

Willie waved the gun erratically. "You think this is all a joke?"

The keeper slowly shook his head, but his smirk remained glued to his face.

"Say it. Say your music is nothing but shit!"

A car door slammed.

"I'll silence you and your stupid music."

Someone slapped the trunk of the Impala. "Hey retard, get this junk box the fuck out of here!"

Willie leaned out the window and waved his gun.

The toll keeper lowered his sunglasses and winked. Willie recoiled from the deadness in his eyes. He flung the gun on the passenger seat and floored it. The Impala lurched, but stalled. The toll keeper snickered. Then in a voice so haunting that Willie froze, the keeper sang:

And now, the end is here
And so I face the final curtain
My friend, I'll say it clear
I'll state my case, of which I'm certain.

The keeper took a deep drag of his cigarette, disappearing into a haze of smoke. The Impala started and Willie screeched out. The horns receded as Willie peered back in the rearview mirror. Then from out of the smoke the toll keeper's arm emerged, flipping Willie a two-finger salute.

Shaken and wobbly, Willie continued eastward, the highway transformed into a no-man's zone. Drivers whipped past him with icy stares, as he toiled to keep up. Everything was happening too fast. Walls of raw shale blasted through cliffs eclipsed the fledging morning light, creating shadows more ominous than night. Willie leaned closer to the windshield. Water oozing from fissures coalesced in black pools that seeped onto the highway. Monstrous machines thick with grime loomed everywhere, their mechanical arms lurking over the highway like gallows. A car crossed two lanes and cut him off. Willie swerved and pounded his horn, but no one heard, no one cared. The road funneled down as cement barriers crept in from both sides. He hit a pothole and his front end rattled. He hit a second and lost his breath. He weaved to avoid something lying in the road, horns barking at his heels.

Willie caught his reflection in the rear-view mirror, and in that glance realized the charade was over. He was just an old man lost with no place to go. He looked for a place to pull over and wait for the troopers to take him back to the Morningside. But construction equipment was scattered everywhere, the breakdown lane an obstacle-course filled with steel machinery. He narrowly missed hitting a car. "Just pull over!" he shouted. He clutched the steering wheel harder. "Pull over!" The walls of shale were closing tighter, what remained of the morning light had turned to darkness. He struggled to breathe, as fear clogged his throat. A truck bore down on him, flashing its headlights.

"Stop!" Willie rasped.

Drowning in indecision, Willie was late seeing the road fuse into a single lane. He tried to merge, but was repelled by the truck's horn. The truck driver glared down at him. Not enough room! Drops of oily water smeared the windshield, making it impossible to see.

Forced back into the shrinking break-down lane, the truck rumbled alongside him. A second blast of the truck's horn reverberated through Willie's body, causing him to swerve wildly. The driver peered out his window and sneered, his teeth smeared with rot. Willie pumped his brakes. The truck driver downshifted, his monstrous wheels inching closer. Willie struggled to hold on. The driver's tattooed arm reached for the horn. Willie cowered and swung right, his tires squealing through the narrow slit of light drilled in the shale. The truck veered left, the curve straightened, and Willie came face to face with the familiar sign. He grinned. And for the first time since his escape from the Morningside, Willie Easelman knew exactly where he was headed.

Petition the Lord with Prayer and Under the Boardwalk

"DEAR LORD," DORIS began, staring out at the crowded Morningside dining room. "We know that many here believe You have forsaken them, that You no longer heed their call. And I'm not talking about the sinners among us, the harlots, and blowhards who have spent a lifetime forsaking You. No, I'm talking about the good folks in this room who find it difficult to understand how it came to be that the Morningside became their final resting spot in Your Great Scheme of Things. Those simple folks, who raised their children, gave them everything, only to discover that in their hour of need their children had forsaken them. It's a hard pill to swallow, Lord, one that easily gets stuck in one's throat. But I also know, as our Pastor reminds us each time someone passes, that You work in mysterious ways."

Doris looked out at her peers, most of them peering at their plates. She had never prayed publicly before, never scolded others, except in her thoughts. But her words flowed as if on their own.

"Well mysterious ways sounds good in sermons, but it don't help us common folk when what we need is a miracle. Oh, not a great miracle, Lord. No parting of the Red Sea or turning Job into salt. And I'm not asking for myself. Oh, Lordy-be that would be too high and mighty. No, I'm asking you to help one of our own, someone who has strayed from the flock and is in danger of becoming supper for the wolves."

"Amen, let's eat," Walter blurted, picking up his fork.

"Amen," his followers echoed.

But Doris wasn't through, although she had lost her rhythm. One of the administrators coughed, as he pondered putting an end to this nonsense. He didn't like the part about the Morningside being everyone's final resting place, but it didn't seem like anyone cared. "Let her talk," the taller administrator whispered. "It'll play well in the press."

"Yes, Lord, I'm asking you to save our Willie," Doris began again with renewed boldness. "He's out there searching for his freedom but fleeing from your plan, a plan that brought Willie here to the Morningside. He's driving the highways of Jersey, but I know you can find him, Lord."

"God's got G.P.S.," Walter cracked, before being hushed by a stern look from an administrator.

"So as we sit at our Sunday blessing in your honor, Lord, let us take a moment to remember how lucky we are to have you as our Shepherd. You are our light and our staff, without which we're … diddly-squat. And so, if in your infinite kindness you see fit to help an old woman, a woman who has spent her entire life praising you, then please bring my prodigal boy back home where he belongs. Until death do us part …"

As Doris choked on her parting "Amen," Walter Wilder, already past his breaking point, bellowed, "Amen and please pass the chicken." But Doris's "Amen" remained lodged in her throat like a stuck wishbone. She turned and shuffled out of the room, accompanied by the cacophony of smacking lips. Following the same route of Ginny's wheelchair, but avoiding Ginny's blood smeared on the floor, Doris gimped back to the settee, no longer able to hold back the tears that streamed down the hollows of her cheeks.

Through the interrogations of Trooper Scott, the scheming of the administrators, and the prayers of Doris Manheim, Lisa Linksky sat playing the piano in the lobby, the same lobby that as a boy

Willie Easelman had been victorious at playing hide-and-seek. At each disruption, her silver-haloed face, complete with "rough-and-ready" lipstick, popped out from behind the piano like an inquisitive puppet. She always played on Sunday mornings and, unless coaxed by one of the residents into old-time favorites, Lisa always played Broadway. Her music was soft, ambient and it was her enormous repertoire that started the rumor that once upon a time she had appeared on Broadway.

But Lisa never performed there, even though she possessed the talent. She had been a performer—that much was true, but it hadn't been on Broadway, for when you're a sixteen-year old runaway from some piss-ant town in Ohio, you don't end up on that stage, even during the devil-be-damned days of war. Broadway required parental consent, required birth certificates, required letters of recommendation from dance instructors, none of which Lisa had.

Seventy years later, Lisa chuckled at those prerequisites. Who would have provided them—her parents, teachers, or possibly her minister? No, girls like Lisa had only one place to strut their stuff—Atlantic City. Atlantic City didn't care about birth certificates and they sure as hell didn't care about letters of recommendation. Atlantic City only cared about one thing—tits. And in an era before surgeons provided what nature failed to nurture, tits were a gift from the gods. You either had them or you didn't. Talent and legs might get you into the back row of the chorus line for chump change, but if you were young, willing, and filled your bra, stage time at Atlantic City was a sure bet. And Lisa's bra overflowed, stuffed to the envy of every flat-chested girl in her high school and the prayers of every high-school boy slipping their hands beneath their sheets at night.

Lisa wondered why her fingers were behaving so naughty today, drifting from the familiar touch of Broadway to the music of the forties. The popular music of that era always carried memories. But today her fingers wouldn't listen, and Lisa found herself slipping back to a world best left forgotten.

Yes, Atlantic City had been her ticket out of that two-faced town she no longer remembered the name of. It was a town like her parents, whose self-righteousness came before love. Seventy years later she still saw their pious faces, shaking their heads with judgment.

Yet she had been their darling, coveted by every mother in the town when, at age fifteen, she got the role of Mary at the Easter pageant, a role always played by a woman. She remembered her solo, a song about a mother's love for her child. It was the first time she had seen her mother cry. But the Lord giveth and the Lord taketh away, and Lisa playing the piano in the Morningside lobby grinned at the irony of the proverb.

Atlantic City during the war was the last stop for sailors and soldiers about to be shipped to the front, there for a final week of cavorting before the war sobered them up. The city was crammed with young men from small towns only too eager to sacrifice their own to the calls of freedom. Of course these brave boys didn't see it that way. They were young and invincible and bent on conquering a world their parents told them had gone insane. The war offered adventure, something that was sorely lacking in their dull hometowns. Yes, these boys were ready to take on the sinister world, but only after a refreshing dip in the pool of carnal pleasures, which had been denied them back home.

And in the pools of carnal pleasures, Atlantic City was as vast as the ocean from which it was named. Many a first-timer dove head-first into that sea, splashing in its invigorating waters, although sadly for many this plunge would be their last.

Lisa Robertson was a fast learner; after stepping off that bus from Ohio she changed her name to Linsky, believing that red-blooded Christian boys secretly yearn to fuck Jewish girls. So she placed herself in a position to find these boys. She could still see their choirboy expressions, their peach fuzz and cowlicks. Some days as she sat in her rocker at the Morningside she wondered if those boys still remembered her. Doesn't everyone remember their first, even that bucktoothed private from Illinois who wept when she confessed to him she was a virgin?

Yes, everyone remembers their first, even if it was a clumsy ride in a sidewalk motel in Atlantic City. But she wasn't like the other girls, mere tramps without theater. She was a performer and those soldiers got their money's worth, even if they didn't know it at the time.

Lisa drifted to last night, how Walter Wilder stomped into her bedroom full of bravado, only to fall asleep fully dressed on top of her. The sound of his snoring still nauseated her. Let him gloat in his story; after all, what good would be served by the truth? What good was ever served by the truth? Let him live out his days like those soldiers had, believing they had seduced an innocent Jewish girl in Atlantic City on their way to conquering the world.

Lisa glanced up from the piano to the Morningside lobby that always had a pull on her. The country fireplace, the pine paneling, the hand-carved newel post all spoke of a lost era. It was rumored to have once been a hotel. The half-octagon portal must have been where the hosts greeted their guests, and the fir stairwell, so steep only the Haitians now take it, led to the guest rooms. How odd that a house built for holidays and adventure ended up as this. Looking beyond its present gloom, Lisa often heard the sounds of the hotel's past as she played the upright piano. Once music filled this lobby with levity and laughter, music that ignited romances in the guests, freed from the restraints of their daily routines.

Lisa wasn't friendly with Doris and didn't know her circumstances. She knew Doris despised her, but Doris despised almost everyone at Morningside and Lisa never took it personally. She watched Doris's tears gathering, unscripted and real, and was overcome with the genuineness of her grief. Lisa began playing the opening number Dinah Shore sang on her weekly variety show. The jingle had been worming through her brain for weeks. "Drive your Chevrolet through the U.S.A." she sang before petering out of lyrics.

No, Lisa was different from the other girls in Atlantic City. She was an actress, a performer, a facilitator of dreams. She would meet her man on Mondays, usually at a bar, and it was over by Sunday when her soldier-boy shipped out. Sadly for many, a lifetime was acted out during those seven days. And as Lisa's left hand leaped over her right to perform a difficult chord change, she reflected on how she had played her role more patriotically than those girls back home, girls who promised marriage and not their bodies to the pleas of their departing lovers.

Lisa never chose the best-looking man, nor the worst. She rarely had to make the first move; her demure gaze was encouragement enough. She never drank, finding it interfered with her role. Tuesdays they strolled the boardwalk. There she listened to his story, which sounded pathetically similar to that of her last boy. On Wednesdays she allowed him a good-night kiss, and then heavy necking on Thursdays in the coat room of an expensive club where they danced till dawn to the tunes of the Big Bands. Fridays he watched her perform, dancing on stage in the flimsiest of outfits. During her routine she would smile at him, making him feel special as he sat on a barstool pondering his move. Her dancing excited him. She could sense the change, his desire, while sipping soda with him between shows. But she feigned fatigue and made him take her back to her motel. It was tricky, since her dancing spurred his craving. She agreed to see him on Saturday, which in his dwindling days stateside seemed like a distant dream. With a parting kiss her hand strayed down his leg, a touch that promised deeper pleasures tomorrow.

Saturdays, after her matinee, they walked the beach. Often, as they stood staring out at the Atlantic, her soldier confessed his fears about dying in a war he barely understood. She was sympathetic while they talked as if the war would soon be over. On Saturday night, after her final show, she called him "Honey," and snuggled into his arms as they took in the brilliance of the boardwalk's lights. Eventually they found a secluded spot and sat to watch the stars. Weeping at his imminent departure, tears as real as any shed by the Hollywood starlets on the silver screen, she praised his braveness and, in the spirit of the moment, let his hands move freely over her breasts. Usually she had to help him unclip her bra, for this was uncharted territory for most. As their passions grew heavy under the stars, she sometimes found herself going too far too fast—after all, she was still just a kid of seventeen.

But she caught herself, adult enough to know that true seduction was theater, and as in theater, drama is everything. Turning to him, she made him promise to return to her after the war and as they lay on the beach barely dressed, there was never a promise made with such conviction. Some spoke their lines eloquently, others convincingly, but in the end they all promised. Then she let their hands roam deeper, freer, their groans of passion prayers in the night.

But then her tears started again and she begged him to stop. Like a wounded animal, he sat confused and disoriented. If the soldier was experienced, which was rarely the case, it was difficult for her to pull away as the tug of war between lust and performance became blurred. But she was professional, reveling in her soldier's pleas, pleas that often would make a Shakespeare blush.

She never tired of those soliloquies, how her soldier loved her more than he had ever loved. Some cursed the girl they left behind, others simply cursed. She sometimes wondered if leaving them wanting on the beach would make them remember her forever. You never forget your first, but maybe it's the girl who got away that keeps the colors of imagination bright when all else fades. But her script never ended on a beach. She wanted that climatic final scene, the curtain closer, and for that she needed the sanctity of her bed.

Sometime between tears and first light, she turned and whispered, "Yes." It was a reticent "yes," a surrendering "yes," and in those rare times that she found her voice from deep within, a prayerful "yes." Some of her subtleties, like her blush, were lost to the chaos of desire, but isn't that the case with all theater? And theater it was. Even now as she played the piano in the empty lobby of Morningside she felt the exaltation as her soldier and she dashed through the narrow streets of Atlantic City, their shadows glued together with lust. Oh, how she loved that dance, the chase that carried with it a lifetime of memories. Sometimes she lingered to arrange her blouse in a storefront window, the two of them breathless with the anticipation, cloned by craving. Watching herself in the glass, she marveled at the rising crescendo of her performance, the magic by which lust was transmuted into love—even if the lust lasted just for one night.

Back in her motel room and out of their clothes, she made her soldier confess one more time. She swooned to the chorus of his yeses, closed her eyes to the theater of lies of their soliloquies. When she drew his body upon her, nothing else mattered—not war, not death, not the girl waiting back home. No, she wasn't like the other girls. She never tired of that moment. She was once playing the role of the virgin in the Easter pageant—the body of Christ penetrating her with his sanctity.

In the morning, mere hours before departing for the war, he would feel the tug of guilt and turn to her. Now it was her time, her soliloquy. She spoke to him of her hopes and of her failed circumstances. She was careful not to overplay her hand, already knowing at seventeen that most men wanted to help her as much as they wanted to help themselves. And having helped themselves to the delights of her body, they opened their wallets and promised more in the mail. And so the deal was struck, the curtain closed—dollars for forgiveness—both parties parting on good terms.

Lisa continued playing as one by one the residents of Morningside left the dining room for a well-deserved nap. Walter Wilder and his pep squad lingered in the lobby talking. She heard their schoolboy snickers and felt their mocking glances, as Walter boasted about last night. "She's there for the taking," he said to his cohorts. "But she don't want no limp dick," he added, shaking his vial of blue pills. Eventually they too left for naps.

Alone, Lisa let her fingers free on the keyboard. They flew on their own, finding snippets of melodies and tidbits of verses that had always been dear to her. She began to sing, her voice confident, until she became stuck when the lyrics and the music didn't jive. She was singing the words from "Maria" in "West Side Story," but the notes seemed all wrong. Over and over she sang the name, "Maria," but it just didn't fit. When she sang "Say it loud and there's music playing—say it soft and it's almost like praying," she knew something was amiss and so she stopped singing and just played.

Glancing at Doris sleeping beneath the amber light, Lisa noticed Doris's lips were moving. Lisa could hear the slight sonance of a song coming from her. It was "Ave Maria." She shook her head. It had been "Ave Maria," not "Maria," she had been playing. Lisa changed keys to better suit Doris's fledgling voice.

Not raised Catholic, Lisa was unfamiliar with the song. It always sounded like the moaning of a jilted woman. But as Doris's voice grew more assured, Lisa added a touch of bravado, making the song sound more like a victorious processional. She watched the blood seep back into Doris's cheeks as she rose from the settee and strolled over. Doris placed her arm around Lisa and together they performed, Lisa on the piano, Doris with a voice that no one imagined was inside her. When Doris hit the high notes, Lisa felt the thrill of the music, the cry for love that had been silent for so long. She sang with heart of missed opportunities and of a story sadly coming to an end without fruition. Doris continued singing in Latin, imbuing mystery into the music. Lisa's fingers played on their own, as she brought to life remembrances of things that might have ended otherwise. The two continued as one, a duet that filled the room with yearning, each for a different reason, each with the same song.

I Am Pegasus

MEMORY'S A STRANGE thing, Willie mused, as the tranquility of the divided road settled upon him. The Merritt Parkway was an old friend and a smile creased his face as the June sun evaporated what remained of the low-lying mist. The Merritt. Jeanie upright in the passenger's seat, sitting like royalty, the kids squirming in the back seat. Jeanie was with him the day he brought his first car home, a used 1946 Chevy, a "woodie" Fleetmaster wagon, one of the first cars off the assembly lines after the four-year hiatus of the war.

Still in Brooklyn, still in a cramped two-bedroom flat, so excited he had no idea where to drive. He piled the two boys into the back seat and, with a pregnant Jeanie, headed north. They ended up on the Merritt. He remembered the boy's faces pasted to the windows. Every curve, every hill, every passing car was an adventure. The dogwoods were in full bloom and Andy thought they were giant flowers.

"Does Jack and the beanstalk live here?" he asked.

Years later Andy said that trip changed his life.

Willie rolled down the window, basking in Sunday's quiet. The trees were so thick they crowded the highway. He was the sole car on the road. Andy said the Merritt was a road *of* nature, not *through* nature. A warm wind washed over his face bringing the spirit of song.

> *My little town blues*
> *They're melting away*
> *I'm gonna make a brand new start of it*
> *In old New York*
> *If I can make it there*
> *I'll make it anywhere*

Images were rushing by with the speed of the passing trees. The split-level ranch with green shutters. Anna was a baby and the boys shared a bedroom. The house only had one bath. Jeanie rose early and cooked "birdie-in-the-nest," then drove him to the railroad station in her night robe. "Someday the police are going to lock me up for indecent exposure," she would joke. Money was tight, but he thrived on the long hours. He owned Manhattan, knew every crack in the sidewalk. He worshipped the scent of the deal. He was a closer—all his bosses said that. "Get Willie in the room and he'll sell them the paint off the walls." Fifteen-hour days. Six days a week. No sweat.

Yeah, but did Anna appreciate it? The first chance she got, she took my car. She's in cahoots with that cop. I bet she's fucking him.

Willie inhaled the moist summer air that hinted of mushroom and decay. Relaxing, he saw Anna through the windshield, a five-year old on her birthday. He bought her a Sears and Roebuck Happi Time tricycle. Top of the line. It was in perfect condition, never out of the box. He and Jeanie spent the night putting it together. Andy helped. A red, white, and blue trike with cut louvers on the front fender and egg-shaped pedals that made it look like it could fly. She loved it, hugged the handlebars with all her childish might. Plastic streamers attached to the handle grips made a funny sound when she went fast. "Zoom," she called the bike. "I'm going to fly Zoom to the moon."

"Did she remember that? Couldn't wait to get rid of me so she could shop. That's all she ever talks about. Shopping is her day job, a bargain her reason for living. Did she thank me? Would one stinking "thank you" be too much to ask?

Nobody believed I could do twenty million. No one had ever done it. The bean counters said it was impossible. Not enough hours in the day. But I did it. Soon we were living in a four-bedroom colonial with a lawn so big it took all Sunday to mow. We vacationed at the Cape. The I95 was the newer and faster highway, but we still traveled the Merritt. Andy's orders.

The sign up ahead read Greenwich.

"Greenwich." Willie said out loud. Andy's poem. The kids were older. How did his poem go?

The Ox and the Moron set out one day
To see the long lost sea
When they came upon a tollgate
Which the blue witches of Greenwich lock with a key.

So to a shortcut along Long Ridge Road they ride,
Avoiding the hobgoblins that steal.
And the fairies all give ferry rides
On the backs of slithering eels.

To the east of Westport our li'l champs row
Then ten miles up Five Mile River,
Past the foul forests of Fairfield
Carrying treasure they're sworn to deliver.

But trapped inside the iron tunnel at Woodbridge
A mighty dragon roars,
Sending our trembling heroes instead
Scampering off to bed.

Fifty years ago. Who said my mind is slipping? They talk behind my back, but I still remember each homer Duke hit in '55, still remember my Brooklyn phone number. The actuaries were impressed. Said I had the mind of a spreadsheet. Knew every client's name, their kids' names, too. All part of the game. Sell a man on his legacy and you've got him by the balls.

Willie spied a twelve-year old Andy sitting in the back seat of the Impala.

You remember those days, Andy. The streets were noisy but the laughs were louder. 1955. The World Series.

We listened to the game on the radio, Andy. You skipped school. A 2:35 start time. Game seven. Didn't get any better than that. Podres took the mound. History. We witnessed history that day, Andy.

The Duke hit two home runs; Jackie stole home.

Willie slapped the dashboard hard. In two years those bums would sneak off in the dead of night to L.A., leaving Brooklyn high and dry.

No one has allegiance anymore, Andy. No commitment left in the world.

Willie passed under an overpass, its wrought iron railing a bucolic blend of ferns and flowers. How many bridges does the Merritt have? Ninety-six and each one different. They don't make bridges like that any more. American steel is now made in China. The Merritt was the highway of the future. The thrill of the open road. Willie remembered Andy's college thesis.

The Merritt takes you through man's history by way of architecture—the brilliance of man's designs blending with the cleverness of his engineering. Every architecture style can be found in its bridges: Classical, Neo-classical, Art Deco, Art Moderne, Rustic, Arts and Craft—and every building substance: stone, steel, iron. But the joy is driving. Over hills and around curves one experiences not the bravado of man but the radiance of nature. Every ray of sunshine, every tree that hugs the road, every songbird nesting is captured in the road. Man triumphs when his cities, his houses, and his roads pay homage to nature. It's in nature that man finds the solace of place.

As the sun climbed higher, Willie felt its heat working deep into his neck. It was still early, the highway still deserted. Best time of the day. Out of the house by five. The early bird catches the worm—the slacker gets to squirm. Maybe he hadn't watched the kids grow, but he was the provider. Raised myself up by the bootstraps. Sold magazines. Saved my nickels and dimes. Yes, the dream was alive with Willie Easelman.

Won't Andy be surprised? After Jeanie's death, Andy begged me to move to Maine. Said he'd build me a cottage. He had been foolish to refuse. Andy needed help running his company. Architects have their heads in the clouds; they ignore the details. He could have taught him a thing or two about closing the deal. Architects draw, but businessmen deal.

His gas gauge was dipping below a quarter, as Willie pulled into one of the old-fashioned gas stations that lined the turnpike. Located just a car-length off the highway, these were the original stations built on the Merritt. They were quaint brick structures with pearly-white trim and steeples with clocks. Andy was impressed that the builders of America's first highway had the foresight to place gas stations alongside it. Willy sat gazing up at the steeple, its clock frozen at 4:13. Andy's thesis came back.

The Merritt architects saw these gas stations as refuges that allowed the dream of the open road to become a reality. A driver could head off into the unknown without fear of running out of gas. The architects wanted to imbue a sense of sanctuary on these gas stations and so they built the steeples. To the soldiers returning from the war the suburbs was the Promised Land and the highway their way to get there.

Willie pulled out his wallet. Twenty-nine dollars, including the five ones the toll keeper had given him. He squinted at the steep price of gas and tried doing the math. He didn't know how much gas he needed to get to Maine, but he knew he was short—way short. And then there were tolls—highway robbery for those crooks in Washington. He shook his head and recounted his money.

Willie remembered an article about a scam, how teenagers were filling up their gas tanks, then acting shocked when they didn't have the money to pay. His chutzpah energized him. After all, the station couldn't take the gas out of his tank. He removed a ten-dollar bill from his wallet and slipped it behind the visor for tolls and then filled his tank, cringing when it topped-off at over $50. Should he skip out? Head for the highway?

No, he'd talk his way through this; after all, he was Willie Easelman, the man who in 1955 became the first agent in America to top twenty-five million. The chairman presented him with a plaque. Jeanie was so proud she kissed him in public. Where is that plaque? Anna took it. She's jealous like that. What did she ever win? A third-place softball trophy on a team she warmed the bench for.

Willie found a skip in his step as he headed to the gas station. Pushing hard against the weather-worn door, he was immersed in a cacophony of bells strung on a leather strap and nailed to the door. Bounding into a room noticeably lacking in snacks, he let the door close behind him.

But planning a con and pulling it off are two different things; ask anyone in the insurance business. Willie tried to quell the twitch in his eye as he strolled to the cooler. Appearing casual, he grabbed a bottle of spring water, noting the "Eternal Springs water 2 for $1.00" scribbled on torn cardboard. He felt watched as he shuffled over to the register and opened his wallet, a dollar bill falling to the cement floor spotted with chewing gum.

"That'll be $54.13 for the gas and a buck for the water," a voice rang out.

As Willie swooped for the dollar bill he tried to track the direction of the voice.

"Let's call it an even $55 for cash. Cash being king these days."

Willie's eyes darted around the room for the voice. "I thought the water was two for a dollar. I only want one."

After a calculating silence the voice echoed back. "The first water's a buck. The second one's free."

"Well that's a pretty stupid way of conducting business," Willie replied.

"Don't make the rules. I just attend to them."

Willie's eyes fell on a chubby man slouched in an armchair. The man sported a full white beard and was wearing bluejean overalls with brass buckle buttons, a red bandana hanging from his rear pocket. Across the top of his soiled shirt the name "Pete" was embroidered with bright red letters under the logo of a flying horse.

The man's age relaxed Willie. Certainly one old man wouldn't be suspicious of another. Old men don't lie to each other, there's a gentleman's code. Willie pulled the bills from his wallet and started to count. For theatrical effect he recounted the money and then gazed skyward, hoping the man would construe it as a baffled look.

"Problem?" the clerk asked.

Staying on script, Willie replied, "I thought I had a fifty."

The attendant ran his hand through his beard. "That so?"

"I swear I had a fifty," Willie replied, hoping he wasn't overplaying his hand.

"No need to swear."

"But I swear …"

"Happens all the time," the attendant said, as he leaned back into the soiled vinyl cushions.

"Maybe my wife …"

"Maybe your wife swiped it when she did the laundry."

"Maybe …"

"Maybe the dog ate it? A man walks into a gas station thinking he's got a fifty. You think this is the first time I've heard that one?"

Willie wasn't sure if the man was being sarcastic.

The clerk folded up the newspaper and slapped it against his knee. "No problem. We might appear old-fashioned, but we do take credit cards."

Willie fumbled through his wallet, a second-rate actor who forgot his lines. "I don't carry cards."

The attendant shifted his weight as he let his newspaper drop to the floor. With a tug of his beard he turned to Willie. "Now we have a problem."

Willie stood at the register with his head bowed, wondering if he appeared guilty or confused.

"Indeed, we have a problem," the attendant repeated.

Willie nodded, glaring into his empty wallet.

"Can't take the gas out of the tank."

Willie shook his head.

"Can't get blood from a stone."

Willie peeked sheepishly at the attendant. "I can mail you the money … Pete."

The attendant glanced at the embroidered name on his shirt and chuckled. "That's not my God-given name."

"Oh?"

"The last attendant left dozens of these shirts."

"Well I can mail you the money anyway."

"Perfectly good shirts. Not a stain on them until I got my hands on them. He was a bit of a neat freak. Thought he'd be here forever."

Willie extended his hand. "Then we have a deal?"

"Yes, I suppose we do," the man said, ignoring Willie's outstretched hand.

Anxious to change the subject, Willie said, "You look familiar."

The man let out a bellowing laugh. "I hear that a lot."

"Been here long?"

"Longer than the last guy."

Willie folded his wallet closed. "I used to travel this road. Years ago when the kids were young."

"I probably pumped your gas. In those days service mattered."

"Those were the days."

"A quarter got you a gallon of gas and a clean windshield."

"I'll mail you the money," Willie blurted, slipping his wallet back in his pants.

The attendant squinted at Willie, who fought the urge to look away. The attendant patted the empty chair next to him. A hush permeated the store as Willie ambled over and sat down, careful to avoid the tear in the cushion where the padding spilled out.

"Tell me about yourself," the old man invited.

"I'm … I'm an honest man."

The attendant laughed. "I thought we already established that. But are you a man of honesty?"

"I'm not sure I know the difference," Willie said, avoiding the man's eyes.

"Most people are honest when they don't have a choice. It's when there's a choice that a horse shows its true colors."

Uncomfortable with the conversation, Willie nodded.

"I met a man once who stole his widowed mother into the poor house. When I enquired why, he said because his mother didn't tell him not to."

"Kids steal."

The old man chuckled as he took a hefty chunk out of an apple he pulled out of the top pocket of his overalls. "Oh, I've seen my share of thieves, heard my share of confessions. Even the murderer swears he's a victim." He took a second, smaller bite. "We had a saying up at the pen. "Innocence is in the eyes of the beholder and the guilty are a bit farsighted." I wasn't always just a gasoline attendant, you know."

Willie tugged at the padding, a handful of which fell to the floor. "Second career?"

"Corrections was my first. Put my time up there at Attica. Parole was my expertise."

"You must have gotten an earful with those characters."

The attendant inspected the apple for a choice spot and, finding it, crunched down. "They all sound pretty much the same after awhile. You know, the prisoners think we make a list. Check it twice like we're Santa."

"But?"

"Well, the truth is we're pinched for time. Besides, I'd rather stare a man in the eye than read a ledger sheet. You develop a sixth sense up there."

Again Willie fought the urge to look away. "I bet the murderers are something else."

"In the big house we don't play favorites. Of course things are different now, what with computers."

Willie felt the weight of the attendant's huge hand on his shoulder. His touch was comforting and Willie felt the unexpected urge to confess. Thankfully, before the urge turned to a confession, the attendant pushed himself out of his armchair, his soiled imprint left behind on the cushion. He was taller than Willie imagined, well over six feet, and favored his left leg as he limped over to an old-style TV propped on a bureau missing drawers. Grabbing a pair of needle-nose pliers, he turned up the volume, then fidgeted with the clothes hanger dangling, the screen remaining thick with static.

"It's a show about turtles, sea turtles. Damn if those fellas don't swim halfway around the world to lay their eggs at the exact spot where years before they had hatched. Talk about finding one's way home. And scientists don't have a clue how they do it. They talk hogwash about the earth's magnetic field, but it might as well be voodoo."

The commentator's voice emerged from the background music. "How many of our heroes perish on this seemingly senseless voyage is anyone's guess. Ten-thousand miles lie ahead of its first stroke. Every predator in the sea awaits them along their perilous journey. Even Darwin would be at a loss to explain why these critters have survived. And yet here's our brave little traveler swimming with the sharks, as if he's out for a Sunday drive."

The attendant continued fiddling with the antennae. Willie watched, waiting for the turtle to appear out of the sea of static.

Without turning, the attendant said. "The world is overflowing with these mysteries, don't you think?"

Willie squinted into the static.

Still fussing with the hanger, the attendant went on. "Someone once told me we each carry a piece of an exploding star within us. Forget what piece they said. Imagine carrying a chunk of a star inside you."

The attendant slapped the side of the TV and gave up. Leaving the core of the apple perched on the bureau, he gimped over to a sink jammed with dirty dishes.

"I guess it gives new meaning to inner light," he added with a twinkle.

He picked a bowl out of the sink and ran it under the faucet. With his back turned, Willie examined the place. The room extended further back than he expected. Apparently the man lived here. Yet there was no bed, only a tattered couch strewn with blankets. Piles of dirty laundry covered the cement floor and a scattering of trash cluttered the counter. Above the sink, a shelf crammed with cereal boxes was built with the same knotty pine boards that lined the walls of the room. A handmade picnic table lashed with deep gashes was the catch-all for everything from open cartons of canned goods to useless automobile parts. Oddly, a finely carved wood chess set sat on the corner of the table.

"You play?" the attendant asked.

"Chess?"

"Ain't talking no Tiddlywinks."

"I'm not the chess type."

"No?"

"Memory's a bit rusty," Willie said, tapping the side of his head.

"You know a grandmaster has no better memory than a waitress and a worse one, in fact, than a cab driver?"

"Really?"

"The most important quality of a chess player is not memory

but his ability to sacrifice. Doesn't matter to a chess master if he forfeits a pawn or a queen. Every piece on the board is there for one purpose—service to the king."

"I guess."

"If a swap brings an advantage, well, then it's 'off with his head.'"

"All for one."

"Kind of simple that way."

After rinsing a few bowls under the faucet, the attendant lost interest and flipped the towel over his shoulder. Willie thought the man's chat about chess had something to do with his skipping out on paying the gas, but couldn't figure out how.

The attendant, however, dropped the subject and gimped back to the TV. He poked the clothes hanger and amazingly the screen cleared. The turtle was swimming in a sea of waves, looking insignificant as it moved its flappers in methodical semi-circles. It was nothing more than a speck. Then, as if to highlight the point, the camera zoomed back, revealing the absolute vastness of the ocean—the absurd scale of the turtle's journey. When the turtle dissolved back to static the attendant shut off the TV and turned towards Willie, who sensed he was about to receive a lecture.

"So a scientist walks into a gas station," the attendant began, with the ease of a polished comedian, "and asks for a dollar worth of gas. The puzzled mechanic asks him why so little and the scientist says that last night he had a premonition that he was going to die in a car accident, and since he's a frugal man he didn't want to die with a surplus. The mechanic ponders this for a second and then asked the scientist. 'If you think you're going to die in a car accident, why drive at all?'

"The scientist didn't hesitate. 'If I didn't drive, how would I know if my premonition was right?'

"'But you'd be dead-right.' the mechanic replied.

"'But at least I'd die with the satisfaction of knowing that Einstein was right, that God doesn't play dice with the universe.'

"Well, as it happened, the scientist did die in a car accident that day and upon arriving at the Pearly Gates he sees Saint Peter and thanks him for revealing the great truth of the universe. A perplexed Saint Peter asks the scientist, 'How's that?'

"The scientist says that the forewarning of his death proved that the universe is ordered, that everything happens for a reason.

"Saint Peter thought for a second before bursting out laughing. 'That's the great truth? And I thought we were only warning you to drive carefully.'"

Willie laughed along with the attendant even as he wondered if joke was aimed at him. The attendant slapped Willie on his back and said, "I'm sure you're an honest man." Taking the bills out of Willie's hand and counting them he said, "Mail me the other thirty."

The attendant was still chuckling at his joke as he limped back to his armchair. Collapsing into a sea of dust, he picked up his newspaper as if accounts had been settled and Willie was free to go. But Willie felt the weight of the moment, as if his guilt required him to say something genuine. So they remained in a stalemate, the attendant absorbed in his newspaper and Willie struggling to say something true.

"Iron," the attendant snapped, slapping the newspaper on his knee.

"What?"

"Iron. That's the part of the sun we carry within us."

"Oh?"

"Can you believe it? Iron's forged from exploding stars. It's the ashes of burnt suns."

"I thought it came from inside the earth."

"Things aren't always what they appear, Willie. We're masters of the universe and we don't even know it."

"Sounds like science fiction."

"That's only half of it," the attendant said, pointing to the newspaper. "Scientists now believe the whole universe came about in less than a second, in a nanosecond, whatever that is. Imagine that—the whole kettle of fish in less time than this." He snapped his fingers so crisply Willie jumped.

"Would have loved to see those fireworks," the attendant added through a spat of laughter. He took a swig from his bottle of spring water. "A nanosecond. What will they dream up next? Reminds me of a riddle," the attendant went on. "What if you slice a second in half, and then cut that half-second in half, and then cut that quarter in half. Well, a man could slice time in half forever and never find the other end of it."

Willie was perplexed.

"Think much about time, Willie? I mean you have the time, then you lose time, then you gain time, then you're plain out of time. Hell there's half-times, full-times, and time outs, not to mention running out of time. Time's as slippery as that turtle."

"I never thought about it."

"The prisoners in the pen say time flies. Say a year passes faster than a heartbeat."

"Thought it'd be the other way around."

"We had an inmate, a lifer, who said he lived outside of time. A real strange one. Read *Alice in Wonderland* over and over—loved the part when the Red Queen shouts, 'They're killing Time.'"

"Thought she said, 'Off with their heads!'"

"She said that too. But, what is time?" The attendant mused, holding his bottle of water up like a crystal ball. "Can't see it, can't feel it, can't taste, smell, or hear it. And yet it runs our lives. Every wonder what would happen if time stopped?"

Confused, Willie thought this might be a good time to leave so he let the attendant's question fade. He thanked him for trusting him and promised to mail the money at his first opportunity.

"Mail it when you find the time," the attendant laughed.

Willie reached the island of gas pumps when the attendant, who had followed him out, slid a bottle of spring water into his hand. "The second one's on the house." And both men shared a hearty laugh.

With his tank topped-off, Willie was impatient to get back on the road but the attendant stood between him and his car, admiring the Impala. "An '86?"

Willie nodded proudly.

"You know I bought one of the first Impalas," the attendant revealed. "Just had to have her. A '58 sky-blue convertible with a 348 turbo thrust V-8. Straight from Detroit. I swear the car had wings not fins, not to mention a king's ransom of chrome. Damn if that car didn't drive like it was riding on clouds. You know I drove her out of the showroom and headed south, like a bird fleeing frost. No

highways back then, just Route 1 weaving its way through every
two-bit town on the coast. Had the ragtop down and the music
blaring. Nothing but blue skies and the scent of orange blossoms to
guide me. Didn't stop till I reached Key West. Damned if I didn't see
the sun rise and set while perched on the hood of my car."

The two men stood over the Impala like old friends reliving
their separate memories. Willie, too, had taken Route 1, making it
as far as Miami in a Chevy station wagon with three kids slug-
ging it out in the third seat. Years later, Andy commented something
about a burger and milk-shake competition with his brother. Willie
tried recalling the trip, but all he could remember was the sound of
screaming kids, the smell of musty motel rooms, and a rear window
smeared with snot.

"Iron," the attendant snapped, shaking Willie out of his trance.
"Who'd imagine?"

"Guess it's got to come from somewhere," Willie replied.

The attendant gave Willie a five-finger salute and stepped back.
Willie slid into the front seat, careful not to wrinkle his army blanket. The attendant shut the door.

"Don't forget your seatbelt," the attendant called over the whine
of the Impala's engine. "It only takes a second."

Willie put the car in gear.

"You know the way?"

"Like the back of my hand."

The attendant slapped the quarter panel of the car and beamed.
"They don't make them like this anymore."

"You can say that again," Willie said, wearing his pride.

Willie waved through the open window, watching the attendant shrink in the rearview mirror. Willie swelled with the smugness
of pulling off the scam. "I still have the magic," he beamed, giving
Andy the OK sign.

I wasn't there, Andy, because I had business. You have to pay the
bills, right Andy? But you got to skip school. Hey, Andy, you remember hitting the streets after *the* game? Freddie Fitzsimmons Bowling
Alley was the place to be. Everyone was there. The Dodgers had just
won the World Series, just beaten the Yankees, and there we were
bowling with Hodges, Reese, even Jackie was there. The Duke gave

you a sip of his beer. Try getting those over-paid whiners of today to throw you a ball.

The attendant stood hugging the gas pump, as he watched the Impala slip back on the highway. His hobble was more pronounced as he limped back to his station, grimacing as he pushed open the door. He struggled to make his way past the Formica counter worn thin with age, then, shaking his head, he stuffed the bills into his register.

Honor, Duty, Fidelity

TROOPER SCOTT COMPLETED the sweep of the second rest area and was back on the highway when his cell phone beeped. Elaine.

"Allie can't make it. Morning sickness."

Now there were three. "And Dad?"

"Glued to his beloved Mets, but he'll come, grumbling and all."

"Honey, you've got to drive yourself to Mass. I'm going to be late."

"Like I wasn't expecting it?"

"They've got me on a wild goose chase."

"Hey, what's all this Silver Alert stuff? It's been breaking news every five minutes on the TV. Some guy named Willie?"

"Willie Easelman. He's old and a tad confused, and take a guess who's got the job of finding him?"

"Sounds thrilling."

"More so than you think. Is Allie OK?"

"She's overwhelmed. I don't know how she's going to handle a third. Says she still wants to work."

"She loves teaching. It's part of her."

"Her salary barely covers two days of day care."

"In September Renee will be in kindergarten."

Scott listened to the worry in his wife's voice. He knew that Elaine would pick up the slack. She calls it her day job. Three days a week 7:00 to 4:00, not to mention cooking dinner. Scott didn't care if it meant eating take-out or stale leftovers. The grandkids fulfilled Elaine—she's never been happier. When they were raising their kids, Elaine worked. Forty hours. She was overwhelmed. But retiring after Allie's first child, Elaine's day was devoted to child care. It warmed him the way she talked about her grandbabies. How this one did this or that one did that. "Geniuses" all of them, a word she never used with her own kids. Often he wondered what Elaine and he would talk about if it wasn't for the grandbabies.

Elaine and Allie always had a special relationship. A mother and daughter have a unique bond, but theirs deepened with the grandkids. Sometimes Elaine didn't get home till 10:00. Turning on the nightlight Scott would ask her, "What do you girls talk about?"

"Oh, women things."

And as Scott pushed aside the three comforters piled on his side of the bed, he mused, how lucky a man he was.

"There it goes again." Elaine shouted. "Willie Easelman. They've got a picture of him on TV. How old is the guy?"

"Eighty-six."

Elaine burst out laughing. "He's not a day over forty in the photo. He's standing on the steps of a fifties split-level with his arm draped around the wrought-iron railing like he's royalty. The man looks prouder than a peacock."

"Well, today that Willie is out joy riding in his '86 Impala."

"HE'S DRIVING!"

"Rumbling down the highway, dementia and all."

Scott heard Elaine sigh and braced for her predictable response. "Jim, you've got to do something with Dad. He's going to hurt someone. You can't let him drive."

"I'll speak to him at the cookout."

"I'm sorry for him, but he shouldn't be driving."

"I'll have the talk."

"Promise?"

"You're the man, Jim. The one I fell in love with in 10th grade biology lab."

"When we were dissecting frogs?"

"That and other biological things. Be safe out there, Jim."

"Always."

Scott felt the pang of his betrayal ripple through Elaine's parting words. Why hadn't he told Elaine then? Fifteen years have passed. Why was the cover-up worse than the crime? He was pigheaded, saw it in terms of honor, his word. But what good is duty and honor if your marriage is a fraud?

Honor, duty, fidelity—the code of a cop. Was the code worth destroying a family for? Fifteen years ago their marriage would have limped on for the good of the kids. He might have been exiled to the couch for a month, but Elaine would have forgiven him. Had his lie just been the easier path? But was it a lie? Is omission the same as a lie? Panic gathered in his chest. Would reconciliation be impossible? Thankfully his phone saved him.

"Hello."

"Davis here; we've got a situation. An unconfirmed report from a civilian puts a vehicle matching our suspect's at the Montvale rest area. How far are you away?"

The trooper calculated. "Thirty miles."

"Figures he went north. It's like these old people have a compass strapped to their foreheads."

"A reliable tip?" Scott asked.

"Fuck if I know," Davis groaned. "Caller said his kid's a wiz with numbers. Memorizes any number he sees. The call came from a pay phone so we can't confirm. Who the hell doesn't have a cell phone these days?"

"I'm on it, sir."

"Probably some kook trying to get his kid on 'America's Got Talent.' Trust me, this Silver Alert crap is going to bring out more jokers than a Vegas dealer. It's going to be a three-ring circus out there today, you watch."

"I can handle it, sir."

"And that's the good half. Apparently the governor was in Connecticut when the tip came in. Up at Foxwoods at a business convention, although odds are girls were the only business at hand."

Trooper Scott heard the satirical lead in the colonel's voice but didn't follow it up.

"The governor's taking his freak show on the road, speeding to the rest area as we speak. You know how the governor likes surprises."

"I ...."

"Well, the gov likes good surprises, Scott, not real surprises. According to his press secretary he's called in the media. Seems like this pow-wow is gonna convene in about fifteen minutes. Scott, you're the closest."

Trooper Scott checked his watch. At 120 MPH he would arrive just about when the governor did.

The colonel had also done his calculations. "You've got to make it in twelve, Scott. Who knows what shit is waiting for the governor in that parking lot. We can't have a fuck-up, not with the media breathing down his neck. It's an election year, for Christ's sake."

Trooper Scott didn't need to do any math to know that the colonel was talking 150 MPH, 30 over police protocol.

"Can do."

"Great, Scott. Pull this one out and we'll fatten that little retirement package of yours."

"Sir," Scott said, uncertain how to continue.

"Yeah."

"I have a funny feeling this Easelman thing is going to end badly."

"Of course it is. Just a matter of how badly."

"But ..."

"Listen Scott, I'd give my right testicle to have the media arrive and find the governor's arm draped around his new pal, talking that 'Greatest Generation' crap as only he can. Would bring tears to my sorry ass eyes and probably ten points in the polls for the gov. Are you moving, Scott? I don't hear your engine."

"I'm doing 120, sir."

"Ford must be doing something right these days."

"But this Easelman," Scott struggled to say. "He's lost."

"Christopher Columbus was friggin' lost and he ends up finding America. We're all floating around in row boats without maps."

"He might not be the guy the governor expects to find. He's confused. Wants to keep his car."

"Scott, we can handle this."

"He believes the world has changed for the worse. He might get carried away with this freedom fighting thing. He might see it as ... as his destiny."

"Destiny? Let me tell you a little tale about destiny, Scott. You know the governor and I go way back. Old college buddies."

"I've heard."

"What's your speed?"

"140."

"We were inseparable back then. So we're going to a Halloween party and we decide to go as Tweedledee and Tweedledum. Don't ask me why. We scrounge around and find everything: the buckled shorts, the suspenders, the patent-leather shoes, everything except those stupid beanies. So we're off to the party hatless and this guy stops us on the street, a bum really, who says, 'You two gentleman want to buy some hats?' And there they were: two leather beanies with the letter T embroidered on them. Think about the odds, Scott. Fucking astronomical. Me, I think this is one whale of a coincidence and if we play our cards right, it might get us some action with the sorority chicks. But the governor thinks otherwise. Thinks it's a sign from above. Believes the bum with the beanies was the Big Kahuna in disguise and proceeds to have a God-damn religious experience right there on the spot."

"Doesn't sound like the governor."

"Keeps it tucked in his back pocket. Later that night he tells me he's going to be president some day."

"I'm not sure I see the significance."

"Significance? There is no God-damn significance other than we're talking a holy war, a crusade, and we all know how that fiasco ended. Word on the street has him running in four years. Vegas has him at 2-1. Politics. Go figure."

"Sir, I talked to Mr. Easelman's daughter. I think there might be something serious."

"Good. If this mess goes down the tubes, maybe we get the media to portray her as the heartless daughter, a made-for-TV Lizzy Borden."

"Not that, sir. The daughter thinks her father might be armed."

"What?"

"Says she can't locate his gun."

"Tell me this is another of your stupid voodoo jokes."

"Says her father's not the violent type."

"That's comforting. We have a friggin' fruit cake out there with the mind of a two-year old packing and the governor's looking for him."

"POSSIBLY armed."

"Glad you make that distinction, Scott. As if no one's ever been shot by a suspected gunman. Got more good news for me?"

Scott was having doubts about covering up the Simone situation. If Easelman did pull a gun on the governor, then all bets were off. It would turn into a media freak show. The anchors would dig in their heels. They'd find Simone and her idiot friend. They'd pressure the poor girl till she confesses … confesses to anything. She might be an illegal, but she's a poster child for cuteness. Mix in a pinch of personal tragedy and a splash of exploitation by some rich administrators, and you've got the recipe for an American pie the media loves to dish out. As for Willie? What a combo the two of them would make on the talk show circuit. Christ, they'd have their own publicist.

But mention the voodoo and he'd be the laughing stock of the force. No way could he alert the colonel about Simone without mentioning voodoo. The colonel would see him as a joke. No, he had to find Easelman before he finds the governor. Everything rides on it.

"I'd call the gov personally," the colonel broke in, "but he'd take it as a college prank. I mean this Easelman guy's got to be a hundred or something."

"Eighty-six, sir."

"A real Charlton Heston type, is he? Doesn't he know the governor's stand on gun control? Christ, he voted for assault rifles in state parks."

"It's not about guns, sir. It's about his car."

"Christ, the kook is going to shoot the governor over an '86 Impala shit box?"

"It's all he has left."

"A friggin' Chevy. Tell me we're not on reality TV, Scott."

Scott's stuttered silence spoke for him.

"Well, you better find the quack. Find him quick!"

"You can count on me, sir," the hollowness of Scott's words gutted by the colonel's parting, "Fuck me."

Trooper Scott had never done 150 MPH before, hardly ever gone the 120 the department deemed safe. Usually anything over 100 meant a chase or accident, both carrying a healthy dose of adrenalin. But this wasn't a chase, unless time was his adversary.

This stretch of the Garden State was well known to Scott, having been assigned this section as a rookie. He knew each rise and fall of the road, could remember each incident that happened that first year. It was less than a mile from here.

They say you never forget your first and in twenty-five years Scott had never driven by that overpass without thinking of them. They were returning from a Christmas Party, kids really. They had won the centerpiece at their table, but when they went to leave, some jerk from accounting tried to claim it. A quarrel erupted, but the kids won, triumphantly heading off with the booty—a waving ceramic Santa Claus, carrying a sack stuffed with red and white carnations. The girl was clutching the centerpiece when she fell asleep. The boy reached for it and the car spun out of control, crashing into the overpass. It was all over in an instant. Scott was the first at the scene. He knew they were dead before he pried open the door. Later Scott discovered he had a certain sense, a sixth sense, when he approached a crash. The old-time troopers call it "the chills," and now, as he raced toward the Montvale rest area, he felt the chills creeping through his veins.

He overtook a trio of vans—the media. Hopefully he'd get there and find a confused old man begging to go home. They'll snap a few pictures and the dog-and-pony show will be over. The governor will get his photo shoot and Willie a free ride back to the Morningside. But if the governor got there first and surprised Willie, the governor might get the shoot he wasn't expecting.

Lost in his velocity and the turmoil of spinning consequences, Scott suddenly felt the futility of it all. The Silver Alert, the gun, Simone's sexual allegations, his father's fall from grace, his fifteen-year deception to Elaine—they were racing through his brain faster than he could drive. But suddenly everything stopped. So what if Willie

Easelman is packing? So what if an eighty-six year old man had sex with a sixteen year old? So what if his dad fought him for his keys? So what if ...

And then it struck. Death was no longer the monster to be feared. Death simply was. It was as ordinary as changing a tire. But what came crashing down on Trooper Scott as he struggled to keep his cruiser between the lines going 150 MPH, was that it was old age to be feared—old age was the serpent of the modern world, the bogyman hiding under one's bed at night.

Scott glanced to his left and saw a flock of geese heading north. They were flying in a V-formation, flapping their wings madly, but falling behind. The sky was crystal blue, not a hint of the predicted thundershowers that threatened to wash out Elaine's cookout. The highway glistened with the prospect of summer. His thoughts drifted out to where the geese were specks on an infinite canvas and his marriage had been reduced to a farce.

Scott entered the curve too shallowly. Lost in dream-time he failed to brake. Thoughts of Elaine swirled. Time slowed, allowing him to compose the letter he would never send, the speech he would never speak. Why, after thirty years, couldn't she understand what it meant for him to give his word? He heard a voice deep within him bellow: "Till death do us part" before the screech of the tires drowned out the voice.

My Heart Will Go On

"NEAR," SIMONE HUMMED softly, as she glided weightlessly to the window in her bedroom. She parted the curtain and blinked. The sun was strong as she watched for Alberto's departure. Somewhere out on a distant beach her friends were playing soccer, celebrating the arrival of summer. She thought she heard their laughter, the joy which will never return to her. A breeze whirled through the overgrown pines whose limbs scrape the house, sounding like demons clawing to get in. She covered her ears, but it is too late; her thoughts are cascading towards that day and there's no way to stop them.

Why did God make the earth move on Tuesday? Had it been on Monday, my brothers would have been outside on the soccer field, instead of inside playing video games. Had it been on Saturday, my mother would have been outside steaming fish on the grill, instead of inside in the kitchen. Had it been on Sunday, my father would have been outside drinking beer on the pier, instead of inside napping on the couch. Why couldn't the earth move on another day?

"Far," she exhaled, as her eyes started to close. She tried to keep them open, knowing the men in black robes would torture her if she fell asleep. Why couldn't she rid them from her dreams? Why didn't she know she was dreaming, that those men weren't real? She was sleepy and even the noonday sun couldn't keep her awake. Thankfully it wasn't those horrid men who came—it was her family.

"Help me slice the string beans, Simone. Crosscut them as your father likes."

She feels the knife in her hand, hears the thump of the blade striking the cutting board.

"I've found wild mushrooms growing near the shed. Tonight I'll make a stew."

A string bean tumbles off the table. It grazes her leg. Sirius snatches it before it hits the floor.

"The sun is returning to his throne," her mother chimes. "The wildflowers are blooming."

Sirius cocks her head, hoping that the food gods from above will send her another string bean.

"Maybe you'll pick us some wildflowers, Simone?"

She fills the bowl with cold water. Her mother sprinkles in salt, which she watches as the crystals sink to the bottom.

"Get your father a pillow. He's snoring like a train."

Sirius waits, her tail slapping the door with impatience.

Simone hugs her baby brother goodbye. Strapped in his highchair, he grips his wooden spoon like a prince. He giggles to the touch of her kiss and smacks the spoon on the table in a spasm of jolliness.

The sky is the color blue that makes one sigh, as if the world is too beautiful for breath. The ocean is still. Her mother hands Simone her rusty scissors and her favorite bottle. The sun streams through the green glass, illuminating the cord of bubbles frozen there. She walks along the lane with Sirius, singing:

> My black-eyed Susans have all lost their heads
> Their tails are naught to be found.
> But come next year
> They'll reappear,
> And blanket the dusty ground.

Has God ever made a more perfect flower? She fills the bottle with these petals of sunlight; their tiny faces smile back at her. She walks home the long way, dallying in the meadow where the bougainvillea always bloom. It's almost five o'clock and her mother will start to worry. If she lingers any longer her mother will send her brothers. At the broken gate she pauses to listen to her father's snoring. The kitchen window is held open with a broken broom handle and she hears her mother singing to her baby brother:

> *Sweep the floor my baby boy*
> *Whisk away the crumbs,*
> *Don't grow up like your lazy Dad*
> *That no good son of a gun.*

One more step and she'll be inside. Sirius nudges her aside with her nose, afraid she might steal any crumbs the food gods dropped in her absence. Her foot rises over the threshold. The snap on her sandal is undone and she kneels to fasten it. The ground moves and something strikes her on the head, pinning her in the doorway. The chickens in the yard go silent, the rooster even stiller. She sees nothing. Rumblings roll through her body, something on her chest restricts her breathing. She hears screams. They're distant, remote, as if coming from another world.

Her mother calls for her sons. Her voice is weak, moaning. "Where are my beautiful boys?" she says over and over. "Why don't they come for me?"

She lies, tells her mother that her boys are on their way, but she can't hear her. They are just a few feet apart. In the rare times she hears Simone's voice, she says, "Do your homework, Simone." Her voice grows weaker. Simone no longer tells her that her sons will come. In Haiti when they speak to the dying they tell the truth, so when they see them again in the next world the dead won't be angry.

"Be a good girl, Simone," her mother whispers, her voice masked by the wind. "Be a mother who loves—it's too easy to hate."

Simone dreams in color—colors she has never experienced before. Time dissolves into disorder. Day no longer follows night. She can't tell the difference between imaginings and memories. She lays there entombed with her dreams, dreams that have become real.

The sun warms her shoulders as she struggles to keep up with

her brothers. The ocean is bright and sea salt taints her lips. Laughter
is everywhere, as the waves sneak up behind them and washes their
footprints. They come upon a deep hole in the sand whose steep
walls roar with storm. Her oldest brother smiles and, holding his nose,
jumps in. Her other brothers follow. They call for her, telling her how
beautiful everything is inside. Simone tries to leap, but her feet are
stuck. The harder she tries, the deeper her feet sink in the sand. The
hole closes.

She hears her father's voice. "Tonight it will storm, my li'l princess. Open your mouth to the rain."

When the thunder comes Simone opens her mouth. The rain
moistens her parched lips and she feels refreshed.

Her father asks her, "Do you remember when you were a child,
how you danced for us, how your belly-laugh tickled the walls of
our room? You were barefoot, my sweet pea, the patter of your feet
on our dirt floors brought delight to everyone. You were so light, I
thought you would float away."

"I'm still your li'l princess, Daddy."

"Then dance, my li'l princess, dance with the joy of life."

As she dances she hears her father sing:

> Soar with the sparkle of the morning star
> Soar with the secrets of a shooting star.
> Dance with the Spirits
> Dance with the Gods
> Dance to the bliss of your baby's first smile.

> Dance, li'l princess, dance
> Till your feet float from the floor
> Dance, li'l princess, dance
> Till the angels chant: nevermore.

They say her mother suffered many days. But her father and
brothers were lucky.

Simone opened her eyes. Alberto's white van was rounding the
house. She was dreaming, her eyes shut but for an instant. Yet in her mind
a lifetime had passed. The van swerved as Alberto stuck his burly arm out

the window and waved good-bye. Awake, Simone ached for her family.

"Wherever you are," she sang, releasing the curtain as the van disappeared down the hill.

Simone tiptoed to her bed, fearful she would awake the men in robes if she fell asleep. But she needed the comfort of her family, and dreams were the only place to find them. Closing her eyes she smiled, as a wisp of an ocean breeze enveloped her. Space and time began to shrink. Softly she whispered "Father," with a sweetness that silenced the spirits swirling in her head, as she slipped beneath the sheets to find him.

Our House

THEIR CONVERSATION HAD grown long in the weakening afternoon light and the pauses threatened to consume them. Andy's thoughts were being pulled by the waves growing in the Atlantic. He hadn't spoken to Anna for months and now this. He tried to sound worried, tried to play the part of the concerned son, but all he could think of was that Joan was out there with the waves. As their silence grew exhausting, he said "Things will work out" in a tone that implied "goodbye."

Anna ignored his innuendo, sensing an end to their conversation would bring an end to everything. "Do you," and here Andy felt a tinge of his sister's anguish, "do you think he ever loved us?"

The question took Andy off guard. He glanced at his distorted reflection in his silver cell phone before stumbling through an awkward, "Of course, he loved us."

But Anna pressed, disregarding their understanding never to get too personal about the past. "Do you think he ever loved anything?"

"He loved Sinatra, loved his Chevys."

Anna brushed aside Andy's attempt at humor. "But did he ever hug you?"

"That wasn't Dad's style."

Anna heard the waves crashing in the background and dove deeper. "Do you think he loved Mom?"

Her question required a serious answer. Andy watched a seagull fly off in a huff, chased from its perch by a wanton wave. "Dad loved Mom as much as he could love anyone."

His words sounded hollow. "Don't worry, Adda, they'll find him." Adda, he hadn't used that name for Anna in years. Striving to sound more upbeat, Andy added, "Dad knows those roads like the back of his hand."

Andy heard the little girl in his sister's voice ask, "You think so?"

"Of course, I think so."

Anna's voice broke. "I'm not so certain," as she hung up without a good bye.

Andy hit the "favorite" button on his cell phone and watched the list of names flash across the screen. His thumb hovered above his brother's name. Anna wouldn't have called James about Dad's escape. They hadn't spoken much since Mom's funeral—something about college money. James, who did not go to college, believed he was owed his share of the inheritance plus the college tuition he never spent. James and Anna were always teasing each other about the inheritance, a teasing that, after Mom passed, had turned to bickering. Andy, who had more than enough money, always thought this quibbling childish, but he also understood that issues of inheritance were woven into his family's folklore. Hadn't his father received the lion's share of Papa Easelman's stock because he was the oldest son, and hadn't his uncle tried to bribe his grandfather with a fancy steak dinner, a ploy that almost worked? There were even stories about how his grandfather had absconded with the family gold sewed into his pant leg when he escaped from Russia. The words "the will" always seemed to worm their way into conversations; especially during Christmas, a holiday that had become the preferred gathering time of the family after all three siblings married non-Jews. Inheritance—hadn't he told Anna a thousand times that in the end only the Impala would be left?

Andy's thumb continued to hang over James's name. If he called James about Dad, he could already hear his brother's snide retort, "So what does this have to do with me?" James had visited the old man only once since he entered the Morningside, even though he lived in Trenton. Anna told Andy that Dad and James had quarreled about the will. "It's all going to the government and this God-damn nursing home," were Dad's parting words. Andy, who received his father's banking statements, knew his father's funds were dwindling. He'd have to make a decision: keep Dad at the Morningside and ante up five thousand a month or put him in a state-run facility. The screen on his cell phone went dark and Andy folded his phone and slid it into his pocket.

Andy looked towards the ocean. The waves were swelling, a storm coming up quickly from the south. Joan was competing in her sailboat, out where the waves were cresting. He leaned against the mahogany railing that wrapped the three-level deck and gazed at the Atlantic. Views of the ocean had always been his golden goose, his income stream in designing houses for the vacationing wealthy who needed a third house on the Maine coast. But as he watched the power of the sea building he was also aware of the sea's caprice.

Dad was missing. The Jersey police thought he might be in Brooklyn, something about returning to a familiar place. But Dad never wanted to go back to Brooklyn. Always called it a cesspool. Even if he wanted to go back, he'd never make it over the George Washington Bridge. The cops thought he was in Brooklyn because they couldn't find a senile old man driving an '86 Impala in Jersey.

Anna had mentioned Dad's Maine license plates. An alibi formed in Andy's mind and he relaxed. If the police asked, he'll tell them his father stay here regularly before he entered the Morningside. Who'd argue otherwise? Andy shook his head, remembering how his father reveled in beating the system, how every Thanksgiving he told the same story of duping the boneheaded insurance regulators. "Bludgeon the bureaucrats," he'd cry, as he sliced the turkey. Insuring his car in Maine was chump change, probably saving him a couple hundred dollars in insurance. Yet it bought him more satisfaction than money could buy. But as Andy stared out at the churning Atlantic, he wondered if those hundred bucks might have bought him a lawsuit.

If Dad was anywhere, he was on the road. Dad loved the highway. The driver's seat was his throne. Everywhere else he was just a tag-along, a chauffeur in Mom's station wagon. But on the highway Dad was king.

Andy rolled out the architectural drawings he was reviewing when his sister called. His assistants had done well. They knew his style, could mimic his touch. His clients would be pleased. They wouldn't suspect he had absolutely nothing to do with the drawings. The torch had been passed, concealed beneath the blurred lines of the blueprints. He no longer had the appetite for these houses, these monuments to obscene amounts of money. How did it come to be that a three-car garage was not enough? He took his pen out of his shirt pocket and inserted two eyebrow windows in the massive roof. He slanted the windows slightly, sensing his Asian client might find it subliminally appealing. He wondered if the great artists of the past spent their final years signing their names to their assistant's work. He resisted the urge to turn the colossal chimney into a bulbous clown's nose and instead scribbled his name to the appropriate box at the bottom.

Dad was missing. Was he supposed to feel something, join in the chase? Was Anna looking for him? Or had Dad simply become New Jersey's problem, a headache they hoped to pawn off on New York? Brooklyn? Why the hell would Dad want to go to Brooklyn?

Andy ambled over to the stainless steel bar and opened the $60 bottle of a Napa Valley Chardonnay he was saving for dinner. He found white wine more flavorful at room temperature. Joan liked it chilled, especially after a race. Andy peered at the waves. Out beyond the ring of islands, where Joan was racing, the waves would be stronger. He hated being jostled, but Joan loved it. She was a Maine girl at heart and fiercely independent. Her father had been a down-east lobsterman who instilled in her both a love of sailing and a stubborn self-reliance. Today she was in her element and Andy felt sorry for those rich Ivy-League boys she was racing against. They might have the fancy sloop, but Joan had the grit. On a calm day those kids might stand a chance, but as for today the race was over. Andy chuckled, knowing he had lost his share of commissions to the parents of those cocky college boys unaccustomed to losing, let alone to a woman. He would love to see the glum in their bronzed faces when Joan crossed the finish line first—little league losers from a world that had always revolved around them.

Yes, Dad was king of the road. Mom rarely drove and when each kid was old enough, Dad bought them a car rather than share his. No one sat in Dad's seat. Andy remembered finding the car unlocked one day. He was young, eight or nine. He sat behind the wheel pretending to drive. He shifted gears for hours, the adrenalin of getting caught flowing in his veins. In the end Andy didn't inherit Dad's fascination with driving. To Andy, a car was only a machine. But for Dad driving was heaven, the gateway to the open road. There was something sacred about how he treated his cars. How he polished them for hours on Sunday mornings. How he religiously bought Chevys.

Sunday drives. The Palisades Parkway, the Saw River Parkway, and, of course, the Merritt—all yellow brick roads leading to the emerald countryside where traffic lights and stop signs were forbidden. Mom packed a lunch and they cooked hot dogs at the picnic sites overlooking the Hudson. Since charcoal was a luxury, Dad had the kids gather twigs. Frankfurters, Dad always called hot dogs frankfurters. He loved mustard. Shoveled it on by the spoonful. "A burnt frankfurter is a thing of beauty." What did Dad call the Hudson?

Things were different after Mom died. How is it that a family dies? Dad couldn't keep it going. The few times Andy visited him, he barely mentioned Mom. Taxes and corrupt politicians had replaced the family stories. Andy remembered finding a stack of photo albums stashed in the closet. Maybe it was when the photo albums were packed away that a family passed.

Andy refilled his glass. He watched the white caps raging in the distance. The race would take longer. They would stop it if the waves climbed much higher. He remembered a few summers ago when they cancelled a race. Joan was leading. She ignored the horn and completed the race, taking the last buoy tight to the wind just to show off. When she crossed the finish line her face was electric. They celebrated with lobster and champagne, then went home and made love on the living room floor. Yes, Andy pitied those Ivy-Leaguers today.

He should have built Dad that cottage.

Andy took out his sketch pad and drew four rustic walls, with deep casement windows. Always the artist, the one who stayed with pen and ink long after his contemporaries sold out to computers.

Andy always felt life flowing through his hand when he drew, a life form that connected him to the great architects of the past. He added detail to the cottage: a Puddingstone façade, a Gothic doorway with sidelights cut from thick diamond glass. He sipped his wine as he capped the cottage with a steep pitched roof laced with brick-fired tiles. "Perfect for dwarfs," he exclaimed.

He should have built it for Dad.

With a few strokes of his pen he opened the door. The hearth was big enough for a small man to stand up in. A single hand-hewed timber formed the mantel from which cast-iron pots hung. He stared at his drawing, amazed how a couple of lines on a sketch pad could create feeling. He added a few sticks of firewood, then lit them with his pen. This was all Dad ever wanted.

He knew the spot. In the southwest corner of his land where a hollow outcrop of granite was deep enough to retain water. Years ago he put a few goldfish there and they thrived. The pool caught the western light, holding the palette of the sunset until the sun disappeared behind the grove of burning bushes. In autumn the weak sun made the pond appear black and mysterious, as the fiery leaves of the bushes sank sluggishly to the bottom and goldfish snapped at the surface.

He sketched the outline of a pond and then connected the pond to the cottage with a cobblestone walkway with grass sprouting through the joints. Utilizing a trick of viewpoint, he altered the rendering so the pond became the focal point and the cottage conversely shrank in importance. Shrubs sprung up from the foundation, further diminishing the cottage's solidity. The cottage and landscape become woven together—nature and home becoming one. Above the pond a dragonfly hovered, a gigantic freak of perspective, lurking over the daylilies, its bulging, faceted eyes pulling the viewer into its vision. Andy was drawing an arched footbridge, the kind found in children's storybooks, when his phone rang.

Lisa's Song

LISA DISMISSED ALL benchmarks of time as she drifted with the sound of her piano. Her body ached. She had played through Sunday supper, a gloomy affair—the inevitable let-down after a day filled with the promise of family visits, but usually ending with disappointment. Walter Wilder and his peanut gallery of want-a-be perverts were chuckling in the far corner of the lobby and the three administrators were conspiring in the opposite corner, composing a letter to submit to the local paper. Doris lay on the settee, valiantly trying to stay awake for her man, her head popping up at any stray sound. Lisa, having exhausted her repertory of songs, was playing snippets of an unfamiliar melody.

The taller administrator went over to mingle with Walter's group. Lisa had never known the administrators to stay so late, nor talk to any of the Morningside residents in private. She eyed the administrator when he put his arm around Walter. Walter basked in the attention, his arms flailing with child-like enthusiasm. When the administrator went back to his corner, Lisa watched Walter sneak a swig from a flask, which brought gasps from his followers.

The administrators were wrapping things up. The one jotting down notes cleared his throat and read aloud.

"The administrators and staff at the Morningside Nursing Home were heartbroken to learn early Sunday morning of the disappearance of one of their long-term residents. Willie Easelman, a retired insurance salesman and father of three, was reported missing during the morning rounds by the home's devoted staff."

Lisa started to play louder. She glanced over at Doris, thankful she was asleep. Each word the administrator spoke dripped with deceit and echoed with the numbing politeness of an obituary. Towards the end of the article the administrator's tone rose.

"Residents of Morningside held a vigil for Willie on Sunday, where Mr. Easelman's special friend Doris Manheim led them in prayer. Her inspiring words gave hope to Willie's friends who have been worried sick by his disappearance. Another close friend, Ginny Blanchard, was wheeled from the room, having collapsed with grief. The service was followed by a festive Sunday dinner complete with roast chicken and potatoes, after which Willie's buddies swapped stories about Willie's younger days in Brooklyn. One of the favorite stories that circulated was Willie sharing a beer and hot dog with the legendary Bronx Bomber, Babe Ruth. 'They're the best,' Willie often exclaimed, as he watched his beloved Yankees on Morningside's new 50" flat screen."

Satisfied, the administrators stood and headed for the door. Walter and his group of four mingled briefly at the doorway and then the administrators left. Brushing shoulders with Lisa, Walter couldn't resist showing off in front of his boys. He draped his arm around Lisa and cooed. "You play like Liberace. A Liberace with a very nice pair of knockers."

Lisa nodded and Walter leered. "Make sure you leave your door unlocked tonight."

This brought a round of heckles from his entourage. Emboldened, Walter's voice swelled. "And this time I'll bring along my little blue buddies." He pulled the vial from his trousers and placed it on the piano. Smugly striking a few keys on the piano, Walter added with a wink, "Something to make our special moment last."

Lisa glanced at Walter's foolish grin, finding, however, Walter's intrusion of her keyboard more upsetting than his crass comments.

She contemplated putting him in his place with a biting retort; after all, she had made a career dealing with jerks like him. Instead she slid her hand sensually up Walter's shirt sleeve and drew him closer. Walter's boys whistled. Walter, soaking up the moment, turned and said, "I think my gal is calling my name."

"Walter," Lisa spoke, her voice hoarse from singing.

Walter winked at his buddies.

Lisa smiled tenderly, before grabbing hold of the flab on Walter's arm and pinching it so hard he dropped to his knees.

"Look, he's proposing," one of his boys mocked.

"It doesn't look like it's agreeing with him," said another, noting Walter's grimace.

"Now Walter, you should know I'm not the marrying kind," Lisa chided, as she tightened her grip. "Although I do admit being partial to the benefits."

Tears flowed down Walter's flabby cheeks as he tried to squirm his way out.

With her free hand she picked up Walter's bottle of pills and shook them. "And next time let's make it a tab longer," she quipped. Realizing the pun was lost on Walter, she added, "And that's a manly kind of longer I'm talking about."

Walter broke free and sheltering his throbbing arm against his chest he stuttered. "I'll show you … you … bitch," as he stumbled for the exit.

Lisa tossed the vial Walter's way. "You forgot something."

Walter bobbled the throw, the plastic vial skidding across the room with Walter in pursuit.

"You'll never get to first base catching like that," Lisa laughed, and turning to Walter's boys she added, "He's a Bill Buckner in the making."

Snatching up his pills, Walter attempted one final retort as he reached the door. "I'll show you … you, nutcase."

"Watch out, li'l boy." Lisa chastised. "Or I'll pull down your knickers and show everyone your peanut."

And with that, Walter and his boys vanished.

Alone, Lisa returned to her piano. Stuck on this unfamiliar melody, she changed a note here and a chord there. Suddenly it occurred to her she was composing and lyrics followed. "Heaven can wait," she intoned and looking over at Doris she added "Got a band of angels locked up in my heart." She played it again. Liking the lyrics, she sang them more boldly before noticing the red and orange afghan covering Doris had slipped to the floor.

Lisa rose and walked over. Asleep, Doris looked so innocent, her hands folded beneath her head as if in prayer. Reaching down, Lisa tucked the afghan around Doris's diminutive body. Draped in sleep, Doris clutched the blanket with her tiny fingers, whispering a drowsy "thank you." More lyrics came to Lisa and she intoned "Will take me through the lonely nights, through the cold of the day."

Watching Doris, Lisa, who had spent a lifetime in the arms of men, couldn't grasp a life spent without them. Maybe it hadn't been love, but she knew closeness, felt a man's yearnings. As she had grown older, her clients had also, and in her later years sex was mostly replaced by conversation. The old Italian men were her favorites. Often all they wanted was to sit at her kitchen table and sip her tea—or she would sit on their laps with her arms around the necks as they told stories about coming to America. One of her suitors confessed that as a boy, growing up in Sardinia, he actually believed that money grew on trees in America. "Money everywhere," he had whispered in broken English, as he closed his eyes to the dreams of his youth.

Doris's eyes were flitting back and forth. Was she dreaming of him? Hopefully Willie wouldn't return. Lisa knew the look. In the span of one day he had become the lover Doris never knew. But Willie in the flesh would never measure up. "Let him live in your dreams where all men are perfect," Lisa chimed, as she brushed a strand of hair off Doris's face.

"Heaven can wait," Lisa sighed, pleased with the irony of her lyrics. Then unexpectedly came, "And all the gods come down here just to sing for me. And the melody's gonna make me fly—without pain—without fear." Lisa rushed back to the piano, her fingers feverish to find the right chords. But as she began playing her body began to shake.

It was the splash of a tear striking the keys that made Lisa aware of how much trouble she was in. Her song was taking her back to a place she never wanted to revisit. She tried to stop. She lifted her hands off the piano, but the music continued to swirl in her head. Her song was becoming her. Her past was freefalling before her and as tears continued to fall she found herself drowning in memories long buried.

That small town in Ohio had been her comfort, a childhood of innocence. When he chose her to play the part of Mary in the Christmas pageant, she was thrilled. She could still feel his touch on her shoulder as he explained how music, like love, comes from the soul. She carried his touch back home, like a thief, taking it to bed so his hands could roam freely in her dreams. On rehearsal nights she couldn't eat, and when her mother dropped her off at church she scarcely found the breath to say goodbye.

Being cast as Mary at sixteen brought tributes from the other mothers—and perils. She was developing into a woman, and the groping hand of an uncle or a hard kiss by an older cousin were all part of the show. Even her brother's friends were tongue-tied by her beauty—beauty understood as extraordinary even in a farm town in Ohio.

Yes, she could still feel the thrill of his touch when he told her to breathe deeper. When she sang, she sang for him. Her voice was young and untamed, but powerful. When he placed his hand on the curvature of her back to force her to stand straight, her whole body quaked. They added extra rehearsals at night; after all, the part of Mary had always been played by a woman, not a girl.

Sometimes he held her hand in his and they talked about her role. How Mary had sacrificed, how the Annunciation had been the greatest sacrifice a woman could make. She played her naïveté well, asking questions like, "What is a virgin?" or "How could it happen?" And though he blushed, he answered as best he could, stumbling when she asked, "What part did the other Mary play in Jesus' life?"

As the pageant grew near, they added still more rehearsals, more questions, until one night they found themselves alone. She was playing the church piano when he came up behind her. She was practicing her solo, the song where Mary struggles over her decision to carry God's child.

"Sing as if you ARE Mary," he urged. "Feel her dilemma in yourself. She wants to give herself to God. Every part of her body yearns for His touch. But she resists because the laws speak otherwise. God appears in the form of the archangel Gabriel and tells her that her worries are warranted, but her desires are just. Gabriel kisses away the tears of indecision from Mary's cheek. 'The Messiah comes,' he coaxes, as he takes her body into his."

He remained standing behind her till she shivered with expectation. When he reached around her waist, she continued playing. His hands trembled as he clumsily unzipped her blue gown. She closed her eyes, humming her song in his ear. The touch of his fingers made her nipples hard and when he reached through the slit of her gown she went weak. She unclipped her bra, sighing with its release. His hands were suddenly everywhere. She rose, letting her gown slip to the floor. He started to speak with his preacher's voice, but she drew his mouth to hers and silenced him. Playing with a man's lips for the first time, she brought his hands back to her body, wanting more.

She quivered, praying for his touch to go deeper. She greedily unbuttoned his pants. Reaching inside she felt his softness harden, heard him gasp as she drew him to her. Breathless for closeness, she leaned back on the piano, pulling him upon her. The dissonance of random notes filled the church as he tugged on her panties.

When he entered it was like God himself was penetrating her. She closed her eyes to the bliss, the joy Mary had experienced as she was transformed into a woman. She wanted more—infinitely more, wanted him to stay buried between her thighs, buried to the core of her soul. She grabbed him by his hips and drew him deeper, their bodies becoming one. Immersed, anointed, baptized, she wept for him to melt into her.

Falling off the piano bench, they tumbled to the floor. Her sense of emptiness was immediate. She wrapped her body around him, desperately trying to recapture their rhythm

When they were finished she rose and put back her robe. He turned away, but she took him by the chin until he met her gaze. "I will always be yours," she cooed. "Always be your virgin beneath my robe."

Over the months that followed, their desire turned deception into a game. They would find each other after choir rehearsals and between church services. It was daring—sometimes only a few minutes in his private vestibule behind the altar. They rarely talked, finding their passion was language enough. As an assistant minister, he had few duties. So they went on church retreats together, sneaking away into the woods to spend the night in each other's arms. Free beneath the stars they discovered the infinite wonders of their bodies, as the universe shimmered acceptance upon them. Sometimes when their hunger made them reckless, they met after school and fled to the wheat fields that enveloped the town. There, with the sun radiating down on her naked body, she rejoiced at the pleasures of being a woman. And afterwards they would lie amid the grain bending in the breeze and fantasize about their future.

When they were caught, she never expected the town would blame her. His church whisked him away to a new congregation, never to be heard from again. But she stayed. Jealous mothers turned judgmental, and the girl with the remarkable looks and talent became marked. But Lisa coped with their pettiness; after all, she was no longer a girl playing the role of a woman.

Did he still remember those moments? Does he keep that girl of sixteen alive in his thoughts? She wouldn't have aged. Does she still come to him as freely in his dreams as she once did in life? The mind remembers passion as it forgets pain.

Yes, she could have survived their stares and whispers, their petty gossip. Even now, as Lisa's tears fell unabated on her piano, she knew she could have endured her mother's rage and the endless lectures to follow. She could have accepted the separation from her lover; after all, it was just a matter of time before she discovered that all men were replaceable, especially an assistant minister from a small-time parish in Ohio. But what she hadn't expected, and what made her board that bus for Atlantic City on that rainy day, was her father.

Lisa watched the keyboard puddle with tears. A grating silence replaced the music that only minutes ago had been glorious. She gripped the piano, consumed by the urge to smash it.

Why? A father's love was supposed to be different, was meant to last forever. It didn't matter if you stole from the cookie jar or raided his wallet; he was to be there, always there. Life was a collection of details and snapshots that faded with time; it's love that reigns eternal.

This was the true lesson of the Annunciation, a truth carved in the soul, not in stone.

In the aftermath of her affair, her father's love was supplanted by silence. He sat at his chair reading his paper, never looking up when she entered. How could something so never ending, end? Alone in her room, she was banished to a lifeless world. Love had become conditional, the columns of care lay scattered in ruins.

She entered that bus bound for Atlantic City, a broken girl of sixteen, but stepped off a woman. If this is life, then she accepted the verdict that fairness was just another childhood fantasy, a tale told at bedtime. She never called, and never heard from him again. Once or twice she thought she caught a hint of him on the boardwalk, but she never gave him a second glance. He had become a shadow on the edge of wakefulness, a player from a fairytale she had long ago closed the book on.

She wiped the keys with her sleeve. Then half chanting, half as a lullaby, she sang:

> *And all the gods come down just to play for me.*
> *And the melody's gonna make me fly*
> *Without fear—without pain.*

Christmas

THE SUN STRUGGLED to slice through the summer-thick branches of oak and maple trees forming a canopy over the Merritt Parkway. Off to the side of the road, but dangerously close to the Impala's passing wheels, two woodchucks nibbled, their spring-fed bellies round as cherubs. Too bad the dogwoods have passed, Willie sighed. How perfect it would be if the dogwoods were in full bloom. "A roadway to heaven," Andy called the Merritt that day as the pink and white petals swirled beneath the station wagon.

Willie spied a grown Andy sitting in the back seat.

You're right, Andy. There's something special about the Merritt. They sure don't build roads like this anymore, hey Andy?

I can help you with your business. Business is business; doesn't matter if you're flogging insurance or Tiddlywinks, it's all the same. You know the old man's still got some petrol left in his tank. You saw me bamboozle that gas attendant back there? I'll teach you tricks, ones they don't teach at Harvard. There's an art to closing the deal; it's a dance. You can't merely go through the motions. Like a car, a lot goes unseen under the hood. But you're a natural, Andy, you've got my blood. Not like your sister. You can't trick the client. They can smell a lie a mile away. I'll let you in on a secret, Andy. The great salesman believes he's selling something good.

Willie looks in the rearview mirror. Andy is stretched out with his eyes shut. But Willie knows he's listening.

Everyone says you're a chip off the old block. You're a winner, Andy. You were a winner in little league when you hit that home run. The guys still talk about it. Two outs, bottom of the ninth— doesn't get more pressure-filled than that. Must have been something watching that ball sail over the fence. Andy, you're a winner.

If you ask me, business comes down to detail. That's why I wasn't there for your home run. I was taking care of details. Did I tell you I hit thirty million in '55? They say if you can sell insurance, you can sell anything. How hard can it be to sell a house? Everyone wants a house. It's not about want, it's about belief, Andy. You've got to make people BELIEVE they want life insurance.

You remember the time I took you back to college. Your mother was sick and we headed out together, father and son. I never cheated on her, Andy, never once. And, hey, it's not like I didn't have opportunity. Those Wall Street wives were animals, strip you naked in a New York minute. I still get stares when I stroll down the street. It's the walk of confidence. A woman wants to be wined and dined. You show a woman a good time and she'll let you peek at her secrets. Compliment her breasts and she'll let you dip further. You should know that, Andy. I wanted to tell you these things when we were driving the Merritt. In Brooklyn the girls couldn't get enough of me. Every girl enjoys a good story, wants to be talked *to* not *about*. I wish you were there in Atlantic City. We were shipping out to Europe, to the Great War, and your old man got the girl. Pegged her on the beach. People believe its looks or money, but it's neither—it's how you tell your story, Andy.

I wanted to tell you so many things on that trip. How great of a son you are. Harvard, Andy, it's not like they let anyone in. I paid the bill, but you got the grades. Oh, how I reveled in telling those bigwigs at work my son goes to Harvard. That shut those blowhards up.

I can help you with the business. It will be our business, our legacy. Nothing like a family business, something you can pass along to the kids, What do you say Andy? Andy remains silent and when Willie turns around he's gone.

Willie's grip on the steering wheel weakened. He had only been to Andy's ocean house a couple of times. Andy built it when his youngest child went off to college. Willie vaguely remembered visiting there when his granddaughter married. A snapshot of the bride in her white gown flashed in his mind. He had risen at dawn and watched her walking barefoot on a rocky outcrop. A barefoot bride, imagine that. Her image remained in focus, untouched by time. What became of her? He heard the piano playing as she walks down the aisle, each note drawing her closer to the altar.

Willie spoke the word "house," out loud, hoping the word might somehow guide him to Andy's house. Bridges were flickering above him, shadows reminiscent of an old-fashioned locomotive chase in the talkies. Willie knew he was speeding. Why not? Andy said the original designers of the Merritt wanted no speed limit. They banked the curves so cars could attain unimaginable speeds. Speed, the designers recognized, was a unique experience, something unknown to the pedestrian world of the past.

Thrilled with the sensation of weight amassing on his chest, Willie continued to accelerate. His wheels screeched, the road curved, then dipped. He fought the car's drift with both hands, smiling each time he swung the Impala back into line. Youth was seeping into his bones.

There it was—Hero's Tunnel, the spot where Andy was convinced the engineers wrestled the project away from the architects. To the engineers, Hero's Tunnel was their exclamation point, the display of their brut power. They could have built the road around the hill, or over it, but instead they went through it. How did Andy put it in his thesis?

"Mohammad moved the mountain, while the engineers wanted to smash it. They pierced the mountain's core with their steel. The harmonic curves of nature were no match for man's linearity; the gospel of his modern world. The architect's vision of a road reconnecting man with nature was lost before the first highway was completed. Hero's Tunnel will stand forever as a testament of man's supremacy over nature, a monument to man's ingenuity. The highway would not be the way back to Eden, rather it would become the roadway to hell."

As Willie sped down the descending trek towards the tunnel, his thoughts raced out of control. Everything he had ever experienced, ever known, was converging. Every insignificant sight, every insignificant conversation flashed in his brain with perfect sense. He saw his visit to the psychiatrist with his daughter, heard Dr. Weiner's explanation of his condition. He grappled with the urge to return to the psychiatrist's office and tell him how it all began. How a few million years ago a fledgling pathway connecting the basal forebrain and the hippocampus allowed an upright ape the rudimentary processing of time. Or how 200,000 years ago this pathway became enmeshed with memory, culminating 10,000 years ago with dawn of modern consciousness, a simple mix of past and future tenses that synchronized time with the agricultural clock of the sun and moon, which in turn became the timeline of mankind's story.

Or maybe he should reveal to the doctor how Homo sapiens became human in the nourishing harbors of the Arabian Sea. Safe within the shelter of the sea, they survived in caves, shielded from the Darwinian struggles of the jungle. They basked in warm waters, were nourished by the ocean, and over time grew naked. And in their nakedness they came to understand that the tribe was richer than the one.

Pictures flew through Willie's mind like pages scattered from a novel; yesterday became today and tomorrow had already passed. He saw the chessboard on the gas attendant's table, saw checkmate without touching a piece. He watched the turtle end its journey before it began. Understood the riddle of "iron."

Time, he now realized, was both illusion and real. A second could be split forever because it never passed out of existence. Just as the entire universe can fit on the head of a pin, so too can time. Time is not just a passive watchdog, the keeper of clocks: it is the maker of universes, the creator of all. Space expands—time contracts, a paradox from which all matter is created. It's not dice that God abhors, it's nothingness. Entropy is an illusion, the nearsightedness of our anthropomorphic minds. Everything evolves. Planets coalesce with the ash of dying stars, as the seeds of life sail silently across the cosmos. Universes burst into existence, a string of pearls that stretch forever across the necklace of time.

How and why this revelation occurred to Willie was a mystery, since Willie was a retired insurance salesman who had little scientific background and absolutely no understanding of relativity. But lost to anyone observing Willie's epiphany was the fact that at this instant all his synapses were firing in his brain, a near infinite amount of connections approaching the number of atoms in our universe. With both hands taunt on the steering wheel, Willie was on the verge of understanding the workings of everything—if a trooper hadn't raced past him in his cruiser.

The flashing blue lights brought Willie back. Up ahead, three cruisers blocked the entrance to Hero's Tunnel. A trooper jumped out and raised his massive hand for Willie to stop. Bright flashes of light and the static of two-way radios rocketed the air. A second trooper, fully helmeted, slapped Willie's fender and gestured him into the breakdown lane. Two troopers approached from the rear. Willie's hand reached for the glove compartment.

"We'll have the road cleared in no time," the trooper told him. Willie was close enough to the tunnel to see something lying in the road.

It's Pokie, Andy, I think Pokie's been hit. I know we should have put him on a leash. Anna's a hippy; she wanted Pokie to run free. It's all her fault. I don't think Pokie's going to make it. The officers will clean up the mess. We'll bury Pokie in the backyard. A dog's got to learn. Once they get hit they'll never go in the street again.

"It's a deer in the road, sir. It'll only take a minute."

You hear that Andy? It's not Pokie. It's just a deer. The officers will clear up the mess.

We're going to make a go of it, right Andy? A family business. Nothing fancy, just solid homes. We'll call our company Easelman & Son Homes. Sounds cozy, like a fireplace. Remember the big house, Andy? Columns. People like columns.

To Willie's side a white SUV with a crunched-in hood stood at an angle; steam rising from the engine. A young couple was leaning against the fender, their kid dressed in plaid shorts with blue suspenders. The boy's head was buried in his mother's skirt. She was smoking a cigarette. Oblivious, she stared into space.

Willie heard a car door open; watched a teenager race by. The boy scampered towards the tunnel. A trooper shouted for him to get back in his car. The boy pointed and laughed. "Road kill," he sneered.

"It's a buck." One of the troopers had his hand on his gun. The troopers approached the deer cautiously. Willie rolled down his window. The kid with his mother started to cry. "Don't worry, they won't shoot Bambi," his father said.

You were never a sissy like your brother, Andy. You didn't cry when Pokie got hit by the car. Took it like a man. The trooper says it's a deer, but I think its Pokie. They trick you like that. Never trust the cops, Andy. They get you chatting and the next thing you know you're spilling the beans. Best let a lawyer do your talking. I'll give you a name of a good Jewish lawyer.

Willie shouted out his window. "Hey, shut that kid up!"

The kid's a sissy, Andy. You've got to be firm with boys or they'll turn into sissies. They should spank that cry baby.

"Shut that kid up," Willie repeated, his face red with fury.

"He just saw us hit that deer," the father called back. "We were playing a word game and the deer jumped out of nowhere."

Playing a word game, Andy. Wimps play word games. Let's see how smart they really are.

"Hey, what rhymes with shrimp?" Willie hollered to the father.

"Excuse me?"

"What rhymes with limp?"

"What's wrong with you, mister? My son has been traumatized."

"You want to talk trauma? Have you ever pried a dead navigator from a cockpit?"

"Please sir."

"The army said we'd see the world, but we saw shit."

"Sir, my son."

You can't let the bullies intimidate you, Andy. You show any weakness and they'll pounce. Got to stand up for yourself. I wanted to tell you that on our trip up the Merritt. A man has to fight. It's not the size of the man; it's the size of his fight. My father was a little man, but if we kids stepped out of line he'd thrash us within an inch of our lives.

So much I wanted to tell you on that trip, Andy. We used to ride the pony with the English girls during the blackouts. If you could get them alone, the least you'd get was a blowjob. I'd dangle my Yankee Doodle Dandy in front of those English wenches. Some bit on the bait.

"You're going to turn that kid into a schlemiel," Willie taunted, slamming his fist on the dashboard.

"Officer, can you do something with this guy?"

The trooper turned to Willie. "What seems to be the matter?"

"They killed Pokie."

"Just a deer, old-timer. We'll have it cleared in no time."

"You said that when Pokie was hit. You should have buried him in the backyard, but you threw him away like trash."

"I'll need to see your license and registration, sir."

"He's unstable," the man near the SUV interjected.

"I'll handle this. Do you have your license, sir?"

"Would I be driving a car without one?"

"I doubt it, sir, but I'll need to see your license and registration."

"It's in the glove compartment, officer. The latch is a bit finicky."

"I'll wait."

He wants my car, Andy. Everyone wants my car. That's why Anna put me in that home. She wants to screw the officer in the back seat of my Impala. You can't show fear. Business is a jungle. I can teach you how to survive.

The compartment flipped open. "It's here somewhere."

"The man's crazy."

The trooper shouted something to his buddies who were sliding a blanket under the deer. The static of two-way radios congested the air. The boy was sobbing louder. His mother lit a second cigarette. Steam hissed from the SUV. The father whispered something to his son who looked straight at Willie and laughed.

Warm tears were rolling down Willie's cheeks. He had been a good father, a good provider. The cars, the house in the suburbs: he paid for them all. He sent Andy to college—Harvard. He worked fifteen-hour days. He worked harder than everyone else. He's not looking for trouble. He just wanted to keep his car.

Dark clouds were rising over the hill. Heavy drops of rain struck the hood with the dull beat of defeat. The mother cupped her hand to the rain, shaking her head with disbelief. The slow sweep of wipers streak the windshield. His hand in the glove compartment, Willie felt the trigger slide onto his finger. "They're not getting my car, Andy."

Shouts and confusion filled the air.

"Watch it old man," the trooper warned, as he stepped away and pulled his gun.

"Not my car, Andy."

The buck kicked. The officers let go of the blanket. The father shielded his son with his body as the deer staggered to its feet. The officers scattered. One officer tripped, the dull thump of his head striking the Impala's bumper as he tumbled to the ground.

Willie pulled out his gun. "They're not taking my car, Andy."

"It's alive!" someone screamed. Wobbly and with blood gushing from its hind quarter, the buck tried to escape to the woods. Blocked by cars, the buck lunged, trampling the officer lying on the ground. The trooper at Willie's window leveled his gun. Disorientated, the buck swung around, slicing the trooper's arm with its antler. The officer on the ground lifted his gun and shot. The mother screamed. The deer dropped on its knees. Another shot rang out. The buck fell to the pavement, its hind legs churning as if still running for freedom. Blood streamed from the trooper's wound. He shouted for help as a third shot rang out. Willie tossed his gun into the glove compartment. The rain was falling harder. Somebody shouted, "Show's over," as Willie put the Impala in gear.

Willie drives by the deer, its eyes blank as Pokie's had been on that day. He feels the weight of Andy's stare on his back. Willie looks in the rear view mirror. "I buried Pokie, Andy, buried him in the backyard myself." Sitting in the back seat, a ten-year old Andy chirps. "You're the best, Dad." Willie flashes two thumbs up and begins singing "Start spreading the news," as he enters the black hole of the tunnel and vanishes.

Amazing Journey

THROUGH THE THOUGHTS and fears screaming for Trooper Scott's attention, through the squeal of screeching tires, Scott felt the front wheels of his cruiser lift off the road. Bracing for a crash, he clenched his abdomen, but surrendered to the inevitability of it all. Time slowed—then stopped. Lost in that frozen instant between life and death, Trooper Scott found himself transported to a trip he took as a boy with his father.

They were camping—his mother's suggestion. They left the main road, traveling the Kancamagus Highway, an old Indian trail passing east to west through the White Mountains of New Hampshire. It was a narrow road that eventually turned into gravel. Parking near a cabin, a plaque told the tale of a settler's wife who placed a lantern in her window every night for thirty years, waiting for her husband to return. "They were tougher back then," his father mused.

Hiking through pines too tall to see their crowns, they found a level spot near the Swift River and pitched the tent. He watched his father hammer in stakes, slowly and methodically. His father told him to pull on the guide line and the tent magically rose. Then his father gripped his shoulders and said, "Good work." He scurried into the tent. It smelled of mildew. "Keep the flaps down, son—the mosquitoes will eat us alive."

The boulders in the shallow waters were worn smooth as he hopped from one to another as if weightless. When he slipped, he slid into icy waters and both he and his father laughed. Later his father took out a fishing rod.

"Patience," he said. "You don't catch a fish; you let the fish come to you."

Scott waited with expectation, the fishing line taunt, filled with the anticipation of catching a fish whose size was scarcely limited by his imagination. But as moments passed into hours and the sun began to set behind the mountains, his enthusiasm waned. He handed the fishing pole back to his dad who laughed.

Scott gathered firewood and his father showed him how to build a fire, then handed him a match. Scott inhaled the scent of burning pine needles and heard the crackling of twigs as the flames rose. In the intimacy of the fire, he asked, "What did you do in the war, Dad?"

His father never talked about the war. TV was alive with war movies and Scott secretly hoped his dad had killed his share of Germans. But having asked the question, he immediately wanted to take it back, as he watched his father's eyes go blank against the silhouette of the darkening peaks.

"Some other time," my father replied, as he opened the flap to the tent and sent him scampering off to bed.

Sleeping beside the roar of the river, he dreams he's fishing. He catches something—something big—and his father helps him reel it in. When they lift the fish from the river, the fish is covered with golden scales.

Excited Scott blurts, "We'll cook it over the fire."

"You can't eat a golden fish," his father says.

Placing the golden fish in a bucket of water, his father explains. "A golden fish is special. We'll bring it home and build a pond for it in the backyard."

At home they start to dig, his father with a pick, Scott with a shovel. "We need to make it deep enough so the water won't freeze in the winter." Although Scott quickly tires and his hands hurt, he keeps digging until his father says, "Enough."

They fill the pond with a garden hose and line it with rocks. Weary, they watch the water slowly rise. "He'll love it here," his father says, then sends him to the basement to find a house for the golden fish. Scott is unsure what to look for, but opening a small door hidden behind the furnace he finds a ceramic castle. "I knew you'd find it," his father chimes, as he wades to the center of the pond and places the castle down.

When they go for the golden fish the bucket is empty. They search the bushes and behind the lattice that aprons the porch. They search the tiny creek that flows near the house. They overturn rocks, finding salamanders with orange eyes and crayfish that grab hold of their fingers, but they don't find the golden fish.

Dejected they return after dark. Mom is in the kitchen cooking dinner. There in her frying pan is the golden fish. "Wash up," she chimes, "Dinner will get cold." He tries to warn his dad, but he's already eating. He doesn't speak until he asks for seconds. "Best fish ever," he mumbles. Mom smiles, "Eat up, Jimmy, children are starving in China."

Trooper Scott awoke to the distant thud of his front tires slamming back on the pavement. A fuzzy black-and-white photo of Willie Easelman feathered his mind, bringing him back to the task at hand. The Montvale rest area appeared like an island on the horizon. Without taking his eyes off the road Scott reached down and patted his gun, quelling the gnawing question of why his father never took him fishing again.

In the Arms of an Angel

SIMONE WAKES TO the crying of a baby. Everything is disorientated. How long has she been sleeping? Is Alberto back? What time is it?

Simone sits up in her bed. She silences her breathing. Is the crying coming from within her or some world she knows nothing about? But as confusions coalesce into thought, she convinces herself the crying is coming from down the hall.

Simone's feet slide effortlessly across the hardwood floors. The crying grows louder as she approaches the room at the end of the hall, a room Simone believes was once a nursery. Maybe it's the unborn child of the people who lived here years ago. Her uncle told her that the unborn try to join the world and play among the relatives they never knew.

Wrapped in a nightgown, Simone moves timidly towards the door. Placing her ear to the gothic door with iron hinges, she listens, but everything is still. She taps lightly and the door opens. Two men in monk's robes are whispering beneath an oval window, standing among the shadows of the torn curtain. They are conspiring in a language that Simone doesn't understand. She twirls to slip back out the door, but the baby starts to sob. The men turn. She wants to flee, but can't—the baby stirs her soul. The taller man motions her in and the door shuts.

The man moves to the cradle, pulls a silver rattle from his pocket, and shakes it. The baby starts to coo and the man smiles. Simone steps closer and peeks at the baby.

"That's close enough," the fat monk by the curtains commands. "Babies are uneasy with whores."

The baby starts to fuss.

"See what you've done."

"I'm not ..."

"What?"

"Not a whore."

"Of course you're a whore, my dear," the thin monk says without taking his eyes off the baby. He shakes the rattle, delighted when the child quiets down. "All women who go to those clinics are whores."

Simone looks away.

"I told you she's a tart," the chubby monk blurts as he steps out from the crease in the curtains.

The monk brings the rattle to his lips and kisses it. "Yes, I was hoping for a tad better. The motherly kind. But Jesus knows what to do with her sort."

"He fucks them, right?" sneers the fat monk, his teeth brown with decay.

"He does enjoy a good fuck," chuckles the other. "One in the hand is worth two in the bush, he was fond of saying to the boys."

The smaller man gimps up to Simone. "A bush in the hand," and he shoves his hand up her gown.

"Don't."

The taller monk turns from the child. "It's not like you don't enjoy it, my precious. We saw you with that boy. How you let him poke you right there on the sink."

"We didn't hear you protesting then," snickers the smaller man, as he gropes higher up her leg.

Simone tries to flee, but the fat monk grabs her and flings her to the floor.

"I like it when the little strumpets struggle."

The baby's begins to cry.

"Be easy with her," the taller monk mocks. Leaning into the crib, he nibbles on the baby's ear. "Our princess likes it gently."

"Tarts take it whatever way they get it."

Simone twists away. "I'm not like that."

"They'll take it up the ass, if you let them."

"I'm not that kind of girl."

"Now, now," the thin monk intervenes. "We heard you lie to that trooper and Sebastian here assumes you lie with everything."

"Once a liar, always a liar."

The tall monk reaches down and tickles the baby with his beard. "Not very nice pinning the blame on a helpless old man."

"A lying hussy is what she is."

"I'm not."

The taller monk coos at the baby. "Naughty girl. Telling the trooper that the old man did it to you with voodoo."

"I …"

"When everyone knows you've been sneaking off and doing it with that boy every chance you can. You know he brags to his friends about doing it with you. Tells them how loudly you moan. They all slap him on the back and call him a man."

"She enjoys it like a slut," spits the fat monk. He tugs her night-gown, exposing her breasts.

Simone tries to cover herself, but the monk rips her nightgown off.

"Be a good little tart and it won't hurt."

Simone rises to her knees, but the fat man kicks her in the ribs.

"Relax my li'l strumpet. We all know how this ends."

Simone starts to cry.

The smaller monk undoes the rope of his robe. He's fat and stinks. He shoves a cross in Simone's face. "Blessed are the righteous, for they shall receive the Holy Spirit."

Naked and on the floor, Simone wraps her gown around her hips. Finding her fear amusing the taller monk leaves the baby and strolls over. He puts his foot on Simone's head. "Blessed are the wretched, for they shall enjoy a healthy helping of the sin."

The fat man shakes off his robe. "Blessed are the whores."

The baby cries.

Simone feels the coarse hairs of the fat man's beard against her breasts. When she struggles he strikes her.

"Please," Simone stammers through her tears. "The Jesus doesn't want you to do this."

"Not do what?" the taller monk asks.

"Not do this to me."

"Not do what?"

"Not make love to me."

The monk taps her on her forehead with his rattle. The baby cries louder. "Not do what?"

"Not make love to me."

He strikes her hard on the forehead. "What!"

"Not fuck me."

"Louder!"

"Not fuck me."

The smaller monk pins Simone to the floor. His smell overwhelms her as he pushes her legs apart. She tastes the salt of her blood trickling from her forehead. The taller monk casts away the rattle. "Maybe the whore's right," and shoves the smaller man off her.

The fat monk scurries on his hands and feet around the taller monk and tries to mount Simone. The taller monk kicks him and he slithers back to the safety of the curtains. The taller smiles at Simone as he removes his robe. Open sores drip from his chest.

"Please don't," Simone whispers. "Please don't ... fuck me."

"Who says anything about fucking?" as he whips the belt upon her. The crack of leather makes the baby erupt in tears.

"Please be merciful," Simone whimpers.

He hits her again.

The smaller man peers out from behind the curtains. "That's for your unborn baby."

Simone lifts her arm.

The baby cries louder.

"Shut up!" the taller monk howls, striking Simone across the face. Dropping the whip he stomps over to the crib.

"No!"

He shakes the baby violently.

"Spare the rod and spoil the child," the fat monk cackles.

"Hit me instead."

The tall monk turns. "You're already soiled."

"Please," Simone wails. "Don't hurt my baby."

The monk picks up the baby. Tickles it under its chin, then slams it against the crib. Simone crawls toward the baby, but the fat monk scampers out. He mounts her, and Simone collapses.

"Please."

The fat monk hisses something in her ear. Aghast, she screams, her tears mix with the blood streaming from her forehead. She tries to get up.

"Please, my baby."

The tall monk is rocking the still baby. In a deep baritone voice, he sings:

> *Swing low, sweet chariot*
> *Coming for to carry me home*

Simone feels the monk trying to penetrate her. "No," she sobs.

> *Got a band of angels coming after me,*
> *Coming for to carry me home.*

Simone sat up, drenched in sweat. She was dreaming, the same dream she had for weeks. Why didn't she know she was dreaming? Why were these men so real?

The shades were pulled tight, but daylight streamed in along the edges. Jacqueline hadn't returned; her blankets lay tangled at the foot of her bed. Simone pushed her face deeper into the pillow, hoping to find relief in its coolness. Her dreams were becoming realer than her life. She tried to still her heart, but it pounded with a suffocating emptiness. The terrors of the night had yet to arrive and now even the day seemed too endless to endure.

"My soul to keep," Simone whimpered into her pillow. She tried to picture her father, her mother, her brothers—but fear overran her imagination. She wiped away her tears; blood puddling in her palms dripped down her arms. Was she still dreaming? Dreams within dreams, the horror of it all stealing her breath. Yet the room resonated with the foreshadowing silence that preceded the earthquake, the perfect stillness from which the horror was unleashed. If only Sirius was here. Simone looked towards the light of the window, hoping for a glint of peace. But there was none, and through tear-choked sobs she whimpered "My soul to take."

Yes, It's Perfectly Understandable

HOPING IT WAS Joan, Andy spilled a few drops of wine as he rushed to the phone. But the voice was gruff and official. Andy nodded into the vacuum of the voice and said nothing. When the man paused, Andy could only muster a parting "Understandable," before the line went dead.

He returned to his sketch and completed the bridge with a minimum number of pen strokes. Smoke now bellowed from the squat plaster chimney, thick and ominous. Using his thumb Andy smudged the ink, an artist's technique which magically transforms day into night. He hung a kerosene lantern in the window, captured the slice of the crescent moon in the antique glass. Starring at the completed rendering, he recognized the cottage.

Fresh out of Harvard, he accepted the commission when none of the architects at the firm wanted it. His clients were an old couple with limited means, but with a choice piece of property deep in the Green Mountains of Vermont. A retired professor of German philosophy, with Heidegger as his specialty, the husband had a strange mental affliction that caused him to speak only in German so his wife had to translate. He could understand English, he just couldn't speak it.

His wife told the story of a highly respected professor, well published in both German and English philosophy journals.

"Once my husband stood at the pinnacle of his profession. Colleagues talked of a Nobel. But he became tormented, tortured by the fact that Heidegger never finished his magnum opus *Being and Time*." The wife became wistful, but after wiping crumbs off her husband's starched shirt, she continued.

"Time led to my husband's decline, time and my husband's obsession to complete Heidegger's book. He had become convinced that as death approaches, Being begins to break down. Finding scraps of Heidegger's notes scattered in his cabin deep within the Black Forest of Germany, my husband jotted down Heidegger's final notes. 'Consciousness, which by its nature is sequential, reverts to its primordial state of Timelessness, much like how a hybrid rose reverts to its native state. Without a timeline, the story which had become the man becomes the story-less man, a blank canvas from which new possibilities arise. Dreams, memories, and reality become interwoven into myth, the physical world surrendering to the spiritual.'"

After that the wife never mentioned her husband's affliction or Heidegger until the couple was touring the completed cottage.

"Of course my husband's mad as a hatter," she casually mentioned, ignoring her husband standing stoically next to her. Rubbing the hickory posts of the cabin, she appeared to find strength in the hand-hewed texture of the crossbeams. Adrift in the magnificent views of the Connecticut Valley, she continued. "His doctors believe that maybe if he completes Heidegger's treatise, things might change for the better."

His wife's mention of Heidegger stirred the professor from his stupor. "Dasein ist zeit," he blurted. Then, as if speaking to the expansive panoramic, he spoke in perfect English. "Timelessness is eternity."

"Understandable."

The word resonated in his chest. Andy turned towards the Atlantic. The waves were higher, yet the air had become disturbingly still. A Nor'easter—one of nature's cruelest deceptions. The storm misses the coast. The skies clear. Everyone relaxes and then the tempest curls around and strikes the coast broadside. Andy looked at the east, facing windows, and made a note to shut them. Joan's father always said you can smell a Nor'easter coming, something about the stink of seaweed.

Hopefully Joan was off water. She had good instincts, but competition clouded them. He imagined her out on the open sea, slamming it out with the waves. They were pulsating higher, but she would be calculating how to use them for an advantage. Problem was, she never factored in danger. Her father taught her how to master the sea, but she taught herself how to master the moment.

"Understandable." The word left a harsh taste in Andy's mouth despite his third glass of wine.

Picking up his drawing pad, Andy added a patch of chrysanthemums bordered by river rocks. It fascinated him how an object could be transformed from two to three dimensions with a single stroke—it was the moment an artist breathed life into his painting. He remembered his fascination with the Hudson River School painters, how he spent Sunday mornings at Harvard waiting for first light to paint along the banks of the Charles. What did Dad call the Hudson? "The Mighty Hudson."

Andy shaded each stone, making every rock unique. He placed a solitary boulder in the center of the flower bed, a counterpoint to the island that preserved artistic balance in his drawing. He scattered daylilies around the island, losing himself, like the Dutch Still Life painters had, in the minutiae of the flower's pedals. Preoccupied, the sun continued to move across the horizon and the waves continued to swell.

There are no ceremonies when a family dies out, no gathering of the tribe. Memories fragment and then the photos are packed up and stored away in a closet. At Mom's funeral, they placed the family albums on a card table. One album marked "England," contained black-and-white snapshots. She was prettier than he remembered, a different woman from the one he called Mom. Her ankle-length dresses with wide belts accented her tiny waist. She was just seventeen in some of the photos. The Germans were bombing London daily, but she was strolling down Park Lane sporting a hat stuck with a peacock feather.

It was an old-style album with the photographs attached by four black paper corners. The captions were in elegant script: "London 1944," "Our Beloved Church," "Duke of Gloucester's Summer Residence," and other sites. The end of the album featured a few pictures of the old tenement house in Brooklyn and then, "Andy Arrives." Mom returned to England after the war, documented by a scattering of pictures of her relaxing on a lounge chair on the deck of the Queen Elizabeth. On the last page of the album there was a picture of him with his mother. They were sitting on a blanket in a park. She was wearing a stylish outfit and heels with straps that snaked above her knees. Her hand was raised, as if protesting her picture being taken. The photo had been cropped. Looking closer, he noticed the fingers of a man's hand wrapping his mother's waist. Taking the photo out, there was writing on the back:

Dear Willie,

Having a splendid time. Andy is the hit of the party. Everywhere we go people want to pinch him. There's so much energy now that the war is over. I have decided to stay a tad longer. Don't be concerned, the travel company says it won't cost you a dime.

Jeanie

The waves were washing over Rider's Rock. Tonight's high tide would spell trouble to the houses he built around Boggler's Bogs. It was getting late and the odor of seaweed was thickening. Andy wasn't prone to worry, but he would like to hear Joan's voice.

He returned to his drawing and added a few geese flying south. A vaporous cloud concealed the moon. He eyed the isle of daylilies and planted a Japanese Queen Maple with branches that wept to the ground; then he cast his pad aside.

Waves were churning, turning the horizon white, and yet still the air was calm. His concern for Joan deepened, but when he re-filled his glass his thoughts drifted.

His dad was behind the wheel of the old Chevy, driving across the Hudson. He was holding a quarter, challenging him to hold his breath. Anna, bookend by her two brothers, giggled, Mom scolded, but Dad beamed. The windows were down and Dad started to sing:

I'm King of the hill
Top of the heap
A number one

He reached for his sketch pad, but dropped it, the sound of breaking glass shattering the silence. He took a deep breath trying to return to the events at hand He glanced at his sketchpad lying in a heap on the deck, pages flapping in the wind. "The Mighty Hudson," he exhaled, as he stared blankly out at the ocean's growing fury.

Unchained Melody
(Memory)

THAT'S SOMETHING THEY don't teach at Harvard, Andy. I bet you thought that trooper had your old man dead to rights. No way Hero's Tunnel was going to be my final resting spot. In business you got to keep cool under pressure. You got to stretch the truth. It's not lying, Andy, if you believe you're telling the truth.

Your mother's so proud of you. The first in our family to go to college. Mom thought we should have some private time together, father and son time. A long drive makes for easy talk. I wanted to chat after you hit that home run. I was so proud. Remember when the Duke hit his home runs in the World Series? 1955. It was magic. I never went to college. It wasn't in the cards. Uncle Sam would have paid my freight. But I'm a salesman, Andy—it's something you're born with.

Did I ever tell you the story of Billy Brodrick? Best salesman that ever trudged the streets of Brooklyn. Taught me everything I know. No, not life insurance. Billy was a legend, made a fortune selling pots and pans. Don't laugh, selling is selling, it's an art. Billy operated in the poorer sections of town, as if Brooklyn was anything but. Carried a list he bought off the rabbis—girls who were engaged.

These brides-to-be didn't have two nickels to their name, but when Billy was finished with them, they were starting their marriage a good hundred in debt. Real money after the war. One day after I threw in the towel on pots and pans, I ran into Billy. We got to talking and the conversation turned to selling. "How do you do it?" I asked him. "These girls are poorer than an Indian penny."

Billy flashed his million dollar smile and puffed on his Cuban cigar. "I don't sell pots and pans—I sell stories." Seeing I was confused, Billy continued. "Marriage is the stuff of storybooks. It's their final chapter of the book called *Childhood*, where surprise endings still happen and happily-ever-after aren't just words. Miss Cinderella might have been dealt a crappy hand, but if she pulled an inside straight she could end up a princess. My job is to tell those girls a little fiction, tell them how pots and pans lead to a well-cooked dinner, which makes for a happy husband and a good marriage. My sweethearts connect the dots on their own."

Stories, Andy. We sell stories and dreams. Package our houses as dreams and we'll be made of money.

Willie rubs the dashboard of his Impala.

Twenty-five years, Andy, and not a squeak or a squeal. Name me a Jap car that does that. They slap them together like Tinker-Toys. Real cars are made in Detroit with Pittsburgh steel. Made in the U.S.A. with old fashioned American know-how and ingenuity. See the U.S.A. in your Chevrolet. It's more than a jingle, Andy—it's a verse.

Exiting Hero's Tunnel, Willie shielded his eyes from the glare. The Impala was driving itself as Willie, guided by instinct, tip-toed around Harford. Boston was little more than a road sign as he skirted the city on Route 128, the Impala winking at him in the mirrored office buildings lining the highway. The ocean came briefly into view as he crossed into New Hampshire. He spotted an access road leading to a tiny brick gatehouse with a steep-sloping copper roof. Straight out of a storybook, the house where the three little pigs cowered and the big bad wolf puffed in vain.

I think Anna's having sex, Andy. She says she's going to the prom, but I know the look. He'll pick her up in his father's car and pin a corsage on her tit. He'll have her dress off and be fucking her in a New York minute.

Willie's thoughts floated with the scenery. At a tollbooth, a girl with streaked blonde hair welcomed him to New Hampshire. "Live free or die," she said and Willie lifted his fist to concur. The girl smiled as Willie carefully pulled two dollars out of his wallet.

Inspecting one bill, the girl chimed, "Well, this bill is well worn."

"It's Will, not Bill," Willie chimed back.

Inspecting the worn dollar, she added, "This one has been well handled."

"Handled my share too," Willie answers with a wink.

She giggled. "I bet you say that to all the girls."

The car behind Willie hammered his horn. The toll girl shooed the driver with a flip of her wrist, then drew Willie closer. "Do you know what you get when you take the 'M' out of Massachusetts driver? An ass-a-who's-its."

Willie slapped the dashboard with his laughter.

The girl gave Willie his change. Her touch lingered as she added, "Be good and be safe."

Willie's thumb caressed her hand. "At my age I don't care about either."

"Mom says we can get another dog," Andy said, as the Impala left the tollbooth.

Willie turned and the Impala swerved. "Did you see that, Andy? I had that li'l pussycat in the palm of my hand."

"An Irish setter would be nice, hey Andy. Ever see a setter run? Like the wind, Andy, like the wind. I'll teach her to stay out of the road. We should have buried Pokie in the backyard. We could have put a stone on her grave—said a few words. I trusted the cops to do their job. In Brooklyn they just throw them out with the trash."

Staring out at the rusting drawbridge at Portsmouth, Willie remembered visiting this old whaling town as a kid. Sailors signed on for two-year voyages. Wives passed the time knitting. No cell phones back then. Life insurance made the wait bearable, that and an occasional romp in a neighbor's sack.

Willie exited at a rest area to look at a map. He knew Andy lived north of Portland and Freeport sounded familiar. A middle-aged woman at the information center bragged about Maine's low taxes: "Ideal for retired seniors." Willie teased the woman with, "Why, are you retiring?"

The woman chuckled and unfolded a map, placing it on the counter. She leaned forward, her breasts leading Willie in a different direction. "I'm not sure if they're where you want to be," she coyly said.

Willie leaned closer. "But the view is breathtaking."

"If you've seen one, you've seen them all."

Willie smiled. "They say each peek is like your first."

Tucking the map in his pocket, Willie started to leave, then added, "No one ever forgets their first," the harmony of their laughter accompanying him out the door.

We're leaving Brooklyn, Andy, getting out of that cesspool. I've put money down on a three-bedroom ranch. It's a real step up. You'll share a room with your brother; girls need their own space. It's got a yard, room for Pokie to run. I'll build a tree fort. We'll play ball when I get home from work. You'll catch on in no time. You're a natural, Andy. You'll be playing for the Dodgers someday. They call them the suburbs. They have supermarkets there that have anything you want.

Willie drove onward, driven by the need to reach Andy's house before dark. Portland whisked by on the right, the sky turning a hazy shade of silver as he crossed the causeway over Casco Bay. Out on the horizon he saw a scattering of islands thick with trees, remembering that Andy once told him that deer swim out there from the mainland.

Taking the Freeport exit he rolled by a string of stores, lured by the sense he had been there before. The road forked and he went right, confident he is heading towards the sea. Weathered houses with colorful flowerboxes crowded the narrow streets. Yes, this was the way. The ocean appeared, then disappeared, flirting with each turn he took. The houses grew larger, shingle-style mansions like Andy built. What had the *Times* called Andy's work? "Shingle Supreme."

Do you know why the Coliseum is round, Andy? So the Italians won't crap in the corners. I used to slay them with that one. Humor makes the deal. Get them laughing and hand them a pen. Fifty million. No one did fifty million back in the fifties. Today's money is worthless. Gold—that's where my money is.

I've given it a lot of thought, Andy. Land's ours for the taking in Maine. They're giving it away. We can buy fifty acres on the cheap and cram a couple hundred houses on it. Three-bedroom splits with two baths—yeah, we'll throw in an extra bath. How about a garage? We'll connect it to the house so the little woman can drive straight into the kitchen. We'll do it like Ford—assembly line. We'll crank them out by the bucketful. I've got people in Manhattan who'll back me, Andy. They've got deep pockets. We won't put up a nickel of our own money.

You always had the gift, Andy. Me, I'm a salesman, but you're a dreamer. When your mother told you to build with your blocks you said, "It's already built." You construct things in your head. Imagination, Andy. You've got the gift. We can't miss, Andy.

How about that cottage, Andy? Have you given it any more thought? I only need four walls and a roof. A fireplace would be nice, with the Maine winters. I'll chop my own wood. Heats you twice. I won't be a burden, Andy. You won't even know I'm there.

The asphalt gave way to dirt and then to sand. The salty air stirred something within him. The Impala rocked as the ruts grew deeper, his wheels reeling with the incline. The road thinned to a single lane, then vanished into the approaching sea. He had gone too far. But where to turn around? He had to keep moving or sink in the sand.

The ocean lurked below him. He floored it, his tires screeching as the Impala fishtailed dangerously close to the cliff. He smelled the stink of his overheated motor but kept going. "Keep the pedal down!" he cursed. The waves were crashing the rocks below, the surf scaling the overhang. "Hold on!" he screamed, "Hold on," as the Impala slid sideways.

He pushed the pedal harder, the engine straining with fatigue. The wheels grabbed, spinning the Impala into a stall. The silence was immediate. Willie climbed out. Amazingly all four wheels stood on solid ledge. "That's my girl," he said, tenderly patting the overheated hood.

It felt like yesterday that the Impala debuted—the car promising luxury for the little guy. He saw the woman on TV, perched on the back seat of a convertible, an exotic bird begging to be stroked. He watched her body arching towards him, her face aglow with the thrill of the open road. He raised his hand to touch her, to feel the electricity of her perky body. Her hair was perfect, her skin pale as the white gloves that laced her arms as she turned. Dinah Shore. He heard the yearning in her voice as she cried out for the "longer, wider, and stronger body of the Impala."

The waves were crashing louder. The late afternoon sun reddened the seascape. His shadow stretched beyond the precipice, disappearing into the ocean where it hung with unanswered questions.

Why?

He leaned against the hood, felt the warmth of the engine flowing through him.

Why?

Willie spied the gun lying on the floor. Reaching through the open window, he slipped his finger tight to the trigger. He brought the nozzle to his cheek. The steel felt soft. He pointed the revolver towards the Atlantic and fired. The aroma of gunpowder heightened his senses. He fired again. He watched the slender wisp of smoke rising from the barrel. "Is this it?" he whispered, as the wind tore apart the smoke.

Willie turned the gun towards himself. The warmth of the freshly fired gun was comforting. He stared into the void of the barrel, felt the pull of the gun's finality. Was there a bullet in the chamber? If he pulled the trigger would he even know if the bullet had been there?

Somewhere across the sea stood England. If life was but a story, then his story was written during those years. He rubbed the chrome emblem on the hood, stroked the legs of the Impala. Closing his eyes, his remembrances came alive with his touch. But it's not England. He's carrying a stack of magazines. On the cover of *Life* magazine an actress wearing "take me I'm yours" red lipstick winks at her audience.

Summer had turned to autumn. He no longer jumped when he heard a voice in the hallway, knowing the chicken butcher never deserted his stall when there was a buck to be made. Liz let him roam her body freely, a joy that seemed boundless. The center button of her dress always remained buttoned. "A woman needs her secrets," she whispered, as he drifted in and out of the bliss of her body.

He was a high school senior and the talk of war was pervasive. Two of his friends had lied about their age to enlist. When he brought up the subject at dinner, his father slammed his fist on the table and shouted in his crude Russian accent. "No son of mine dies in the sewers of Europe. Nothing to do with Jews. It's greed. Always it's about the greed."

Liz's baby was bigger, no longer the newborn who cared only for its mother. The boy had a rattle, a red, white, and blue one made of hard plastic. When Willie shook it, he giggled. It didn't matter how many times Willie shook the rattle, the kid always laughed. One day the boy snatched the rattle from Willie and brandished it. His eyes widened. Over and over he waved it like a scepter, until he struck himself on his forehead. He had never experienced this kind of pain before. His face contorted into tears. Liz swooped him up and started to carry him to her bedroom. As they neared the doorway the boy looked back through his tears. Impulsively Willie blew up his cheeks and made a duck sound. The boy grinned. When Willie did it again the boy stretched his tiny hand towards Willie and burst into a silly laugh. Giggling Liz took her boy into the bedroom.

When Liz returned from the bedroom she was wearing the polka-dot dress. When he asked her how the boy was she put her finger to his lips. The days were shorter and the shadows shrank the room. She started to unbutton her dress. The pearly buttons were large, but her fingers unclasped them with deliberate grace. She was wearing nothing underneath. She hesitated at the last button and then let her dress slip to the floor.

Later, as evening blanketed their bodies, a sense of wholeness filled him. Liz fell asleep, but they breathed together as one. He pulled her closer, falling into her warmth. Her softness engulfed him. He yearned to stay within her softness forever.

When Willie returned to her apartment the next week, the door was ajar. Even before he entered he knew she was gone. Dust balls gathered in the corners and cracks crisscrossed the bare walls. Only the sofa remained, too heavy, to old, to stuffed with memories to take with her. Collapsing, he watched the dust drift like uninhabited planets through slivers of the afternoon light.

It was nearly dark when the lady from across the hall entered. She was one of his customers, a fat woman who snooped. "Did they owe you money?" she sneered.

Willie shook his head.

"She went to Chicago. Her husband found work in the slaughterhouses. She has a boy to care for."

It was late November. Willie had no idea that the Japanese were planning a sneak attack on Pearl Harbor. Within weeks he would ride the patriotic wave, forging his father's name on his enlistment papers. In three months he would be in England. But at that moment he only wanted to lie on the sofa and let the world spin without him.

Willie gazed at the Atlantic. His memory always ended with him going off to war. He had replayed this scene on the couch a hundred times, had asked the same question a thousand different ways. Yet now, as he leaned against the Impala, he remembered more.

The fat lady was leaving. She hesitated at the door and took an envelope from her smock pocket

"It's for you. I found it on the couch."

The envelope had been opened. His name was addressed on it. He reached inside and a single sheet of stationery fell out. It floated to the floor, a solitary leaf falling in the late autumn light. Eclipsing the doorway, the fat woman watched. When he picked up the letter it was blank. Trembling, he turned to the fat woman, demanding an explanation.

She made a slight motion with her head, as if to say turn the letter over. There, written in lipstick were the words:

"Let the Altar Shine."

The Atlantic was heaving as Willie mouthed these words. A seagull screeched, its cry swallowed up by the ocean's fury. The waves crashed against the cliff, lashing him with saltwater. Willie stood unflinching, his mind churning. Was there a message—a meaning that these words would have unleashed?

His eyes burned as he stuffed the letter back into the envelope of his mind. He sank into the front seat of the Impala and turned the key. The engine whined but started. He threw the gun back into the glove compartment. Putting the car in gear he headed back down the rutted road, his mind racing through a picture book of remembrances, semblances, and transcendences of what was and wasn't to be.

Eleanor Rigby

WHEN LISA WAS a child, her mother took her to choir practice rather than leave her at home with her father. Choir practice was in the basement, leaving Lisa free to explore the empty church above. With the sanctuary dimly lit, Lisa played hide-and-seek with herself beneath the pews and behind the pulpits. Lisa, who was already taking piano lessons, played hymns for her imaginary congregation. To avoid being caught, however, she played softly, bringing her ear down to the keyboard, which created a sense of serenity deep within her.

Tonight, as Lisa played in the faint light of the Morningside lobby, she felt that bliss. She was tired and weak; her playing was so gentle that the notes resonated within her. Doris was half awake on the settee, still waiting for her man to return. Everyone else was asleep.

The song she had been composing excited Lisa, making her aged fingers vibrate with life. She needed more lyrics, but the melody was there. "Heaven can wait." Her laughter echoed through the empty lobby with a touch of irony. Aren't we all here waiting? Maybe we came to the Morningside by different paths, but the road out was the same. Except for Willie. God speed, Willie.

Heaven can wait

It amazed Lisa how the core of a melody was merely a couple of notes. And yet, with the right song those few notes ignited emotions that could survive a lifetime. She continued with one finger:

Heaven can wait
And a band of angels wrapped up in my heart

Lisa felt the angels gathering in her heart. Every experience, every disappointment, every tick of life's clock felt insignificant compared with this moment.

Will take me through this lonely night
Through the cold of the day

She looked over at Doris, her hands clasped under her head. Did she go to bed each night praying for a man, hoping that God would send her one? How many nights had her prayers gone unanswered? Lisa, who went to bed each night with a different man, hadn't prayed since she left home. What was that prayer she used to recite with her mother?

Now I lay me down to sleep

I pray my Lord my soul to keep

Lisa hesitated. Her head tilted upwards with meditation. What do children know about their soul? About God? Words without meaning grow up to be verses without rhymes. Bedtime stories are meant to soothe, keep the evils of the world away. Lisa remembered the comfort of her mother's bed, how the warmth of her mother's body made her feel safe after awaking from a bad dream.

If I die before I wake

I pray the Lord my soul to take.

As if to erase the prayer from her thoughts, Lisa turned to her song, singing:

Give me all of your dreams
And let me go along on your way
Give me all your prayers to sing
And I'll turn the night into daylight.

Consumed with spirit, consecrated with her song's creation, Lisa struck the piano with all her might and sang:

Let the altar shine

It was well past midnight when Lisa turned off the piano light. Her body ached as she rose from the bench, the same bench that half a century ago had been the hiding place for a victorious Willie Easelman. She would carry drifts of her song to her bed, into her dreams. Rising, she peered over at Doris. Her afghan lay sprawled on the floor. Weary, Lisa smiled and walked over.

The blueness of Doris's lips spoke of a truth more final than her unanswered prayers. Lisa placed the comforter over Doris's body and then folded her icy hands upon it. For an instant Lisa believed she saw Doris's eyelids flutter. But there was only a deathly stillness. She thought about waking the Haitian aide on duty, but no ... let Doris spend her last night waiting for her lover.

Lisa leaned over and kissed Doris on her forehead, tucking her in with a mother's gentle care. The walls of the lobby were lifeless as Lisa turned to leave. Passing the piano, she struck a single key, letting its sound hover, as she sang:

Eleanor Rigby picks up the rice in the church where a wedding has been
Lives in a dream.

Lisa reached for the newel post, hoping the steepness of the servant stairs might stretch her twitching legs. At the landing she paused. She surveyed the couches and chairs that tomorrow would be filled with the soon-to-be-dead. She noticed the stained-glass window, black and foreboding, awaiting daylight to burst back to life. Lisa struggled up the last stairs ... breathless, she hesitated. She gripped the railing, and looking down on the empty room she whispered, "No one was saved."

Forever Young

THE CRUNCH OF tires on seashells caused Andy to turn towards the driveway. Andy stood, shielding his eyes from the daylight that lingered on this the longest day of the year. Andy's hair gave the intruder a hesitant wave. He took a couple steps down the stairs and stopped. "Dad?"

He raced down the driveway. His hand griped the chrome handle of the Impala and he flung open the door. "How?"

"I did as you always told me. I followed the Merritt."

Andy paused before breaking loose with a laugh that challenged the crashing waves. Leaving the car door ajar, he led his dad to the deck, dumfounded by his father's nimbleness when climbing the steep stairs.

A half-filled bottle of Chardonnay sat on the railing. Andy slipped into the house, leaving Willie to survey the sea. The waves were breaking against the immense boulders that lined the shore. Further out, seals bobbed like a pack of playful pups. Willie inhaled deeply. He felt like pinching himself. This was the view of privilege. "Harvard," he said to himself, proud of his son's accomplishments.

Andy returned with a glass. "To my dad. May his amazing journey last forever." They touched glasses, the clink of their toast harmonized with the waves.

Andy's phone beeped. Joan. She was off water. "Bring home an extra steak, we have a guest. A surprise."

Surveying the broad expanse, Willie said. "You've done well. I always knew you were the special one."

Andy emptied the bottle into his father's glass, a bit uncomfortable with his father's compliment.

Willie held his crystal to the sky, its faceted glass created a rainbow over the two men. "The others didn't have your chutzpa, Andy." Willie downed his wine. "If I were to tell you the tortures your sister put me through. You have no idea what it's like in that cesspool."

Andy watched the tear gather in his dad's eye and felt the guilt in his gut of having agreed to let Anna put his father there.

"I'm telling you, son, never grow old. Stay forever young."

Andy, at a loss for words, picked up the roll of architectural drawings, holding them down against the wind with cobblestones.

"Shingle-style," Willie said, looking over his son's shoulder. "You still have that Richardsonian touch." The two clinked glasses again and laughed.

Willie continued to amaze Andy, pointing out the two eyebrow windows that Andy had just added. "They look like they're watching," Willie noted. "And I see a hint of the Orient."

Andy saw none of the dementia his sister whined about. Dad seemed younger—vibrant. Maybe he had been too quick to agree with his sister about the Morningside. As for taking away his car, hadn't Willie driven here from Jersey?

As father and son stood watching the clouds swallow up the horizon, they swapped stories that had remained dormant for years. Jeanie had been the family storyteller, and so many of the family stories had died with her. Willie, who could remember every client, policy, and claim he ever processed, always felt he was hearing her stories for the first time. When Andy went inside for a second bottle Willie grew gloomy, realizing that Andy's family had their own stories that didn't include him.

Joan returned from the race, more shocked than Andy by Willie's visit. After celebrating Willie's odyssey with a toast, she told the tale of her race in a pirate's accent. "The winds were strong and the waves bleeping high as we awaited the gun's report. The seas were nasty and them college kids cringed as they bobbled through blown tacks to marks wide enough to sail a fleet of schooners through. It was over by the third leg."

"Victory!" shouted Willie.

Andy popped the cork on a bottle of Champagne. "To my wife, the goddess of the seas."

"Row, row, row your boat," Willie piped in, mimicking Joan's pirate accent.

Joan raised her glass to the reddening sun. "To college kids everywhere. May they tremble at Neptune's fury."

"Before Aphrodite's fury," chuckled Andy, as he pulled his wife in for a kiss.

"Life is but a dream," added Willie.

Joan went to the kitchen and dropped the corn cobs into boiling water.

"Don't overcook the corn," Andy cautioned, as the two men stood arm and arm grilling steaks. "Two minutes, no more."

"We'll have lobster tomorrow," Andy told his dad. "We get them from a lobster man who swears he can tell their sweetness by the color of their gills. Just don't mess with his traps, though. Believes he has rights to the ocean, divine rights."

"Amen," Willie added, and the two laughed.

To the delight of Joan, Willie teased Andy over dinner.

"We were at Coney Island and Andy made an incredible sand castle turrets, towers, even a drawbridge made from a cigarette pack. He protected his castle with a moat, but when the tide came in a wave whooshed over it and the castle got swept away. Andy cried like a baby."

"That's because I was a baby."

"Should have known then you'd be a famous architect."

"At least my castles don't get swept away anymore."

"That's because you stopped making them out of sand," Joan chimed in.

"A pinch of cement never hurts."

Willie lifted his glass. "To castles that last ten-thousand years."

"I'd be happy with a hundred," laughed Andy.

"Just the ten years our lawyers write into our house contracts," Joan added.

"To the end of contracts."

"And this from a man who made a fortune for his company out of the small print."

After dinner Willie helped Joan prepare strawberry shortcake. While she whipped the cream, Willie sliced the berries Joan had bought home from a local farm.

"They're early this year," Joan explained. "First pick was always the fourth of July. Some say it's global warming, but I think the farmers are tinkering with genes. Soon we'll have fresh strawberries at Christmas."

"Well, then, they'll come fresh frozen," Willie added with a laugh.

The juice dripped through Willie's fingers as he painstakingly sliced the strawberries one at a time. Joan watched patiently, as her whipped cream soaked into the biscuits. When Willie reached for a napkin, the juice ran down his arm. Joan grabbed a dishtowel, but it was too late. Willie stood helplessly as the juice spread through his shirt sleeve. Joan laughed. "Like father, like son." And the three returned to the deck to enjoy the sweetest strawberry shortcake ever.

Andy saw the fatigue advancing across his father's face and suggested he sleep in the den where he could hear the waves. Willie snuggled into the arm of the leather sectional. A hint of light gathered at the window. Was it the moon or the sun? Then Willie remembered: today was the longest day of them all, the summer solstice.

Willie listened to Andy and Joan talking in the kitchen. "I can build that cottage," he heard Andy say. "He's really nothing like Anna makes him out to be. To hear Anna you'd think he was in diapers."

Joan sounded unconvinced. "He'll be a handful."

But her objections were weakening and Willie's face broke into a smile when he heard Andy say, "After all, how bad can he be if he drove here from Jersey?"

Willie lay on the sofa drifting in and out of sleep. He recalled the old days in Brooklyn, a family of five crammed into that apartment and Pokie just a pup What would have happened if they never left Brooklyn? Would Andy be a famous architect? Would Jeanie have passed away so young? Where would he be? Maybe he'd still be working. Didn't old man Zimmerman sell flowers from his stall on Flatbush well into his nineties?

Tomorrow he'd tell Andy his big plans about building houses—split-level ones that can't miss. Andy will be impressed; he'll love the idea of two full baths. They'll sell houses by the bucketful—a father and son team that can't miss. Dreams, they'll sell dreams and stories. Andy was already designing his cottage in his head, adding windows and doors like a magician. Maybe Andy could build it out of stone? Willie saw Andy and him playing catch in the back yard, Pokie chasing down errant throws. Willie showed Andy how to grip the bat, how to swing for the fences. "That's the way you do it," he said, as Andy hit the ball out of the park.

Willie sank deeper beneath the comfort of the covers. He imagined the warmth of his cabin in the winter with a fire blazing. A few light taps on the pane made him turn to the window. It was winter and the snow was drifting high above the cottage windows. There was laughter in the air, the sound of children playing hide-and-seek. Willie struggled to stay awake, to keep drawing in his imagination the pictures in the storybook he was creating. His life played like a never-ending Sinatra record. He was a kid again, trying to fall asleep on the eve of his big birthday.

Fall on Your Knees
(O Holy Night)

AM I AWAKE? Am I dreaming? I no longer can tell the difference.
My mother told me to pinch myself to tell if I was dreaming.
I do that now and I feel pain. But I feel pain when those men in
black robes hit me and I'm dreaming then. Each night when I wake
I believe they're real. I smell their stink, feel the coarseness of their
hairy bodies. But they're not real.

When I was a girl my mother told me I sleepwalked. My eyes
were open, but I was asleep. My mother would follow me around
the house, believing it was dangerous to wake a sleepwalker. She
worried I might walk down to the ocean and drown, so she had my
father put special locks on the doors.

If I'm dreaming, I will soon hear my baby cry. I'll get up to look
for her. She'll be down the hallway in the nursery with the two men
in robes. They'll torture me and punish my child. But my child is
innocent. I am the evil one.

My uncle was a powerful voodoo houngan in our village. When
he heard about my sleepwalking he told me I could be a mambo some
day. "Dreams are cut from the fabric of the universe that covers us all.

Only in dreams does time stand still and Loa is free to visit us. Sleep-walkers are messengers who connect the world of spirits and man."

But my dreams have become poisoned. The sins of my past are kept alive in my nightmares of today. These men in robes inhabit a realm outside that of spirits and man, a lifeless land of sand. They will never release me, never free me from the bondage of their evil. Their hatred spreads a plague that infects everyone they touch. They will inherit the earth. Their stink lingers on my body. I wash my hands till they're raw but their stench remains. I no longer hold out hope of ever being cleansed.

Jacqueline believes that Legba has taken over Willie's body. But she is wrong. Legba is a kindly old man with a dog. He is a wander-er, who wants to help you. I was wrong to lead her on. I used her superstitions to conceal my sins.

My mother hated the voodoo. She filled our house with pic-tures of Jesus to keep the evil spirits away. In Sunday school they told me stories about Jesus. How he saved the woman from being stoned. "Let those without sin cast the first stone." My priest said the gospel of Jesus contains but one word: love.

My baby will start crying soon. I feel her fussing in my heart. I must be sleeping. Maybe the men won't be there and I can soothe her. Will she know I'm her mother?

When my mother refused to let my uncle see me, he visited me in dreams. He appeared as a donkey and told me voodoo is the way the first Christians worshipped, before they began worshiping the Word.

"Words," the donkey told me, "create a vision of time, a sto-ryline we trick ourselves into believing is 'I Am.' But in voodoo the past resides in the future and the present holds the possibility of all things past and future. Bondye is the All of that possibility, the mist in the morning, the dryness of death, the starry flow of the Milky Way. Beware of words, the donkey warned. The priests preach 'In the beginning was the Word.' They marvel at the cleverness of their verses, the craftiness of their rhymes. But they are tricked by their own cunningness. Find meaning in the timelessness of spirit, the miracle of one's yesterdays resurrecting in tomorrow. God is more than words, as the breeze is more than air."

My baby is crying. I call out to her, but I don't call soft enough. I get out of bed and go down the hallway. But something is different. Maybe this isn't a dream. I hear voices and slip into the bathroom.

My treasure box is open—my precious things are scattered. Fingerprints smudge the photo of my family, careless greedy fingerprints. The sand from my beach at home is spilled. I whisk a few grains back into the vial, but most falls on the floor.

My uncle says the only way to tell if you're dreaming is with words. You can watch yourself being born in a dream, see yourself smiling in your mother's tummy, but you can never read in a dream. Words reside outside the spirit world. They lead to the altar of false idols.

I must make amends for my sins before it is too late. There is a pen in my treasure chest and begin to write.

Dear Trooper Scott,

I am sorry for lying to you. I did not have sex with Mr. Willie. He is a kind man who tells funny stories. I don't believe in voodoo. I believe only in Jesus. I could tell you that Jacqueline made me lie, but that would be a bigger lie. I lied to her because I had sex with Alberto and didn't want her to know. She is like an older sister, the only person I have who loves me.

I wish I could go back to my house in Haiti. When I was a child my mother pinned pictures of Jesus on my walls. She told me Jesus would protect me. I pray now for his help for I am lost, as lost as Mr. Willie. Maybe if you can find Mr. Willie you can find me. My uncle spoke of pathways through time, roads that connect the past to the future, death to life. These pathways can lead you to me. I can't take this horror anymore. I grow weaker by the day. I hear my baby crying. I can't comfort her. No one knows my pain.

The men in robes grow bolder by the day. They have begun to visit me during the day. I wish I was stronger. My baby wishes I was stronger. I no longer sleep. My dreams make me weary. There's blood on my hands. Please help me.

Simone

Simone looks at the stationery. It is blank.

At the bottom of her treasure chest lays a tiara, a gift from her father. She lifts the crown out of the box. Once upon a time she wore it as she danced on the dirt floor. Her father said she was the prettiest ballerina in the world. When her father gave her the tiara it sparkled, its tiny diamonds created rainbows, which filled the room as she danced.

Simone goes to the pedestal sink and turns on the faucet, fills the basin with hot water. Music is playing, the strumming of her father's guitar. She smiles at the face in the mirror. Placing the tiara on her head she feels the sharpness of its shards. She curtsies to her reflection that is clouding over in the rising mist. Bringing her hands over her head she twirls, inhales the fragrance of her youth. With her finger, she makes the sign of the cross on the mirror, glimpses the beauty of her face in the narrow slits of silver. Blood drips from her forehead.

She pirouettes to her family hidden behind the mirror. She hears their applause and curtsies. Sirius barks and her brothers shout her name. She closes her eyes to the sound of her father's song.

Dance among the morning star
Dance beneath the evening sky
Dance with the spirits
Dance with the Gods
Dance with the joy of your baby's first smile.

The razor blade glistens as it slices across the flesh of her throat. Simone lifts her finger to her neck, surprised how slowly the deep wound fills with blood. "Forgive them, Father," she cries, as her tiara falls from her head.

Her head slams forward, striking the porcelain sink. The blade tumbles across the tile, cold steel echoing through empty space. She grips the sink, trying to pull herself up to the mirror where her family is watching. Her legs buckle. "Forgive," she murmurs, feeling wisps of frost flow through her flesh. She struggles for air, but finds none, her innocence breath enough for a thousand suffering angels.

Simone lifts her arm for one final twirl. The guitars screech, angels harmonize. Simone sees her child and smiles. She gathers herself for her final dance. She smiles. Twirls. His little princess is coming home.

Dance princess dance
Till the angels all proclaim.
Dance princess dance
Till the heavens call your name.

Simone falls awkwardly to her knees, the promise of a forgiving Jesus frozen on her lips.

We Will Rock You

TROOPER SCOTT SKIDDED to a stop upon entering the Montvale rest area, a mile shy of the New York border. No sign of the governor. The parking lot was overcrowded with sunburned day-trippers returning from the Jersey shore and busloads of seniors exaggerating their winnings after a hard day at the casinos. With all these grey heads loitering around, it would be impossible to pick Easelman out of the crowd. No, the key to finding Easelman rested with the car. How many '86 Impalas could still be on the road?

Scott weaved cautiously through the labyrinthine maze of the main parking lot, forced to stop for groups of giggling teens loitering in the lanes and for seniors backing up without so much as a glance. He peered at the calendar on his watch. The 21st. Good. Gambling would be light. Next week, with Social Security checks in hand, it would be different. He shook his head, bewildered by the elderly's obsession with gambling. How many times had his dad rambled about buying a Russian bride or a Bangkok maid when he hit the jackpot? The young bet for the future, the old bet for a second chance. And with stakes that high, the police were often called to break up spats over the slots. Lucky machines were something to battle over and the old fought surprisingly dirty. He remembered administering first aid to one elderly woman, who after a nasty brawl refused to go to the hospital. "That's lucky blood," she spat, cramming quarters down the machine with both hands.

As Trooper Scott turned into the auxiliary lot, he heard the wail of approaching sirens. Through a screen of pine trees he could see the string of black SUV's speeding down the turnpike from the north. The governor was minutes away. If Easelman did have a gun, things could get ugly real fast. The governor might not take too kindly about being shot, but he also would have issues watching one of his state troopers frisk an eighty-six year old man on TV. And what if after frisking Easelman on Breaking News he didn't have a gun? What then? Gun or no gun it was a rousing start to the governor's Silver Alert campaign.

Scott's phone beeped. The colonel. "You there yet?"

"I'm moving into the auxiliary lot, sir. The governor's just arriving."

"Shit. You find him?"

"Not yet, sir. The place is stuffed with seniors. It's all coming down to luck."

"And I'm not feeling my Vegas luck today. Have you searched the rest rooms? These old guys gotta pee every five minutes."

"No time for that, sir, I'm concentrating on finding the car."

"Christ, Scott, the man's driving an '86 clunker. How hard can it be?"

"If he's here, I'll find him, sir. But his car's not in the main lot."

"The auxiliary lot?"

"Doesn't appear to be there either."

"Crap. Have you checked the commuter lot?

"It's Sunday, sir."

"You think seniors give a shit what day it is?"

"Sir, about the gun..."

"Fuck the gun. If you find the old geezer, pin a medal on his chest, and call him a hero."

"But the governor?"

"I know the governor. He'd rather take a bullet then watch some old codger spread-eagled on the hood of a cruiser opening up the six-o'clock news.

"But …"

"I'm betting a leg wound would raise the governor's polls fifteen percent. Besides, old people can't shoot straight."

"Sir?"

"It's a joke Scott, loosen up."

"But if he does have a gun, sir?"

"Listen Scott, the gov's got a shit load riding on this Silver Alert crap. Thinks it's his wagon he can drive all the way to Pennsylvania Avenue. These old folks vote like lemmings. Nursing homes, not soccer moms, pick presidents."

"But…"

"If he comes out shooting, duck."

"Sir?"

"Just find the God-damn guy. He's driving an '86 Chevy for Christ's sake."

"But I won't have time to disarm him."

"Then find the friggin' time.

"But …"

"You want that sweet-ass pension, Scott? Then find him." And the phone went dead.

Trooper Scott gunned his cruiser, knowing he was down to minutes. Damn, was he going to loose his pension? His tires squealed as he rounded a curve, barely avoiding a group of teenagers in spandex bathing suits frying hot dogs over a can of Sterno. He reached for his siren, but thought otherwise. No, they'd scatter like rats. As he turned to enter the commuter lot a man leaped in front of him frantically waving his arms. "God," Scott groaned, as he screeched to a halt.

"My son found him," the man stammered.

"413-782," the boy at his side proudly recited.

There, parked at an awkward angle with the nose of the car smothered in pine limbs, stood the '86 Impala, a Maine license plate dangling from a single screw.

"My son's a wiz with numbers," the father added. "Remembers everything."

As Trooper Scott got out of his cruiser he was drawn to the boy's expression. He had seen that look before. Autism.

"You've done well, son," Scott said, dismissing the boy.

Scott crouched alongside his cruiser as he studied the Impala. He slid his hand down his pant leg and unstrapped his gun. Scott heard the sound of approaching sirens; the governor's party was closing in.

The kid shadowed Scott. "Is that gun real?"

Scott raised his palm to silence the boy, but the kid continued. "Is your gun loaded?"

Scott ignored the question, but the kid persisted. "Are you going to shoot him?"

The father stepped in. "Danny!"

Trooper Scott flashed the father the GET YOUR STUPID KID THE HELL OUT OF HERE look, as he crept closer. Someone was sitting in the driver's seat.

"Am I going to get a medal?"

"Danny!"

"My dad said I'm going to get a medal."

Scott moved forward, next to the Impala."

"Are you going to kill him?"

"Danny!"

The boy stomped his foot.

"I promised you a hot fudge sundae."

"I don't want a sundae, I want a medal."

Scott halted at the rear bumper of the Impala. His instincts told him to draw his gun. The colonel might not care, but if this turns into a shootout the fallout would land on his lap.

"I want a medal," the boy persisted.

Scott resisted the urge to slap the kid. "The governor's on his way. I'm sure he'll give you an award, kid."

"I don't want an award, I want a medal."

A black SUV skidded into the lot. The sirens were nearly drowned out by rock music. What ... and then Scott remembered that the governor liked to travel to music. Rumor was he had his vehicles outfitted with a sound system deafening enough to wake the dead and as the SUV bore down on them the bravado of bass speakers reverberated in Scott's chest.

Scott turned back to the Impala. If Easelman was sleeping, maybe he should rush the car and yank him out. But Scott remembered that frail woman in the nursing home. Careful—he could snap the old man's arm with a tug. But a confused old man waving a loaded gun was worse, especially if he was defending his God-given right to drive.

Scott gripped his holstered gun.

The kid giggled, "You can't kill him."

"Mr. Easelman?" Scott called out, hugging the rear panel of the Impala.

"You can't kill him," the kid repeated.

Scott wheeled and shoved the kid to the ground.

A string of SUVs were now closing in on him.

"Fuck!"

Laying on the ground the boy covered his mouth and snickered. "You said the "F" word, mister."

"Mr. Easelman?"

"Officer," the boy's father said. "I think we have …."

"Shut-up!" Scott barked.

Buddy you're a boy, make a big noise
Playin' in the street be a big man some day
You've got mud on yo' face
You big disgrace
Kickin' your can all over the place

The music was earsplitting as the lead SUV slid to a halt. Scott inched closer to the door. Both of Easelman's hands were on the steering wheel. Excellent, the music would wake the old man up. He drew his gun.

As if choreographed, the van crammed with media rounded the corner, nearly tipping over.

Surrounded by sound Scott stood and raised his gun, coming face to face with the profile of the old man's face in the side view mirror. "Step out of the car, Mr. Easelman."

"You can't kill him," the boy chuckled.

We will we will rock you
We will we will rock you

"Officer," the father went on.

"Get that kid out of here. The guy's armed."

The tinted windows of the SUV rolled down, releasing a wave of music that engulfed the parking lot.

Buddy you're a young man hard man
Shoutin' in the street gonna take on the world some day
You got blood on yo' face
You big disgrace
Wavin' your banner all over the place

Lying on the ground, the kid was choking on his own laughter. "You can't kill him."

"Danny! Please."

Scott heard a car door open, but resisted the urge to look. "Mr. Easelman," he demanded, "Come out with your hands up."

We will we will rock you

Nothing. Scott gripped the handle of the door. "Mr. Easelman!" Adrenalin pumped as Scott tightened his clasp. Should he rip open the door and … what? Point his gun at the old man's head? He heard the media pouring out of the van.

We will we will rock you

Scott leveled his gun.

Someone near the media van shouted, "Shooting."

Scott glanced back at the SUV. The press secretary was advancing towards him, a cell phone glued to his ear. The governor stood leaning against the fender of the SUV, casually watching.

"Hey officer," the kid on the ground snickered. "You can't kill someone who's already dead."

Scott hesitated.

Someone near the media van called out, "You got this?"

Scott needed to act, needed to act know.

The kid stood up. "The old guy is deader than a doorbell."

Trooper Scott flung open the door. There sat Willie grinning, his body propped against the steering wheel at an unnatural angle. Scott reached over and felt the old man's hand. Cold.

"Told you," the kid sneered, as he weaseled past Scott for a better look at the dead man.

The press secretary was approaching as Scott slid his gun back into his holster. Stepping in front of the smaller man, Scott muttered something to him.

"Really?" Peering into the partially open window of the Impala, the press secretary shook his head and chuckled. "At least he won't be plowing into our tourists." He rushed back to the SUV. The governor motioned to someone in the SUV to turn down the music. The secretary whispered to the governor who nodded. The governor's smile never changed as his gaze drifted skyward.

"That's a wrap," the press secretary barked to the parade of reporters and cameramen.

The governor strolled over to the Impala. He tapped his fingernails on the driver's side window, as if to wake a sleeping motorist. He turned to Scott. "You believe that? Two hands on the wheel."

"The man's a poster child for highway safety," his secretary quipped, as he signaled to the chauffer to keep the motor running.

The governor turned away as if he hadn't heard the comment.

Trooper Scott stepped towards the governor. "Sir, this is the boy who found … the car. The Silver Alert."

The governor sized up the boy's condition with a single glance. He nodded to his photographer and then hugged the boy as the photographer shot away. The boy craved the attention. The governor spoke to his secretary, who announced to the media they'd get five minutes. As the cameramen scrambled to set up their equipment, a woman jumped out of the SUV and applied makeup to the governor's face. It all happened so fast that Scott had to be told to get out of the way of the rolling cameras.

"First of all," the governor began, "I'd like to thank my new friend, Danny, for calling in on the Silver Alert line. It was Danny's heroics that saved lives here today. His quick thinking, along with our vigilant state troopers, averted a disaster. A man who should not have been on the road, and was a danger to himself, has been found. And I'm happy to report his family no longer needs to worry."

The governor paused and, in a magician's blink that even the cameras failed to catch, gently pushed the boy into the waiting arms of his press secretary.

The governor turned and faced the Impala, stroking its fender. "American ingenuity. Some say it's a relic of the past. That we've sold out to the foreigners, that we can't get things done anymore. But I believe otherwise. I remember my father returning tired and worn from a hard day's work. We didn't have much in the way of material things, but we had each other. My mother was a housewife, which in those days meant something. It meant that her two kids would grow up to go to college."

As the cameras moved for a close-up, the governor strolled to the opened door of the Impala. He appeared at a loss of words, as he placed his hand on Willie's inert shoulder.

"But I say the American dream is not dead. It lives on with people like Willie Easelman, whose life was … is … a testament to that dream. A man who helped build the greatest nation the world has ever known. Once upon a time America made great cars. Our factories were the envy of the world. We won wars. Cured diseases. Put a man on the moon. We were the chosen ones."

The governor rubbed his eye as he turned to face the cameras dead on.

"They say America doesn't make cars like these anymore. But I say we can and we will. With God's guidance, with your vigilance, and with the political wisdom of our forefathers, we will awaken the American dream from its slumber and once again drive the byways and highways of this great nation."

The governor stared straight at the cameras, with a street-fighter's toughness, challenging them to respond. He took a deep breath, his shoulders broadening, as if by some photographical sleight of hand of the camera lens. He slammed the Impala's door for affect—a theatrical gesture that shut the door on debate.

"That's a wrap," the press secretary cried, shutting down the media who craved for more. The governor stood slightly breathless, leaning on the Impala, fingering the chrome emblem on the hood. Without looking up, he said, "I owe you one, Scottie."

The boy broke free of his father's grasp as the governor was stepping into his SUV. He raced over to the politician and stammered, "The policeman said you'd give me a medal."

Without turning to the boy, the governor motioned his secretary who reached in his pocket and handed the boy a crisp five-dollar bill. The boy turned it over as if suspecting counterfeit. The governor waved to no one in particular before shutting the door. The music went ballistic, reverberating through the parking lot as the SUV sped away, the governor's silhouette pounding on imaginary drums in the rear window.

> *We are the champions — my friends*
> *And we'll keep on fighting — till the end*
> *We are the champions*
> *We are the champions*
> *No time for losers*
> *'Cause we are the champions — of the world.*

"This isn't a medal," the boy coughed, as he chucked the bill on the ground. "You said the governor would give me a medal."

"The governor's a very busy man, Danny," his father interjected.

"The governor's an asshole."

"Danny!"

Turning to Scott the kid spat. "You lied," struggling with his private demons to go eye-to-eye with the trooper.

"We need to get Mr. Easelman to the hospital," Trooper Scott replied.

"He's dead, stupid."

"Danny!"

"The hospital will make him feel better," Scott sheepishly added.

The kid gathered enough courage to look Scott in the eye. And holding Scott captive with his gaze, the kid slowly shook his head and smirked.

"Danny, let's get that ice cream sundae."

The boy released Scott from his stare and stomped his foot, scuffling up dust as he trailed his father back to the car. The father whispered something to his wife, who looked exasperated by the whole ordeal. As the father put the car in gear, the boy rolled down his window.

"What's an American dream?" he asked the trooper.

Trooper Scott remained stoic, appearing as if he hadn't heard the question.

"What's an American dream?" the kid repeated.

"It's something we all want," his father interjected.

"Like a medal?"

"Like a medal, son."

The boy appeared satisfied and started closing the window. But stopping halfway he seized Scott's stare and held it. "You know we're all going to die someday."

Scott froze.

"You're going to die," the boy smirked.

But before the father could "Danny," the kid again, the kid grabbed hold of his father's neck and hugged him. "Can I have two cherries on my sundae?" And after a nod from his father, the car sped off.

Trooper Scott surveyed the parking lot. With the abrupt departure of the governor's entourage and the media, the area took on a crime-scene stillness. He radioed headquarters who told him the coroner was tied up with a bad accident, a carload of teenagers returning from the shore. Police policy was clear—the coroner needed to declare Mr. Easelman dead before Scott could call an ambulance. Till then nothing could be touched.

On the ground Scott spied the five-dollar bill. Picking it up, the portrait of Lincoln stared back at him. Turning it over, the words, "IN GOD WE TRUST," rang like a verse from the governor's rock music.

> *God hates pennies*
> *God hates dimes*
> *God wants five dollars*
> *All the time.*

Scott checked his watch and scribbled 4:13 into his notebook. He had long ago given up on the idea of sneaking in a quick nine before the cookout. As for his dad, let him watch the second game of the doubleheader on his lucky TV—the Mets were going to lose it anyway.

Flipping through his notepad Scott found Easelman's son's phone number and dialed it. Easelman's son answered and said nothing as Scott described his father's situation and how no one could have prevented it, adding "He died with both hands on the wheel," because it sounded good when the governor said it. At the end of his spiel the trooper paused, expecting the son to have a few unanswered questions. But after an awkward silence punctuated by the sound of waves breaking in the background, Easelman's son could only muster a parting, "Understandable."

Trooper Scott stood filling out his report on the hood of the Impala when his phone beeped. Elaine.

"Hey, guess who I just saw on TV?"

"Can't."

"My man. You were standing behind the governor looking pretty dapper."

"It's been a long day."

"Seems like that Silver Alert thing works. Hey, why wasn't the old guy there? Willie, why wasn't Willie there?"

Scott's hands trembled but he caught himself before he shouted "because the old guy is dead!"

"I've cancelled the cookout. I'm sure your Dad wouldn't have remembered anyway. I'm heading over to help Allie with the kids. She's got a migraine. Pregnancy—you men will never know what you're missing."

"Some things are best left to the imagination."

"Men. Oh, I almost forgot, Jim. Guess who held mass today? Father McKenna, I mean Archbishop McKenna. Everyone says he's headed for Rome. "

Scott noticed Easelman's keys dangling in the ignition.

"Can you believe it, Jim? The priest who performed my confirmation is going to Rome."

With rain imminent, Scott wondered if it would it be against regulations if he shut the Impala's window before the coroner arrived.

"He spoke about the rights of the unborn. How every life is precious in the eyes of God. He says those who kill the unborn will be punished on Judgment Day."

Scott opened the door and rolled up the window, avoiding eye contact with Easelman.

"Sometimes I think hell is too good a place for them."

"Is Allie OK?"

"Nothing a good cup of tea won't cure."

"Tell her hello from me."

Scott's thoughts drift westward to where black clouds crowded the waning sun. Almost on cue he heard the roll of thunder. He hustled back to his cruiser and gathered his paperwork. He felt oddly relieved. With Easelman apprehended, or at least found, he could avoid bringing up Simone's situation to the colonel. "Let sleeping dogs lie." His phone beeped. The colonel.

"Good work, Scott. The gov couldn't praise you enough. You know, he had planned to open the car door and shake Easelman's hand. Would have been a real show stopper seeing Easelman tumble to the ground with the cameras rolling. Talk about going viral. The Democrats would have pissed in their pants."

"Thank you, sir."

"You saved the governor's butt."

"Glad to be of help."

"Big time, Scott, we're talking big time."

"Sir, you were friends with the governor at college. His father, did he work at a factory?"

"Factory? Did Tom give you his American dream bullshit? Hell, his father was a professor. Law. And his mother was loaded. Inheritance. Her family owned half the factories in Ohio. Textiles. Or maybe it was shoes."

"I see."

"He did, however, party his ass off. The man was a legend. But there is something you should know about the governor. He believes it."

"Sir?"

"When he says his father toiled at a factory, he believes it. His life is so intertwined with myth that he can't distinguish the two. The shrinks call it 'delusion,' but it's got him where he is today."

"Not sure I follow, sir."

"Neither do I, Scott, neither do I."

Weary, Scott hoped to hear the colonel's abrupt exit.

"One more thing, Scott. You interviewed a girl at the Morningside today. A Simone?

The mention of Simone's name clogged Scott's throat.

"You have your notes?"

"I haven't filed them yet, sir."

"Good."

"Is there a … problem?"

"Apparently she did a real number on herself. A bloodbath, the medics are calling it. She left a suicide note addressed to you. An apology or some crap like that."

"Suicide? A note to me?"

"Haven't seen the note. Anything I should know, Scott?"

"She seemed a bit confused. Maybe I should have taken her more seriously."

"She say anything about Easelman?"

Scott took a deep breath. "Said his voodoo spirit mounted her."

"Sexually?"

"She was rambling. Said the old guy did it to her … twice."

"Christ, everyone's taking those blue pills. Put it in your report, Scott. We'll try to deep six it, but you never know when something like this sprouts legs. Reeks of a media bonanza. Illegals?"

"Assume so."

"Haitians, right?"

"Yes, sir."

"They're a crazy lot. All that voodoo crap. In New York they busted a ring dealing in shrunken heads. What the fuck does anyone want with shrunken heads?"

"Beats me, sir."

"Dangle them from their rearview mirror like the Ricans do."

"Maybe I should have dug deeper?"

"You dug deep enough. One more thing, Scott. Did Easelman have a gun?"

"I didn't check."

"Well, check it out. These citizen review boards are stacked with Democrats. They can mess us up big time. It's good to have a little ammo of our own stashed away. A gun tends to put everything in perspective."

"Yes, sir."

"Oh and, Scott?"

"Yes?"

"How does it feel to go 150 MPH?"

"It's an experience, sir."

"You nipping death in the ass and you call it an experience?"

"It did raise my blood pressure."

"Some call it a life changer."

"I guess."

"You're the best, Scottie, you're the best." And the phone went dead.

Trooper Scott returned to the Impala and opened the passenger door. He felt strange rummaging under the front seat looking for a gun, while trying to ignore the dead man sitting in the driver's seat. Scott found a weather-worn leather briefcase engraved with initials W. E. He unzipped it and pulled out a legal pad of yellow paper with curled corners. Handwritten in script was page after page of names, dates, amounts, beneficiaries, terms, and payout amounts. The first entry was July 18, 1945, the last June 2, 1994. Other than the yellow pad and a copy of the *Daily News* dated July 4, 1994, with a front page printed in red, white, and blue exploding firecrackers that spelled out "HAPPY BIRTHDAY" the briefcase was empty.

A crack of lightening brought a downpour, forcing Scott to take refuge in the Impala. He watched the old people scattering in the parking lot, their dreams of hitting the jackpot dashed for another week. The storm was blowing in from the Atlantic, unusual for this time of the year. The undertow had been reported as strong and accounts of drownings were starting to come over the radio, causing Scott to wonder if this would further delay the coroner.

A gust of wind rocked the Impala, forcing Scott to shut the door. The glove compartment door popped open. "Jesus," he muttered, as he spied the .45-caliber, its hammer cocked. He turned to the man in the driver's seat. Would he have shot the governor?

From the angle that Trooper Scott peered at Easelman, he noticed a childish grin on the old man's lips, as if he was getting away with something. Last night must have been some ride. The ride of his life and he must have died happy—in his car.

Scott's thoughts returned to his short conversation with Willie's son and wondered if his own children would someday refer to his death as "understandable," the thought of which was repulsive.

Sitting side-by-side in the front seat of the Impala, Scott resisted the temptation to move the old man's hands off the steering wheel.

What kind of life did this Easelman have? What adventures? He noticed the key chain dangling in the ignition. The 546 Bombardment Squadron, a screaming eagle stamped in the tarnished brass. Had he seen action in the war? Had he seen death?

Understandable. Something about the word haunted him, wouldn't leave him alone. Did his kids understand him? Does anyone ever understand anyone? Would Elaine understand him? Would she understand how it happened? Understand why it happened? Would she forgive?

The windshield was fogging over as Scott's thoughts returned to that rainy day fifteen years ago. He could accept his role in the affair, if only Elaine wasn't blind to her own.

Scott turned to the man sitting next to him. The night was pounding with questions, some answered, some not. The patter of rain on the hood was exiling, taking Scott to a place where nothing much made sense. Scott's mind swirled with contradictions—the taking of his father's keys, the taking of a young girl's life, the confession he must make to Elaine. But as he sat in the front seat of the Impala, a solitary word emerged from the cacophony of accusations and implications churning in his head. "Understandable." As the word wormed deeper into his skull, Scott felt a loneliness of brutal consequence as he pondered why his father never took him fishing again.

Revive

What a Wonderful World

WILLIE AWAKES ON the couch, aroused by a nagging sensation that he is losing his sense of time. He desperately scours the room for a clock, but finds none. A glow beneath the kitchen door spreads along the hardwood floor, its light too weak to illuminate the walls of the cavernous room. Andy and Joan are in bed, the house resonates with a slumbering silence. Willie sees his reflection in the panoramic window, as he searches for a sign of first light. His face is oddly distorted by the glass and he sticks out his tongue to reaffirm it is him he is looking at. A silvery glint paints the sky. "The solstice," he exclaims, aware that at this time of year and latitude the sun lingers on the horizon deep into the night. He slides open the door, and steps out into the full glory of the cosmos.

Outside the stone outcrops are under the assault of high tide. The granite monoliths shimmer beneath the strange light, sentinels of the coast that will survive for millenniums. Nobody at the Morningside would believe he had driven this far. Willie shakes his head at his feat, this seemingly miracle comparable to the fifty million he did in '55. He raises a fist to the night, his mind reeling with visions of the cottage Andy will soon be building for him. "Start spreading the news," he sings as the prospect of renewed life pumps through his veins.

Slivers of clouds partially eclipse the moon as Willie walks to the deck's edge cantilevering over the surging Atlantic, defying gravity. He leans against the railing and peers into a vastness that stretches along a pathway of stars that exceed imagination. He breathes the nighttime air, thick with the onset of summer, the scent of wildflowers and moist earth. The surf carries the drift of music. As he skips down the steep stairs, the music grows louder. He catches the cry of a runaway sax, the triumphant of a trumpet.

She appears in a breeze: American royalty perched on the back seat of the convertible. He knows her by the desire woven into the platinum waves of her hair. Dinah Shore, the Queen of General Motors, the darling of America, the one who brought glamour to the black-and-white TVs of America. Red gloves wrap her arms, a red streak of lipstick emboldens her pale complexion.

She summons someone with a wave and out of the darkness strolls Sinatra, suave and debonair. Their fingertips touch and he lifts Dinah, swirls her around as if she's weightless. She offers her cheek and he kisses her. Placing her back on her throne, she blushes while rearranging her dress.

Sinatra steps into the front seat of the Impala and lights a cigarette. Gripping the wheel, he surveys the landscape with confidence. Dinah reaches over and snatches his cigarette, inhales deeply before exhaling a cloud of pure pleasure. She is radiant, her body quakes with life. She raises her arms, her voice strong and clear:

See the U.S.A. in your Chevrolet
America is asking you to call.

And Frank answers:

Drive your Chevrolet through the U.S.A.
America's the greatest land of all.

Dinah blows a kiss Willie's way, along with a wink that buckles his knees. Frank tilts his martini to Willie and motions him over. Di-

nah tosses Willie a cherry from her Manhattan, which Willie catches
with his teeth. Everyone cheers.

Out of the woods they come and Willie knows them all. Satchmo on the trumpet, waving his handkerchief, Benny Goodman
lighting up the night with his licorice stick. Dinah claps wildly,
twirling in the back seat, like an exuberant cheerleader. When the
strap of her gown slips off her shoulder she pouts to Willie, who
slides it back on, aroused by her supple skin.

Benny tosses Willie a baton and begs him to conduct. Buddy
Ammons, Al Cohn, and Hoss Page join in, as Willie bobs to the
beat. Peggy Lee sits on a rock near the wood's edge, snapping her
fingers, as Ray Charles serenades her with his tearful version of
"America." He sings it slowly and Willie mouths along, watching
the amber waves of grain bend in the breeze, the purple mountains
glisten in his imagination. Then from deep within the woods comes
the haunting voice of Billy Holiday, singing "When Jonnie Comes
Marching Home Again." Accompanied by the single beat of a drum,
she sings in a slow gospel way, as the two legends fuse their separate
melodies into a single song. Their voices harmonize, woven together
with mutual pain and irony. Dinah sheds a tear and Willie draws her
fur wrap high around her slender neck.

Willie tells Sinatra how grand he is. Sinatra laughs, saying it's
Willie, not him, who made this country great. Dinah concurs and
kisses Willie on the forehead. She wraps her toe around Willie's leg,
drawing him in to her.

Satchmo hands Dorsey his trumpet and wipes his forehead. He
nods to the band and they stop. In his unmistakable gritty tone,
Satchmo continues:

> *The colors of the rainbow...so pretty...in the sky*
> *Are there on the faces...of people going by*
> *I see friends shaking hands...sayin'...how do you do*
> *They're really trying to say...I love you.*

Dinah is ecstatic and kisses Willie again, leaving her mark on his
cheek. Sinatra downs his martini and whistles. Someone in a rabbit's
outfit hops out of the woods and refills his glass. When Willie places

his hand on Dinah's exposed back, she looks aside, bashful and smiling. Sinatra nods. The band joins in and Satchmo continues:

I hear babies cry…watch them grow
They'll learn much more…than I'll ever know
And I think to myself…what a wonderful world.

Willie sticks his key into the ignition, the thrust of 358 horses
rush through his body. From her roost on the back seat Dinah clasps
her arms around Willie. "Honey," she murmurs, as she nibbles on his
neck. He stiffens to the feel of her breasts, pressing against him. "Take
me away," she swoons, sliding her hand through the slit in his shirt.
He puts the Impala in gear and beeps goodbye to the band. Dinah
giggles. Framed in the rearview mirror, Sinatra salutes Willie with his
martini. As they near the end of the driveway Willie hears Satchmo's
parting, "What a wonderful world."

"We've still got it, old buddy," Willie chimes, as he rubs the
dash of his Impala. Dinah's hair remains perfect, even as the Impala
gathers speed and her fur wrap flutters wildly in the breeze. "See the
U.S.A. in your Chevrolet," Willie bellows into the night. When he
turns to hear Dinah's snappy retort, a twelve-year-old Andy is sitting
in the backseat alone.

Not missing a beat, Willie says. "Not bad, hey son? Told you the
girls have a hankering for your old man."

"Dinah Shore, who would figure, Dad. She was wrapped around
you like a bandage."

"It's all in the delivery, son. Like selling pots and pans."

"You're the maestro, Dad."

Willie, who is still holding the baton, taps it on the dashboard.
"Benny and I swing with the best."

"I saw you with Sinatra."

"We're pals, Andy. We speak the same lingo."

"Tell me about that girl back at Atlantic City."

Willie caresses the curves of the steering wheel with his memory. "She could have had anyone in the squadron, but she chose me.
Nailed her under the boardwalk."

"She was some cool cat, right Dad?"

"A regular kitten. We could have been arrested for indecent exposure."

"You mean you got your pocket picked by a prostitute."

Willie swerves. The front tire sinks into the sand, but Willie plows through it. "She's a fine car, Andy. The best Detroit has to offer."

Andy hops into the front seat "You'd buy a tricycle if it was stamped made in Detroit."

"I sent you to Harvard, Andy."

"You couldn't spend one weekend alone with me."

"I had to work. Had to pay the bills."

"Yeah, like listening to game seven of the World Series together. Business is business, right Dad?" Andy pushes in the cigarette lighter.

"You shouldn't smoke, Andy."

Andy takes a cigarette pack out of his rolled-up T-shirt sleeve and lights up. "You drive like an old lady."

"It's dark I can't see, Andy."

"This car's like a morgue." Andy switches on the radio.

"We're going into business together, right Andy? Build houses."

"Yeah, we'll build split-level shit-boxes, like the ones you stuck us in."

"What about the Big House? It had columns taller than the White House."

"It was made for Disney."

"It was solid as stone."

Andy starts to sing. "When you wish upon a star, makes no difference what's your car."

"I drove Chevys, Andy."

"NASCAR, Pace car, even an Avatar—nothing plays truer than an acoustical guitar."

"We'll build houses by the thousands. We'll be millionaires."

"I build dreams, not nightmares." Andy changes the station on the radio and the car floods with the strumming of a guitar. Andy knows the song and begins nodding to the familiar chords. "You walk into your house, with your pencil in your hand. You bow to your shit box, a shack that should be banned. You scratch you head, but you don't understand. Just what's happening to your homeland?"

Andy slaps Willie on his back. "They threw out those three-bedroom splits with the photo albums."

Near tears, Willie sucks it up. "We'll make new memories. I'm a natural born closer. Everyone at work says so."

"You didn't bury Pokey out back, did you?"

"I did, Andy. Cross my heart and hope to die."

"It's Mom who's buried out there."

"Andy!"

The guitar grows louder.

"Pokey's in the trash pit rotting like a beef steak—Mom's in the kitchen pounding out a fruitcake."

"In Brooklyn they throw your dog out with the trash. There's no place to bury them. No yards."

"You traded a street full of neighbors for a stinking patch of crab grass."

"I did it for you, Andy. Fifteen-hour days, for Christ's sake."

"You did it so you didn't have to be with us. Pull over, pal, I'm out of here."

The slashing guitar chords grow louder, confusing Willie. The strumming in his head won't stop. Driving on the wrong side of the deserted ocean road, Willie steers the Impala onto a tract of sandy grass. Andy flings open his door and hops out. The waves clash with the strumming guitar. Andy takes the last drag of his cigarette and flips it aside. He leans his elbows on the hood of the Impala, letting the smoke seep out between his lips.

Facing his father, Andy asks, "Who are you?"

"I'm your father."

Andy smiles from within the cloud of cigarette smoke that encircles him.

"Yes, but WHO are you?"

"I'm Willie—Willie Easelman."

Andy salutes his father. He steps back into the cloud of exhaust. Disappearing into the night, he chants "There ought to be a law about you coming around."

"Andy."

"Oh, my God, am I here all alone."

Willie dashes out of the car to where Andy was standing, but

Andy is gone, his smoldering cigarette all that remains. Shaken, Willie stumbles over to an iron railing that guards the steep drop to the ocean below. It's late and the moon hangs huge on the horizon. The Milky Way glimmers, a river of light flowing to the ends of the universe. Willie grips the railing with both hands and leans deep into the night, the sole spectator of this cosmic splendor. Below on the beach a bonfire glows, sparks spiraling skywards join the constellations. Willie sighs. Tired from this endless day, this endless drive, Willie scours the sky for relief.

"Quite the ride, hey Willie boy?" a voice out of the darkness speaks.

I Shall Be Released

"FORGIVE ME, FATHER," Trooper Scott whispers, his eyes avoiding contact.

Years ago, when I was a cadet, I found a novel in a bookstore, *Crime and Punishment.* Thinking it might help my police career, I took it home. From that book I remember one thing: those who commit a crime harbor an inner need to confess. Over the years I have used this to my advantage. Whether it's a drunk driver or a wife beater, I found that befriending the suspect is more effective than being his adversary. Playing the tough cop makes for great drama on TV, but a kinder cop gets his man. You don't force a confession, Father, you allow it to unfold.

I still remember walking home from my first confession. Maybe my sins were simply inappropriate thoughts, but those ten "Hail Marys" cleansed me.

"Be patient, Father, there's more."

Elaine goes to confession; it's part of her weekly ritual. For years I wondered what sins she had committed. I imagined a secret affair. On patrol I'd swing by our house and watch. Was her lover a neighbor, someone I knew? My fantasies became detailed, and the cooler our sex became, the hotter my imagination burned. I scoured her closets for clues, checked our bed for ropes. Sometimes I'd close my eyes and hear her moaning with her lover.

"Is coveting your wife's imaginary indiscretions a sin, Father?"

When we were kids, barely seventeen, Elaine and I would make out on her couch. With her parents upstairs sleeping, we discovered desire. Those nights became a seesaw, passion versus her Catholic upbringing. But during that summer the seesaw became weighted to lust. The back seat of my father's car became our shrine, our refuge from a disapproving world. The radio was our choir, its music our rapture.

After a Saturday night rich with cravings, I would accompany Elaine to mass on Sunday. She always wore a veil. When she rose for communion, she glided down the aisle, her dress flowing with innocence.

"I'm getting to the point.

Fifteen years ago I sinned, father. Elaine was away visiting her sister. I'm cooking spaghetti, hamming it up with Allie. I throw the spaghetti to the ceiling, and say "If it sticks, it's not done." Allie is giggling. My police instincts tell me she's laughing too hard. I throw the spaghetti again. "Done."

Allie is sixteen, an honor student who already knows she'll be a teacher. She's magic with the kids. She's bubbling over, telling me about the daycare where she volunteers. Something about a bully, a big kid from a broken family who takes out his personal nightmares on the smaller kids. Yet, Allie's gotten the bully to cooperate, to become a member of the group. She's electric as she basks in her success. A tear forms, but I ignore it, privileged to be allowed into her world. In the middle of describing the bully's hidden talents, she bursts into tears. Allie mumbles something, her braces clogged with spaghetti. I ask her to repeat herself, but I can't make out what she's saying. She stutters, her eyes unable to focus. I grab her with my massive arms, but she breaks away. A loop of spaghetti plops from the ceiling.

"I know I'm stalling, Father. But both God and the devil reside in the details."

Allie rushes to the kitchen sink. She opens the faucet full force, drowns herself in its stream. She chokes. Struggling for air I gasp. Turning, her childish curls dripping, she blurts, "I'm pregnant."

The rest is a blur. She huddles in a corner, a wounded animal. Her words reverberate in my mind, but they don't make sense. I ache to close the distance between us. "Allie," I call. She wipes her nose with her sleeve and pivots towards me. "I'm having an abortion." Her tone is not defiant—it's definitive. "He's taking me to New York."

"How is it, Father, that you can see your whole life play out in an instant and you're helpless to act?"

While Allie's voice hangs in the kitchen, I know my complicity will one day cast me as the sinner. The arguments against keeping this quiet from Elaine are overwhelming. Her voice echoes in my head. "A mother has a right to know." "Trust is the foundation of a marriage." "Life is sacred."

I am silent to her accusations. Elaine is entrenched with the church. Abortion is a sin against God, the sole unforgivable sin that even Christ can't forgive. For Elaine, faith fosters family. Allie's youthful resolve will crumble under her mother's will.

I see the dimple in Allie's cheek she's worn since birth.

"Mom can't know. Please." the plea of her words is more solemn than a sermon.

I nod. She steps into my embrace as I tell her. "I'll take you to New York."

All is settled in those few words. If our marriage ends, if trust ends with those few words, then so be it. The burden is less for Allie; for me it has just begun. Looking down at the child I have adored since the day she entered this world, I smile knowing she will be safe.

"Why is it, Father, that salvation for one is a crime for another?"

I no longer can bear to hear Elaine's voice without reliving that day. I must confess. It is a tumor tearing at my throat. Our marriage will collapse. Our family will end.

… What God has joined together will turn to dust.

Scott felt the touch of the man's elbow sitting to his side in the Impala. The rain had subsided. The parking lot was graveyard still. The quietude of the evening seeped into the void left by his confession. Willie stared straight ahead, oblivious to the marvels of the cosmos that earlier in the day he had witnessed. Scott gently removed Willie's hands from the steering wheel and warmed them in his. Fog clung to the windows, shielding the two from the empty chill of the universe.

"Forgive me, Father, for I have sinned."

Scott's blood surged, as images of his first confession sprung alive in his body. No longer interested in what kind of life Willie Easelman had lived, all that mattered was that he was here—here to listen. Whether saint or sinner, a good father or scoundrel, the simple act of touch was enough. Scott sighed, his breath filled with the moist summer's air of the solstice. The episode with his daughter, the guilt from his deception of his wife, the taking of his father's keys, even the suicide of a troubled girl, all were washed away as Scott stared through the windshield at the moon peering through an opening in the clouds.

Out of the accompanying silence, a hum rose. The radio was on, teetering on the threshold of hearing. He reached over and turned up the volume. A single note, a single strike of a piano key was all Scott needed to hear. Years ago Elaine and he pledged their love to this song, while lying naked in his father's car. "Allie's Song" they called it.

The moon glowed over the landscape, casting Willie's face with the chimerical light of life. Scott drifted with the music, reliving the unbelievable sense of unity he experienced years ago with Elaine. Closing his eyes to the mysteries of the song, opening his body to the magic of the moment, Scott felt cleansed. He rubbed away a tear, and in a tenor's voice, a voice that as a choirboy had made his mother cry, Scott sang into the nighttime air:

> *And all the gods come down just to sing for me*
> *And the melody is gonna make me fly*
> *Without pain*
> *Without fear.*

Whaling Stories

WILLIE WHIRLS TO confront the voice addressing him out of the darkness. "Who are you?"

"No way were they going to keep old Willie Easelman down."

Willie takes a step towards the voice. "Who are you?"

"You are THE Willie Easelman?"

Willie strains to see his face. Scouring the darkness, Willie replies. "I am. And you?"

"I am whoever you want me to be."

Willie rubs his chin. "That's not much of an answer, mister."

"Not much of a question, either. But you, Willie, your escape from the Morningside was extraordinary."

"You were there?"

"At the tolls. I was certain you were going to give that poor boy both barrels."

"He was killing the music."

"A sin, Willie?"

Willie glares at the shadow. "It is, in my book."

"Amen, Willie, amen."

"You've been following me?"

"Let's just say we've taken an interest in you."

"Are you taking me back?"

"In a way, yes."

"But ... but Andy's building me a cottage."

"Yes, I know."

"It'll be my home."

The man strikes a match against the iron rail. The night bursts with brilliance. He lifts the flame skyward, his silhouette blacker than the night.

"Funny, what some call infinite, others believe can fit on the head of a pin."

The flame swells; a sphere of light which engulfs the two men, but leaves them both in shadow.

"Imagine, in the blink of an eye the stuff of a trillion suns explodes into existence. And yet by the time this match extinguishes, ten-thousand suns will pass away. Time. It's the story, Willie. The only story."

The sky begins moving, circling the two men. Willie is awed by the child-like patterns in the rotating stars: animals, warriors, and goddesses. The man's voice brings Willie back. "Oh to hear again the melodies of the spheres, the perfection of planets unfettered by time."

An ash breaks loose from the bonfire. Willie watches the ember rise; it hovers in the air, then goes dark.

"It's enormous—this sea without shores."

Willie suddenly recognizes the voice. "Have you come for the gas money? I can explain ... I'm innocent."

"We're all innocent, Willie. But no, I haven't come for the money. I've come for you."

"Iron, chess, the swimming turtle, I remember them all."

The match dims as the shadow turns towards the ocean.

"I even got the joke about St. Peter—and I'm Jewish."

"They're just stories."

"I don't care about stories. I want to stay."

"Today on the highway you glimpsed something—call it a truth. How iron is part of a remarkable design. And yet iron isn't the story, Willie, you are. You're unique beyond imagination, a galaxy unto itself."

"I want my cottage."

"You're unrivaled in the universe."

The man blows out the match.

Willie watches the void of the man appear in the canvas of stars. The hush of anticipation stops the moment. But when the man speaks again, his tone is gentle and soothing, a storyteller breathing the flame of life into his tale.

"Once upon a time there was a village of fishermen. In those days boats were small and rickety and hugged the coast for protection. Storms were frequent and rose without warning, and often ships were lost. Storytellers spoke about an island far to the west, so bountiful with fruit that anyone landing there never wished to leave. Once or twice in a generation a brave sailor from the village sets sail for the island, promising to return, although none ever did. 'See,' harkened the storytellers to comfort the villagers. 'This confirms the legend of the idyllic island.'

"Over the centuries, however, another version of the story grew popular, one that spoke of sea serpents and monsters that guarded the island and destroyed any vessel attempting to reach it. Then, when sailors failed to return, the storytellers said, 'See, this confirms the saga of the beasts and the fate awaiting anyone who ventures west.' And for centuries, sailors rarely strayed from the safety of shore, as storytellers spiced their tales with dragons that tortured and horrendous ogres that devoured sailors foolish enough to try."

The silhouette pauses. Willie peeks at his Impala, barely visible in its bellowing exhaust. He contemplates escape. Certainly the man wouldn't stop him. But as Willie fidgets, the man continues, captivating Willie with an indescribable desire to know the ending.

"Over time," the man begins again, "the villagers grow uncomfortable with both versions. Storytellers are summoned who now allege no island exists; it never did. It's a fantasy, a tale told by idiots of long ago. In the new narrative, sailors brash enough to venture westward vanish into the abyss. Most find this tale disturbing and a malaise sweeps the village. Villagers yearn for the past, the barbed tales of paradise and bolted castle towers. But the new legend fascinates the storytellers. They embrace its starkness and relish the spell it casts over their audience."

"So which of the three versions is right?" Willie sheepishly asks.

The man sighs. "Somewhere out in that vastness a turtle swims, one who has no idea where it's headed."

"But it makes it to shore. It lays eggs. It survives."

"Some do."

"But ..."

"It's time, Willie. Your time."

"But I don't feel it."

"No one ever does."

"I'll pay for the gas."

The man laughs. "I'm sure you would, Willie; after all, you're an honest man."

"Just a bit more time. Quality time with Andy."

"I don't make the rules."

Far off the waves gather.

"There're no other legends?" Willie pleads, a child stalling for time.

The silhouette's gaze drifts seaward.

"One story has begun to circulate. In it a sailor lands on the island, but discovers only desolation. He finds remnants of ships, remains of previous voyages scattered on the beaches. He sees footprints in the sand, but no sign of life. He feverishly searches the island end to end but it's uninhabited—nothing. Overwhelmed with sorrow, he curses the day he set sail. Time passes. Then one day he begins to build a sand castle."

"That's it?"

"The story isn't finished."

"Does he complete the castle?"

Willie feels the man shrug.

"Certainly the storytellers know the ending?"

"The storytellers tells his tales spun from the imagination of others. You, Willie, are that other."

Waves start to splash, slashing each other as they jockey for position.

"Tomorrows arise from the ashes of today. It's the storyteller's promise, the hope woven into a young mother's lullaby."

When the man speaks again his voice is distant.

"It's a song, Willie—your song. Hear it. Breathe it. Nourish it within."

"But what if ... I am ...I can't...I'm not." Willie stops. He knows the man is gone. He grips the railing, cocks his ear to the sound of receding footsteps. Far off a voice sings:

Close the doors and bar the gates, but keep the windows clean
God's alive inside a movie, watch the silver screen.

Somewhere Over the Rainbow

WILLIE IS DRAWN to the bonfire glowing on the beach. Using the iron railing for support, he ambles to where the wind formed a bridge of sand over the fence. The faint sound of a piano frolics with the surf. He casts off his shoes and gingerly steps over the fence, stumbling when his foot snags a picket. Safely on the other side, his stride widens as he glides down the steep incline. He closes his eyes; his feet barely touching the ground.

The sky is worn silver—the moon is nowhere to be found. As he approaches the bonfire, he comes upon a grand piano askew in the sand. The lid of the piano is propped open and through the gap Willie glimpses a young woman. She is wearing a sequined dress, the kind worn on Broadway in the '40s. As Willie nears, a solitary sequin catches the glint from the fire and bursts to life.

"Evening, soldier boy." She doesn't look up, instead launches into a medley of Sinatra songs. "Remember these?"

"Could I forget?"

"He was some crooner."

"The best."

She looks up and winks. "No slouch in the sack either."

Willie finds her alto voice familiar.

"Did you do it your way, Willie?"

"Do what?"

She giggles and changes keys.

> *I've lived a life that's full*
> *I've traveled each and every highway*
> *And more, much more than this,*
> *I did it my way.*

"Did you travel each and every highway, Willie?"

"I've loved, I've laughed and cried," Willie retorts. And then as a duet they sing:

> *I've had my fill — my share of losing*
> *But now, as tears subside,*
> *I find it all so amusing.*

"Was it amusing?"

"Parts."

"And the other parts, Willie?"

"That's life."

"Touché. You're slick with the lyrics, soldier boy."

"To me, they're the national anthem. But I've heard you sing before; I never forget a voice."

"Me, I never forget a face. When they brought you into the Morningside screaming like a newborn, I knew it was you."

"I'm sorry, miss, but I think you're mistaken."

"Skip the 'miss,' buster." She stops playing and stands up, sliding her hand down her tight fitting dress. Even in the thin light Willie is aroused by the sensuous curves of her hips.

"You don't remember these?" she boasts, her profile highlighting her voluptuous body. "Come here, soldier boy."

Willie shuffles over, awkwardly standing behind her. She reaches behind her and draws his hand to her breasts.

"Feel familiar? Atlantic City. Spring of '42."

Willie's memory of that week in Atlantic City nearly knocks him over.

"But you haven't aged."

"Memories never do. The 546 Bombardment Squadron, right?" Willie salutes her. "Front and center, ma'am."

Lisa salutes back. "You know I watched those newsreels at the movie house every Friday looking for you. Watched you bomb those Nazi cities. Carpet bombing, I think they called it. You were my pilot, my hero, Willie."

"I wasn't exactly a hero."

"You're modest, Willie. She turns, peers into his face. What was the war like?"

"I ..."

"You were just a kid."

"I didn't ..."

"You know all the girls loved the pilots. When I told them I had one over there, they were jealous."

"But I wasn't actually a pilot."

"No?"

"I was just a private. I folded shirts in the laundry."

"Oh."

Willie forms a question mark in the sand with his toe. "And you, miss, you weren't that poor little orphan girl from Kansas?"

"How'd you know?"

"I saw the movie in London."

Lisa stops playing. "I'm from Ohio."

An uncomfortable pause follows, which Lisa tries to fill with a jazzy Sinatra riff.

"Was I the Scarecrow or the Tin Man?" Willie jokes.

"The Tin Man. You were a bit on the squeaky side."

"Is Lisa even your real name? Why not Dorothy?"

"I was sixteen when 'The Wizard of Oz' came out. Everyone in my home town said I looked like her, with the exception of these." Lisa's eyes drop to her well-developed breasts. "And then there was my voice." Lisa plays a short introduction, and then sings:

Somewhere over the rainbow
Way up high

Her voice is bolder than Garland's, but soft, more descriptive in its range. Lisa turns reflective. "You know when Dorothy woke up in Oz, and the movie came alive with color—I believed my life was about to do the same."

A wave sweeps out of the darkness, halting at Lisa's bare feet. Curious, she watches the water bubble as it disappears in the sand. Tilting her head, she continues plucking the keys with one finger.

There's a land that I lived in
Once, in a lullaby.

Willie leans over and kisses Lisa on her neck.

"There's no place like home, Willie." Lisa laughs and starts playing "As Time Goes By" from "Casablanca."

"Time goes by, Willie, with or without you. Kind of the un-written rule of nature and lovers. She pauses, letting the silence connect them. "I see you got your jalopy," nodding at the Impala jutting over the ledge, its headlights distant points of light in the fog of the car's exhaust. "Never met a boy so smitten by wheels. You talked all night about wanting one. A girl gets pretty jealous listening to a man talk about a car that way."

"I still remember my first."

"How we hid in the coat closet at the Claridge Hotel? I thought I was going to have to undress myself."

"I was nervous."

"You were greener than a grasshopper. Hopefully you've learned a trick or two along the way."

"You'd be surprised."

"Show me, Willie."

"What?"

"Let me feel your hands again."

Willie undoes the snap of her dress—then unzips her.

Lisa sighs. "A girl's got to breathe."

He slides his hand through the opening.

"No bra, Willie. Woman's lib."

Willie closes his eyes, letting his hand follow the contour of her back. Reaching around, his hands find her breasts.

"A woman knows when her body pleases. You know I almost let you do it right there in the coat room. I was still a bit, shall we say, inexperienced—still learning my craft. We were lying on a pile of furs with the saxophones screeching and I got to thinking, why the hell not?"

"Duke's band was on stage."

"Remember rushing back to the motel in the rain? Goose bumps of anticipation. We were shouting 'Singing in the Rain,' at the top of our lungs."

"Dancing around puddles."

"You were hop-scotching, trying to keep your hushpuppies dry."

"We were Rogers and Astaire."

"You swung me around."

"I never knew dancing could be so ..."

"You grew up pretty fast that night, hey soldier boy?"

She turned around and pressed against him. "I keep those memories alive. Some nights I drift back to that motel. I grip your hips, pull you into me."

"I never tire of seeing you lift off your wet blouse."

"We were just a couple of hep cats. Kittens, really."

"I remember watching your breasts rise and fall as you slept. In a way you were my first."

"Don't get cute with me, Willie boy. A woman knows when she's being played."

Willie rolls the top of Lisa's dress down, his hands shaking with desire. He leans into her and touches his lips to the slender bend where her neck greets her shoulders. He warms to the softness of her skin and aches for more.

"You have learned a thing or two," Lisa giggles. She continues playing with one hand as she slides her free hand up his pant leg. "Now there's the little Willie I once knew," she purrs, as she cups her hand around his stiffening body. Willie arches into her, craves to take her here on the beach.

"Not so fast, soldier boy. We're not kids anymore."

Willie pushes harder, but when he reaches to loosen his belt she grabs his wrist.

"Some things are best left as memories," she balks.

Willie hesitates; the shrieks of distant seagulls echo his frustration.

"Of all the boys, I thought you'd be the one to come back to me." She waits for Willie's fondling to return before adding, "But all I got was a check in the mail with 'Final payment" scribbled on the bottom. That hurt, Willie."

Willie feels the grit of the sand between his toes. "Life got in the way."

"It always does, Willie."

"I met someone over there."

"In England?"

"She worked in the laundry."

"You mean you didn't marry the butcher's wife?"

Willie's hand slips from Lisa's breasts.

"What was that girl's name? Liz. You never went back to Liz?"

"I got married over there."

"Tell me you didn't."

"I ..."

"You told me your story, Willie. How you went to her apartment and found it empty. Do you know I still stay awake some nights, agonizing about you sitting on that stupid sofa alone?"

"There was a war going on. People were dying. I was eighteen in a strange land and she comforted me."

"You mean she pulled down your britches."

"She ..."

"And pulled on your plum."

"My Jeanie was the light in a world gone dark."

"Spare the poetry, Willie. Your last name ain't Shakespeare."

"She was my better half, the honey that sweetened my tea."

"But did you love her?

"I ..."

"Did you love her like you loved the butcher's wife?"

A chill sweeps through Willie. He falters towards the bonfire, stumbling on a piece of driftwood. Grabbing it, he casts it into the waning fire which explodes with sparks.

"That night on the beach when you told me about her, about her softness, her touch. Never had I heard love spoken of like that. No warmed-over poetry, no light in a world gone dark. You made me cry, Willie. Do you have any idea how hard it is to make a girl like me cry?"

"I never stopped thinking about her."

"Thinking!" Lisa stands up, struggling to zip up her dress. Willie tries to stop her, but she slaps him. "A woman doesn't want to be THOUGHT of. She wants to feel your body next to her. She wants you near when she wakes with a fright, the reassurance of your scent on her pillow."

A wave races out of the shadows and strikes the side of the piano. Startled, they both hold their breath until it slips back to sea. Lisa, the fringe of her dress dripping, brings her hands to the piano, but hesitates.

"I've been working on a song, my first," she says, striking a few chords. "Let's call it 'Your Song.' This one's for you, Willie."

Heaven can wait
And a band of angels wrapped up in my heart
Will take me through the lonely nights
Through the cold of the days

She pauses, searching for the right notes to continue. "It's those lonely nights, the sadness that overwhelms a woman when the sun goes down." She turns. "Were you at least a good father, Willie?"

"Raised three," he replies, thankful of the change in subject. "I was the provider."

"I mean ... "

"I sent Andy to Harvard. He's a famous architect now. I worked sixty-hour weeks. I commuted hours every day so the kids could have a yard. You should have seen my houses. Columns as tall as the White House. And cars, a new one every two years, like clockwork. Maybe they weren't Cadillacs, but they were Chevys. I lived the dream. I did it my way."

"You did it the way *they* wanted you to!"

A second wave rocks the piano. Sea foam smacks Lisa's face. Stunned she shakes her head, saltwater drips from her curls. She wipes her face with the back of her hand, determined to continue. When she plays again, her tempo slows, her voice deepens, the alto of a gospel singer crying to be free:

Heaven can wait
And all the gods come down here just to sing for me
And the melody's gonna make me fly
Without pain
Without fear

Her song hovers in the air. Seagulls shriek, the ominous fore-shadowing of an approaching nor'easter. Lisa turns towards the sea. "What would it take to make you fly?"

Willie stares blankly at the smoldering bonfire.

"What would it take to make you fly without fear, Willie?"

Willie, lost in the implications of her question, watches the piece of driftwood he threw in the bonfire burst into flames. He turns, their eyes lock in the moment. "She would. She would make me fly."

Lisa scoffs. "You're too much, Willie. You leave a woman and a half-century later you say something like that."

"She left me."

"This wasn't a game of hide-and-seek. This was life, your life, Willie. Did you even try to find her?"

"In my dreams I still search."

Lisa jeers and somewhere hidden within the darkening sky seagulls scold. The tide is rising fast; the sea swirls at her ankles. She ignores the surging waters, pressing both pedals with her feet.

Give me all of your dreams
And let me go along on your way
Give me all of your prayers to sing
And I'll turn the night into the daylight
I got a taste of paradise
I'm never gonna let it slip away

"You let it slip away, Willie. You know she left that joker, the butcher who craved chicken liver more than he did her."

"What?"

"I tracked her down in Chicago."

"Why?"

"Call it curiosity. Even a woman like me has her jealousies."

A renegade wave breaks without warning, staggering Willie. He waivers, but stands his ground.

"She left him?"

"Oh, don't stare at me with those puppy-dog eyes. Of course, she left the schmuck."

"If I had called? Would she have …?"

Willie's being goes weightless. Lisa, with her make-up washed off, appears not much older than a girl. She shakes her head to the absurdity of Willie's question, then sings:

I'm never gonna let it slip away

"NEVER, Willie. It's not just a stupid word."

"But I'm …"

"Never. It rhymes with forever."

Laughter erupts from behind the stone outcrops, challenging the raging sea. Lisa's piano sways now with each wave. Yet she plays on—her piano, her world, her providence.

"One never forgets the music of youth," she says as her fingers trace through a sequence of Sinatra songs. "Music touches you where nothing else can. It paints your dreams. It becomes part of you—it is you."

More laughter escapes from behind the rocks. A woman and man prance out in the nude. Others follow, carrying driftwood that they heave into the fire. When one couple strays too close to the surf, a wave crashes upon them, slamming them to the sand. He picks her up and they kiss, their lips finding each other with the greed of youth. The fire blazes anew, as the couples join hands and dance. They're joyous dancing naked, the glow of their bodies highlighted with flame, their shadows fleeing across the beach with lightness.

"Amazing how fleeting youth is," Lisa sighs, with a tilt of her head. "One day you're dashing off to be alone with a man and the next day you're sitting alone at the Morningside."

A thunderous wave strikes the beach, streaming to the edge of the bonfire where it hisses into vapor. The dancers are ecstatic. Circling in and out of the rising vapor, their bodies gleam with sweat and desire. Euphoric, they swirl with the poetry of Lisa's song, clinging to each other.

"You could have opened that girl's heart," Lisa shouts over the crashing surf. "It wouldn't have taken much. She fell asleep at night, dreaming about the thrill of your touch. When you didn't return, she took her kid and hitchhiked to L.A. She carried that red polka-dot dress across country. Ended up designing dresses for the movie studios."

Lisa strikes the keys harder, her piano rising above the thunder of waves. The dancers twirl faster, tightening their circle, they stray closer to the flames. With faces rapt, their shadows stretch into the distance, where they're swallowed up by the surrounding darkness.

"She made it to L.A.?"

"All the way."

"Is she still there?"

"How would I know?"

"But I have time," Willie pleads.

Lisa salutes him, humming the refrain from "Over There."

"That's the old fighting spirit, soldier boy."

"Tell me I have time."

And all I got is time until the end of time
I won't look back
I won't look back

A rogue wave hits the piano broadside, smashing them both to the ground. The dancers halt and peer over. Lisa lifts herself up, giggling, her hair tangled with seaweed. Groping for the keyboard, she plays on. The dancers embrace with glee.

Willie remains on the beach, gasping for breath. He struggles to one knee. His mind is aglow. Images of Liz's polka-dot dress, the softness of her body, and the tenderness by which she balances her child on her hip swirl in the cavern of his mind. He grips the piano and hoists himself up, meeting Lisa's gaze head on.

"She would have loved me?" he clamors, somewhat afraid of Lisa's answer.

Lisa's laugh startles a flock of seagulls sleeping in the outcrops. "She already did."

Willie reels under the weight of Lisa's words. "Can I see her one more time?"

Lisa lifts her hands off the keyboard and the music ceases. The dancers halt.

"Are you sure?" Lisa asks.

Willie looses his grip and falls. He opens his mouth to speak as a wave swells over him. Choking, he reaches out and clutches the piano leg.

"Are you sure?" Her dress in shreds, Lisa is a goddess, waist-deep in foaming waters. She brings both hands over her head. The piano lists in the surging tide. The dancers are aghast, quivering in the flames they hold their breath, as wave after wave lash the beach.

"Are you sure?" she cries a third time, her voice challenging the core of the sea. Seagulls swoop, flashes of white flicker in and out of the night.

Willie lifts himself to his feet. Faint, he grips the piano. Leaning towards Lisa, he finds her eyes amongst the chaos swirling surrounding them.

"I am."

Everything that has made him Willie, everything that is and has ever been, collapses in that instant. The sky tears. Thunder rolls. Lisa smiles, then pounds the keyboard with all her strength. The dancers break forth in joyous song. The piano begins to drift out to sea. Willie scrambles up the side of the dune. He watches Lisa cling to the piano. He calls, but his voice is drowned by the approaching sea. The fire screeches, as wave upon wave rain down upon the dancers. Lisa pulls herself on top of the piano. Standing, she raises a defiant fist, challenging the sea with the strength of her song. Lyrics gush from her soul, a fountainhead of ethereal water signifying everything.

> *I got a taste of paradise*
> *That's all I really need to make me stay*
> *I gotta taste of paradise*
> *If I had it any sooner, you know*
> *You know I never would have run away*
> *From my home.*

Willie stands transfixed by the monstrous wave building on the horizon. It rips free from the sea, streaming towards the shore with hellish consequences. It rises skyward, a tower of water that swallows up Lisa. Racing across the beach, the wave gathers speed as it ascends the dune. Falling to his knees, Willie lifts a feeble hand to the surf soaring above him. The wave crests, eclipsing the sky as it plunges upon him.

Arrive

Heaven Can Wait

THE CALL OF a solitary seagull wakes Willie. He reaches out and blindly grasps a handful of sand, its warmth sifts onto his naked body. Sitting up, he shakes his head of the vestiges of last night. What had been real, what an illusion? Questions now as meaningless as these grains of sand.

His eyes burn as he opens them. Squinting through the haze, the mounds of desolation extend to the horizon, everything the endless rise and fall of dunes. He peers skyward. The clouds blend seamlessly with the sand, surrounding him in a sphere without beginning or end. He sets out into the unknown, driven by a thirst to find the sea.

Night no longer follows day. Devoid of hunger he pushes onward. Color has evaporated; there is only the constant monotony of sand. Sometimes when the wind dies down he thinks he hears the whisperings of waves. But it's a sham, the hum of a seashell pressed to a child's ear.

One day, long after he began walking, Willie approaches a mount that rises higher than the others. Scurrying up the steep peak on hands and knees, he reaches the summit where the haze thins and the views stretch forever. In a valley he spies a river. Knowing it leads to the sea, Willie stumbles after it, to where the ocean's scent hangs heavy and wet sands cool his feet. He hikes along the sinuous curve of the coastline, waves lapping playfully at his heels. But the beach is desolate. Looking back, he sees the waves wash away his footprints, feels the ache of loneliness.

Eventually he comes upon a rowboat, silvered with age. The boat is splintered but floats in a narrow outlet of fresh water with reeds crowd its bow. Whoever abandoned the boat planned to return, for a thick seaman's knot secures it to a post hammered into the ground. Willie scours the underbrush for oars, but finds none. Finding bamboo, he straps together a mast, then lashes it to the boat with vines.

On its side, the boat provides shelter from the storms that frequently blow in from the sea. The storms last for days, during which Willie huddles beneath the rowboat. When a storm passes, he rummages the shore for scraps of fabric that cling to thorn bushes, convinced that one day he will gather enough cloth to weave a sail. And so it is after a fierce storm that Willie comes upon the shattered remnants of a piano. Placing a finger on the keyboard, he plays. The notes are faint, but audible. He strikes harder, failing to resurrect the song he has carried all these years in his head.

Watching the sun cross the sky, he senses her approach. He lifts his head to the wisp of shuffling feet. Her red polka-dot dress bellows in the breeze, a painting stripped from its canvas. Gliding across the sand, her stride is confident and bold. She kneels next to him, her fragrance fertile with memories. Willie closes his eyes to her touch, the hint of salt on her lips as she whispers, "Like this."

Taking his hands in hers, they play. The music thrums within Willie, flowing through and throughout him. The melody restores life to his age-racked body, breath to his suffocated memories. They remain at water's edge, watching the sky slowly swallow the sea. As daylight turns to nightlight and the stars peer down upon them, she cups his hands and fills them with sand and together they start to build.

Day breaks. Silently they stroll past the majestic towers and turrets of sandcastles that lead to the sea. The rowboat bobs in the waves, indifferent to the vastness that stretches before it. Slipping out of her polka-dot outfit, she drapes the dress over the mast. A simple tug undoes the seaman's knot. Standing in the boat they cling to each other as a breeze gathers in the lowlands and fills their sail. The sun rises, an ocean of liquid light that warms them. Bathed in the glow of their naked bodies, they set sail—out into a new day.

Raymond Ahrens is a baby boomer who grew up in the soon-to-be-congested suburbs of New York City. He did OK by his parents' standards, but was left with a nagging uneasiness of having achieved not enough to fill a respectable obituary. Finding wisdom in Thomas Jefferson's writings that a man ought to accomplish three things with his life: raise a child, build a house, and write a book, Mr. Ahrens feels a sense of fulfillment now that he has completed the trifecta. Or so he thinks.